TSARINA

TSARINA

A Novel by Ellen Alpsten

B L O O M S B U R Y   P U B L I S H I N G

LONDON · OXFORD · NEW YORK · NEW DELHI · SYDNEY

Bloomsbury Publishing
Bloomsbury Publishing Plc
50 Bedford Square, London, WC1B 3DP, UK

BLOOMSBURY, BLOOMSBURY PUBLISHING and the Diana logo are
trademarks of Bloomsbury Publishing Plc

First published in Great Britain 2020

A catalogue record for this book is available from the British Library

ISBN: HB: 978-1-5266-0641-9; TPB: 978-1-5266-0643-3; EBOOK: 978-1-5266-0642-6

2 4 6 8 10 9 7 5 3 1

Typeset by Integra Software Services Pvt. Ltd.
Printed and bound in Great Britain by CPI Group (UK) Ltd, Croydon CR0 4YY

To find out more about our authors and books visit www.bloomsbury.com
and sign up for our newsletters

To Tobias: Thank You

RUSSIA UNDER PETER THE GREAT 1689–1725

Legend:
- Russia c. 1725
- *AZOV* Provinces established by Peter the Great
- Area ceded to Russia by Sweden 1721

Barents Sea

SWEDEN

White Sea

Gulf of Bothnia

• Archangel

ARCHANGEL

SIBERIA

Baltic Sea

Gulf of Finland

Tallinn •

• St Petersburg (founded 1703)

• Vologda

• Viatka

• Novgorod

ST PETERSBURG

R U S S I A

• Riga

Volga

Nizhniy Novgorod •

KAZAN

Volga • Kazan

LITHUANIA

• Vilna

Smolensk •

• Moscow

MOSCOW

Dnieper

Minsk •

• Orel

Tambov •

• Penza

Samara •

Orenburg •

C O S S A C K S

Ural

POLAND

Kursk •

AZOV

KIEV

• Kiev

• Kharkov

• Poltova

Don

• Tsaritsyn

Volga

Azov

Astrakhan •

KHANATE OF CRIMEA

C O S S A C K S

Danube

GREAT KABARDIA

DAGESTAN

Caspian Sea

Black Sea

CIRCASSIANS

To Russia 1723–32

O T T O M A N   E M P I R E

N

P E R S I A

0 100 200 300 400 500 600 miles

0   300   600   900 kilometres

Cast of Characters

Peter the Great's family

Peter the Great, Tsar and Emperor of All the Russias; also known as Peter Alexeyevich Romanov, *batjuschka* Tsar, Peter I

Marta Skawronski, mistress and then wife of Peter the Great; also known as Catherine Alexeyevna, Catherinushka, Tsaritsa and Empress of All the Russias

Evdokia, Peter's first wife, mother of Alexey, formerly Tsaritsa

Tsarevich Alexey, Peter's son and original heir

Charlotte Christine von Brunswick, known as Charlotte, Alexey's wife

Petrushka, Alexey and Charlotte's son

Tsarevna Anna, Tsarevna Elizabeth and Tsarevna Natalya, Peter's surviving daughters by Catherine

Ekaterina, Peter and Catherine's daughter who dies in infancy

Peter Petrovich aka Petrushka, Peter the Great's preferred heir, Catherine's and his son, dies young

Regent Sophia, Peter's half-sister

Tsar Ivan, Peter's half-brother

Tsaritsa Praskovia Ivanovna, Ivan's widow

Tsarevna Jekaterina Ivanovna, Tsarevna Anna Ivanovna, Ivan's daughters; also known as the Tsarevny Ivanovna (plural form)

Duke of Courland, husband of Tsarevna Anna Ivanovna

Duke of Mecklenburg, husband of Tsarevna Jekaterina Ivanovna

Duke of Holstein, marries Tsarevna Anna, Peter and Catherine's daughter

At the Russian Imperial Court
Count Alexander Danilovich Menshikov, general in Peter's army and his trusted friend; also known as Alekasha, Menshikov
Daria Arsenjeva, noblewoman, mistress and then wife to Menshikov
Varvara Arsenjeva, sister to Daria
Rasia Menshikova, sister to Alexander Danilovich Menshikov
Antonio Devier, husband of Rasia Menshikova, head of Peter's secret service
Feofan Prokopovich, Archbishop of Novgorod, confessor to Peter
The Princes Dolgoruky, supporters of Alexey's son, Petrushka
Blumentrost, Paulsen and Horn, doctors to Peter
Anna Mons, the German former mistress of Peter
Wilhelm Mons, her brother, a courtier and Catherine's lover
Marie Hamilton, courtier, Peter's mistress
General Marshal Boris Petrovich Sheremetev, Peter's leading general
Alice Kramer, German mistress of Sheremetev, later lady-in-waiting
Count Peter Andreyevich Tolstoy, courtier and confidant of Peter
Alexandra Tolstoya, Count Peter Andreyevich Tolstoy's sister, lady-in-waiting to Catherine
Pavel Jagushinsky, master of Peter's household, Privy Councillor
Peter Shafirov, Jewish courtier, Privy Councillor
Ostermann, Peter's Chancellor
Jakovlena, Cherkessk maid to Catherine
Boi-Baba, washerwoman, mistress to Peter
Afrosinja, washerwoman, mistress of Alexey
Andreas Schlüter, master builder and architect, creator of the Amber Room
Domenico Trezzini, architect in St Petersburg

In the Baltics
Christina, Fyodor and Maggie, Marta's half-siblings
Tanya, Marta's stepmother
Vassily Gregorovich Petrov, Russian merchant in Walk, buys Marta to be a house serf
Praskaya, Vassily's mistress
Nadia, Vassily's housekeeper
Olga, another of Vassily's house serfs

Ernst and Catherine Gluck, Lutheran pastor and his wife
Anton, Frederic and Agneta Gluck, their children
Johann Trubach, Swedish dragoon, first husband of Marta

The Europeans
King Charles XII of Sweden, Peter's enemy in the Great Northern War
Marshal Rehnskjöld, Charles XII of Sweden's principal general
Augustus the Strong, Elector of Saxony – Peter's ally
Frederick William, King of Prussia, the Soldier King
Louis XIV of France
Louis XV of France
Jean-Jacques Campredon, French Ambassador to Russia
Prince Dmitri Kantemir of Moldovia
Princess Maria Kantemir, his daughter, Peter's mistress

INTERREGNUM, 1725

He is dead. My beloved husband, the mighty Tsar of all the Russias, has died – and just in time.

Moments before death came for him, Peter called for a quill and paper to be brought to him in his bed-chamber in the Winter Palace. My heart almost stalled. He had not forgotten, he was going to drag me down with him. When he lost consciousness for the last time and the darkness drew him closer to its heart, the quill slipped from his fingers. Black ink spattered the soiled sheets; time held its breath. What had the Tsar wanted to settle with that last effort of his tremendous spirit?

I knew the answer.

The candles in the tall candelabra filled the room with a heavy scent and an unsteady light; their glow made shadows reel and brought the woven figures on the Flemish tapestries to life, their coarse features showing pain and disbelief. The voices of the people who'd stood outside the door all night were drowned out by the February wind, rattling furiously at the shutters. Time spread slowly, like oil on water. Peter had imprinted himself on our souls like his signet ring in hot wax. It seemed impossible that the world hadn't careened to a halt at his passing. My husband, the greatest will ever to impose itself on Russia, had been more than our ruler. He had been our fate. He was still mine.

The doctors – Blumentrost, Paulsen and Horn – stood silently around Peter's bed, staring at him, browbeaten. Five kopeks-worth of medicine, given early enough, could have saved him. Thank god for the quacks' lack of good sense.

Without looking, I could feel Feofan Prokopovich, Archbishop of Novgorod, and Alexander Menshikov watching me. Prokopovich had made the Tsar's will eternal and Peter had much to thank him for. Menshikov, on the other hand, owed his fortune and influence entirely to Peter. What was it he had said when someone tried to blacken Alexander Danilovich's name to him by referring to his murky business dealings? 'Menshikov is always Menshikov, in all that he does!' That had put an end to that.

Dr Paulsen had closed the Tsar's eyes and crossed his hands on his chest, but he hadn't removed the scroll, Peter's last will and testament, from his grasp. Those hands, which were always too dainty for the tall, powerful body, had grown still, helpless. Just two weeks earlier he had plunged those very hands into my hair, winding it round his fingers, inhaling the scent of rosewater and sandalwood.

'My Catherine,' he'd said, calling me by the name he himself had given me, and smiled at me. 'You're still a beauty. But what will you look like in a convent, shorn until you are bald? The cold there will break your spirit even though you're strong as a horse. Do you know that Evdokia still writes to me begging for a second fur, poor thing! What a good job you can't write!' he'd added, laughing.

It had been thirty years since his first wife Evdokia had been banished to the convent. I'd met her once. Her eyes shone with madness, her shaven head was covered in boils and scabs from the cold and filth, and her only company was a hunchbacked dwarf to serve her in her cell. Peter had ordered the poor creature to have her tongue cut out, so in response to Evdokia's moaning and laments, all she was able to do was burble. He'd been right to believe that seeing her would fill me with lifelong dread.

I knelt at the bedside and the three doctors retreated to the twilight at the edge of the room, like crows driven from a field: the hapless birds Peter had been so terrified of in the last years of his life. The Tsar had called open season on them all over his Empire. Farmers caught, killed, plucked and roasted them for reward. None of this helped Peter: silently, at night, the phantom bird would slip through the padded walls and locked doors of his bedchamber. Its ebony wings blotted up the light and, in their cool shadow, the blood on the Tsar's hands never dried.

His fingers were not yet those of a corpse, but soft, and still warm. For a moment, the fear and anger of these past few months slipped from my heart like a thief in the night. I kissed his hands and breathed in his familiar scent of tobacco, ink, leather, and the perfume tincture that was blended in Grasse for his sole use.

I took the scroll from his hand. It was easy enough to slide it out, although my blood thickened with fear and my veins were coated with frost and rime like branches in our Baltic winter. It was important to show everyone that I alone was entitled to do this – I, his wife, and the mother of his twelve children.

The paper rustled as I unrolled it. Not for the first time, I was ashamed of my inability to read. I handed my husband's last will to Feofan Prokopovich. At least Menshikov was as ignorant of its contents as I. Ever since the days when Peter first drew us into his orbit and cast his spell upon us, we had been like two children squabbling over their father's love and attention. *Batjuschka* Tsar, his people called him. Our little father Tsar.

Prokopovich must have known what Peter had in mind for me. He was an old fox with a sharp wit, as comfortable in earthly as in heavenly realms. Daria had once sworn that he had three thousand books in his library. What, if you please, can one man do with three thousand books? The scroll sat lightly in his liver-spotted hands now. After all, he himself had helped Peter draft the decree that shocked us all. The Tsar had set aside every custom, every law: he wanted to appoint his own successor and would rather leave his empire to a worthy stranger over his own, unworthy child. Alexey ...

How timid he had been when we first met, the spitting image of his mother Evdokia, with his veiled gaze and high, domed forehead. He couldn't sit up straight because Menshikov had thrashed his back and buttocks bloody and sore. Only when it was too late did Alexey grasp his fate: in his quest for a new Russia, the Tsar would spare no one, neither himself, nor his only son. *You were no blood of my blood, Alexey, no flesh of my flesh ...* And so I was able

3

to sleep soundly. Peter, though, had been haunted by nightmares from that day on.

My heart pounded against my lightly laced bodice – I was surprised it didn't echo from the walls – but I met Prokopovich's gaze as calmly as I could. I clenched my toes in my slippers as I could not afford to faint. Prokopovich's smile was as thin as one of the wafers he would offer in church. He knew the secrets of the human heart; especially mine.

'Read, Feofan,' I said quietly.

'Give everything to …' He paused, looked up and repeated: 'To …'

Menshikov's temper flared; he reared as if someone had struck him with a whip, like in the good old days. 'To whom?' he snarled at Prokopovich. 'Pray tell, Feofan, to whom?'

I could hardly breathe. The fur was suddenly much too hot against my skin.

The Archbishop shrugged. 'That's all. The Tsar didn't finish writing the sentence.' The shadow of a smile flitted across his wrinkled face. Peter had liked nothing better than to turn the world on its head: and, oh, yes, he still had a hold on us from beyond the grave. Prokopovich lowered his gaze. I snapped back to life. Nothing was decided. Peter was dead; his successor unnamed. But that didn't mean I was safe. It meant quite the opposite.

'What – that's it?' Menshikov snatched the paper out of the Archbishop's hands. 'I don't believe it!' He stared down at the letters, but Prokopovich took the scroll from him again.

'Oh, Alexander Danilovich. That's what comes of always having had something better to do than learn to read and write.'

Menshikov was about to give a stinging reply, but I cut him off. Men! Was this the moment for rivalry? I had to act fast if I didn't want to live out my days in a nunnery, or be forced aboard a sledge to Siberia, or end up face down in the Neva drifting between the thick floes of ice, my body crushed and shredded by their sheer force.

'Feofan – has the Tsar died without naming his heir?' I had to be sure.

He nodded, his eyes bloodshot from the long hours of keeping vigil at his lord's bedside. In the manner of Russian Orthodox clerics, he wore his dark hair plain; it fell straight to his shoulders, streaked with grey, and his simple, dark tunic was that of an ordinary priest. Nothing about him betrayed the honours and offices with which Peter had rewarded him; nothing apart from the heavy, jewel-studded cross on his breast – the *panagia*. Feofan Prokopovich was old, but he was one of those men who could easily serve many more Tsars. He bowed and handed me the scroll. I thrust it into the sleeve of my dress.

He straightened up. 'Tsarina, I place the future of Russia in your hands.' My heart skipped a beat when he called me by this title. Menshikov, too, raised his head, alert, like a bloodhound taking scent. His eyes narrowed.

'Go home, Feofan, and get some rest. I'll send for you when I need you. Until then, do not forget that the Tsar's last words are known only to the three of us,' I said. 'I hope you will serve me for many years,' I added. 'I bestow upon you the Order of St Andrew and an estate outside Kiev with ten – no, twenty – thousand souls.' He bowed, looking content, and I thought quickly about whom to send into exile, whose property I would have to sequestrate, in order to reward Prokopovich. On a day like today, fortunes were made and lost. I gestured to the servant standing guard next to the door. Had he understood our whispers? I hoped not.

'Order Feofan Prokopovich's carriage. Help him downstairs. No one is to speak to him, do you hear?' I added in a whisper.

He nodded, his long lashes fluttering on his rosy cheeks. A handsome young boy this one was. His face suddenly recalled that of another. One I'd thought the most beautiful I'd ever known. Peter had put a brutal end to that. And afterwards, he'd ordered that the head, that same sweet head, be set at my bedside, in a heavy glass jar of strong spirit, the way apples are preserved in vodka in winter. The wide eyes stared sadly out at me; in the throes of death the lips, once so soft to kiss, now shrivelled and drained of blood, had pulled back from the teeth and gums. When I first saw it and, horrified, asked my lady-in-waiting to remove it, Peter threatened me with the convent and the whip. And so there for a time it had stayed.

Feofan Prokopovich laughed softly, his face splitting into so many wrinkles that his skin looked like the parched earth after summer. 'Don't worry, Tsarina. Come, boy, lend an old man your arm.'

The two of them stepped out into the corridor. The footman's pale, narrow-legged silk breeches clearly showed the outline of his muscular legs and buttocks. Was there any truth in the rumour that Prokopovich liked young men? Well – each to his own. I blocked the view of the Tsar's bed with my body. Pale, frightened faces turned to gaze into the room: both noblemen and servants sat there like rabbits in a snare, craning their necks, awaiting their destiny. Madame de la Tour, my youngest daughter Natalya's scrawny French governess, was hugging the little girl close. I frowned. It was much too cold in the corridor for her and she'd been coughing since yesterday afternoon. Her elder sisters Elizabeth and Anna were there beside her, but I avoided their eyes. They were too young; how could they understand?

Nobody knew yet whether I was the one they had to fear. I searched the crowd for young Petrushka, Peter's grandson, and the Princes Dolgoruki, his followers, but they were nowhere to be seen. I bit my lip. Where were they ... busy hatching plans to seize the throne? I had to lay hands on them as soon as possible. I snapped my fingers and the closest guard leapt to attention.

'Send for the Privy Council – Count Tolstoy, Baron Ostermann and Pavel Jagushinsky. Look sharp, the Tsar wants to see them,' I said loudly, making sure that my last words were heard the entire length of the corridor.

Menshikov pulled me back into the room, closed the door and sneered his disbelief at my audacity.

'Come,' I said curtly. 'We'll go next door, to the little library.' Menshikov picked up his embroidered coat of green brocade from the chair in which he had kept watch at Peter's bedside for the last days and weeks. A peasant household could easily have lived for two whole years on just one of the silver threads woven in its cloth. His ivory-handled walking stick he clamped into his armpit. In the hidden door that led to Peter's small library I turned to the doctors. 'None of you may leave this room and you are to summon no one.'

'But ...' Blumentrost began.

I raised my hand. 'It cannot become known that the Tsar has passed away. Not yet.'

Peter would have approved of my tone.

'As you command.' Blumentrost bowed.

'Good. You shall be paid later today. The same goes for your colleagues.'

Menshikov swayed a little. Was it tiredness that made him unsteady on his feet, or fear?

I walked ahead of him into the cosy little library. Menshikov followed, but only after seizing the tall carafe of Burgundy he had been drinking from, as well as two Venetian goblets. 'This is no moment to be either sober or stingy,' he said with a lopsided smile before kicking the door shut like a common innkeeper. The fire had burnt down in the grate, but the wood-panelled walls retained its heat. The colourful silk rugs we had brought back from our Persian campaign – easily adding a dozen baggage carts to our train – depicted all the flowers and birds of God's creation in their full splendour. The plain chairs standing by the desk, the fireplace and near the shelves, had all been made by Peter himself. Sometimes I would hear him lathing and hammering far beyond midnight. Carpentry drove out his demons and gave him his best ideas, he used to say. His ministers feared nothing so much as a night Peter spent doing carpentry. He would fall asleep, exhausted, across his workbench. Only Menshikov was strong enough to hoist the Tsar onto his shoulders and carry him to bed. If I were not there waiting for him, Peter would use the belly of a young chamberlain as his pillow. He always needed skin against his skin to keep the memories at bay.

The high windows were draped with lined curtains that he had bought as a young man on his visit to Holland, long before the Great Northern War, those two decades of struggle for survival and supremacy against the Swedes. The shelves sagged beneath the weight of the books, which I was told were travelogues, seafaring tales, war histories, biographies of rulers and books on how to rule, and religious works. He had leafed through each and every one of them time and time again. It was a world where I could never follow him. Scrolls still lay open on his desk or piled up in heaps in corners. Some books were printed and bound in thick pigskin; others were written by hand in monasteries.

On the mantelpiece stood a model of the *Natalya*, Peter's proud frigate, and above it hung a painting of my son, Peter Petrovich. It was painted months before the death that broke our hearts. I had avoided this room for years because of it, the painting was too real; as if at any moment my son would throw me the red leather ball he held in his hands. His blond curls tumbled onto a white lace shirt; his smile hinted at a row of little teeth. I would have given my life to have him here, now, and to be able to declare him Tsar of All the Russias. Still a child, certainly. But a son of our blood, mine and Peter's. A dynasty. Isn't that what every ruler wants? Now there are only daughters left, and a dreaded grandson, little Petrushka.

The thought of Petrushka took my breath away. At his birth Peter had cradled him in his arms and turned his back on the unhappy mother. Poor Charlotte. She had been like a nervous thoroughbred, and like a horse her father had sold her to Russia. Where was her young son now? In the Dolgoruki Palace? In the barracks? Outside the door? Petrushka was only twelve years old and Peter hadn't even granted him the title of Tsarevich, but I feared him more than I feared the Devil.

In the library, Menshikov conceded: 'You did well, calling for the Council and getting rid of Feofan, the old fool.'

I turned to look at him. 'We're the fools. I hope he keeps his word.'

'What promise did he give you?' Menshikov asked, astonished.

'You see! You only hear what is spoken, but so much more than that is said.' I seized him by the shirt collar and hissed: 'We're both in the same boat. God have mercy on you for every second you waste right now. I saw neither Petrushka nor his charming friends in the corridor, did you? And why is the rightful heir to the Russian Empire not here at his grandfather's deathbed, where he belongs?'

Menshikov looked uncertain; he wiped his forehead.

'Because he's with the troops at the Imperial barracks, where soon they'll hoist him on their shoulders and give him three cheers when they find out the Tsar is dead. What will happen to us then? Will Petrushka remember the people who signed the judgment on his father, albeit with just a cross next to their name because they couldn't write?'

I let go of him. Menshikov refilled his goblet and took a long slug of wine, his hands trembling, strong fingers weighted down with heavy rings. His natural wiliness was blunted by fatigue, but I was not yet finished with him: 'Siberia will be too good for us in their eyes. The Dolgorukys will feed the four winds with our ashes. No one but us knows that the Tsar is dead,' I whispered. 'That buys us time.' Time that might save us. We couldn't keep the Tsar's death secret for too long; it would be out by morning, when a leaden dawn broke over Peter's city.

Menshikov, the man who had turned so many battles in his favour, whose neck had slipped so many times from even the most perilous of nooses, seemed dazed. My dread was contagious. He sat heavily in one of the armchairs, which Peter had brought from Versailles, and stretched out his still-shapely legs. A marvel that the dainty piece of furniture was able to bear his weight! He took a few sips and then turned the coloured glass this way and that in front of the fire. The flames warmed the goblet's smooth, tinted surface; it looked as if it were filled with blood. I sat down opposite him. Tonight was no time for drinking games.

Menshikov raised his goblet to me in jest. 'To you, Catherine Alexeyevna. It was well worth gifting you to the Tsar, my lady. To you, my greatest loss. To you, my greatest gain.' Suddenly he laughed so hard that his wig slipped down over his eyes. It was like the sound of wolves in winter: high and scornful. He pulled the wig off and flung it away. I calmly took his insolence while Peter would have had him flogged for it. Menshikov was suffering like a dog: it was his lord and love, too, who had died. What was in store for him now? His anguish made him unpredictable. I needed him desperately. Him, the Privy Council and the troops. The Tsar's last will and testament was wedged up my sleeve. Menshikov's face was red and bloated under his shaggy, still dark-blond mop of hair. He stopped laughing and eyed me over the rim of his glass, his gaze unsteady.

'Here we are. What an extraordinary life you've lived, my lady. Divine Will is the only explanation for it.'

I nodded. That's what they say about me in all the courts of Europe. My background is the running joke that always puts envoys in a good mood. But for Peter, whatever he willed at any given time was normal and so nothing was extraordinary any longer.

Menshikov's glass slipped from his fingers, his chin dropped onto his chest and the wine spilt, leaving a large red stain on his white lace shirt and blue waistcoat. The last weeks, days and hours caught up with him. A moment later, he was snoring and hung as limp as a rag doll in the chair. I could grant him some rest before Tolstoy and the Privy Council arrived. Then he would be carried back to his palace to sleep off his stupor. Menshikov already held the Order of St Andrew, as well as far more serfs and titles than I could grant him. There was nothing left to promise him. He had to stay of his own accord: *Nothing binds people more powerfully than fear for their own survival, Catherine*, I could hear Peter say.

I walked over to the window, which looked over the inner courtyard. The golden icons sewn to the hem of my dress tinkled with each step. When little Princess Wilhelmine of Prussia saw the way I dressed on our visit to Berlin, she had laughed out loud: 'The Empress of Russia looks like a minstrel's wife!'

I pushed aside the heavy curtain that kept at bay the inky chill of a St Petersburg winter night – our city, Peter, our dream! Alexander Nevsky Prospect and the Neva were shrouded in the darkness that now held you forever in its arms, the darkness that hid the breathtaking beauty of what you had created: the icy green shade of the waves blending to perfection with the rainbow hues of the flat façades of both palaces and houses, such a novelty twenty years ago. This city that you raised out of the swampy ground, by the sheer strength of your incredible will and the suffering of hundreds of thousands of your people, nobles and serfs alike. The bones of the forced labourers lie buried in the marshy earth as the city's foundations. Men, women, children, nameless and faceless; and who remembers them in the light of such magnificence? If there was a surfeit of anything in Russia, it was human life. The morning would break wan and cool; then, later, the palace's bright, even façade would reflect the day's pale fire. You lured the light here, Peter, and gave it a home. What happens now? Help me ...

Candlelight moved behind the windows of the fine, tall houses, gliding through rooms and corridors as if borne by ghostly hands. In the courtyard below, a sentry stood hunched over his bayonet, when with a clatter of hooves – sparks flying off the hard cobble-stones – a rider dashed past him and out through a gate. My fingers clenched the catch of the window. Had the doctors obeyed my order? Or had the rider left to confirm the unthinkable? What would happen to me now? *Volya* – great, unimaginable freedom – or exile and death?

My mouth was dry with fear: a feeling that knots the stomach, turns sweat cold and bitter, and opens the bowels. I hadn't felt it since – stop! I mustn't think of those things now. I could only focus on one thing at a time, whereas Peter, like an acrobat, would juggle ten ideas and plans.

Menshikov was mumbling in his sleep. If only Tolstoy and the Privy Council would come. The whole city seemed to be lying in wait. I bit my fingernails until I tasted blood.

I sat down again close to the fire and took off my slippers, stiff with embroidery and jewels. The warmth of the fire made my skin prickle. February was one of the coldest months in St Petersburg. Perhaps I should order some mulled wine and pretzels instead of the Burgundy; that always gave me a swift boost. Was Peter warm enough in the room next door? He couldn't stand the cold and we had always been freezing on the battlefield. Nothing is frostier than the morning after a battle, be it lost or won. I could only keep him warm at night when he sought refuge in the folds of my flesh.

People asleep look either ridiculous or touching. Menshikov, snoring open-mouthed, was the latter. I drew Peter's last will from my sleeve and the scroll lay in my lap, so close to the flames. Its letters blurred as my tears came: real, heartfelt tears, despite the sense of relief. I still had a long day and longer weeks ahead of me and I would need to shed many more tears. The people, and the court, would want to see a grief-stricken wife with tousled hair, scratched cheeks, a broken voice and swollen eyes. Only a show of love and grief from me could make the unthinkable acceptable, my tears more powerful than any bloodline. So I may as well start weeping now. The tears weren't hard to summon: in a few hours I might be either dead, or wishing I were, or else I'd be the most powerful woman in All the Russias.

I

My life began with a crime. Of course, I don't mean the moment of my birth nor my early years. It's better to know nothing of life as a serf, a soul, than to know but a little. The German souls – *nemtsy*, property of the Russian Church – were more wretched than you can ever imagine. The godforsaken place in which I grew up is now lost in the vast plains of Livonia: a village and a country that no longer exist. Do its *izby* – the shabby huts – still stand? I neither know nor care. When I was young, though, the *izby* that lined the red earth of the village street in rows, like beads on a monk's rosary, were my world. We used the same word for both: *mir*. Ours looked just like many other small villages in Swedish Livonia, one of the Baltic territories under the rule of Stockholm, where Poles, Latvians, Russians, Swedes and Germans mingled and lived together, more or less peacefully – in those days.

Throughout the year, the road through the village held our lives together like the belt on a loose *sarafan*. After the spring thaw, or the first heavy rains of autumn, we would wade knee-deep in slush coloured like ox-blood from our *izba* into the fields and down to the Dvina river. In summer, the earth turned into clouds of red dust that ate its way into the cracked skin of our heels. Then, in winter, we would sink up to our thighs in snow with every step, or slide home on ice as slick as a mirror. Chickens and pigs roamed the streets, filth clinging to their feathers and bristles. Children with matted, lice-infested hair played there before they came of working age, when the boys stood in the fields, chasing away the wild birds with rattles, stones and sticks, and the girls worked the monastery's looms, their delicate fingers serving to make the finest fabrics. I myself helped in the kitchens there from the age of nine. From time to time a loaded cart, pulled by horses with long manes and heavy hooves, would rumble through the village to unload goods at the monastery and take other wares to market. Apart from that, very little happened.

One day in April, shortly before Easter – the year 1698 according to the new calendar the Tsar had ordered his subjects to use – my younger sister Christina and I were walking down this road, heading through the fields towards the river. The pure air was scented with the greatest wonder of our Baltic lands: the *ottepel* or thaw. Christina was dancing: she spun around in circles, clapping her hands, her relief at the end of the darkness and cold of the winter palpable. I clumsily tried to catch her without dropping the bundle of washing I was carrying, but she dodged away.

Throughout winter, life in the *mir* was on hold, like the shallow breathing of a bear who lives off the fat beneath its fur until spring. In the long season, the leaden light dazed our minds; we sank into a listless gloom, soaked with *kvass*. No one could afford vodka, and the bitter, yeasty drink fermented from old bread was just as intoxicating. We lived on grains – oats, rye, barley, wheat and spelt – which we baked into unleavened flatbreads or made into pastry on feast days, rolling it thin and thinner, before filling it with pickled vegetables and mushrooms. Our *kasha*, the gruel on which we subsisted, was sweetened with honey and dried berries, or salted with bacon rinds and cabbage; we prepared vast amounts of this vegetable every autumn, chopping, salting and pulping it, before we would eat it every day. Every winter I thought I'd be sick if I had to eat sauerkraut one more time, but we also owed our lives to it. It helped us withstand a cold that would freeze the phlegm in your throat before you could hawk it up.

Just as the snow and frost were becoming unbearable, they would slowly fade away. First, it might stay light for a moment longer, or the twigs straighten under a lighter load of snow. Then, at night, we woke to the deafening crack of the ice breaking on the Dvina; the water spurting up, free, wild, and tearing huge slabs of ice downstream. Nothing could withstand its power; even the smallest brooks would swell and burst their banks, and the strong, scaly fish of the Dvina leapt into our nets of their own accord. After a brief, scented spring, feverish summer months followed and our world was drunk with fertility and vigour. Leaves on the trees were thick and succulent; butterflies reeled through the air; bees were drowsy on nectar, their legs heavy with pollen, and yet in too much of a hurry to linger on any one blossom. No one slept during the white nights; even the birds sang throughout, not wanting to miss any of the fun.

'Do you think there's still ice on the river, Marta?' Christina asked me anxiously, using the name I was known by back then. How many times had she asked me this since we'd left the house? The Spring Fair was tomorrow and just like her I longed to scrub off the stench of smoke, food and the dull winter months in readiness for what was to be the highlight of the year. There would be amazing sights, delicious foods of which we might afford some, and the arrival of all the people from the neighbouring *mir*, as well as the odd handsome stranger, a thought that was never far from Christina's mind. 'Shall we race each other?' she asked, giggling. Before I could answer, she set off, but I tripped her up and just managed to catch her before she stumbled and fell. She shrieked and clung to me like a boy riding a bull at the fairground, pummelling me with her fists; I lost my balance and we both fell onto the embankment, where primroses and rock cress were already blooming. The sharp young grass tickled my bare arms and legs as I struggled to my feet. Oh, wonderful – the clothes were strewn all over the dusty road. Now we really had good reason to wash them. At least we could work beside the river: only a few weeks ago, I'd had to smash the ice on the tub behind the *izba* with a club and push the icy lumps aside as I scrubbed. My hands had frozen blue with cold, and chilblains are painful and slow to heal.

'Come on, I'll help you,' said Christina, glancing back towards the village. We were out of sight of the *izba*.

'You don't need to help me,' I said, though the laundry was heavy on my arm.

'Don't be silly. The quicker we wash it all, the sooner we can bathe.' She took half the washing from the crook of my arm. We didn't usually split the chores because Christina was the daughter of Tanya, my father's wife. I'd been born, nine months after the summer solstice, to a girl in the neighbouring village. He was already engaged to Tanya when my mother fell pregnant and he had not been forced to marry her: the monks had the final say in such matters, and they, of course, preferred to marry my father to one of their girls. When my mother died giving birth to me, Tanya took me in. She had little choice: my mother's family had stood on the threshold of the *izba* and held my bundle of life towards her. They would have left me on the edge of the forest as fodder for the wolves if she had refused. Tanya didn't really treat me badly, considering. We all had to work hard, and I got my share of our provisions such as they were. But she was often spiteful, pulling my hair and pinching my arm over the slightest mistake.

'You've got bad blood. Your mother would spread her legs for anyone. Who knows where you really come from?' she'd say if she was feeling malicious. 'Look at you, with your green, slanted eyes and your hair as black as a raven's wing. You'd better watch your step.' If my father heard her, he wouldn't say anything, but just look even sadder than usual, his back hunched from working in the monastery fields. He could only laugh his toothless chuckle when he'd had a few mugs of *kvass*, which brought a dull light to his sunken eyes.

Before we walked on, Christina took my arm and turned me towards the sun. 'One, two and three – who can look at the sun the longest?' she said breathlessly. 'Do it. Even if it scorches your eyelids! Between the spots that dance in front of your eyes, you'll see the man you're going to marry.'

How eager we were to know him then: at midnight, we'd light three precious candles around a bowl of water and surround them with a circle of coals; we'd stare and stare, but the surface of the water never reflected any faces but our own. No midsummer ever went by without us plucking seven types of wildflowers and placing the spray beneath our pillows to lure our future husbands to our dreams. I felt the afternoon sun warm on my face and spots danced senselessly golden on the inside of my eyelids. I kissed Christina on the cheek. 'Let's go,' I said, longing for the warm rocks on the bank. 'I want to dry off when we finish bathing.'

In the fields souls were bent double at their work and I spotted my father among them. Only part of the land was cultivated in spring, for the first harvest. In summer, turnips, beets and cabbage were planted in the second part; all crops that could be harvested even in winter, when the earth was frozen solid. The last third of the ground lay fallow until the following year when the crops were rotated. The time we had to make provision for the rest of the year was short and a few squandered days now could mean famine later. In August my father might easily spend eighteen hours a day in the fields. No, we didn't love the earth that fed us: she was a merciless mistress, punishing us for the slightest mistake. Six days of the week belonged to the monastery, the seventh to us. But our obligation to God allowed no rest to us souls. The monks walked back and forth between the workers in their long, dark robes, keeping a sharp eye on their property, both the land and the people working it.

'What do you think is underneath a monk's robes?' Christina asked me now, saucily.

I shrugged. 'Can't be much, or you'd see it through the cloth.'

'Especially when they see you,' she answered.

Her words reminded me of Tanya's insults. 'What do you mean by that?' I asked tersely.

'Aren't you meant to be older than me, Marta?' she cried. 'Don't say you haven't noticed the way men look at you. They'll all want to dance with you at the fair and no one will pay me any attention.'

'Nonsense! You look like an angel. An angel in dire need of a bath. Come on!'

Down by the river we settled at the shallow spot we'd found the previous year. A little path wound down through a birch grove and some low bushes. Early buds were on all the twigs; wild iris and bedstraw would bloom here soon. On the riverbank I sorted the laundry, putting all the men's good linen shirts and breeches on one side and the *sarafan* dresses and linen tunics we women wore on feast days on the other. We had spent many a long winter evening embroidering colourful floral motifs on the flat collars. Perhaps we could swap some of Father's woodcarvings – small pipes, bowls, spoons and cups – for new thread at the fair tomorrow. I wound my hair into a loose knot so it wouldn't dangle in the dirty foam, and folded my faded headscarf to shield me from the sun. Then I knotted my *sarafan*'s wide skirt around my knees, though the fabric was lined and quilted against the cold, and tugged at the long strings threaded through the seams of my sleeves, gathering the cloth into countless pleats. From afar I must have looked like a cloud on long, bare legs.

'Let's begin.' I reached out for the first of the linen and Christina handed me the precious soap. I dipped the washboard in the clear water and painstakingly rubbed the soap over its sharp ribs until they were thickly coated with a slippery layer. Making soap was hard work; your whole body ached afterwards. Mostly Tanya gave me this task in autumn, when the monks had been slaughtering to pickle, smoke and salt meat for the winter larder and had bones to spare, or in spring, using ashes gathered throughout the winter. All the women would help mix rainwater and ash with pork or beef lard and ground animal bones to make a caustic lye, which they boiled for hours in great cauldrons. The grey, slimy brew – its big, hot bubbles bursting on the surface with loud splashes – thickened slowly from one hour to the next. We had to stir it constantly until it felt as if our arms were about to fall off. In the evening we poured the liquid soap into wooden moulds. If we could afford to add salt to it, we ended up with a solid lump. But mostly we needed the salt for the animals, or to pickle meat and cabbage for the winter, so our soap was more of a slime that you added to the washing water.

The river glittered and Christina and I worked fast: the prospect of bathing spurred us on, as we dipped the clothes in the water, scrubbed them hard, beat them on the flat stones – 'Imagine it's the Abbot,' I goaded Christina so that she would beat them harder. She threw back her head and laughed, her blonde hair slipping free from its bun. We wrung out the garments and hung them to dry on low-hanging branches along the shore. 'On your marks, get set, go!' Christina shouted, as I was still straightening and smoothing the last of the shirts. She undid the knot of her belt, pulling the simple *sarafan* and rough tunic over her head as she ran, and stood naked in the spring sunshine. How different she looked from me. Christina's skin was as pale as skimmed milk, her body slim, with narrow hips and high budding breasts that looked as if they'd fit just so in the hollow of her hand. Her nipples were like little raspberries. She was already able to bear a child: her blood had started to flow the previous year. I, on the other hand – well, Tanya was probably right about me looking like my mother. My hair was thick and black, and my skin the colour of wild honey – or dried snot, as Tanya used to say. My hips were wide, my legs long and strong, my bosom large and firm.

Christina was splashing about in the shallow stream close to the bank. Her head bobbed up and down between the rocks where water gathered in pools. The sand of the riverbed shone white between her feet when she rose. 'Come on, what are you waiting for?' she laughed, then dived headfirst into the waves, allowing the current to sweep her off into the deep. I undressed as fast as I could, loosened my hair and hurried after her. We splashed and dived and – deliciously forbidden! – scrubbed our bodies with the precious soap; I opened my eyes underwater, grabbed at water snails, broke off sharp reeds from the riverbank to try to spear an eel and tweaked Christina's toes, pretending to be a fish – anything to have a laugh after the dreary winter months!

The water was still icy. I was the first to get out, goose-bumps instantly rising on my skin. I shook my hair and flying drops of water sparkled in the sun before I wound it into a bun. 'Better than the bathhouse,' gurgled Christina, still drifting in the shallows. 'At least you don't get whipped with twigs here till you're all sore and almost bleeding.'

'Oh, I can see to that,' I said, snapping a switch off a bush. Christina squealed and ducked underwater. Just then we both heard sounds: horses neighing, stones crunching under cartwheels, men's voices. 'Stay in the water,' I ordered her, and looked up the road. Three riders surrounded a cart covered over with pale canvas. The man in the driver's seat had pulled the horses to a halt in their traces. In spite of the distance between us, I felt him scrutinising me and desperately wished I could reach my long *sarafan*.

'Who is it?' Christina whispered, drifting back and forth in the shallow water.

'Shh! I don't know. Stay where you are!'

To my alarm I saw the man get down from the cart, throwing the reins to one of the other riders. I counted three armed men while he turned down the little path towards our stretch of riverbank. I ran to the bush where my clean *sarafan* was drying. It was still damp, but I slipped it on nonetheless. I had just managed to pull it down over my thighs when the man appeared before me.

He must have been the same age as my father, but had certainly never worked as hard. His long Russian coat had a dark fur collar and his breeches were cut from soft leather and held up by a richly embroidered belt. His high boots were spattered with mud and dirt. I shielded my eyes with my hand. Sweat glistened on his forehead, although his face was shaded by a flat beaver-fur hat. He had a full beard, as all Russians did in those days. He looked me up and down, then took off his gloves. He wore several rings with bright stones on his short, thick fingers. I'd never seen anything like it: not even the Abbot wore this much jewellery. I took a step back. To my dread, he followed me.

'Can you tell me the way to the monastery, girl?' he asked in harsh German. He still had all his teeth, but his gums were stained dark red from chewing tobacco and he smelt of sweat from the long ride. It would have been rude of me to make a face and offend a travelling stranger, though, so I stood there uneasily while he looked me and up and down. I sensed that the outline of my breasts was visible beneath the thin, wet linen. Feeling my hair slipping from its knot, I instinctively reached up to tighten it, and the dress slipped, baring my shoulder.

His tongue darted across his lips, which made me think of the snake my brother Fyodor and I had spotted the previous summer in the undergrowth of our vegetable patch. It was pale green and we could almost see its intestines shining dark beneath the taut skin. It had slithered towards us, slowly at first. Although he was smaller, Fyodor pushed me behind him. The reptile looked deadly, but my brother bent down and picked up a heavy stone. At the very moment the snake darted forward, jaws agape, he smashed its head in. The nerves in the beast's dead body made it go on twitching and wriggling for some time afterwards.

The man took another step towards me, and Christina screamed: 'Marta, watch out!' from the water.

He turned his head and I bent to grab a mossy stone. I might have been a virgin, but I knew all too well what he wanted. We had a cock and hens in the back yard, after all; and my father had to hold the mares for the stallions in the monastery stables. Besides, in the *izby*, where families all slept together on the flat oven, bodies and breaths mingling, there was little room for secrets. I knew what he wanted and I wasn't going to let him have it.

'The monastery's straight ahead, just down the road. You'll be there soon if you hurry!' I said curtly, even though my shaking voice gave me away.

He didn't respond but took another step towards me. 'Your eyes are the same colour as the river. What else is there to discover about you?' he asked. There was little more than a breath separating us.

I stood firm and hissed, 'If you come any closer, I'll smash your skull in and bake a pie with your brains. Get back to your cart and go to the damned monks.' I weighed the stone threateningly in my hand. Out of the corner of my eye, I saw his three companions dismounting, shaking out their limbs after the long ride and allowing their horses to graze. I bit my lip. One skull I could smash, but we didn't stand a chance against four men. My heart pounded in my breast as I tried not to give in to the fear of what might happen. The first of the men seemed about to head down the path. The stranger smirked, sure of an easy victory. Christina sobbed in the water and the sound made me furious: anger laced with strength and courage. 'Get out of here, Russian!' I snarled at him and he hesitated; then, all of a sudden, he held up his hand, stopping the other man in his tracks. The traveller smirked at me.

'By God, girl, you amuse me. We'll see each other again, and then you'll be kinder to me.' He stretched out his hand as if to touch my hair. Christina screamed. I spat at his feet. His face grew hard. 'Just you wait,' he threatened. 'Marta, eh? That's what she called you, the little minx in the water?'

I was mute with fear as he turned and walked back up the embankment. Only when he had urged on his horses with a flick of his whip, and the clopping of hooves and the clattering of wheels had died away, did I breathe again and let the stone slip from my sweaty, sticky fingers. My knees buckled and I dropped onto the rough grey sand, shivering. Christina waded out of the water; she wrapped her arms around me and we held each other tight, until I was only shaking with cold and not fear anymore. She stroked my hair and whispered: 'Marta, you're so brave. I'd never have dared to threaten him with a silly little stone.' I glanced down at the stone at my feet. It really did look silly and little.

'Do you think we'll see him again?' she asked, while I struggled to my feet. I bit my lip in worry. He'd asked the way to the monastery to which all of us belonged – our *izba*, our land, the dress on my back, we ourselves. I chased away the thought.

'Nonsense,' I said, hoping I sounded surer than I felt. 'We'll never see that tub of lard again. Let's hope he falls off his cart and breaks his neck.'

I tried to laugh but couldn't. Christina didn't look convinced either. Clouds covered the sun, veiling the daylight with the first blue of dusk. I was shivering in my damp dress, which was covered in dirt again. What a nuisance: I would have to wash it tomorrow, early in the morning before the feast. I brushed sand and pebbles off my shins. 'Let's go.' Silently, we slipped into our old clothes and gathered up the still-damp washing to hang it over the flat oven at home to dry. It made the air in the hut even more humid and worsened my brother Fyodor's cough.

'Let's not tell anyone, shall we?' I said to Christina, hoping I could pretend to myself the encounter by the river had never happened. But in my heart I knew this wouldn't be the end of it. Nothing in this world happens without a reason. That afternoon my life changed course, like the weathervane on the monastery roof spinning in the first blast of a sudden storm.

2

It rained the night before the fair. The monks didn't make *nemtsy* like me attend their church on Sunday as the other souls did: I had been baptised Catholic, but to me faith was just mumbled prayers and a constant crossing of yourself with three fingers. On the day of our death, this – or so we hoped – was supposed to gain us entry to the freeborns' Heaven.

Walking to the fairground by the monastery, our feet sank into the warm mud of the road, a soft sucking sound accompanying each step. We carried our sandals of wood and raffia in our hands so as not to ruin them. My younger sister Maggie, who was only four, could barely keep up with us, so I took her hand and slowed my steps to match her scuttle. The morning had been damp but this afternoon was sunny, the sky big and blue. At the village green, men were still levelling the ground for the evening's dancing, and some women were stretching ropes between high birch trees for children to swing on. Others were standing around in groups in their long, bright dresses, laughing, talking, singing songs and clapping along. The fairground was already a lively hubbub as people from all over the province had come for the market.

A bear was tethered to a post outside the first tent I passed, his pelt dirty and dishevelled, and the teeth in his jaws as well as his claws filed down. Still, better he was kept away from the captive animals: their angry, unpredictable natures were merely slumbering, unconfined by their chains. In winter, the travelling merchants who kept them often froze to death by the roadside; the bears would rip their chains from the dead men's hands when hunger drove them to the nearest houses and farms. So Maggie and I gave Master Bruin a wide berth as he uselessly whetted his claws on his post. Maggie glanced round quickly for her mother but Tanya was at a stall, looking at necklaces and bracelets. Putting her finger to her lips, the little girl curiously lifted the flap of a tent, its cloth mended and darned with colourful patches.

'Maggie!' I was about to tell her off, when she gasped and shrank back in dread. I took her place and peered inside: a gruesome creature with two heads, four arms and two legs was tied up in the middle of the tent. I suppressed a cry as one head turned to look at us, while the other hung helplessly to one side. Saliva dribbled from one slack mouth, while something like a smile spread across the other sad, slightly crooked face. A hand stirred; fingers reached out to me. I counted them: there were six! I stepped back. It was horrid, but I couldn't take my eyes off it. Maggie squeezed in again beside me. At that moment a voice boomed behind us: 'Aha, young ladies, so curious already about my Tent of Wonders?'

We were so startled, we almost tumbled right into the tent. Behind us, a man held on to a dwarf by a short chain wrapped around his neck. To his other side stood a girl in a dress of bright green and blue patches with a rope about her waist; her hair was wrapped in a torn fishing net. I had not seen make-up before and she looked frightful to me: her face seemed to have been pressed in lumpy flour, two garish red patches were painted on her cheeks, and she had outlined her eyes and eyebrows with a lump of coal.

The man bowed. 'I am Master Lampert, bringing the wonders of the world right here to your sorry little village.' I frowned: only we were allowed to badmouth the *mir*, not some random stranger! Master Lampert now kicked the dwarf in the side, whereupon he did a somersault and the bells and dull coins sewn on his jacket clinked cheerfully. 'No one else has dwarves, mermaids and ghastly creatures like mine. Come to my show this evening, ladies!'

Ladies? Maggie and I giggled. No one had ever called us that. Master Lampert ignored our foolishness and carried on, 'There's a fun competition planned, throwing rotten fruit at my monster. Whoever hits it bang, smack in the face, wins.' He pointed at the miserable being in the middle of the tent. Timidly, I glanced at it again. Both its heads were hanging once more, and its arms dangled uselessly. The 'mermaid' – whatever that was supposed to mean – smiled at me, revealing black gaps between her teeth. Dear God, I was glad when at that very moment an angry Tanya dragged Maggie and me out into the open.

'What are you doing, loitering with the travelling folk? Are you one of them?' she snapped at me. 'Come, Christina and I are watching the fire-eater.' In spite of the harshness of her tone, she pressed a few honey-roasted nuts into my hand. God knows how she'd smuggled the money for them past Father who'd surely feel we'd deprived him of a drink or a plug of chewing tobacco. This was a proper feast day and no mistake.

A troupe of musicians came down towards us along the muddy paths between tents and stalls, and the jolly noise of drums, flutes and bells mercifully swallowed Tanya's scolding. I fed a couple of nuts to Maggie and followed Tanya and Christina to the stalls with the fire-eaters, jugglers and a magician in the midst of pluck-ing a red ball from a farmer's grubby ear. The crowd cheered and clapped furiously. Other men pressed forward, wanting to have balls conjured from their ears, too.

Christina pointed to the fire-eater. 'Have you seen those muscles? He eats fire all right,' she giggled. I sighed inwardly. If the monks didn't find a husband for her from among the serfs in the village soon, we would be the ones leaving a little bundle on the edge of the forest.

I strolled on a few paces to a juggler with a long white beard and a bare chest weathered by the sun. A vermillion dot was painted on his forehead, heavy earrings had weighed his lobes down and his white hair was slicked back and plaited: still, his eyes shone bright and clear. He must have seen so many things in his life! I, on the other hand, would always stay here in this village. The crowd fell silent as he added a fourth and fifth club to the three he already held and said in broken German: 'Two clubs – for bunglers! Three clubs – for fools! Four clubs – is good! Five clubs – for masters!'

Christina squeezed in beside me and Maggie's little hand slid into mine. Tanya joined us, too. The clubs flew straight up in the air, high and fast, their wood shimmering in the sun. As he juggled, the old man got his helper to throw him a sixth club, and a seventh. I gasped and then watched breathlessly; the colourful musicians marched noisily past again.

When the juggler took off his cap to ask for money, we walked on, past the barber-surgeon, where people with all sorts of aches and pains queued up. I heard a man's horrified gurgle as the barber pulled the wrong tooth, while there was cheering from the puppeteer's stall: I headed towards it. The play was in full swing. We sat down on the grass with the other onlookers. Surely we could watch for a little while without having to pay? It seemed to be set in a fortress. One puppet wore a glittering round cap, with the Russian double-headed eagle embroidered on its jerkin. That must be the young Russian Tsar. A soldier puppet stepped out in front of it and the man beside me burst into laughter.

'What's this about? Is that the Tsar?' I whispered.

The man beside me nodded. 'Yes. Two years ago, Tsar Peter wanted to visit the fortress in Riga. He's hardly ever in Moscow, did you know that?' I shrugged and he carried on, 'But the Swedes wouldn't let him. An ordinary soldier barred the way to the Tsar of All the Russias, and the King of Sweden –' here he pointed to a third puppet, sitting on a stool '– refused to punish the man. The Tsar is said still to be furious about the insult. He's sworn revenge on all Swedes.' He blew his nose into his fingers. The Tsar-puppet was having a temper tantrum, stamping wildly on its crown. I laughed loudly, along with the others, and was feeding Maggie the last of the sweetened nuts when a shadow fell across me, blocking out the sunlight. A voice said in Russian, 'That's the girl.' I looked up. It was the man from the riverbank.

3

Surrounded by his three companions and a group of monks, he looked even wealthier today amidst us souls, peasants, idlers and scoundrels. His low-slung belt was richly embroidered, and despite the warm spring sunshine the wide collar of his dark green velvet coat was once again trimmed with fur. Tanya jumped up, dragging me to my feet along with her.

One of the monks pointed to me. 'Tanya, is that your daughter?'

'No, *otets*.' We addressed everyone who had power over us as 'father'. 'Marta is my husband's daughter. But I've raised her. Or tried to anyway,' she added bitterly. Her grip on my wrist was painful. 'Has she done something wrong?'

The Russian stroked his beard and smiled at me. I couldn't see his eyes, shaded by his large, flat beaver-fur hat. The monk seized me by the chin. He stank of pickled onions and vestments that had been too long in the wearing. I wrinkled my nose. Couldn't priests wash themselves, or at the very least change their underwear? The monk stared at me brazenly before letting go of me. He turned to Tanya. 'Go home. We'll come to your *izba* early this evening.'

'But it's the dance this evening,' Christina cried out. 'I've been looking forward to it all winter.' All of us had been looking forward to it all winter.

The monk gave Tanya a searching look. She shrugged, turning her face plain and blank. It was the serf's only and oldest weapon against our masters, whose power inevitably made them our enemies. We had to bear their constant meddling in matters sacred to us: family or work. How often were their orders frustrated by the mental void in which we took refuge?

On the way home Christina sulked and Tanya's face was pinched with anger. She spat noisily, and repeatedly, as she walked. When I tried to tell her what had happened beside the river, she just said, 'Shut your mouth. I knew it – all someone like you does is make trouble for us!' Maggie cried, and fell over three times on the short walk. After the third time, I picked her up and carried her on my hip, her warm little body pressed close to mine. Already I sensed it was the last time I would hold her like this.

I was almost relieved when at last, towards evening, there was a knock at the door of our hut. The silence in the *mir* was eerie as everything that was able to walk was at the fair. Waiting for the unknown is a punishment in itself. My father had asked what had happened, but all he learnt was that the monks wanted to come and see me. He sighed, got up from the oven, which took up a whole corner of the *izba*, and poured himself more *kvass* into a shallow bowl. Then he sat on the bench in the 'red' corner of the hut – meaning the good, clean corner – dusting the icon of St Nicholas that was painted in cheap earthen colours on a rough wooden board. He looked at the plain wooden cross beside it and frowned, as if thinking for a moment. In the end he shrugged his shoulders and left both objects hanging there, side by side. My father patted the bench next to him and I sat down.

'What have you been up to, Marta, hmm? It's all right, you can tell me.' To my surprise, he was smiling.

I shrugged. 'Nothing special. A Russian who's staying with the monks wanted to grope me by the river yesterday. So I threatened to smash his skull in.'

My father laughed so hard he began to cough. The smoke from the flat oven that filled our hut had made him sick a long time ago. 'You call that nothing special, eh? Good,' he wheezed, when he was able to breathe again.

Tanya eyed me coldly. Nothing more was said until the men came.

They pushed the door open themselves. As they stepped over the raised threshold my father's face suddenly emptied of expression, just as Tanya's had done earlier. He rose briefly, crossed himself with three fingers in the Russian manner, and then sat down again.

The man from the riverbank for a moment covered his nose with his elbow – coming in from outside, the stench of six people living in a small space hit him full on. He looked around in disgust at the *izba*, whose four walls held our pitiful life together. Boiled moss was wedged between beams to keep cockroaches away. His gaze took in the modest heaps of clothes and blankets we left folded on the floor. Our six coarsely carved wooden bowls were stacked in the corner, beside the vat of water. We relieved ourselves in a second bucket that we emptied onto the street. The corners of his mouth twitched before he wiped his muddy heel on the straw that covered the floor. I hated him for this haughtiness. This, after all, was my home.

'*Brat*,' said the monk to my father. Brother.

My father murmured, 'Welcome, *otets*.'

The monk bowed to our icon and crossed himself. 'Good that you keep your icon clean.'

My father smiled and the monk continued: 'We have a guest at the monastery. Vassily Gregorovich Petrov, a merchant from Walk. He needs a maidservant and has been so gracious as to think of your family.'

Gracious! I almost choked with fury, but Tanya leapt up and pushed Christina forward. She curtseyed clumsily to Vassily and licked her lips. 'My lord. Big houses need many servants. I'm telling you, my lord, no one works as hard, no one is as skilful, as my Christina. Look at her, my lord, isn't she an angel?' She tugged at her daughter's plait until her blonde hair fell loose over her shoulders. 'Her delicate skin ... and such beautiful teeth!'

She forced open Christina's narrow jaw to reveal her teeth, like at the cattle market in spring! It was so revolting even the monk raised his eyebrows. My father turned his face to the wall. Vassily seized Christina's wrist, where the veins shimmered blue through her pale skin. He shook his head.

'She'll die after a single winter. I can't afford to feed useless mouths.' He pinched her narrow hips, making her wince. 'She's no good for childbearing either.' The monk stroked his matted

29

beard. 'No, I want that one. She's healthy and strong as a horse.' He pointed at me. I felt faint.

Tanya cut in again: 'She has bad blood and she's stupid and lazy to boot.' She didn't mean to give up that easily.

'Shut your mouth.' Vassily reached into the leather pouch that hung on his belt beside a dagger and pistol. With a cart full of wares, any journey was long and dangerous. He gave the monk a few coins. Tanya pushed herself forward one last time. 'And what about us? We lose a worker if she goes!' She held out her hand. My father's face darkened. Vassily hesitated, but the monk shrugged, so he gave Tanya one silver coin. She bit it quickly and pocketed it.

Vassily turned to me. 'Pack your things, girl. My cart's already outside. We're leaving right away.'

Tanya nudged me along. I was wearing my good linen tunic, its collar embroidered with a floral pattern, over a clean *sarafan*. Walk was about a three-day ride away; my clothes would be ruined on the journey. When I undid my belt, the monk turned away. Vassily, however, appraised me from top to bottom as I slipped out of my under-dress and put on my simple, long-sleeved day dress with an old tunic on top. My cheeks burned with shame as I wound my braid into a knot and tied my scarf tight around my head. I swore to myself that I wouldn't make it easy for him.

'I'm ready,' I said.

My father hugged me, for the very first time. 'Look after yourself, my child. Your mother was a good woman. We'll see each other in the next life, God willing,' he whispered in my ear.

'What am I to God?' I hissed, to stem my tears. Vassily seized me by the wrist. Maggie started to wail. Tanya slapped her face, which only made her cry even more. The monk made the Sign of the Cross over me and I snarled at him. Then I was out of the door and sitting beside Vassily on the driver's seat. His three men, who hadn't even dismounted, eyed me briefly. They must have known beforehand that the deal would not take long. I felt sick with humiliation.

Most of the journey to Walk I spent crying beside Vassily. He didn't say a word to me, but clicked his tongue at the horses that were bridled in single file, driving them at a fast trot along narrow roads between fields where the clods of earth were already dry and gleaming. In the flat, open countryside his companions rode in front of and behind the cart, so that from afar we must have looked like a skein of wild geese in the sky. In the forest, though, they shielded the cart with their horses' bodies to ward off thieves and wolves. I hardly dared to look around. I knew nothing beyond our *mir*. In the guesthouse where we spent a night, I was given my own room. Vassily locked me in. I had never been in a room alone before. The straw bed was more comfortable than the hard oven I slept on at home. One of his men settled outside my door, while the other two guarded the cart. Was Vassily afraid I would run away? But where would I go? There was no way back.

4

The first sight of Walk was overwhelming to me. Noise and smoke rose up into the dense blue of the sky and the houses here were much bigger than the ones in our *mir*. Most were crowded inside the town's walls, while others sprawled over wide plots of land between the road and the river, built on stilts against the yearly flooding during the *ottepel*, like the houses in my *mir* that stood too close to the Dvina. I tried to count all of Walk's chimneys but gave up as we trundled through the town gates.

I had never seen so many people at once before: the bustle on the streets reminded me of the anthills we used to smoke out in autumn; the insects would flee, running in all directions, which always made me laugh. Farmers were carrying cages of geese and chickens on their shoulders, or driving calves and pigs before them. It must have been market day. Well-dressed gentlefolk placed their shiny leather shoes carefully, avoiding the muck on the streets. Women hurried home with their purchases from the market and red-cheeked boys hawked fresh bread and pastries from laden trays hanging around their necks. Beggars and riff-raff hung about furtively; I had seen their like before on the fairground, probably ready to pilfer an apple here, a bulging purse there. Dogs fought, barking and yelping, over the rubbish thrown in front of the houses; coachmen on other carriages cracked their whips and cursed one another.

This scene beat Master Lampert's Tent of Wonders hands down, even though my nose was already numbed by the stench. In our *mir* all smells – slops, stray cattle, rotting vegetables – were lost in the vastness of the plain. Here, the midday sun was trapped by the alleyways, its heat hanging in suffocating clouds. The people of Walk, I later discovered, simply emptied their chamber pots out of windows, right onto the heads of passers-by. But mercifully the smell of human waste was masked by the alluring scent of delicious foods: soups and sauerkraut, cabbage- and meat-filled *pierogi*, roast chicken, fresh flatbreads, and many, many more things that I, in my poverty, was unable to name but would get to know in the weeks to come.

Vassily saw me staring at a group of men with dark hair and slanting eyes above high cheekbones: 'Those are Tatars from the East. Bloodthirsty, lazy scoundrels, all of them.' They frightened me with their bold gazes and the rough animal pelts they wore, wrapped even around their calves. 'Those fellows over there,' he said, pointing to fairer-skinned men in tight knee-length breeches, silver-buckled shoes and narrow jackets, 'they're Poles.' The tall, blond soldiers were Swedes from the town's small garrison; they winked at me before eyeing up the good German girls going from stall to stall with their mothers and maids. Their hair was worn neatly tucked under stiff, puffy bonnets, yet the bodices of their high-necked dresses were laced almost indecently tight, moulding their bosoms and slim waists. I felt like a savage beside them.

A group of Orthodox priests greeted Vassily, and I saw other Russians, too, in their trailing, belted robes with wide collars, their matted beards still sticky from their lunchtime soup. They grinned at me brazenly. I stuck out my tongue at them behind their backs.

'Is it far?' I finally dared to ask as I had lost all sense of direction. The sky above us was a mere square, concealed by the towering buildings. Where was the horizon, where a forest or a river? How should I ever find my bearings in such a place? I was wondering when Vassily abruptly pulled on the reins. He whistled and a gate opened in a long, high wall. With a clattering of hooves, the horses turned into a cobbled yard.

'We're here,' he said curtly.

His house was inside the town walls, yet near the river. It was so big – surely several families must live in it. Beneath the house, pigs and chickens were penned in among the wooden pilings. To the right and left were stables for the carriages and horses – I caught the animals' warm whiff – with a vast vegetable garden laid out behind. Vassily tossed the reins to a young serving boy and lifted me down, brushing my breast with his hand as he did so. I jumped, but he said calmly, 'Here's Nadia. Go with her into the house and do as she says.'

I looked up, clutching my bundle. A woman was coming towards us across the yard. Her dark hair was streaked with grey and her eyes bulged slightly in their sockets, like the toads we children used to blow up with straws until they burst. Three hairs sprouted from a wart on her chin; fresh blood and feathers were stuck to the apron around her comfortable waist.

'Who's this, my lord?' she asked, frowning, not even looking at me. She placed her hands on her hips as she spoke to him.

'A new maid, Nadia.' Vassily avoided her gaze. 'She's called Marta.'

'Marta what?'

He shrugged. 'I don't know. Does it matter?'

Nadia showed me to my room. She was short of breath after climbing the sturdy timber ladder leading up to a small, draughty chamber. The floor was bare and between two bedsteads stood an open Russian chest made of oak and studded with iron bands and slate. In a corner of the room, I spotted a bucket. When we entered, another girl rose from her bedstead and hastily placed the tunic she was embroidering into the open chest. I could not help but notice the fine colourful thread she used. She curtseyed quickly to Nadia.

'Move your stuff, Olga, there's a new girl. Her name is Marta,' Nadia said, and turned to me, seeing my face: 'What? Did you think you'd have a suite of rooms to yourself? Olga is also a kitchen-maid here. She can break you in, teach you a thing or two.'

Olga lowered her eyes, blushing. I noticed how scrawny she looked next to Nadia. Her clavicles were hard-edged beneath her slender neck and her wrists mere bones. She clutched her hands tightly over the ends of her long, thick blonde plaits.

'Settle in, girl, and don't give me any cause for complaint,' Nadia said to me, ready to leave.

'I will not,' I said hastily. I had to get along with these women. 'I work hard. In the monastery, I cleaned the ovens and the floors and kept the store for the monks ...'

'Good. I have no time for idle hands,' Nadia said curtly. 'Olga, make some space in the chest, will you?' Olga obeyed, shoving her things to one side. My blouse and spare *sarafan*, which I had worn at the fair, certainly would not take up much space. But when I folded my clothes inside the chest I was surprised: next to Olga's neatly folded clothes lay a dress in Western style, some balls of wool tinted the colour of the sky, a comb in a dark and shiny wood, as well as some softly gleaming large buttons, tied together like a posy.

'Any more questions?' Nadia jangled the bunch of keys on her belt. She certainly looked in charge and was impatient to get on with things.

'Yes,' I dared to say.

She raised her eyebrows. 'What?'

'How will I not get lost here? The house is so vast,' I said, yet I felt it might not be vast enough to hide me from Vassily. The sight of that narrow bedstead terrified me: would he come for me here tonight? Did the other women know why I was here?

Olga smiled at me, but Nadia's reply was curt. 'Do your work well and you will not lose your way. Olga, the fire needs rekindling for the master's samovar and *chai*. Don't forget the vodka in his cup, to warm his bones.' Olga slid out of the room. When Nadia made a decision, there was no contradicting her.

Taking care to stay on the housekeeper's good side, as well as sharing the bedchamber with Olga, might shield me from Vassily, I hoped, yet my stomach clenched with fear. How should I sleep a wink and still be strong enough to do my chores? I remembered his words from the riverbank all too well, and he did not seem like a man to make idle threats.

5

Nadia, Olga and I cured meat and fish, pickled mushrooms and root vegetables, marinated fruit, vegetables and herrings in alcohol and vinegar, and stuffed *verst* after *verst* of sheep's intestines with spiced meat to make sausages. Chickens, geese and piglets ran around my legs, and the huge, glowing oven added to the summer heat, making it unbearable. As soon as Nadia turned her back on me, I would nibble at things and stick my fingers in all the saucepans, which made Olga warn me, only half-jokingly: 'Stop eating, otherwise you'll grow all fat and Nadia might slaughter you in autumn as well.' But I'd never dreamt such delicacies existed. I had worked in the monastery kitchen on feast days, but what was the monks' simple food compared to this heavenly fare?

Vassily's pantry had to be kept well stocked for his many guests, who often arrived and stayed several days. The shelves were stacked with jars of vinegar, oil and gherkins. Milk was left in barrels to sour into *kefir*, or hung in muslin cloths to make cheese, if I didn't have to skim it and churn the cream into salted butter. Greaves, flour, red and white onions, nuts, lentils, peas and beans – thin green ones, as well as the fat white ones Tanya used to boil into a slimy stew – were all stored in sacks. Hanging from the ceiling, beside lightly salted sides of ham, were bundles of herbs and spices, all except the saffron, which Nadia kept locked away in a casket. When I'd asked why, she'd told me it came from a country in the East and was weighed and priced like gold. 'Once we had a maid who pinched a bit and Vassily had me break her fingers. They didn't quite grow back together again,' she said, with the hint of a smile.

The rest of the time I beat skins and carpets, turned or changed the straw on the floor or waxed the floorboards until they shone and smelled of honey, and dusted the gilded frames of the icons on the wood-panelled walls. I was uncomfortable about having to air the bed in Vassily's room in the mornings. So far he almost seemed to have forgotten my presence, yet the cruellest hunter puts its prey at ease before striking suddenly. Nadia taught me how to sprinkle the washed and thoroughly dried linen with a brush of feathers dipped in water in which she had soaked peeled and sliced potatoes – afterwards I would touch the starched and herb-scented sheets in awe. Even the monks' cells that I had cleaned in the monastery just offered bare planks or stone hollows for beds. At home I'd slept together with my family on top of the big, flat oven in our *izba*, burrowed deep in warm straw, like pigs in a sty. I tried not to think of them and of days past, as it made me too miserable. I longed so much for my family. Often I cried into my pillow and at first Olga would leave me be, folding her hands as in prayer on top of her thin blanket.

Vassily traded in anything that made him money: linen from Russia, French velvet, and another cloth called silk. Once, Olga held one of the bales against her cheek, sighing at its shine and softness: 'Did you know that its threads don't come from fields like cotton, or animals like wool?'

'No?' I snorted. 'So do they fall from the sky or what?'

'Well, almost. Vassily told me it is spun by big, fat caterpillars that do nothing all day but hang around on certain trees, munching leaves.'

I laughed. 'How stupid do you think I am? Show me a caterpillar like that and I'd swap places any time!'

'It's true,' she said, her voice plaintive, as she placed the bale of silk back on the shelf. Vassily kept a careful inventory of his goods: wax and honey, salt, sugar and flour, meerschaum, fats and oils, leather – and little pouches of a strange white powder that had a powerful effect. I could always tell when he had sampled it. He would then be in high spirits and go to town together with friends to a *kabak* – an inn that served only vodka – his whip dancing playfully against his shiny, freshly polished boots.

There was a second storeroom that he kept tightly locked. 'What's in there?' I asked Nadia on my first visit to the warehouse. 'Why should I risk my neck by telling you?' she asked, before telling me anyway, proud of her knowledge. This was where he hid forbidden treasures: sable, ermine, vodka and caviar in buckets of ice to keep it cool. Only the Tsar was allowed to trade in these goods and even here, outside the Russian Empire, Vassily could have his nose cut off for his misdeed, or be broken on the wheel. No Tsar was to be trifled with where his income was concerned – not even Peter, despite the strange things we heard about him.

When Nadia wasn't around to forbid it, Olga and I would lure the servants of Vassily's customers into the kitchen, calling to them from the window, laughing and teasing them by blowing kisses. Then, over a mug of *kvass*, they would tell us everything that was going on in the world outside.

'You won't believe it, my girl. They say the Tsar isn't even in Russia! He calls himself Peter Mikhailov, lives on cabbage like you and me, and is learning how to build boats in Holland.'

What nonsense, I thought, but politely held my tongue. No one in their right mind would swap the richest of lives for our daily drudgery.

Or: 'If Peter carries on like this, Charles of Sweden is going to show us what for! He's still a child, but he exercises with his troops from morning to night. They're great towering fellows who adore him and obey his every order. Now *that's* a real king.' Their own Tsar bewildered them: he had just issued a decree ordering them to cut off their beards. Had Peter lost his mind? Being clean-shaven was sheer blasphemy: every icon showed Christ with a beard. Was he a changeling after all like the old stories said, one his mother had smuggled in from the German Quarter on the outskirts of Moscow, desperate for a son after the birth of a daughter? Or was the influence of his German whore, Anna Mons, to blame? He was with her in spite of his marriage to a good and god-fearing Russian noblewoman, who'd given him a healthy son as heir to the throne. Even I had heard rumours that Peter was a false Tsar.

One evening at the end of May when I was lying awake – crying as usual while listening to the white night outside, full of birdsong and longing – I heard the floorboards of our room creak. I was so scared by the noise that I even stopped sobbing, my heart pounding. Was this Vassily coming for me? Olga stood by my bedside, the light pooling around her bare, thin feet, and her threadbare nightshirt hanging like a limp flag on the pole that was her body.

'What?' I asked, sitting up, wiping my nose and feeling almost defiant.

Olga reached out and her long, slender fingers caressed my hair. 'Stop crying, Marta. You exhaust yourself and you have to be strong,' she whispered before withdrawing, her expression like a veil when she turned and climbed back into her bed. She could only offer words to comfort me, but after them I fell deeply asleep as I never had before in Vassily's house, exhausted from all that had happened and all the new things I had to learn. Perhaps it was because of her unaccustomed tenderness and the brief solace she had offered me that I neither heard the steps coming up our narrow flight of stairs, nor the feet coming along the corridor, heavy with drink and lust. I only woke when the door was thrown open, shrieking on its hinges as it never seemed to do in daytime. I sat up, startled. Vassily stood on the threshold, the milky light of night showing him a clear path to my bed.

Though I was unable to move, my thoughts raced. The moment had come. What exactly would happen, what would he do? If he only lets me live, I thought. Vassily stood there, swaying a little in the doorway, steadying his heavy body against the frame with one hand. I did not stand a chance against him I knew, and pulled my knees up tight. Vassily was still catching his breath after the climb and I yanked the blanket over my head, shielding my eyes from the sight of him, and my head against any blows or else him taking me by the scruff of the neck. At least I would not see him come for me; it would be awful enough to feel him and to suffer his wrath. Had the long wait before it fell on me been part of my punishment for defying him?

'Come here,' he said hoarsely, his voice thick with drink. 'Or shall I come and get you, girl?'

6

Perhaps it would be better for me to give in. I looked towards Olga; all was quiet from her bed. How could she sleep through this – or was she stricken by sheer terror, as I was? I took a deep breath and prepared to peel back the blanket. The time had come and now the only thing to do was to survive it. If I could just stop shaking. I didn't even know how I'd stand in this state.

A loud creak from Olga's bed surprised me. 'I'm coming,' she said, in a voice brittle as dead leaves. I held my breath, stunned, and then hiccupped with surprise as I peered out from beneath the edge of my blanket and between my spread fingers. She rose from her bed as if dressed in a flaxen sheet, her light blonde hair flowing to beyond her hips as she stepped towards him. He grabbed it, wrapping it around his hand and pulling. She let out a short, pained scream. He led her out of the door, which he did not deign to shut, and into the corridor.

I heard it all. When Olga stumbled back into our chamber, her thin legs trembling, clutching her torn nightshirt to her like a drowning person might a piece of driftwood, I was by her side before she fell down on her bed. I held her head, felt her tears on my throat and her slender body heaving, stroked her hair and dabbed her cut lip until the blood clotted.

'Why is he doing this?' I asked, hearing the helplessness in my voice.

She tried to shrug but winced: I saw bruises blooming on her shoulder. 'This is nothing. It gets him going. If I put up a fight, it's even worse.' Her blue eyes were huge in the moonlight. Was this what Nadia had meant by Olga being able to teach me 'a thing or two'? Her hot cheek pressed into my palm, she whispered: 'Don't help me. You can't. Help yourself.'

The following day, I saw her dip her fingers in a tub of pork lard and sneak up to our room, where she greased the door's hinges. I understood: the shrieking sound when Vassily came for her made her shame worse. A couple of weeks later, I did not wake from my restless slumber when he summoned her, but from the sound of her retching over the bucket in the corner of our chamber. In our chest, I spotted a new pair of soft green gloves on Olga's pile of clothes, next to her other treasures.

'Have you been in Vassily's service long?' I asked Nadia one afternoon in August in my still clumsy Russian, which caused endless laughter in the house.

We were shredding cabbage for a pie of bacon and vegetables. The kitchen was sweltering in the summer heat. My hair stuck to my forehead and I had shortened the sleeves of my *sarafan* as much as possible, pulling on the strings there. I took care to do my chores swiftly and with a smile, so Nadia would not cuff me. That day she seemed in a good enough mood to chat.

'My family belonged to his father so I grew up in his service.' She gave me a short, sharp look. 'Even though I wasn't pretty or charming, I was allowed to work at their house. I could be trusted. When Vassily's mother died giving birth to him, I raised him.'

I almost dropped the cabbage stalk I was holding. 'So you are like a mother to him?'

Instead of answering, she cast me a glance and I busied myself with the cabbage, guarding my tongue. Nadia was at Vassily's beck and call as any housekeeper worth her salt would be, bowing to his every demand while mercilessly keeping us in check. That she had raised him as her own child shocked me nevertheless, as I only knew love for my younger siblings. Exactly how close was Nadia to the master?

'Doesn't he have any family then?' I asked, stirring the chopped cabbage that floated in a shallow bucket of water, cleaning it thoroughly, as both earth and small slugs loved to stick to its layered leaves.

'He's a widower and childless,' she replied. 'His wife died three years ago of consumption.' She checked another cabbage stalk for blemishes and then halved it with a single chop.

'What about Olga?' I dared to ask. Olga, who tied her tunic more loosely these days and nibbled sour gherkins and pickled Baltic herring when she thought no one was looking.

Nadia split the next cabbage stalk with a powerful blow that made me jump. 'Olga was bought a year ago, a bit like yourself. Our lord has made her pregnant.'

'Our lord?' I said stupidly, lowering my own knife. 'But that only happens in the Bible.'

'Fool,' scolded Nadia. 'Vassily's a man like any other. And Praskaya can't keep an eye on him all the time.' She chuckled, which made the hairs on her wart quiver in rhythm. 'But she'll be back soon.'

'Who's Praskaya?' I gathered the discarded leaves to feed the chicken and pigs later.

Nadia clicked her tongue. 'Praskaya's a snake. She's Vassily's mistress. Can hold her own in any drinking game, and her jokes would make even a soldier's ears burn. She allows him to stray, but only as long as no other woman is a threat to her ...' She fell silent, because at that moment Grigori, the young stable boy, came into the kitchen, followed by Olga herself, who had been washing and darning the horse blankets. Grigori was about fourteen or fifteen years old, with arms and legs that seemed too long for his skinny body, and angry pustules blooming across his cheeks and neck. To me he resembled a cross between a puppy and a colt, like my brother Fyodor had.

'I'm starving, girls. Can I have some of the vegetable soup?' He eyed the cauldron where the pea soup – lunch for everyone – was bubbling on the open fire. Its scent was laced with bacon rind, heavenly, thick and moreish.

'Cats and maids eat in spades, servants and dogs wait by the bogs,' Nadia said with a scowl, but then filled a wooden bowl for him anyway. Grigori sat with us, slurping his soup contentedly. I was tempted to point two fingers like a pair of horns to ward off the evil eye when Olga crossed herself with three fingers behind Grigori's back. I noticed scratches and deeper marks like cuts on her arms. As little as she spoke about herself, she knew things about others and had told me all about Grigori: 'Keep well away from him – he's got the evil eye.'

In the milky evening light of our chamber her words had crawled across my skin like spiders' legs. 'Really?' I'd sat up, pulling the threadbare blanket high as my chin.

'It comes over him all of a sudden, when he's exhausted. He screams and twitches and thrashes about before throwing himself on the ground. Then he foams at the mouth, as if the Devil himself were in him.'

'Has he always been like that?' I'd shivered, in spite of the blanket.

'Yes, he used to have these fits as a child. But he's been much worse since Vassily punished him.'

'Punished him? What for?' My throat had suddenly gone dry, thinking of the maid who had pinched saffron. Severe measures were taken for even small mistakes.

'Grigori wasn't paying attention. Vassily's stallion scraped its flank on a rusty hook in the stable and died of blood poisoning. Vassily whipped Grigori senseless. Since then we've often had to tie the boy up when he goes into convulsions, to stop him from hurting himself.'

Did I really think that Vassily would forget and forgive any offence, least of all from a girl who had threatened him in front of his men?

'Some soup, Olga?' Nadia offered her, but she shook her head, turning her face away in disgust. 'You have to eat,' Nadia scolded, while Grigori sat hunched on his stool, eating his soup and smiling shyly at me whenever I caught his eye. Nadia glared at us, sieved the rest of the flour, chucked away tiny pieces of gravel and husks, and weighed out the precious salt before giving me my orders. 'Go to the chicken shed and collect the eggs,' she said, and I sighed: Vassily's chickens were foul beasts that put up a fight for each and every egg they were obliged to yield. Nadia added: 'Then chop the white onions.' White onions! They always made me cry my eyes out.

*

When Praskaya returned from her travels, she hated me on sight. I had to tie my hair back tightly, hide it under a scarf and keep my eyes lowered at all times. She gave me the hardest tasks. 'Carry the coal bucket!' 'Sweep out the fireplaces – look at the state of them!' 'The pigs have to go out in the field – don't dawdle, go on, go, go, go.' If I showed the slightest clumsiness, she would box my ears, dig her nails into my arm or pinch me hard, twisting my skin, leaving blue and blackish bruises. Once she pushed me as I was carrying boiling water for her bath; I stumbled and almost scalded my hands and feet. In the evening, she would lock our bedroom door. Olga and I were prisoners every night, which also meant Vassily wouldn't come to us. 'Thank you, Praskaya,' we laughed, before, despite our fear, we sank into deep, dreamless sleep.

It was the hottest, driest summer in living memory. Under the burning sun, corn caught fire in the fields and the harvest failed. I worried desperately: from all over the country we heard dreadful stories. Souls died during their work in the fields, and their masters – against every law of man and country – first closed their ears to their serfs' pleas and then their cellars and pantries to the starving. Corpses lay bloated in their *mir* or floated downstream, to be eaten by fishes and bears. Still, I also heard that those who could left the stricken villages. At night I did not draw the curtains and looked up to the sky, hoping for my family to find a new home elsewhere, in peace and safety.

Olga gave birth to a boy: Nadia chased me from our chamber as labour started. All I was allowed to do was heat vat upon vat of water. For hours her agony pierced both my soul and the kitchen walls, where I sat, my head buried in my arms, my hands on my ears. Her son Ivan was never christened. Praskaya let the newborn slip from her hands while bathing him in her tub. Perhaps it was for the best. With a bit of luck, a nice young man might still marry Olga and make an honest woman of her. But a few months later, during a late, windy spring with the river frozen longer than usual, she was pregnant again. Clearly, Vassily did not need the key to our chamber to get to her. I tried to comfort her; her pale eyes welled up and she turned away.

When the master left on his travels, using the warmer months to fill his storerooms, Praskaya found some ridiculous reason to give Olga a whipping. The next morning, Olga's bed was empty. How and when did she tiptoe out? I cursed her greasing of the hinges: we looked everywhere for her, but in vain. Two days later the Dvina washed up her body. Weeds hung in her hair; fish had nibbled away her eyelids. Her big blue eyes stared out at nothing, and her little hands were clenched above her swollen, but sagging belly as if in prayer. As Olga had taken her own life, she wasn't buried in sacred ground, but thrown into a clay pit outside the city walls, where animals were known to dig up the corpses and eat them. I felt like clinging to Nadia when the town warden sent two coarse men to collect Olga's body. They threw her corpse onto their cart, but the housekeeper made no protest, just turned and went about her work. The following week, Vassily drove Praskaya away. What became of her, I do not know. Then, at night, he came for me.

7

Living in constant fear would not allow me to sleep properly. Still, the floorboards creaking under Vassily's feet woke me from an exhausted slumber. He was on top of me before I could scream, pressing his hand over my mouth, pulling me to my feet. I felt instantly wide awake with terror, biting down on his stubby fingers. He let go but slapped me so hard that I fell backwards onto my bed. I tasted blood on my lips and gave a sob.

He sat on my thighs, pinned my hands above my head and tore my nightshirt from my body: my breasts shimmered pale in the moonlight. Panting, he tweaked my nipples and sucked greedily at my flesh, biting me and gasping, 'By God, you're beautiful. Your Tatar slut of a mother must have chewed wild garlic, your eyes are so slanted and green. And how splendidly you've fattened up. It felt like poking a bag of bones when I was with Olga.'

I struggled under his weight, but he slapped me again, and harder than before. I thought of Grigori, and kept still: did I want to be beaten foolish, like him?

'I knew it. You want it too,' said Vassily smugly, taking off his nightshirt. His naked belly hung down over his small penis. 'Besides, I like a wildcat like you.'

'Please, don't,' I begged, although I knew it was pointless. Vassily's cock was bent and wrinkled; he rubbed it, but it stayed tiny and red, like a stray dog's. He saw me staring at it and screamed, 'You've hexed me!' He yanked me to my feet and cursed, probably praying in vain to all the saints in Russia to make him go hard. I was flooded with relief: perhaps he would go away again and leave me in peace for good. But no. He dragged me off the bed and pushed me to my knees, forcing open my jaw. I felt sick. Surely he couldn't ... ! Yes, he could. He shoved his limp thing into my mouth, grabbed my head and dug his fingers into my hair.

'Lick it. Suck it, my little witch; nice and slow, deep and firm. That's how I like it.' He pushed himself deeper and deeper down my throat until I gagged, but he tugged my hair and threatened, 'Bite me and see what I do to you.'

I closed my eyes and timidly sucked and licked at the disgusting thing in my mouth. Vassily began to groan and I felt him swell. I wanted to die. Hopefully it would soon be over – whatever 'over' meant.

Just then he pulled away and said hoarsely, 'Turn around now.' Vassily threw me face down on the bed, spread my thighs and shoved two fingers between my legs. He gave a satisfied laugh.

'You're like a bitch in heat, yet you're still a virgin.' Then he opened my legs wider and spat on my most secret spot, before he started forcing himself inside me, each movement agony. Please God, if only he would stop! He was right on top of me, scraping me raw inside. Still he thrust, again and again, panting and slapping my buttocks. He spanked me harder and harder, so that I bit my pillow, before he kneaded my breasts and buried himself inside me. Had Olga had to endure this, over and over again? Perhaps Praskaya wasn't the reason she had killed herself after all. My voice cracked; I could neither scream nor cry. Vassily reared up, then fell on top of me. His breath rattled as he slid out of me, and it felt sticky and damp between my legs. Olga had told me that this was when it was most dangerous. His weight was almost crushing me.

Time dripped past; everything inside me ached. When Vassily finally started snoring, I struggled out from beneath him. He grunted, and I limped over to where a bowl of water stood in the corner of the room. I leant against the wall and held on to the door handle before sinking onto a stool. All my limbs were shaking. It was awhile before I stroked my tangled hair off my face and licked at the dried blood on my swollen lips. Vassily lay sprawled across my bed. I couldn't look at him, but broke the thin crust of ice on the water and washed carefully between my legs. The rag was soon red with blood.

Every month, thank God, my bleeding still came. After that first terrible night, Nadia turned a blind eye to me sneaking into the room where Praskaya's bathtub still stood, and left the kitchen when I stoked the fire to heat bucket after bucket of hot water. As I carried the last bucket to the tub, a piece of camphor-scented soap lay on its rim. I ladled the hot water over my body countless times, hoping to cleanse my soul.

In the kitchen afterwards she glanced at me before saying in a matter-of-fact way: 'It won't be nearly as bad from now on.'

I wasn't sure that was really a comfort.

Vassily visited me almost nightly. I learnt how to give him pleasure, which disgusted me but made him come more quickly, so that he would leave me sooner rather than later. He gave me presents as he had done with Olga, which made me feel like a whore: another dress in the German style, which I put on a scarecrow in a field, or boxes of sticky sweets from somewhere far south of the Black Sea. I burnt them in the oven; the sugar melted and I breathed in the bitter-sweet smoke with flared nostrils. Sometimes, at night, I dreamt of Olga. Had it been she who had kept me at bay, never confiding in me or asking me for pity, or had I stayed away from her, lest her bad luck might spread, trying to survive just like everybody else here?

During my rare breaks, I walked to the riverside where her corpse had been found. Where she was now, no one could hurt her anymore. It was a tempting thought that made me sad, but also angry. Several times I waded out into the waves until my skirt grew wet and heavy. But I didn't have the courage; or perhaps I didn't feel the true, deep despair needed to surrender myself forever to the waters of the Dvina.

In November of the same year, the sharpness of the air was crystal-lising the breath on my lips. The blue ice on the Dvina glistened in the bright sunshine when I left the house by the kitchen door. I wrapped a blanket over my woollen dress, slipped into the servants' boots standing next to the door and went out to the stables to bring Grigori fresh hot *chai*. The poor lad had to make sure the water troughs for Vassily's horses didn't freeze over. To stop himself from falling asleep, he always held a sack full of pieces of metal. If he nodded off too deeply, so that his muscles relaxed, the sack would fall to the ground with a clang; then Grigori would shake himself awake, seize his club and smash the thin layer of ice that had already formed on the water in that brief moment of rest. Two of his toes had already frozen off, and he was constantly exhausted from the lack of proper sleep. I hurried, because the bowl of *chai* was very hot, but at the stable door I stopped. What was that strange noise? I heard a whistle, and rattling breaths.

'Grigori, are you there?' I asked, but shrank back as Vassily flung open the stable door. He was wearing nothing but breeches and knee-high boots, and despite the cold he was drenched in sweat. In his hand he held his long horsewhip with the silver pommel.

'What do you want?' he snarled. For the past two days he'd had an infected tooth that must have been hellishly painful. His cheek was red and swollen.

I held out the bowl. 'I've brought *chai* for Grigori. It's so very cold . . .' Then I looked over Vassily's shoulder and fell silent, horrified. He had tied Grigori to a wooden beam with his arms stretched above his head, and had ripped the boy's shirt – already far too thin for winter! – right down to his belt. Was Grigori still alive? The skin of his back hung down in bloody strips. My stomach turned and I retched at the sight of it. What could the poor boy possibly have done?

'Oh my God!' I dropped the clay bowl; it smashed, and spattered *chai* all over Vassily's boots. 'Why have you done this?' I asked, aghast. I pressed my fingers over my mouth to force back the rising bile.

He spat out, 'Lazy, useless creature! He fell asleep, and now the troughs are frozen. How are my horses supposed to drink?'

'You've beaten him half to death because he fell asleep? He's just a boy. Stop –' These days, I could get away with a number of things with Vassily, but instead of answering he went back inside the stable. Grigori merely sighed as the whip sliced down on his raw flesh once more. He was still alive, but barely so, and Vassily was about to strike him again. I couldn't stop myself; I hurled myself onto his arm and tore the horsewhip from his hand. 'You animal! You're killing him,' I shouted.

Vassily shoved me; I stumbled, fell over backwards in the straw and dropped the whip. He grabbed it and hit me with it, two or three times. I curled up, shielding my head with my arms. The whip licked across my hands. It felt like an animal clawing at me, and I howled. Vassily wiped the sweat from his brow and his eyes almost popped from their sockets. 'Just you wait until tonight. I'll teach you to behave like that with your master.' Then he left the stable.

I sat up slowly. The whip had torn both the blanket and my dress. Warm blood trickled down my arm, but I could deal with that later: Grigori's head was hanging back, his whole body rigid, and he was gurgling and foaming at the mouth. When I loosened the rope, he collapsed on the straw with a sigh. Vassily's shirt lay nearby: I folded it to make a cushion for Grigori's head.

Then came the seizure, more terrible and more violent than I could ever have imagined. His face twisted and his eyes bulged; he did look possessed as he thrashed about, arms and legs jerking, gurgling incomprehensible words. Suddenly a stream of blood mingled with the foam at his mouth and he spat out a piece of pink, spongy flesh. I shrank back and crossed myself, before taking pity on him and overcoming my fear. What could I do? I thought of how I used to calm my younger siblings when they screamed, and I grabbed his lolling head. His eyes rolled back until only the whites were show-ing. I mastered my dread and pressed his face firmly against my breasts, rocking him back and forth, crying silently as he gradually quietened in my arms. At last he lay still. His life was now in God's hands. I felt his breath go cold between my breasts, in fits and starts, before it stalled.

Moments later, Grigori was dead.

8

For the rest of the day, I was strangled by a fear that curdled my blood and twisted my guts. Never before and never again have I known such terrible foreboding. I saw Vassily neither in the house nor in the yard. Nadia and I stood and watched as Grigori's body was dragged from the stable. I wept: what would Vassily do to me now?

Nadia eyed me but said nothing. She knew well enough what was going on and tonight of all nights, it was my turn to keep watch over the fire in the kitchen, which in winter could not be allowed to go out. I couldn't lock myself in the maids' room; I was utterly at Vassily's mercy. When Nadia wanted to go to bed, I clung to her against all reason.

'Can't you stay with me, Nadia? Please.'

She loosened my grip. 'What on earth have you done? I have never seen him so angry.' My heart sank: she should know, she had raised him after all. He ought to be like a son to her. I knew I couldn't expect more from her than that square remark.

Feeling doomed, I moved around the dark kitchen like a sleep-walker, pointlessly scrubbing the top of the stove again and again with a sprinkling of ash and a coarse brush. As long as I was doing something, no one could do anything to me, I thought foolishly. Eventually I wrapped myself in my blanket, exhausted, on the warm floor in front of the stove. I couldn't sleep, listening wide-eyed to the silence. Pictures were chasing madly through my mind:

Olga's heavy belly, swollen with Vassily's bastard. Ivan's little limbs sinking into the depths of Praskaya's tub. The terrible sight of Grigori's battered body. I didn't want to die: not like that, not now. Then I heard Vassily's footsteps approaching, swift and threatening. Before I could hide, he grabbed me, dragged me to my feet and pressed me against the wall.

'Look at me before I kill you. Look what I've got for you.' He dangled a whip with several knotted straps before my eyes. I hiccupped in horror. Executioners used lashes like these to flay thieves and swindlers alive. A single blow would tear off layers of skin. 'Yes.' He enjoyed seeing my despair. 'Do you know what the Regent Sophia did with disobedient souls? She flogged them, rubbed them with vodka and set them on fire. I am still her loyal subject and I spit on the false Tsar Peter. You're going to make a beautiful torch, Marta.' He pulled me over to the big kitchen table and bent me across its heavy wooden top. He kissed me then, which made me gag, and bore down with all his weight.

Vassily's head on my throat and chest almost choked me and I gasped for air. He was pushing up my dress and spreading my legs. He didn't think I'd put up any real struggle. In the dim light I frantically swept my hands over the table, first beside me, then behind my head. That afternoon, Nadia had been crush-ing herbs, right here where I was lying; she'd used the heavy brass pestle and mortar, because the frozen greens didn't give up their flavour lightly. Vassily pulled my hips up. As he threw himself on me, my fingers stretched back as far as they could and brushed against the cool metal of the mortar. Quickly, I pulled it towards me.

'Turn over,' Vassily groaned, and started yanking me onto my stomach. No! I'd be lost then. And so I raised the pestle with all my strength and brought it crashing down onto his skull. There was a hideous, crunching sound, like cartwheels on frozen snow. In the faint glow from the fire, Vassily's face changed: turning first aston-ished, then empty. He opened his mouth and spat over me, spilling not words and hatred, but blood. His skull had split in two like a walnut. But that was no longer enough for me: I hit him again, and a third time, spurred on by my fury, my helplessness and the shame he had made me suffer. He should not go to the next world with the face of a man.

Vassily slumped, fell sideways and lay still on the cold stone floor. I slid off the table and knelt beside him. His face was a pulp. I was still holding the pestle; I smashed it down one last time, just to be sure. I felt sick, the kitchen spun all around me and I passed out on the floor next to him.

9

Someone was wiping my face with a damp cloth. I came to and blinked: Nadia was kneeling over me in her nightdress, her hair braided in two long plaits. Her nightlight – a piece of rope dipped in rancid pig fat – flickered on the floor beside us. It gave off an evil stench, but there was another, more nauseating smell: the kitchen reeked of blood and death, just like slaughter day in the village.

Nadia shook me. 'Marta, wake up.'

I tried to sit, but everything hurt. Then I saw Vassily: all that was left of his face was a bloody mess. Had I done this? I pulled myself onto my knees, closed my eyes and rubbed my temples with trembling fingers. My whole body shivered now and I felt so weak I could barely move.

'He wanted to kill me, Nadia. He threatened to flog me, rub me with vodka and set me on fire,' I stammered, looking up at her. The nightlight drew strange shadows over her face with its bulging eyes and lips pinched in steady disapproval. What had I done? The kitchen closed in on me. I tried to steady my head by holding it and gasping as if coming up for air after having been held under-water. 'Please, Nadia –' I started, and cowered away, but she didn't say anything. Mine was the worst kind of *volnenye*: any form of disobedience by a soul towards their master. Men were broken on the wheel for it, women were buried alive up to their heads and left to die of thirst and starvation. Only in milder cases were they condemned to a life of hard labour in the spinning mills. But killing Vassily was no milder case.

My teeth were chattering. I wrapped my arms around my knees to hold them steady, but my legs were trembling too much with cold and fear. 'Please,' I said again, as she took a step closer, ready to seize me. On her face, emotions chased each other: stunned surprise, shock and then, sheer hatred. I wrapped my hands around my head, ready for her blows. Would she finish Vassily's work and pour vodka over me before setting me alight? I peered through my elbows, sobbing.

Nadia kicked Vassily's faceless body with all her might, once, and then again. His ribs crunched and she stomped on his fingers. 'Serves him right, the dog. He should be fed to his sows.' She stopped, breathing heavily, and looked at me, thoughtful and stern-faced. I hiccupped with surprise. 'Someone should have done this long ago,' she said. 'What are we going to do with you? They'll torture you, and then you'll be executed. Come with me,' Nadia said, pulling me to my feet. I stumbled up, wiping snot and tears off my face with my sleeve. 'We have to be fast. It's almost morning.'

I tried not to step in Vassily's blood, which was all over the kitchen floor. Nadia shuffled ahead of me down the corridor, her candle dancing like a will-o'-the-wisp, and I followed. She was leading me not back to my room, but deeper inside the house.

'Where are we going?' My voice cracked.

'Come,' she said. Finally, she stopped outside the room where Vassily met his customers. Only Nadia had access to it. She pushed the door open and raised her nightlight. The curtains were drawn and last embers glimmered in the iron grate. On a wide wooden desk a quill was stuck in an inkwell. The letters and numbers on the papers and scrolls looked to me like mouse droppings; next to them I spotted an empty carafe of vodka. Nadia sniffed it scornfully: was this how Vassily had summoned up his courage, and his cruelty? One of the small bags of white powder lay beside it, open and still half-full. Nadia moistened her finger, dipped it in the powder, sniffed it hard up her nose and rubbed some on the roof of her mouth and her gums. Then, she grinned, and swept her arm across the desk, making Vassily's bills and papers whirl up into the air. His books flew across the room; their pigskin bindings came off and they lay there, tattered and open, as she kicked them about. I sneezed from the dust.

'Help me,' she said, tipping the contents of the desk drawers onto the floor. Quills, slide rules, coins, knives, inkpots, leather pouches, bullets and pipe tampers tumbled out at my feet. I gawped, too surprised to cry, as Nadia finally tore down one of the curtains and kicked over the chair behind the desk. 'What are you doing?' I stared around at the chaos in the room.

Nadia shrugged. 'We've had burglars in here, Marta.'

'Burglars?' I was dumbstruck.

'Yes,' she said, as if speaking to a child. 'The ones who killed Vassily. Such a terrible thing. Our good and generous master.' Her bulging eyes glittered with cunning. Suddenly, she seemed capable of anything and was no longer a servant, but the one who gave the orders.

'What are we going to do with you, Marta? You have to leave, right now, and never come back. You've only got until dawn.'

'Where would I go?' I begged. 'I have no one, Nadia.'

'I can help you with one thing only. After that, you'll have to trust in God.' Her hand slipped under a shelf: she found a little key and unlocked the casket on Vassily's writing desk.

'How did you know it was there?' I was stunned.

'I know everything that goes on in this house, Marta.' She counted out a small handful of coins, although the casket was full of them. 'Do you have another dress, apart from those rags?' She pointed at my torn and bloodstained *sarafan*.

'Not a plain one. Olga's clothes are still in our room, but her dress is not made in the Russian fashion.'

She pressed the coins into my palm. 'So much the better. Pack your bundle. No one will remember one maid more or less in Walk. The carts set off from the town gates at daybreak for Marienburg. You'll buy a ride. Do you understand? That's far enough away. I'll wait till sunrise to call for help. The money's enough for the journey, and for you to live on for the next few days. After that you'll have to fend for yourself.' Nadia grabbed my chin and stared me down. 'I never, ever want to see you here again, Marta. Is that clear?'

'Marienburg?' I said dully. The city was many *versty* and many worlds away.

'No one will think to look for you there,' she repeated.

'What will happen to you?' The coins lay cool in my hand; only a few, but it was more money than I had ever seen.

Nadia smiled. The candlelight flickered in the draught from the open door, drawing lines on her round, smooth face. She pointed to the casket. 'There's enough for me here. When all this is over, I'll move in next to my sister's *izba*, with a little garden. I shall die honoured and loved,' she said. 'It's more than I could ever have wished for.'

There was nothing else to say.

Nadia led me back to my room through the silent house. She watched while I hastily washed my face and packed: a good *sarafan*, my woollen tunic and a last pouch of sticky sweets that Vassily had given me just a few days ago. 'I'll have these,' Nadia decided, and took Olga's buttons, the balls of wool and the dark, shiny comb. 'These you'll have better use for,' she said, and gave me the green gloves. 'Let's get you dressed and out of the door.'

Putting on Olga's dress was harder than I'd expected; it was tailored for when she was not pregnant. Nadia squashed my flesh into the bodice and laced me up. The bones in the seams pinched my waist until I could hardly breathe. Then I put on the *tulup*, a heavy sheepskin coat – another of Vassily's presents – as well as two pairs of thick woollen socks so I could wear the boots that were kept by the front door for the menservants. I twisted my hair into a knot and tied the scarf tight around my ears and chin.

Nadia clapped her hands. 'How wonderfully ugly you can be. Nobody's going to look at you twice. But be sure to lower your eyes, my girl,' she said. 'There's not another pair like them in all of Walk. Slanted and green, like a cat's.'

I nodded, forgetting to lower my eyes, and Nadia cuffed me. We walked in silence to the front door, where she gave me a blanket of double-knitted wool that I rolled up under my arm. Then she grabbed me by the shoulders. 'This night, Marta, will forever be our secret. If ever you should speak of what has happened, may the Devil cut off your ears, nose and hands, and roast you alive.'

Nadia's curse was heartfelt and frightening. She kissed my forehead and unbolted the front door. An icy gust of wind made me shrink back, but Nadia forced me over the threshold, out into the dark and the cold. I clutched at her tunic, in vain; she pushed me away. I watched her pick up a stone and walk around the house to beneath Vassily's study. She hurled it and I heard glass shatter. 'That's how the burglar came in,' she said, before pointing to the gate. 'Carts for Marienburg leave at dawn. Go now. Farewell. It's people you should fear, not the Devil.'

Those were her last words to me before the door to Vassily's house closed behind me forever. There was no contradicting her.

I stood there, alone in the night, in possession of nothing but my life. Thick clouds smothered the stars and the snow was falling like a curtain, hiding Nadia's tracks. I could barely make out the stable where Grigori had died that morning. It felt like a lifetime ago. I trudged down the icy steps to the courtyard, crossed it and, using all my strength, pushed back the iron bar on the gate. When I stood in the empty street, snowflakes stuck to my eyelashes and the tears froze on my cheeks. An icy wind cut through the seams of my coat. I couldn't see or work out which way to go. Where were the town gates? I lumbered on and when I looked back, snow was already filling my footsteps as if I had never existed. Had I ever been so lonely? Still, I took a deep breath and stopped crying, because it only wasted my strength. With a handful of snow, I rubbed the last of Vassily's blood from my face, making my cheeks burn.

Then I set off.

10

The wind cut right through me, biting down to the bone; by the time I reached the town gate, my lips were white with rime. I was comforted neither by burying my fists deeply in the *tulup*'s fur-lined pockets nor by the memory of poor Grigori's frozen feet. The thought of them made me wiggle my toes in my much-too-large metal-capped boots.

Despite the early hour, the gate was teeming with life: horses bit on their snaffles, their breath steaming up into the clear winter air and their heavy, hairy hooves scraping on the icy cobblestones. Torch flames cowered before the freezing wind, the hot tar fuelling them dripping and sizzling in the snow. Men who were drenched with sweat despite the biting cold heaved bundles and bales onto carts, shouting orders and cursing. Swedish soldiers were grouped close to the town wall, leaning on their weapons and keeping an eye on everything and everyone. Their uniforms looked like they were cut from cheap, thin cloth and they warmed themselves by crackling fires. A couple of weeks earlier the footman of one of Vassily's customers had told me that Augustus the Strong, Elector of Saxony – was it true that he squeezed an apple to sauce with his bare hands and bent horseshoes straight? – had declared war on Sweden. Along the Livonian border to Courland the first skirmishes were said to have taken place, but that felt very far away. Still, Augustus had more than once tried to take Riga from the Swedes; among Vassily's customers everyone believed it wouldn't be long before he came knocking on the door here too, asking for his due. As Russians, they didn't mind; he was a puppet of the Tsar, a puppet with a mighty army at his back.

No wonder the mood in Walk had been sullen and downcast in recent weeks and people in both the streets and the market had been going about their business hurriedly.

Along the wall, old women sold hot *chai*, boiling up the bitter broth in huge black cauldrons on beds of smouldering coals. The tea's coarse leaves drifted in maelstroms on the simmering surface: you had to strain them through your teeth when drinking it. Other *babushky* offered flat sourdough bread, topping it sparsely with salted meat and sauerkraut. I felt faint with hunger and, while I wanted to stretch my money as far as possible, I bought both *chai* and bread. When I counted the coins into her palm, the trader raised her eyebrows: my ill-fitting clothes and over-large boots were unusual in someone walking around with a small fortune in their pocket. Better to have counted it earlier, out of sight, I scolded myself, suddenly panicked. What if someone knocked the coins out of my hand? Both dawn and the crowds, who were all on their way somewhere, made the town gate a target for pickpockets and other loafers all too ready to pilfer.

Feeling faint with hunger, I first ate the salty meat and sauer-kraut. When that was gone, I dipped the chewy bread into my *chai* and sucked hungrily on the softening crust while looking around. 'Not so greedy, my girl!' The woman laughed toothlessly as she poured me more tea. 'Keep your ardour for your lover, as long as you are young and beautiful and men will still look at you.'

I barely heard her. My muscles ached with tiredness but also with fear and strain. Had Vassily's body been found yet? What if Nadia didn't stick to her story; who, after all, believed a serf? Crimes by souls against their masters – especially a master such as Vassily – were commonplace and the punishment usually swift and brutal. Dread made me feel even colder. I fingered the coins in my pocket again. Their weight and number reassured me.

The first carts were ready to leave; the drivers pulled themselves up onto their boxes. Soldiers circled them, asking their origin and destination so loudly, I could hear it from across the road. They seemed to check loads repeatedly. They, too, were not wholly welcome in Walk anymore. Vassily had hoped that very soon, not only Saxony but also Russia would fight the Swedes. But when I listened to gossip in the market I'd learnt that meant only one thing for the Baltic people: we'd be helplessly caught up in a war that was neither ours to fight nor to win, and we'd be crushed when the big powers clashed. Every day I survived from now on would be a miracle I must cherish.

The heavy-hooved carthorses were ready to leave, neighing and flicking their ears, and their drivers shouted out their destinations, hoping for last passengers.

'Pernau!'

'Dorpat!'

'Marienburg!'

I hurried to a cart that was just about to pull away. 'How much will it be for you to take me to Marienburg?' I asked, grabbing the reins and tilting my head back to look up at the driver.

He grinned and tapped a stubby finger against his cheek. 'It's for free, my girl, if you add a kiss and agree to spend a night with me.'

He seemed harmless enough all the same so I hissed. 'Tell me, old man, or I'll ask someone else.'

He shrugged. 'If you squeeze between the barrels, it will cost you a *denga*.'

A *denga*. That was half a kopek for squeezing between some barrels in a cart! It was daylight robbery but I had no alternative, so I picked out a coin; the money was warm and sticky, I had held it so tight. The man bit into it with one of his three yellow teeth and slipped the coin out of sight. 'Let's go,' he said, and pulled me up. I crawled back inside the covered cart. When it jolted forward, I leant against the barrels and stretched out my legs.

Apart from some crates of chickens and a young couple, I was the only passenger. The woman was very pregnant and her husband would hold her steady whenever the cart shook or plunged into a pothole. They seemed to have eyes only for each other and this suited me fine, I was in no mood to chat and answer questions.

When I lifted the waxy flap of the awning, the morning mist and a curtain of snowflakes had swallowed both Walk's town walls and the patrolling soldiers. Soon we were out in the open. The next time I looked, the sun was shining, dull as a copper coin, in a sky that hung low and menacing. The villages we passed through were dark dots against the snowy, shrouded plains.

11

During the day, the couple and I shared a goat's skin full of sour milk and some pieces of cold oatcake with the driver Misha. At night we stopped at a guesthouse that was hardly better than a pigsty. I sat by the open fire with the drivers. I was too fretful to sleep anyway.

We reached Marienburg late in the afternoon. As evening fell it started snowing and didn't look like it was ever going to stop. Nadia was right, nobody would notice me here. The alleyways were crowded. Our cart splashed soggy slush onto passers-by, who jumped away; and rolled over the fingers of beggars who cursed us with fists raised. There were Swedish soldiers everywhere: were these the men who would stop the mighty Tsar? They looked like any other men to me – a bit more handsome, I'll allow, tall and blond in their blue uniforms and cloaks, with a certain pride and confidence to them.

The cart stopped outside a *kabak* just as the innkeeper kicked out a drunkard. The man fell down in front of us and was in no fit state to get up again. Little wonder: a *kabak* served no food. Punters downed as many glasses of vodka as quickly as they could so as to reach a profound stupor. Misha threw the reins to a stable boy, got down from the driver's box, shook his legs in their coarse linen breeches tucked into sturdy knee-high boots and took off his high rabbit-skin cap.

'Marienburg. Off you go, hurry up or I'll kick you out,' he said, eager for his visit to the *kabak* after stabling his cart and horses.

The husband helped his pregnant wife out of the cart and then extended his hand to me. 'May God protect you,' I said when we parted ways, he standing protectively between his wife and the filthy road. I felt a crushing sadness to see the care and tenderness between them. Constant hardship drains away hope and leaves no room for anything but deep sorrow. Loneliness lunged at me like a wolf at a lone traveller, burying its claws in my soul. I swallowed my tears and grabbed my bundle. Where should I go? Who needed a maid, and how to find out about them?

Misha had his horses fed and watered and their hooves searched. He eyed me while picking between his teeth, checking now and then to see what he had found. 'Don't you know where to go, girl?' He tucked a pinch of chewing tobacco underneath his upper lip and sucked noisily, then spat red saliva into the snow.

'No ... Yes,' I said. 'Well, I am looking for work. I don't ask for much ...'

'Come over here.'

I walked up to him gingerly. He raised my chin with a dirty hand smelling of leather and tobacco, pushed back my headscarf and fingered one of my dark locks. He grunted and said: 'I didn't even notice how pretty you are. Don't lower your eyes like that. And what has happened to your lips? Has a bee stung you in the mouth?'

I blushed and held my bundle tight, but he seized my elbow. 'Where is your family?'

I didn't answer, forcing back the tears that welled up. 'I'm look-ing for work as a maid,' I said instead. He hardly seemed the type to know a family in need of staff but I didn't know where else to start.

'Do you know how to read or write?'

'No.'

'Perfect. Too much learning spoils a pretty head,' he laughed. 'I might have work for you. Come, follow me,' he said, before telling the stable boy, 'Watch the cart and keep me a bottle of vodka or I'll have your hide.'

I hesitated. But could I afford not to try in case it turned out to be true? I followed him blindly through the streets of Marienburg, one leading into another, for what felt like forever until finally we reached a small door with a candle glowing cosily behind the red glass casement. The coachman knocked, waited and then pushed the door open. When I peered inside, seeing only a dark and dingy corridor, he shoved me in. When I turned back in surprise, Misha bolted the door behind us.

Somewhere in the house I heard a woman laugh as if she had been drinking. Misha barred my way out with his body and forced me up the narrow, creaking stairs ahead of him. It was warm inside and I tried to loosen the belt of the *tulup*, without losing my grip on my bundle. I could hear first another woman scream, and then the sound of a hand hitting flesh. The sound reminded me of Vassily. I froze in my tracks but the coachman pushed me along further until we reached a dingy upper floor.

'*Matushka*? Sonia?'

Could this be his mother? Had he brought me home? Did she need a maid? Even vain hope is better than no hope at all. One of the doors to either side of the corridor opened, and then another. Girls peered out, their faces painted as garishly as the mermaid in Master Lampert's Tent of Wonders. The girls' hair was loose and unkempt. I saw naked breasts, shimmering pale in the house's dusky light, and thighs in greying lace drawers.

A Swede poked his head out of a door and looked at me, wrapping a sheet around his nether regions. 'Can I try her?'

'You'd think you'd be busy enough with me,' the girl standing in the room behind him scolded. She looked to be Tatar, with a firm, lithe body. He laughed and dragged her back into the room.

I froze. Olga had told me about a house of sin in Walk, but I hadn't believed her. That was surely what was going on here. I looked around quickly and saw no way out. The girls closed in on me, taking off my scarf and touching my hair.

'Look at that, all thick and shiny ...' one girl said.

'And she's all nice and fleshy too. Who has fed you so well, my dove?' another one said, with a giggle.

They stopped and scattered when a woman came down the corridor. This had to be Sonia. I took a step back, bumping into the coachman. Compared with this woman, even the portly Nadia had been skin and bones. Sonia's red dress was laced tightly around her belly blubber. On her wide, sallow face little hairs sprouted in a fine moustache above her upper lip. A lacy cap covered her bald head and her eyebrows and eyelashes were fine and almost white. I shrank back with fear, but the coachman grabbed my arm and bent it. White-hot pain shot through my shoulder.

'Sonia,' he grinned. 'It's been awhile.'

'Indeed.' She slapped him hard. 'The culprit always returns to the scene of the crime. Don't think that I have waived your debts.' Then she hugged him to her and kissed him on both cheeks. All the while she was looking me up and down. 'Who's this?' she asked finally.

'She came from some godforsaken place to work in Marienburg. She doesn't have a family, but is hard-working, she says ...'

The girls all around giggled. Sonia pushed me underneath a night-light, taking my bundle and tossing it to Misha to hold. There she held me so close I could smell her sour breath, and squinted at me.

'You have eyes like a cat and nice full lips. The men like that.' She forced my mouth open. 'You still have all your teeth, straight and white ...' She loosened what remained of my braid and unlaced my dress to assess my breasts. 'A bosom like a milkmaid's. Delicious. I have new Swedish recruits coming tonight. They won't believe their luck.'

Despair washed over me. Was this to be my punishment for killing Vassily?

'Are you a virgin?' Sonia asked.

I didn't know what to say to this and lowered my eyes. Sonia grinned. 'Ah. Butter wouldn't melt, eh? Who was it? A stable boy? Your former master?' I blushed, all of a sudden grateful for the twilight of the corridor, then the woman slapped me so hard that my ears rang and tears welled up in my eyes. 'Stupid girl. But we'll sort that out. Men are so easy to fool.' She turned to Misha. 'How much do you want for her? I'll forget about your debts, if you like?'

Misha grinned. 'I knew it. She's just what you're always looking for. But she doesn't come cheap.'

'Let's see,' Sonia said, taking a key from the ring at her belt and opening a door. 'There is better light in this room. Come in here.'

I clamped my feet to the floorboards – vowing not even ten horses would drag me into that room. 'I want to leave,' I said. I don't know what I was hoping would save me. Nothing did, of course.

Misha, who still held on to my bundle, pushed me into the room, which was musty and windowless and smelt of mould. The stench reminded me of our *izba* at the end of the long winter. 'You are going nowhere,' he said. I saw a mattress, a few chairs and a table with several candles as well as some empty vodka bottles on top of it. A rat scurried through the open door into the corridor. Sonia breathed heavily as she lit the candles with her nightlight. A dull glimmer spread throughout the room: what was to happen here?

'I want ten roubles,' Misha said. 'And ...'

'And?' the madam asked with suspicion in her voice. 'There is to be more?'

'Yes. I want to be the first to take her. Here and now.'

Sonia pursed her lips, but the girls tittered and clapped their hands.

'That's his due, Sonia. He should be good at breaking her in ...'

'Please, Sonia. Can we watch?' someone called out.

She shrugged. 'Do what you have to do. But we'll stay. I don't trust you – what if you disappear with her afterwards, to sell her elsewhere?' She slumped down on one of the chairs. 'At least we'll be able to see if she's any good. My men like girls who wail like cats. But don't bruise her, otherwise I'll train my new whip on you.'

'No!' I cried when he grabbed my arm. 'Let me go, you swine!' I shouted, pushing against him with all my might.

It didn't stop him. It barely slowed him down. My mind raced as Misha pulled me towards the filthy mattress and tore at my clothes. After striking out blindly a few times to no avail, I tried to take control of the fear bubbling up inside me. There had to be some way out and I had nothing to lose.

Looking up, I could see Sonia counting and recounting the roubles in her palm. The four girls who had followed us into the room were standing behind her, lacing their arms around each others' shoulders and waists. My mind raced. I had to make it out of here or I'd be lost, damned for all eternity. Misha let go of one of my arms to fondle my breast, weighing it in his palm. Now or never! I twisted out of his grip with a jerk, stretched out and hit Sonia's hand from underneath as hard as I could. She screamed: the roubles flew high up in the air and rained down all over the creaking, pitted floorboards. I heard them clink and saw them shine. Misha stopped groping me and the girls lunged for the coins like vultures going for a carcass. Sonia jumped up and started pulling them away by their hair, her mouth foaming with curses. Misha kicked them and shouted, while all the time also trying to grab some coins. I jumped to my feet and ran down the corridor, my hair loose and dress undone, stumbling down the stairs. The heavy bolt scraped against the door when I dragged it up. Then, with a strength born out of sheer dread, I yanked it open and ran outside.

The icy air of the Marienburg winter night hit me like a cudgel. Snow fell so thickly that I couldn't see further than a couple of steps ahead. I kept running, through now empty roads, not looking behind me, paying no attention to where I was going, slowing only to lace up my dress. When I finally felt far enough away to stop, I had a stitch in my side. Icy air stabbed my lungs, tears blinded me and I could hardly breathe for fear. I sank down into the wet slush at the roadside, not caring that my old boots, socks and the hem of my dress were soaked. I was freezing. I leant against the wall of a house and wiped tears and snot from my face. My limbs now felt like lead, my teeth chattering so hard that my whole body trembled. Only then did I understand my utter misery: I had left not only my bundle and my gloves in the whorehouse, but also my *tulup* coat. I quickly checked my pocket: the coins were all missing. I was as good as dead.

I sank onto the threshold of the house and buried my face in my arms, too spent even to think. This was it. I had killed and now I should die. I hoped for a quick, merciful death. Perhaps I'd just fall asleep and feel nothing? Already a drowsiness came over me and I curled up inside the porch.

The street was empty save for a group of patrolling Swedish soldiers who walked past without spotting me. I had withdrawn into the doorway before the light of their lanterns touched me. At this hour, nobody but loafers and beggars were out. The respectable burghers of Marienburg sat around their dinner tables, folding their hands in prayer, even if the little wooden church opposite my resting place was still lit for the evening service. My stomach growled. I couldn't remember the last time I'd eaten. All that wouldn't matter anymore soon. As my eyelids closed, I tried to think of something comforting, such as Maggie's weight hanging on my arms when I swung her around, her little face splitting with laughter in the spring sunshine. It was a memory from a lifetime ago.

With every shallow breath I took leave of life, my hands and feet totally numb by now. My mother had died giving birth to me, and my life was going to end on a street in Marienburg, where I knew no one, was no one. In the past three days my existence had turned into a nightmare, so the prospect of death didn't scare me. Just let it be quick, I prayed, and shut my eyes for what I thought would be the last time.

12

I heard voices so beautiful that I thought I was at the gates of Heaven. Though what business would God have with a murderess like me? I opened my eyes unwillingly. The chanting grew louder and I tried to sit up, my limbs painfully stiff. The warm voices and lyrics of the chorale felt like a cloak against the cold. I gave an involuntary sob. I couldn't even die easily.

The hymn stopped and the church door was flung open. Warm light fell onto the icy pathway leading up to the little wooden building. Candles were lit in its low windows, banishing the cold and darkness. As well-dressed gentlefolk left the church, I moved deeper into the shadows. I was cast out and damned.

A tall man stepped outside the church. Despite the bitter cold, he wore no coat over his black gown with its narrow white band at the throat. He seemed to have a friendly word for everyone leaving the Lutheran church, accepting what looked like small gifts and alms and shaking hands with all the men before parting. People chatted on the street and then took their leave with friendly farewells. Even though I pulled up my stiff knees and made myself as small as possible, some of the churchgoers spotted me as they walked past, the women hurriedly – and somewhat disgustedly – hitching up their wide, thick skirts so as not to touch me and the men crunching through the snow as if they'd not noticed.

Through the open church door I caught a glimpse of the inside. Simple wooden pews were aligned either side of the well-lit nave, braziers smouldered and fresh straw was scattered on the wooden floorboards. Someone had taken the trouble to adorn the altar with stems of willow, their cat's paw buds reaching up to a painting of the Holy Trinity. In the monastery, the sheer number of icons staring down on me with stern, knowing eyes had been as threatening as the clouds of myrrh and incense were suffocating. This Lutheran church looked so homely that I was overcome with longing; it was a true light in the darkness.

The priest pulled the door shut, ready to lock the church. His duty was done: were a well-deserved dinner and a loving family awaiting him? He hesitated on the church's threshold.

'Who's there?' he called out in Russian, raising his lantern. Its light ate into the darkness but hadn't quite reached me when I started coughing. I gasped for air, covering my mouth with my fingers, but he could hear me. He came down the pathway, crossed the road and touched my shoulder.

'What are you doing out here at this ungodly hour? You'll freeze to death, girl,' he said in German. 'Look at me.' He lifted my chin, but my head dropped listlessly. He touched my cheek and then took my wrist, checking my pulse. 'Good God! Get up.' He pulled me up on my feet though I was so limp he had to drag me along the narrow pathway to the church. I stumbled after him, trying not to think of Misha forcing me into the brothel. My clothes as well as my heart felt unbearably heavy. The priest more or less carried me to a small chamber hidden behind the altar. He took a cloak from a hook on the wall. He wrapped me in it, but then frowned and took it off me. 'Get that wet dress off,' he said, and began to unlace the bodice of my German dress and then rubbed my bare arms and back with his hands. I tried to cover my breasts but he shooed my arms away. 'Don't be stupid,' he said curtly. 'I am married with three children. Do you think I've never seen a woman's breasts before?'

He covered me with the cloak anew; its cloth was itchy, but I felt as warm and safe as if in the womb. He left the room and returned with a bowl filled with a steaming, scented drink. 'Drink this, don't scald your tongue.'

I sipped and swallowed, which made my throat hurt, but never before had I tasted something so delicious. Its scent was heady with wine, cloves and cardamom, and the drink itself thick, hot and sweet.

'What is this?' I whispered, and took another sip. It was like drinking life itself. The heat from the braziers made my face burn. Still, he blurred before me when I tried to look at him. Was there only one man or were there two? I wasn't sure and didn't care. I squinted but it didn't help. I had a splitting headache.

'It's mulled wine. My wife makes it for me and for the congregation, if they are lucky. It's one of her many secret recipes. Some work, others don't,' he said with a smile, before asking me, 'What's your name?'

'Marta.'

'Marta. What's your family name?'

I shook my head, avoiding his gaze.

'Hmm. You don't have to tell me if you don't want to,' he said. 'I am Ernst Gluck, the pastor of this Lutheran church. Where are you from?'

'I came from Walk today,' I answered with what I felt was not an utter lie. 'I am orphaned and am looking for work.'

'Honest work, that is?' he asked with raised eyebrows, and helped himself to some of the hot spiced wine, eyeing me over the rim of the cup. I held his gaze; it wasn't difficult, as he had a friendly, honest face, and I hadn't seen too many of those recently. His hair and moustache were the colour of honey and his skin weathered by the Baltic seasons. The little wrinkles around his blue eyes and his mouth – fine white lines in his tanned face – spoke of a happy, good nature.

Or perhaps it concealed something worse. My grip weakened. The bowl of spiced wine slipped to the floor. It broke and a deep red puddle spread over the flagstones, just like Vassily's blood on his kitchen floor. The crimson footprints I'd left in his house spun around me, treading all over me and marking my soul, just as Misha's grip and his greedy fondling had branded my body. Sonia and her girls had been no help to a fellow woman in distress.

Chills seized me, yet I felt boiling hot; my hands searched in vain for something to hold on to and my teeth chattered so hard that I couldn't speak anymore. The last thing I remembered was Ernst Gluck catching me before I fainted.

13

For the next few months I was at death's door. The Glucks weren't sure if I wanted to live, they told me later, when I opened my eyes on a day in mid-March. It must have been noon: spring sunlight fell into the friendly, bright room I was lying in, its rays drawing patterns on a rug braided from many colourful strips of cloth. The walls were painted a sunny yellow and all the furniture was stained white. I turned my head. Next to my bed stood a low chair with a bunch of early daffodils set upon it, blossoming in a small vase. A woman sat at a dainty desk, her blonde hair pleated into a thick braid, big brown eyes scouring the open book in front of her. She frowned and moved her lips silently – was she counting up numbers, ticking them off with a flick of her quill? Next to her stood a girl; her serious little face a smaller copy of the woman's. Her way of leaning on her mother's chair made me think of Maggie, and it hurt me deep inside. She felt my gaze on her, looked up and nudged her mother gently.

'She's awake, Mother,' the child whispered.

The woman rose, her blue-grey cotton skirt swishing around her slim waist and hips. 'Can you hear me? Do you understand me?' she asked, her large eyes full of concern.

I nodded. Swallowing hurt so much, I didn't even want to think about having to speak. She touched my cheek lightly, smiled and slipped out of the door, returning minutes later with a bowl of hot, thick soup. It smelt heavenly. 'Help her to sit up, Agneta. She has to eat otherwise she'll die on us after all,' she said, and Agneta placed her hand behind my neck, while her mother pulled me up and stuffed two cushions behind my back. Then she spooned a soup of comfrey with fleshy lumps of fish into my mouth. Even though it hurt me to swallow to begin with, I gladly finished it and then wiped the bowl clean with the crusty brown bread she offered me.

'Welcome back amongst the living, girl. There isn't much you'll have to fear in life after surviving this,' she said, smiling.

I could only marvel at the Glucks' kindness and generosity. War was drawing close, I learnt; both armies awaited further orders, growing nervous and tetchy. This was not the moment for anyone to take in a stranger. As soon as I was well enough, I did everything I could to thank them, even if I hadn't much to offer but my labour. I darned socks and turned collars on Ernst Gluck's shirts as well as on those of his two sons, Anton and Frederic. After supper, I scrubbed the pots with ash and soap until they sparkled, and following each service I swept the church, gathered wilted branches from the altar's adornment and burnt them in the braziers of the cosy, small vicarage I shared with the Glucks. On market day I drove a harder bargain than Caroline Gluck herself, and each Sunday afternoon I ladled pea or barley soup into the beggars' wooden bowls outside the church, for every week their number grew. During Mrs Gluck's visits to old or sick members of their congregation, I'd carry her bag of medication or alms, and hold her lantern if things got late. Last but not least, I played with Agneta in all my free time, giving in to her every whim. Caroline gave me a chamber behind the kitchen, which was wonderfully warm as the oven was on the other side of the wall. I had it all to myself since the cook went home in the evening once her work was done. I felt like a part of the family and ate at the table with them, watching, listening and taking everything in.

'Marta? Come and see me when you have a moment,' Caroline said one afternoon, peering out of her study. I had been scrubbing the floor, so I wrung the cloth and wiped my hands on my apron. My heart pounded. For a while I'd known I was strong and healthy again. It was only a matter of time till this life of peace and happiness would come to an end. How should I brave the world without the Glucks' warmth and kindness? If she asked me to leave, I hoped she'd give me a recommendation, or, in the best case, would tell me of another family who needed help. On the threshold of the yellow room that looked like sunlight itself, I curtseyed, waiting for her to ask me in. I wore one of Caroline's old high-necked dresses, which I had widened a bit in the seams and tucks to suit my curves. The Russian way of dressing made me feel like a peasant now compared to the more tailored Western style.

'Sit down.' Caroline smiled at me, patting the stripy fabric of the sofa. A fire crackled in the tiled oven – it was April, but winter still had a hold on the weather – and the basket next to it was filled with logs. I waited for her to speak when she closed her accounts book: those numbers were a steady source of despair to her because of her husband's generosity – soon, they'd have to pawn the rectory, she'd say – but they were also a good way of catching a cheating, thieving cook. The rows of numbers looked like poppy seeds on a bun to me. She took my hand; her fingers felt warm and dry.

'How are you, Marta? I'd say you're back to full health now,' she said, her gaze searching my face. I nodded, forcing back fearful tears. I did not want to leave this place. I had had no idea that any family as friendly and welcoming as the Glucks even existed. It couldn't be easy for a kind woman such as this one to turn me out.

'You have been with us for almost four months. What are your plans, Marta?' she asked.

'I'll have to look for work, I suppose,' I said, swallowing my tears and steadying my voice.

'Ernst tells me you have neither friends nor family in Marienburg. This is no time for a young woman to be on her own. You are a good, hardworking maid. Why don't you stay with us?'

I sat bolt upright.

She laughed. 'You should always keep yourself so straight, Marta. You have nothing to hide. Do you want to stay with us, take care of Agneta and keep the house and the church tidy? You don't have to cook, but you can do the shopping. Your bargaining skills have saved me money,' she said, smiling. 'You'll get room and board and a small salary. And when our ways part, I'll give you a good recommendation.'

I threw myself on my knees, kissing Caroline's fingertips, but she hastily pulled away her hands. 'You are more Russian than I thought. Then we have reached an accord? I am happy for you to stay.'

I nodded so forcefully that my bun came loose. 'Of course I want to stay.'

'Good. But let me tell you two things.'

'Yes?' I looked at her in surprise, hearing a new note in her voice.

'I suffer neither lies nor fornication in my house.'

I shrank back, shocked by the openness of her warning, but she patted my hand. 'That's just a general rule, no offence intended. Everyone's heart has its secrets and God has spared me from the sin of curiosity. But if you speak, it has to be the truth. And I see how the young men on the street ogle you. It's not your fault, but I would not suffer an unmarried, pregnant maid. And my Ernst, too, is but a man.'

My cheeks burnt like fire, but I swore to myself to live up to her standards.

'Off you go now. There is a lot to do.' Caroline took up her accounts book again. 'Tell the cook we'll have fish pie and bread for supper. No beer, just water and *chai*.'

I left her to her numbers. The rectory was the first house built of stone I had ever set foot in, and the cold of the granite seeped into my bones when I knelt on the floor beneath the simple wooden cross hanging on the chalk-washed wall. I botched the *Pater Noster*, which I had heard again and again in the past few weeks, but had never learnt properly. My God had sold me to Vassily, but the Glucks' God had saved my life and, more importantly, given me a home and a purpose.

I believed that I could live like this forever.

14

My time with the Glucks was as busy as it was happy. Agneta, an afterthought in the marriage, was spoilt, but I was happy to indulge her. I hardly saw Anton and Frederic; they were a bit older than me and both handsome boys – Anton especially with his curly, honey-coloured hair and bright blue eyes. The girls who'd marry them would be lucky, I thought. The priest taught them, together with the sons of the town's many well-to-do burghers, in a cold room on the upper floor of the vicarage where they scratched on slates with styles and leafed through the many books in his library.

Sometimes I'd linger outside the door to listen: how could a single man know as much as he did? Every day he received a dozen or so letters, and when I cleaned the room, I spotted scroll upon scroll filled with his tiny, neat handwriting. The sheer number of books on his shelves made me despair; by the time I had finished dusting them, they were ready for me to start all over again. He knew about every other country in the world. He taught his pupils history and they spoke, wrote and read in German, Swedish, Russian, Greek and Latin. The priest's true passion, though, was mathematics. Handsome Anton seemed to have taken after him, as he once calculated the number of litres in my bucket with no effort.

Of the many amazing things in Reverend Gluck's schoolroom, the most notable was the drawing of a man displayed on one wall. He wore no clothes and so I had avoided looking at him to begin with, embarrassed. But one day while cleaning the room, since there was no one else there, I stood right in front of the drawing and stared. He looked nothing like our saints but had several pairs of arms and legs outspread like wings; his body looked as sheer as a veil. He seemed ready to fly. I could see everything inside him, everything I had never known: the picture had been drawn by a master who lived in Italy, one of the countries Gluck had told me about. It didn't sound real; apparently the sun always shone there and the air smelt of honey. I was stunned by the drawing: were we all like this on the inside, veins, heart and brain, blood flowing and muscles bulging?

Finally I plucked up the courage to tell the priest that I had studied the drawing and something bothered me. 'But where is the soul, Pastor Gluck?'

He looked at me in surprise. 'I can't tell you how often I have thought that myself, Marta. The soul is God's masterpiece. We have it but on loan; it belongs to Him in eternity. Be careful with it; it's fragile and invaluable, the one thing that makes a man a man. Nothing is more valuable.'

'Nothing? Not even the truth?'

He hesitated. 'Telling the truth might not always save you. But maiming your soul will destroy you for sure. What good is it to conquer the world if in so doing you damage your soul? I can spot such a man from a hundred yards away.'

In my second summer with the Glucks, Tsar Peter of All the Russias together with Augustus the Strong of Saxony declared war on mighty Sweden. I remembered the puppet show I had watched at the last Spring Fair, about a soldier refusing the Tsar entry to the fortress of Riga: Peter used that slight as his pretext for war. He also claimed that he wanted to free the Baltics, provinces of 'olden Russian lands', from the Swedish yoke, which Reverend Gluck said felt like mocking us all, as the Tsar's words were based neither on recognised history, religion nor language. 'We are but pawns,' he said at the dining table one day when further news of the conflict reached us. 'Our peace is broken without waging a direct war. I have heard that Peter has tens of thousands of men in his army. Who over time can oppose such power?'

His words worried us and we prayed longer than usual before dinner that night, thanking God for his provision for us and asking for renewed peace and prosperity. For as long as I could remember, people from Russia, Poland, Sweden and the Baltics had lived together and gone about their business peacefully. Was the world as we knew it coming to an end?

At first, our lives didn't really change. The harvest had been good and barns and pantries were filled, ready for the long winter. Merchants, minstrels and roving tradesmen and handymen were out and about, as they had always been. But the news they brought to Marienburg was worrying. The skirmishing had spread and was said to have reached the *mir* where my family lived.

In late October, shortly before the big autumn storms were unleashed, Charles of Sweden, the warrior king, crossed the Bay of Riga and set foot on Baltic soil. We heard that he jumped from the prow of his ship into the spray of the shoreline to claim our countries for good. By late November his army had reached Narva, a Swedish stronghold, which had been under siege by the Russian army for over a month, as Ernst told me while pointing out the city on the map.

Forty thousand Russians massed outside its high, thick walls, I heard, but was unable to imagine such a horde or what it meant for Narva. The men were exhausted from the long march there; they were short of ammunition, and food was as scarce as clean drinking water. Every *izba* or *mir* on their route had been plundered and the village people had fled, hiding their livestock in the deep forests. Supplies and reinforcements promised from Novgorod never arrived and the generals were at odds with each other. There were drunken brawls every night and the troops' morale was at an all-time low when their cannons, apparently cast from thin, cheap metal, exploded in their faces once they tried to fire them.

King Charles arrived with nine thousand men, a force a fraction the size of the Russian army, but nature was his ally: a thick fog drifted in from the sea, followed by a heavy snowstorm, shielding his men and horses from the enemy's sight. The Russian soldiers ran onto the Swedish bayonets like crazed deer. The Tsar only survived because he was in Novgorod on the day of the battle. The Swedes scornfully minted a coin showing a crying Peter sitting outside Narva, his crown slipping from his head and the words *He sat in the snow and sobbed like a child* engraved underneath. Ernst showed it to me, laughing despite his admiration for the young Tsar. 'Look at his face! It's so well done. The poor man – the very picture of thwarted ambition.' The following Sunday, he held a special service to give thanks that the order of things as we knew them was preserved. We thought the war was over. In truth, it hadn't even started.

15

Food became scarce shortly before the Battle of Narva as two big armies took what they thought was their due, plundering farms and stopping merchants to relieve them of their goods. Fewer and fewer travelling tradesmen dared to be out and about. In the market, I heard women have heated words or saw them even getting into fisticuffs over butchers' bones, shrivelled-up beans, stale bread and bags of sprouting pulses. Thankfully, I did not need to take part in those squabbles as there was always a good loaf as well as a bunch of unblemished vegetables left under the counter for the pastor's household, since all the farmers attended Gluck's service on Sundays. The cook served us a pie of wild mushrooms and red onions for dinner, which was filling, but the difference from the bounty of summer was stark. The November mist shrouded the town and drifted into our hearts.

We bowed our heads for the table prayer. Ernst, whose family were originally from a German princedom, asked for peace and prosperity in the Baltics, for the health of both Tsar Peter and King Charles XII and for the salvation of the soldiers' souls. Caroline sliced the pie and served the largest piece to her husband, then to her sons, Agneta and me. The last and usually smallest piece went on her own plate. We ate in silence, hearing nothing but the scratching of wooden spoons on pewter and the autumn wind whipping the empty roads of Marienburg, making the rectory's shutters rattle.

All of a sudden Agneta looked up and said in her most solemn tone, 'Is it true that the Tsar of Russia is a two-headed giant who eats children for supper?'

We all laughed, grateful for the lighter note, while Agneta looked confounded.

'Yes,' Anton said, smiling, 'and priests' little daughters with blonde braids and blue eyes, crispy yet tender, are his favourite.' As he teased her, I noticed how dark his eyelashes were in comparison to his very light eyes. Yet when he looked up, I lowered my gaze.

Agneta frowned, realising she was being teased, but looked relieved by the shift in the mood and returned to eating her pie. We all glanced at the pastor. We had heard so much about the Tsar of All the Russias and his strange decrees, the *ukazy*, that were set to change his country, cost what it may. His subjects seemed less than happy with his reforms. For instance, despite his law of two years ago that had forced the Russians living in Walk to shave their beards, I'd still spot bearded Russians in Marienburg, who also wore the traditional long, belted gowns, sleeves dragging in puddles, that had been legislated against. Surely in Russia itself it was a different story? There, I had heard, beards were shaved off under threat of hefty fines or hard labour. At every Russian city gate, dolls showed the way men and women had to dress, with tailors taking orders for new wardrobes there and then. If the Russian weather was not conducive to tight breeches, short jackets and low-cut dresses, the Tsar didn't care.

'Peter wants to take the eastern Muscovy and turn it into a western Russia. One should admire him for the scope of his ambition if nothing else,' Ernst Gluck finally said.

'Admire? And why is that?' Anton said, astonished, as ready as always to verbally cross swords, even with a man as learned as his father. Anton's confidence, spirit and fire added to his looks and presence; I had noticed that Marienburg's young maidens lingered longer after services that he attended.

'You'd think I'd explained that often enough in my lessons,' Ernst said with a sigh. Anton rolled his eyes. He caught me looking at him and shot me a smile. I blushed and suppressed a jolt of pleasure.

'Anton,' his mother scolded, but with a gentleness reserved for her favourite child.

'No, Mother, let me speak. The Tsar is our enemy. If he gets his way we'll be but a footnote in history, a story to scare children with at bedtime. Since when does Russia ever give up territory it has conquered? Look at the way the Kingdom of Rus has spread eastward from Kiev, crushing everything in its way. We have centuries of slavery ahead of us. What nonsense to give the fact that we were "always" Russian lands as his reason for waging war! Why doesn't he stay in Muscovy, where he belongs? He's got no business here in the West.'

Ernst shrugged. 'You are right. Neither Peter nor Charles has any true claim on our lands. But without a foothold in the West, Muscovy is doomed, Anton. The Tsar needs an ice-free harbour, to trade and to fight, which Archangelsk doesn't guarantee. Azov on the Black Sea really belongs to the Porte in Istanbul, who will get it back as soon as they can. Peter and Russia risk being crushed between the Ottoman Empire in the South-east and the Swedes in the West. No, he *has* to fight; and he needs the Baltics so as to breathe and to prosper. Considering Peter's heritage, in fact, it's no surprise that he's looking westward.'

'Why is that?' I asked.

'His mother grew up in the household of an open-minded man, who corresponded freely with Western thinkers. And don't forget when his half-sister Sophia was the Regent. She, too, looked to the West for Russia's good.'

'That slut,' Frederic spat out.

His mother raised her eyebrows. 'And why's that? Because she wanted an education and a life for herself instead of rotting in a *terem*? She was a good ruler as long as Peter was too young to reign. His half-brother Ivan, God bless his soul, was frankly an idiot.'

'What is a *terem*?' I asked.

'A part of the Russian house where the women of the family live. The only men allowed in are relatives. Women are kept there in seclusion until they marry. They receive no proper education. If they are ever allowed to leave the *terem*, then it is only in closed carriages and in voluminous, concealing clothes. But somehow Sophia convinced her father Tsar Alexis to allow her to study. At his death, she was the healthiest and strongest-willed of his surviving children, and thus able to seize power as Regent. Peter was but a toddler of three then, and his half-brother Ivan so ill he couldn't keep the Tsar's tiara on his lolling head, it was said. Sophia did good work as Ivan's regent and then Peter's, especially in forging diplomatic ties with the West and corresponding with rulers and thinkers. Really, compared with her, Peter can't count to three. But she's a woman. That's her truly unforgivable fault.'

A woman had ruled Russia, I thought with wonder. 'Is she still alive?' I asked.

'Yes, but in a convent somewhere, probably cursing every day she has left. She and her lover Prince Golitsyn ranged far and wide in their thinking, yet not far enough when they were in power.'

'Prince Golitsyn! That ...' Anton stopped, unable to find an acceptable word that showed his proper contempt for Regent Sophia's lover.

'Be careful,' Caroline said, covering Agneta's ears just in case. The girl immediately wriggled free so as to hear more.

'Think before you speak, Anton,' his father said.

The young man threw his spoon onto his plate, rose and left the room, slamming the door. His father frowned.

'He's such a hothead,' Caroline said, but not especially disapprovingly. Frederic mashed up the mushrooms on his plate, then shifted them from right to left, and Agneta looked at everyone's faces, trying to work out what had made them so angry. The room felt darker and colder without Anton in it.

'Prince Golitsyn,' Caroline said, helping her husband to find the thread of his last thought. He smiled at her.

'The prince lived with Sophia, but was far from ... well, whatever Anton wanted to call him. He is a soldier and a diplomat. Without his groundwork and forward thinking, Peter wouldn't have half the ideas he pursues today: the military and administrative service for the sons of his nobles, building a navy, his travels to Holland, Berlin, England and Vienna, to see life and progress in the West with his own eyes. Peter is restless and his goal is clear: he wants Russia to be a true player in politics – a global power, if you like. I bet that he is looking for a foreign bride for his son Alexey, even though it's not usually the Romanov way.'

'But why didn't Sophia think far enough ahead?' I asked, keen to return to the topic of this female ruler. Had she also been beautiful? It sounded like a fairy tale, albeit one with an unhappy ending. How awful to be sent to a convent, withering away after such a life and such a love.

'Well, her hold on power wasn't safe as long as Peter lived. But she never threatened him, even when he was a young boy and it would have been easy. Who knows why she didn't? I doubt it was from love for her family. Her clan and the family of Peter's mother were forever at odds. Perhaps she simply didn't take him seriously.'

'Where was he while she was the Regent?'

'At first he lived in the Kremlin, until he set fire to it. He is said to love setting fire to things and, fortunately no doubt, even more than that, extinguishing flames. So Sophia sent him to the Nemezaja Sloboda, Moscow's German Quarter outside the city's gates. He lived there peacefully, playing at being a soldier, playing at being at war and playing at ruling as Tsar. That's where it is said he met people from all over the world: tradesmen, merchants, artists, thinkers, doctors and pharmacists. This is where he is believed to have picked up his passion for all things Western. Have we ever before heard of a ruler who leaves his country for more than a year and a half just to travel and to learn? Russians usually hold foreign ways in great suspicion.'

'Did Peter meet Anna Mons in the German Quarter?' I asked, and Caroline shot me a warning glance. This was definitely not for Agneta's ears.

Ernst smiled. 'Ah, women, always interested in love stories. Yes, I suppose that is where he met her, just before Sophia banished him to a village far from Moscow and from any source of power, or so she thought. He, however, took his friends along with him and built up an army to counter hers, a state within the state. Before she knew it, he had men and arms, was married to the daughter of a respectable Russian family, had a son and heir, and had reached his majority.'

'What happened to Peter's wife?' I continued.

'Evdokia Lopukina? The poor soul. From their three sons, only Alexey was to live. Two years' ago Peter sent her to a remote nunnery after she refused him a divorce. He is said to have pleaded with her for hours, but to no avail. She's rat fodder for all her pride while Anna Mons has the time of her life. But she's given Peter no child so far, so who knows what will happen next?'

Caroline shivered. 'Poor Evdokia. How terrible, to bury such a young woman alive. Why didn't he send her back to her family?'

Which brought the Glucks to one of their favourite subjects of conversation: whether divorce should be allowed or not.

The year passed slowly with many small battles between the armies and the people caught in the middle had no peace and little food. I just hoped that my family had escaped with the great famine of last summer after I had been sold and had been spared the war, now living elsewhere in safety and good health. It had been almost three years since I'd left home. I had turned sixteen. Maggie would be seven years old by now, Fyodor almost a man, and Christina for sure married and a mother herself. Every night, I hoped that their life was as blessed as mine was with the Glucks.

16

We decorated the church for Harvest Festival, all the women together. Despite the shortages people brought in sheaves of grain, jars of stewed fruit or pickled vegetables, smoked fish and meat, and twigs of sweet-smelling wood, which we tied together with colourful ribbons. The dozens of home-made candles burnt brightly: we had worked in the evenings, moulding them from beeswax, as the best fat for candles was to be found in whales' heads, but that was very dear and hard to come by.

The pews and floorboards were shiny and clean when the congregation flocked in, and the church air fragrant from the offerings. The men and women were well dressed, though you could only tell that from the cut of the cloth and the thickness of the fabric. Lutherans didn't dress like Russians, who praise their Lord by dripping with velvet, gold and silver. Cleanliness was more important than riches, and the only signs of vanity on show were the vast white lace collars the married women wore. Young girls tied colourful scarves around their waists, and pearls shimmered in their earlobes as well as on their necks. Their hair was plaited into braids and wrapped around their heads like crowns. These girls entered the church with cheeks flushed from the winter cold and pretended not even to notice the young men who were present, though I saw a few of them discreetly casting glances at Anton and Frederic. I had polished their boots to a shine and their breeches were so tight that you could see the muscles of their long, strong legs. They and their friends in turn pretended not to notice the girls, only to eye them up later when they took their places in the pews among their families.

It was a world I would never fully be part of. The Glucks were kind, more kind than I could have hoped, but I would never be courted by these boys from their respectable families. I would not be a bashful maiden guarded by her family, who would never dream of selling a child for a single piece of silver. I was feeling sorry for myself to be sure, and it must have shown on my face. When I looked to the side, I saw Anton smiling at me. He winked and a feeling of warmth ran through me. I *did* belong here. Maybe someday I would belong even more.

Anton was looking right at me, his gaze scalding. I didn't hear a word of the service after that. As the elder son, it had recently been decided he was to start work with a Marienburg merchant in spring. Then he could start to think about having his own family. But at the thought of him leaving the house, ready to settle down with another girl, one he loved and honoured, I almost gasped at my own sudden despair. When the congregation's voices joined in a hymn, I heard it as though from far away. I rose with the others, my knees trembling, without paying attention to the service; when I sat down again, Anton's fingers grazed my hand. I fought back a smile. His fingers held mine, hidden deep in the folds of my dress so that no one around us could see, not even Agneta or Caroline at the end of the pew.

My heart was racing behind my tightly laced bodice but I was attempting to keep a pious expression on my face when I half turned in my seat and met the gaze of a tall blond stranger seated in the pew behind Anton and me. I blushed even deeper: had he noticed anything? I turned away without giving him another glance. The pastor stepped out of the small altar chamber, the congregation rose and the service started. Only when the last hymn was over, and we knelt in prayer, did Anton let go of my hand.

I turned around and caught Caroline's eye. God had already given me more than I could have hoped for, I reminded myself. I must not lose the family that had accepted me.

17

In the following days Anton and I lived for every moment we could snatch together. He spent the mornings studying with his father while I cleaned, and then he'd put on his best attire before presenting himself to one Marienburg merchant after the other. But with war declared and the rival armies encamped, ready to strike, making all travel and trade dangerous, finding employment wasn't easy. Still, somehow he could leave the house just when I had to go on an errand or come to the church when I was there alone, tidying it. I'd drop my work there and then: we'd talk and laugh, hold each other tight – and yes, we'd kiss, kiss, kiss, our lips brushing against each other's and our warm breath mingling in the cold of the nave.

Shortly before Christmas – the busiest time of the year for the Glucks – we were alone together in the rectory. Anton prowled through the rooms and corridors, catching me at every corner, on every staircase, snatching embraces. He held me tight, cupped my face and covered it as well as my throat with kisses, before he sighed: 'Marta, I can't go on like this. I hate all this secrecy and following you around like a randy dog. Be mine. Marry me. Come spring I'll have work and then I can feed us. We can take a small house together and ...'

'What nonsense!' I said, though these were the words I most longed to hear. 'Your parents will never allow us to marry. It is one thing to take in a girl off the street as a maid, and I am eternally grateful for their kindness, but it is quite another to welcome her as a daughter-in-law.'

'But as soon as I have an income, it shan't be their decision to make.' How I loved his pride and confidence! 'It's *my* life, and I want it to be with you, every day and every night,' he said, kissing me more, holding me tight, till I felt his desire through my dress and apron. 'Be mine entirely,' he begged, his breath hot on my skin. 'We love each other. Being together is part of that – part of a love like ours.'

My heart leapt with excitement then plummeted with shame. I thought of the things Vassily had made me do, of Misha holding me down in that hellish house. Was there something else to being with a man? He raised my chin and I met his deep, honest gaze. Anton was exactly what Christina and I had thought of when we plucked flowers and lit candles to seek out our true loves. Just then we heard Caroline's voice calling me and jumped apart. He snatched a last kiss before I hastily straightened my dress, smoothed my hair and walked towards the study.

Anton held me back, his fingers hot on my skin. 'Don't lock your door tonight,' he whispered, before letting me go.

I left, feeling numb with fear, and happiness.

I sleepwalked through my chores that day, thinking only of the night ahead. My fingers trembled so much that I broke the Christmas cookies while turning them out from their copper cutters and had to start all over again, wasting butter and flour. I cut myself while hollowing the apple cores to fill them with raisins and nuts. Finding Caroline's eyes on me startled me, though she behaved as she always had. I remembered her words of warning: 'I suffer neither lies nor fornication in my house.' But surely a soon-to-be husband and wife lying together was not fornication as such? Wasn't I entitled to marriage, happiness and a contented life, just like hers? Although I might not be the Glucks' ideal daughter-in-law, I would repay their kindness to me for the rest of my life, I swore that to myself while touching my lips that were swollen from Anton's kisses. I couldn't fight my feelings any longer. For the first time in my life I knew the power of passion, a flood which tears away all reason, just as the big thaw overcomes the mightiest ice floes.

*

Anton came to me when I had almost fallen asleep, after folding my hands in evening prayer three times over, and then tossing and turning on my straw sack. The door opened just a gap, and mercifully without creaking, and a moment later he held me in his arms. I stiffened when I first felt his weight upon mine, but everything was so different from the way it had been with Vassily! Anton's body was warm, his hands were smooth and his breath sweet when we kissed. I pressed myself against him, wanting to feel him everywhere, and helped him when he gently took off my nightshirt, letting it drop to the floor, and covered us with his coat. Lying so close to him, I dared to discover him. I was hesitant at first, but then I grew more daring: his muscles, the dark and curly hair on his chest and his flat, hard belly. The straw felt spiky on our naked skin, but we giggled together and the feeling of his skin on mine was a caress in itself; how long had my body waited for this delight?

'How beautiful your breasts are,' he sighed, cupping them gently. 'And your skin is as white as milk.' His lips followed the line of my throat, nibbling the tender skin, making my breath fly. Lightning shot through my veins when his tongue found my nipples, sucking and teasing the tender flesh. I sighed and spread myself open as all I wanted was him, more of him: much, much more. The feeling flowed from my head into my limbs, spilling into my belly and then between my thighs. I wrapped myself around his hips and pulled him towards me, trying to guide him. Vassily had always been in such a hurry, once he finally had grown hard. But Anton's fingers met mine, stopping me, and he smiled. 'Not so quickly. You too want to enjoy this, don't you?'

I was not quite sure what he meant, but Anton knelt between my thighs, spread them, licked his fingers and gently caressed me, fondling my curly hair. 'What sweet dark fur you have there, my little cat. I'll like that as long as I live, I promise.' He bent over me, kissed my belly and then gently raised my hips to his mouth. 'Don't move.' His whisper sent shivers over my skin. I felt embarrassed and wanted to push him back when I felt his tongue: I rose with a muffled scream and my whole body arched with shock at what he was doing and what I felt. He traced my wetness, again and again, deeper and deeper, before caressing me in tiny circles. Vassily had shoved himself so many times into my mouth – I'd had had no idea that it could be the other way round as well. Heat shot through my body and my limbs went as soft as butter in August; my fingers laced themselves into Anton's honey-coloured hair. I moaned, then all of a sudden his tongue stopped and he held still. All I felt was his hot breath on my moist, swollen flesh.

'Please,' I sighed.

Anton's tongue-tip brushed a spot I hadn't even known existed. I felt a wave building up in my body, mighty and powerful, and was ready to throw myself into it with abandon. Molten gold seared my veins. I called out and then fell back, my face sweaty and my throat dry. My skin glistened pale in the moonlight, droplets pooled like liquid starlight between my full breasts. Anton slid up to me and kissed me, so that I briefly, greedily, tasted my own scent on his lips, before he entered me, gently, carefully, feeling his way where I was so wet and swollen: Vassily had always brought nothing but pain but I moaned when Anton thrust into me more forcefully, right up to the root, closing my thighs around his hips, and I met his every move, wanting more and more of him. I held his neck, his back, his buttocks, and finally he stifled a scream and fell on top of me, panting, his heartbeat racing. I stroked the hair from his moist forehead and blew the glistening sweat from his face. He smiled, his eyes closed, his lips searching for mine, his hands still cupping my body. This was how we fell asleep.

When he crept out of my chamber shortly before sunrise, my lips were swollen from his kisses, my breasts longed for his tenderness and my heart was full, yet felt light as never before.

The following Sunday in church I folded my hands in prayer and asked God for one thing only: to live a long and fulfilled life at Anton's side. When I raised my head during the last hymn, I met the eyes of the tall, blond stranger whom I had already seen at Harvest Festival. He was not old but whipcord thin, his weathered face lined with many fine wrinkles and scars. He looked just like many of the Swedish soldiers of the Marienburg Garrison did. He stared brazenly at my mouth, as if he knew what had happened. I lowered my eyes, but his gaze burnt holes in my lids.

18

Anton couldn't sneak out to see me for the next few days and at mealtimes could pay me no attention. In the kitchen, I heard that yet another Marienburg merchant had turned him away. Ernst Gluck was said to be angry and helpless. I couldn't believe that: a man like him, with his faith and his patience? The same afternoon Caroline called me into her study. Had Anton spoken with his parents already? That was why he wasn't coming to see me: he wanted to put our love on a formal footing. My fingers trembled as I plaited my braid anew and I felt the blood rushing through my veins, hardly daring to look at my mistress when I entered the room. Would she treat me like family now, or would she be disappointed in the choice her son had made? I knocked on the door with my heart in my mouth.

Both the Glucks were in the room. I was surprised to see the pastor there as he was usually busy shortly before Christmas. But then, of course he'd be there to welcome me into the family! They smiled as I entered and Caroline set her sewing aside. 'Come in, Marta, and close the door. It's such a cold and windy day. We'll have more snow later, what do you think, Ernst?'

The only person missing was Anton himself; was he too nervous to sit through this? He wasn't meant to speak to his parents till he had found work. But I could forgive him his haste, I thought with a little smile, as I, too, couldn't wait to be with him forever.

'Mulled wine?' Ernst asked me. 'It's delicious.' Mulled wine, at noon, in these times? We definitely had something to celebrate. I sat next to Caroline, sinking into the stripy sofa. The bowl warmed my hands; bits of apple and pear bobbed on the surface, soaking themselves full with the steaming red liquid and sinking to the bottom of the bowl.

Caroline broke the silence as her husband stoked the fire in the tiled oven. I saw embers fly. 'Marta, something absolutely wonderful has happened. I'd never have dared to hope for such luck and happiness for you.'

I blushed deeply. 'What has happened?' I asked, my voice husky with feeling. Indeed, how could I have hoped for such happiness? Oh, my strong, honest and most beloved Anton. He had kept his word.

'You know that there are some Swedes in my congregation? Men who live in the garrison? Honest, good men, such as a dragoon called Johann Trubach,' said Ernst, leaning against the oven.

'Yes?' I said, nodding. Had this Trubach some link to a merchant who had given Anton a job? Well, then all was sorted. Caroline smiled and took my hand: 'A soldier will never be a rich man, but Johann has his own room in the garrison, steady pay and a warm heart. That is all that counts, isn't it?'

Well, yes, but for what? My fingers clenched the wine bowl as to not drop it. Where was Anton, and why was he not here to speak up for us?

'Believe it or not, yesterday Trubach asked for your hand in marriage. He was not to be deterred,' the pastor said and his wife beamed at me. 'It's true. He spotted you in church and fell in love, there and then.'

'But that's impossible,' I stammered. All this was a mistake: I was promised to Anton. Another man could not ask for my hand in marriage, I was spoken for. Surely the Glucks had sent that silly dragoon packing?

'I know,' said Ernst. 'And I've been very open with him. You have neither parents nor a dowry. God knows, you don't even have a family name.' He winked at me. 'But for him it's enough to know that you share a roof with us.'

'Can I think about it?' I asked, dry-mouthed. I had to buy time so as to tell Anton and make him stop this from happening. Together we'd find a way out!

'What is there to think about?' Caroline asked. 'We have accepted his proposal on your behalf. Nothing better could happen to a simple girl like you,' she said, and hugged me. 'Congratulations! Ernst will perform the marriage ceremony in the New Year.'

'So quickly? Don't you need my help anymore?' I asked, instead of blurting: *No! I love your elder son and he loves me. We are engaged to marry.*

'Not so much anymore, Marta. Agneta will join Ernst's classes and Anton has finally found work, albeit with a merchant in Pernau. He's leaving in the morning but will visit us for Easter, and then Johann and you must come for supper, too. Anton is sorry not to see you, but he sends you his warmest regards.'

He is leaving without saying goodbye to me? He sent his *warmest regards*? I swallowed hard and tears welled up. I tasted bile. Of course, he had not known that I was to be married off, I reassured myself. I saw concern in Caroline's eyes and she took my hand. 'There, there,' she said. 'I know, it's all such a surprise. Why not marry soon, at Epiphany? Trubach is coming for supper tomorrow evening. He is a nice man, you'll see.' She took up her sewing again and the pastor smiled at me as a father would, proudly and kindly. The talk was over. I turned to leave and saw a quick glance passing between the Glucks: a silent look of agreement and understanding. Were they getting rid of me? No. They had wanted only the best for me, always. Could I disobey these people to whom I owed everything? The answer was clear in both my heart and my mind: I could.

That night I waited only for the right moment. I had no time to lose. Nervously, I checked my bundle twice. I had enough money to take me to Pernau; the first carts were leaving at dawn. I'd walk if I had to. The Glucks would be hurt, insulted too. I couldn't let myself care. Just as I rose for the third time to check my belongings, I heard a tapping against the windowpane. Someone was throwing pebbles against it. I almost stumbled in my haste to reach the window, tearing the lead catch open. A horse was tethered outside, its breath steaming. The winter night hid the rider's face – his coat collar was turned up and his hat pulled low over his forehead – but my heart knew what my eyes couldn't see: it was Anton. He had come to take me with him. He got off the horse and hastened over to the window of my room behind the kitchen.

'Marta,' he said, embracing me. 'I have to go, but I can't leave without saying goodbye to you.'

The clouds moved across the moon and in the sudden white light I saw him clearly: his blue eyes and his strong white teeth. 'No need to say goodbye, Anton. I have packed already. Let me get my boots and my coat and we can go. I shall sit behind you on the horse. We can do this,' I whispered, my voice choked with relief.

'It's not safe to travel with a young woman, Marta. There are two large, marauding armies out and about, just waiting for their next orders. Do you know what bored soldiers do with girls like you?' he said. 'And, besides, what would we live on? Give me time to build my life in Pernau and I'll come and get you then.'

'But time is running out . . .' I pleaded.

'I love you,' he said. 'You are best off here, with my parents. We have time aplenty.'

'Far from it! They are marrying me off to a Swedish dragoon and your father wants to wed us at Epiphany, in only a couple of weeks. But I only love you and I will only ever love you.' I heard the fear in my voice. I remembered something Tanya had said a lifetime ago: men can sense a woman's despair like bloodhounds their prey. Still, I couldn't stop myself from adding, 'Isn't the war almost over? After Narva there shouldn't be any reason for more big battles again, should there? That's what your father says, at least. The Swedes have won and are keeping their hold on the Baltic provinces.' I sounded unsure, though.

'My father knows nothing,' Anton spat out. 'What is Narva to Charles but another feather in his cap? He is crazy about war and France and England are happy to know he is keeping busy here. Charles will only stop when he reaches Moscow.' The church bell tolled and Anton looked around. 'I have to go, Marta.'

I clung to his neck, crying, 'Don't leave me.'

97

He loosened my grip, caressed my face and whispered, 'Don't cry. Let's wait and see, shall we? Perhaps this isn't the worst way forward? After all, I wasn't the first with whom you – well – you know.'

'How do you mean?' My voice was hoarse with hurt.

He shrugged. 'Well, this way we can always meet without anyone being suspicious. You will be an honest married woman and we can do whatever we want.' He kissed me, sliding his warm tongue into my mouth. I pushed him away. 'Take me with you,' I said, through tears, grabbing his cloak once more in my fists and clinging to him.

Something stirred in the rectory's doorway and Anton hastily shrank away from me, relief in his face. 'I ought to go. Don't despair, Marta. We'll meet again.'

He mounted his horse, tipped his hat to me and galloped away through the narrow alleyways of Marienburg, his horse's hooves thundering on the cobblestones, towards a town which was by the wide, open sea; far away from me. Why had I wasted those last moments in quarrelling with him? I should have smiled and lured him in, saying, *Come, my love, let's talk about this inside, shall we?* Pain and shame tore me apart, but I held my breath when the Glucks' cook, who was working late, stepped out on to the snowy street. 'Who's there?' she asked, raising her lantern and squinting into the darkness.

I stepped back, climbed over the window ledge and fell onto my room's cold stone floor where I cried, heaving with sobs. Only when I shivered with cold – despite the warm clothes I had planned to wear while travelling to Pernau – did I remember to close the window. The flagstones were covered with rime as I opened my bundle and unfolded my dresses.

19

I was sick for the first time between Christmas and New Year, throwing up in a kitchen bucket. The cook had surprised us with a heavy goose-liver pie for Christmas dinner: probably that hadn't agreed with me. When I didn't bleed though, I remembered Olga's despair. I was pregnant with Anton's child.

Whenever Johann Trubach came to see me, my eyes were red and swollen from crying and I hardly even thanked him for the small gifts he brought each time, be it some coloured yarn, new needles or boiled sweets. The day before Epiphany – the day Ernst had set for our wedding – I was resolved: I had to end the engagement.

Johann fetched me for a walk through the town. As the war and what might happen next was ever on our minds, I was glad that he wore a simple, dark knee-length jacket over tight breeches and sturdy high boots instead of his uniform. His shirt was spotless, and he even wore a silk neckerchief and a warm fur-lined coat. Dressed like that, he looked like a well-to-do burgher – not that such a man would ever marry the likes of me.

'Lift your hands up high in the air, so they are nice and white,' Caroline had told me, and pinched my cheeks rosy before Johann came. 'There you go. Now you look healthy again. Don't be too long, will you? We have a lot to prepare for tomorrow.'

Marienburg was busy but joyless. The stench of sewage on the icy streets hung in the January air. I took care not to spoil the boots

Caroline had lent me for the walk. Coachmen still drove their oxen and mules on with whips, even though their carts only carried light loads. Baker boys with frozen red faces sold meagre rations of bread, pies and the Epiphany cake, in which a lucky charm was hidden: I bought a cake for the rectory, as we all needed some good fortune in these days. Farmers hawked poached animals such as skinny hares and small deer; they were freshly hunted, blood still trickling from their ears. Well-dressed men tipped their hats to each other, trying to hide the axes they carried while dragging along little handcarts full of freshly chopped firewood. I counted more and more beggars in town, squabbling with the girls of easy virtue for the best places to loiter. A man sold hot chestnuts, turning them over the coals, his fingertips blistered. Johann bought me a handful and we walked on, enjoying the soft, sweet and mushy flesh in silence. Once we had eaten, his fingers sought mine in the muff that my mistress had also lent me.

I hastily withdrew my hand and he looked at me, saddened. 'May I not hold your hand? Do I disgust you so much? What can I do to make you like me more?' he asked. I felt ashamed: at our few meetings, he had treated me with more kindness than I could have asked for.

'You don't disgust me ...' I started to say, but Johann would not listen to me.

'Why then do you always look so sad when I come to see you? It was of your own free will that you agreed to marry me, wasn't it?'

'Yes. And no.'

'No?' He stopped walking, a look of hurt on his open features. I touched his arm.

'Please. You are a good man, Johann. But I simply can't marry you.'

He chuckled and squeezed my arm, which surprised me. 'Oh, I see. It's the pastor's son, isn't it? I have watched the two of you in church. I know it's hard but forget about him. He will marry a Pernau girl who will further his prospects, a rich merchant's daughter.'

I blushed. Had this been clear to everyone but me? Perhaps I was being foolish. It would be easy for me to marry Johann and raise this child as ours. What man in love notices a month here or there? But I didn't want to be a liar, like Anton.

'I am pregnant, Johann,' I said, lowering my voice. 'You won't want to marry a girl who carries the child of another man, will you?'

He stopped and stared at me. My courage gave way to dread. What would he do? Slap me? Drag me back to the rectory and shame me before the Glucks threw me out? I'd be on the streets again, but this time pregnant. I felt breathless and light-headed from fear. I stepped back when Johann embraced me in full view of all Marienburg, kissing my forehead and laughing. A minstrel lifted his pipe from his frozen lips, just to smile at us. Johann tossed him a coin.

'How wonderful, Marta!'

I was dumbfounded.

'I, too, have something to tell you before we get married.'

I looked at him. What could it be?

'I will not be able to satisfy you as a husband should. It's all over for me, perhaps due to an old wound or maybe the cold in the field and the fortress of Riga. I'll only be half a husband to you, but a full father to your child, I swear.'

What was there left for me to say? The following day Ernst married us in his church. I wore a high-necked dress of pale grey cotton and held a small bunch of snowdrops so tightly that my knuckles turned white. For our wedding breakfast we ate chicken stuffed with offal and drank wine and beer: it was the best the Glucks' kitchen had to offer. When we shared the Epiphany cake for pudding, I found the lucky charm inside my piece.

Johann kept his promise and was a good husband, who never raised his voice or hand against me, liked the food I cooked and only came home drunk on a Friday, when I gave him part of his pay to go to a *kabak* with his friends. We laughed together – not a lot, but enough – and for that period of my life, his good nature gave me what I had I had longed for: peace at heart. If this was to be my life, then so be it: his room in the garrison was sparsely furnished with a table, two chairs and a narrow bed; our few clothes hung off two hooks on the wall. I tried to make the place pretty by placing flowers in a bowl on our windowsill. But a month after our wedding Johann left for the field. I felt very lonely after the warmth of the Gluck household, but visited Caroline as rarely as was possible without being impolite.

The only friend I had in the garrison was my neighbour Lisa, whose sons and husband were also away in battle. One evening in May we sat together in her room, turning collars and darning socks for the still-wealthy customers who liked her needlework. We sipped *kvass* and Lisa chewed tobacco – her only joy in life, she said – but I found the spitting of red saliva as off-putting as the tinted gums and rotten teeth the habit gave you. In a break from sewing she spat, neatly for once, in her bucket and then took my palm between her hands.

'Let me read your hand, my sunshine, and see what life has to offer a dove like you. Haggard old Johann can't be all there is, can it?' she giggled tipsily and looked at my palm, where lines criss-crossed, starting low down at the wrist and leading all the way up to my fingers. She shook her head. 'Who are you trying to fool, or have you borrowed your hand from another woman?'

'Why? What is it you see?' I asked eagerly. 'Will I be happy? What about my baby, what will it be?'

She glanced at my palm again. 'I see a big, enduring love and many, many travels. I see a long life – you are as strong as a horse, aren't you, Marta?'

'Travels?' I said, laughing. 'For me? And what about that big, enduring love? Will it be fulfilled?' I honoured Johann; love was not the word for it.

She bent my hand and counted the small folds that formed beneath my little finger. 'Indeed. I see thirteen pregnancies.'

'Thirteen? Good Lord!' I said, but then fell silent. Johann had to content himself with caressing my body whilst I lay on my back, my eyes closed. I felt so lonely and miserable in those moments: where was Anton now and was he ever thinking of me? I was even ready to forget his ugly last words and his betrayal, if he only came back for me.

I rested my hand on my still flat belly. 'What about this baby then? Is it a boy or a girl?'

She dropped my hand. 'I can't see that. Stop asking nonsense and get on with your work,' she said, picking up her needle again.

Two days later I met Caroline in the market. By now, farmers only sold what they didn't need themselves to survive and there were no more foreign merchants and travelling salesmen to be seen. Over a year at the mercy of foraging armies had sent the province into famine: the people of Marienburg paid with strings of pearls for a pound of butter and with emeralds for a side of bacon; most burghers had swapped their flower beds for vegetable patches. With Caroline was a pretty young woman, who carried her basket for her as I had once done.

The pastor's wife embraced me. 'Where have you been hiding, Marta? Finally, we meet again.' Her joy at seeing me warmed my heart.

'Well, you know how busy marriage keeps you,' I said, and glanced at the stranger. She carried herself proudly in her well-cut blue cloak; the colour flattered her light eyes and blonde hair that was wrapped in a heavy bun at the nape of her neck. Small pink pearls shimmered in her earlobes.

Caroline linked elbows with her: 'Meet Louise. She is Anton's fiancée and has moved in with us. As soon as Anton met her – he works for her father – they were head over heels in love. I hope to be a grandmother soon as well.'

She patted my belly and Louise met my gaze calmly, her grey eyes gauging me, before she gave a hint of a smile. I was sure that Anton hadn't so much as touched her fingertips in his wooing of her. He'd be the first man to have her, not like the maid in his parents' house. I nodded curtly and wasn't able to wish her well, as politeness demanded. The sight of her stabbed me right to the heart.

20

After meeting Louise and Caroline in the market I felt a mad longing for a hot bath, wanting to scour the memory of Anton from myself. I dragged bucket upon bucket of water up to the room and lit a fire, counting neither the kindling wood nor the coals. When I poured the last of the steaming water into my wooden tub, a searing pain shot through my lower belly. I bent over double and my knees buckled, and I felt a warm gush between my legs before my skirt turned red with blood. I wanted to get up but pain floored me: it felt as if a giant was squashing me in his fist, breaking my back there and then. I crawled out of my room on all fours and was just able to knock on Lisa's door before I passed out on the galleried landing that connected the billets.

She lifted my feet, told me to breathe and to push. I'd have bled to death without her. Anton's son was stillborn at five months and with him died my love for his father. For days afterwards Lisa was still spooning hot broth and *kvass* into my mouth, to help me gain strength. During these lightest months of summer, my days were as dark as midwinter.

King Charles of Sweden loved war for war's sake. Yet after the first successes, such as holding Swedish Livonia and taking the neighbouring Courland, the war turned sour for him. The Tsar of All the Russias seemed to have learnt from his first defeats. Rumour was rife all over Marienburg: 'Have you heard? General Boris Petrovich Sheremetev is approaching with ten thousand men. He's the son of one of Russia's oldest families and has war in his veins. So far, he has not lost a battle, they say. The Swedes don't stand a chance.'

'Huddle up in the garrison. By July we will be under Russian siege!'

'No, hide in the rectory, it's solid and built of stone. The garrison will burn like tinder.'

The rectory? I would not live under one roof with Anton's fiancée. Instead, I holed up in the garrison, together with the other women and children.

On 25 August 1702, Sheremetev attacked Marienburg and, to me, it seemed as if the day of reckoning Ernst Gluck had threatened us with had truly come. Seen from the garrison's tower, his armies resembled a dark flood coming to swallow us whole; they poured towards us, shouting, screaming and shooting. Hell opened its gates. Cannon maws roared and spat death and destruction; cannonballs howled in the air like wolves – the sound scared me witless the first time I heard it and I hid underneath the table, pressing my hands to my ears. They tore open the town walls, roads and the market square. People were rushing around, crazed with fear, bundling up their possessions and dragging children and animals along. The wooden houses were ablaze; thick grey smoke made people choke and hindered them from saving what they could; there was no quenching the flames. The town lay in ashes, the air reeked of sulphur, and still the siege's steady thunder deafened us.

By noon the Russians were storming the town: when I watched the dirty, ragged Swedish banner being torn from the main gate, my stomach clenched. To a serf, one master was like another but what would it be like to live with the Russians once more now that I had known kinder masters? I heard the whooping and shouting of their army: they fired round upon round into the air and I knew that Marienburg had capitulated. What had happened to Johann? Was he still alive and, if not, what was to become of me? Lisa's sons and husband had not returned from battle. Her wailing haunted the empty garrison. I dared to leave my room to plead with her, but she would not open the door. The next morning, all was silent next door. I hoped she'd made it away in the dead of the night, as in the following days no one in their right mind would go outside any longer. The Russians locked captured Swedes inside stables and set them alight. They plundered and looted, marvelling at the riches they found in the prosperous town, practising their knife-throwing skills on the Holy Trinity above the altar of Ernst Gluck's church, before melting down the silver, guzzling the Eucharist wine and lighting bonfires with the pews.

I felt weak with hunger, as if an animal sat inside me, slowly and steadily gnawing from my guts to my stomach. I rummaged through any cupboard, shelf or pot in the deserted garrison but found nothing save some mouldy pulses and rock-hard bread: in my despair I soaked both in rainwater until there was only pulp; I devoured it, but it gave me stomach cramps. Whoever stayed in this town would starve: hunger finished war's dirty work, undermining your body once the spirit was broken. The Russians ruled the town like a trinity of fire, destruction and death.

Three days after the battle I heard a knock on my door, which I had barricaded with our table and chairs. The hour of curfew was close and I was just about to chop a carrot for some thin soup – I had dug for it in a corner of a vegetable patch in the garrison, like a squirrel looking for last autumn's acorns. I halted, knife in hand. The garrison gates had been taken for fuel and the rest of the building was beginning to serve as firewood. I had lit a fire using cladding from the stables. Who could this be? Dusk and even the early hours of the night were still light, which made it hard and very unwise to break the curfew imposed by the Russians. What was my visitor doing out so late in the day? I hid my carrot and grabbed the knife harder.

'Who's there?' I hissed, my ear close to the door.

'Marta Trubach?' a man asked. 'I have word from Caroline Gluck. It's about Johann.'

Johann! Was he alive after all? I thought of my neighbour's cries and, even more terrible, the silence behind her door afterwards. I moved the table and chairs aside, hiding the knife in the folds of my skirt when I looked at my visitor. Outside stood a haggard man: for many Sundays I had filled his bowl with the rectory's soup at lunchtime and had sometimes given him a forbidden second helping.

'What is going on?' My eyes swept the landing behind him. He seemed to be alone, as he, too, looked around carefully. The Russians had their own sense of humour, liking to cut ears and noses off hapless folk they caught in the street, or else branding them like animals. I had also heard stories of caps being nailed to heads or burghers who had had to run the gauntlet.

'Johann is in the town hall. That's where the priest's wife found him. He is badly wounded and she's not sure he'll last the night. But he calls for you in his fever.'

My husband was alive. I hesitated for a moment: the town hall lay on the other side of town. Curfew was almost upon us and Marienburg's ruins swarmed with Russian soldiers. Despite General Sheremetev's strict orders, they raped anyone in a skirt, be it a seven-year-old girl or a toothless grandmother. But had I ever thanked Johann for showing me love and respect after Anton had denied me either?

The man slipped away. 'I'll be on my way. I hope you see Johann again before he dies.' He hastened down the narrow flight of stairs and then out of the garrison.

Johann had taken me, and loved me, as I was. I wiped my face and hands, twisted my long hair into a hasty bun and wrapped myself in the cloak that he had given me shortly after our wedding. Underneath, I wore a long linen skirt and a belted, sleeveless tunic which I had embroidered with a pleasant floral pattern during my long, lonely evenings. Even if it was for the last time, and if God protected me, Johann should see me neat and pretty. He had given me some peace in life. Perhaps I could do the same for him before he died.

It was the least I owed him.

21

Marienburg was eerily empty. Afternoon had given way to a pale dusk, but the air still reeked of vodka, gunpowder and smoke. The roads and alleyways were torn open and I ran whenever I could, avoiding the worst potholes and hiding behind smouldering ruins. If I saw no one, I told myself childishly, then no one would see me. I held my cloak tightly to me so it wouldn't flap and give me away. Soon, I found myself close to the town hall and felt relief: just one more dash and I'd be with Johann. I pressed myself against part of a blackened wall: all seemed quiet. I took a deep breath and prepared for the last spurt across the open square to the town hall and makeshift hospital. I set off – and was jerked back, smashing into the wooden wall.

'Look what we have here!' Three Russian soldiers grinned at me, forcing me against the timber. Their uniforms were dirty and torn and made up from all sorts of clothing, stolen, found or given – who knew? They all had teeth missing and the one who held me wore a dirty eyepatch. Pus seeped from the wound beneath and his hair was caked with mud and blood. The stench of sweat and shit coming from them made me retch.

'Let me go, you pig. I have to go to the hospital,' I spat at him in Russian.

'To the hospital? Are you a nurse? I have a burning sensation that needs an urgent seeing to,' he laughed, and forced my hand between his legs. I snarled at him like an angry cat, but he covered my mouth with his filthy hand, forcing up my head. 'Of all the girls I've seen in this damn' town you are for sure the prettiest, all clean and nice. And none of the others have complained.'

He forced me against the wall; my cloak slipped and splinters dug into my neck and back. I wriggled and tried to scratch him, going for his face and hands with my nails.

'Damn it, Andrey, hold her. She's a wild one. Juri, you go and look out for Sheremetev's men. I'll go first, I spotted her,' he grunted, pressing my fists above my head and shoving his tongue in my mouth. He reeked. I felt bile rise in my throat and bit his lips as hard as I could. He shrank back, cursing and shouting. I tried to break away, but he caught me by my hair and yanked me back. Pain shot through my scalp and I burst into tears when he forced me against him, wrapping my loosening hair around his fist.

He slapped me so hard that my head was thrown to one side, straining my neck; my vision blurred. I felt him tear my tunic open and rip my skirt off.

'Breasts like a wet-nurse and legs like Menshikov's mare,' he crooned while his friend grabbed me from behind. The man with the eyepatch lifted me up and forced my thighs open, digging his fingers into them. My tormentor's breeches hung around his knees and he pushed into me with a single hard thrust. I screamed until my voice cracked. His accomplice turned my head and forced his tongue into my mouth. The first man thrust and thrust, laughing, swearing and digging his fingers into my backside. These would be the last moments of my life, I thought, the world closing in on me. Everything was erased by blinding pain. Then I heard Juri the lookout scream, 'Guards!' and he ran away as fast as his bow legs would carry him. The two others howled with fury when a crop hit them hard over their heads and shoulders. Horses neighed and voices shouted; the one who had been raping me stumbled backwards, his eyepatch torn off and blood and pus trickling down his face. I sobbed and curled up against the wall, so as to not be trampled by horses' hooves, covering my head with my arms: how many men there were I couldn't say for all the shouting and cracking of whips. A guard gave one of the marauding soldiers an uppercut, before grabbing them both by the hair and thundering their heads together. Their skulls crunched like gravel underfoot. It sounded like music to me.

'Stand to attention!' the guard shouted, himself straightening up. 'For the General Marshal Boris Petrovich Sheremetev. Standing orders decree rape is punishable by the whip and hard labour.'

I made myself as small as possible, gasping and wiping tears, snot, blood and dirt off my face. Both my rapists tried to stand to attention. Hooves hit the cobblestones as a black stallion circled us. By the dying light of the day, I peered to see the face of the rider who towered high above us: the legendary General Sheremetev.

He sat straight on his shiny leather saddle: his silver breastplate sparkled in the evening sun and his fur-lined coat was fastened with a diamond-studded miniature portrait. I squinted to look at it more closely: it showed the face of a man. A blue sash ran across Sheremetev's chest, but he wore no hat and was clean-shaven. His stallion reared as he ordered, 'Cut out that man's tongue and catch the one who made it away. Thirty lashes each with the knout should do.'

Ignoring frantic protests, the guard grabbed the already disfigured man by the jaw, forced his mouth open and cut out his tongue at the root. The sight of him throwing the piece of pink, bleeding flesh in the dust made me gag, but I loved it all the same. 'If you survive the knout, you can fry your tongue for dinner. If it was up to me, I'd add your cock to that stew,' the guard told him.

My rapist held his throat with both hands, gargling, his eyes wide with shock. Blood spurted from his mouth and his knees buckled. Well, now he knew what pain felt like, writhing like a worm, I thought, and almost wished the guard would act on his threat and castrate him, though thirty lashes with the knout should see to that. The troop of guards mounted again and Sheremetev was ready to carry on. I tried to straighten up, but pain shot through my lower body and I cowered again. I couldn't walk. How should I make it to the hospital? Johann had died by now, I feared, but I still wanted to reach him. Perhaps if I just waited for the men to leave? I tried to give them a weak smile as if I was fine, when the guard said, 'What about the girl? We can't leave her behind. It's too dangerous.'

I froze. Sheremetev looked down at me. 'Get up, girl,' he said curtly. I swayed and felt blood trickle down my thighs. Embarrassed, I tried to cover myself with my tunic.

Sheremetev got off his stallion. The world blurred as the tall man came towards me. He tilted my face towards the white night and cursed again, then took off his dark green cloak and wrapped me in it. I had never felt anything as soft and ample. The fur lining caressed my skin and I buried my face in it, suddenly sobbing. Sheremetev mounted and reached out for me. 'Give her to me. She is too hurt to get on by herself. As for those three rapists – fifty lashes each, twenty-five of them on their cocks.'

He placed me behind him on his horse and I held on to him. Sitting astride like that was painful but I leant against his back. The uniform cloth was scratchy; silent tears ran down my cheeks when I buried my face in it. I heard the soldiers plead for mercy, but in vain, as the guard lifted his arm for a first round of lashing. I turned my head to see as much as I could of it.

'Hold on tight, girl,' Sheremetev said. 'We're riding back to my camp.'

I heard my rapists scream until we were well outside the remnants of the town walls: the guard was doing his work properly. Was there some sort of justice at work on my behalf for once? When I took a last look over my shoulder at life as I had known it, smoke billowed out of the garrison's ruins. The first flames devoured the last of the walls and the watchtower. The fire turned the sky a rosy shade of ash and made the horizon glow, giving Johann a hero's send-off. There was no way back there for me, but once more God in His wisdom and mercy had let me live, I understood, just before I passed out.

22

Somebody gently patted my cheeks and lifted my legs; blood rushed to my brain and I came to, looking into the worried but friendly face of a young man. He raised my head by the nape of the neck, dabbing my face with a cloth soaked in spirits.

'Do you remember what happened? You are in General Sheremetev's tent. He has saved you from ...' he said in a soft Ukrainian lilt, and stopped suddenly, blushing. I meekly raised my hand.

'I know,' I said, and looked down, which made him blush even deeper. It was the sort of thing one was unlikely to forget. Was this the person who had stemmed the bleeding, washed and wrapped me in the general's cloak once more? I tried to sit up but felt so dizzy that I grabbed his arm to steady myself.

'I have to go,' I said, trying to stumble to my feet. 'I have to see if my husband is still alive.'

'You are going nowhere. Marienburg is in flames. The people are all fleeing. Sheremetev will be here any moment and he wants to see you strong and healthy. When did you last eat? Are you hungry?'

I couldn't care less about what the Russian wanted, but my stomach growled and I remembered longingly the carrot I had peeled hours earlier. What had happened to it? 'I am starving,' I said. The guard left the tent and when he lifted the waxed cloth that served as a door, afternoon sunshine flooded inside. How long had I been asleep?

I took a good look around: the floor was covered with layers of rugs. Their patterns reminded me of fabric I had seen in Vassily's storerooms. A desk was drowning in scrolls and maps, and one of the three chairs around it was buried underneath a throw made of shiny, dark furs. I had never seen anything like them: were those sable skins? Next to my foldable campaign bed stood a chest studded with slate and iron bands. It was locked with a bar and chain: was that the war chest? Just then I spotted a tray of leftover food on the floor, right next to my bed. Had Sheremetev sat here, eating, watching me in my sleep? The thought troubled me, but I bent down and sniffed at the food like a dog. Some wine was left in the brass goblet, a slice of cumin bread was untouched and half of the white, succulent meat still attached to the bone of a chicken leg. I smelt the crispy skin covering it and felt ill with hunger; I couldn't wait for the guard to return. Instead I lunged at the tray. I gulped down the wine and stuffed the bread into my mouth, crunching the cumin between my teeth. The white meat melted in my mouth, which was just as well, as I didn't take the time to chew. I almost choked with embarrassment when I heard laughter at the entrance to the tent. I looked up, my lips and chin covered with cumin and crumbs, holding a chicken leg in my hand and with my face red from lack of breath.

Boris Petrovich Sheremetev's skin was tanned and shiny, as if he had just had a shave. As befitted the victor of Marienburg, his uniform was freshly laundered and pressed, and his long black cloak had a big white cross embroidered on its back.

'Well, that's a good sign, girl, if you are hungry,' he said, grabbing another bottle of wine from the table to refill my goblet. 'Drink. It heals and helps you to forget. Believe me, I know what I am talking about. Next to a battle lost there is no greater misery than a battle won.'

He pulled up a chair close by, crossing his legs in their tight breeches and high, shiny boots. I eyed him from under my lashes: he was older than I had thought. The dark hair at his temples was sprinkled with white and his wrinkled, scarred face reminded me of the dry, brittle earth of our Baltic summers. Deep lines were carved from his nose, which was as bent as an eagle's beak, to the corners of his thin lips. It wasn't a mouth that smiled easily.

More chicken, bread, pickled fruit and sour gherkins were brought by the young Ukrainian; Sheremetev and I ate in silence, until I dared to ask, 'Why did you save me, General Marshal?'

He looked at me warily. 'I don't know. I have seen it happen a hundred if not a thousand times, what happened to you today. Perhaps I am just tired. I have not been home for three years. Who knows? We'll see.'

He leant forward, locking his fingers, as if deciding what to do with me. I shrank back. Sheremetev laughed. 'No worries, girl. I have never forced a woman to do anything she didn't want. What's your name?'

I felt ashamed: without his help, I'd be dead, torn to pieces by those animals in the alleyways of Marienburg. 'Marta,' I said, wrapping the cloak tighter around my bare shoulders in the torn tunic.

'Get some more sleep and then let's decide what should happen next.' He was making to rise when the flap was flung open and the young Ukrainian shoved aside by the tall, rangy man who entered the tent.

'Stay, Sheremetev,' the stranger said. 'Don't we always enjoy each other's company?' His hair was ruffled and the same colour as the coat of a stray dog, a dark, dirty blond. His features were blunt, almost like the dolls' faces my father had carved from a log for my sisters and me. A steady, curious smile lurked at the corners of his thin-lipped mouth, and his eyes were so dark, you could hardly tell the pupil from the iris. Sheremetev sighed: 'You again, Menshikov. Haven't we discussed this already? I have agreed that you have the first pick.'

Seeing me, the stranger placed his hands on his hips and blew out his cheeks. 'Sheremetev, you old devil. A girl in your tent! Now that's a first. Have you finally forgotten that hag of a wife of yours? And are you not much too noble for this sort of hanky-panky? Who is she? Well, well, to the victor, the spoils, say I.' The newcomer grinned and placed his hands on Sheremetev's shoulders. The taller man's fingers were covered with rings from their base to the first knuckle; gemstones broke the sunlight into prisms. Meanwhile, Sheremetev's guard had steadied himself. Indeed, he stood more rigidly to attention than I'd thought was possible.

'What do you want, Menshikov?' Sheremetev said wearily, but he rose, standing between the new arrival and me. He wasn't as tall as Menshikov but carried himself with pride. I sensed the guard's concern; sweat glistened on his forehead, but Menshikov laughed. 'The usual things. To eat, dance, laugh and love,' he said, dropping into a chair that almost buckled under his size and weight. He eyed me shamelessly; I huddled into the cloak and lowered my eyes. Sheremetev went to gather some maps. 'Do you want to take these with you?' he asked, but Menshikov brushed this aside. 'Forget about your maps, they are only good for lighting a fire. I have the best ones in my tent and will send them over to you later.'

'Too kind. I wonder what you're doing with all these maps if you can't even read, Alexander Danilovich.'

'Careful, Sheremetev,' Menshikov said, sounding only half playful. 'But let me get on with the important business here, will you?' He tugged on the cloak, which I clutched in front of my breasts. 'What's your name, girl? Where did Boris Petrovich find you? I thought my soldiers had scoured every corner of this godforsaken town looking for pretty faces. Open that cloak so that I can see more of you.'

I met Menshikov's gaze stonily and wrapped the cloak even tighter. 'And who are you to stare at me like that? Do you really think I'd show you my body like a whore? Never. You'll sooner see black snow.' Who was this man to walk into a war hero's tent and behave as if he could take what he wanted? I looked at Sheremetev to see if I had gone too far, but he coughed lightly to hide his laughter, studiously reading a map.

Silence reigned. The guard looked at the tips of his boots, his face as red as the apples growing in the orchards outside town. Menshikov stared at me, open-mouthed. Then he threw back his head and laughed until he had to wipe tears from his eyes, and gasped: 'Who am I? You want to know, you dirty little tramp.'

'I am only dirty because circumstances have not allowed me to be otherwise. And my name is Marta.'

Menshikov grabbed my chin hard. I stifled a wince and met his gaze. I would not lower my eyes, whatever the cost.

'I, Marta, am Alexander Danilovich Menshikov, the most powerful amongst the powerful, the Tsar's most loyal and absolute friend.'

'Who loyally and absolutely fills his pockets whenever possible behind the Tsar's back,' Sheremetev added.

'Shut it! We don't need you here.'

'It's my tent, Alexander Danilovich. And I am the victor of Marienburg, not you.'

Menshikov walked up to me. I stiffened. He sniffed ostentatiously. 'You smell all right, though a bath wouldn't hurt. Show me your neck.' He pushed back the hair that covered my shoulders and forced my chin up. 'Ah, it's nice and long. And you seem strong and healthy. Just what I need when I'm in the field.'

Both Sheremetev and I started, but Menshikov just slapped my hip and moved closer. I pulled my legs together and glowered at him.

'Your wine is sour, Sheremetev. I'll send you some from the Rhine together with the maps later on. Give the girl a bath and then she can follow my scribe to my tent. I wouldn't trust your soldiers if she walked alone through the camp. Perhaps she can sleep on the floor next to Daria's bed, as long as they don't squabble. I'm not so much into girls wrestling, unless it happens under the open sky, in the mud.' Menshikov grinned at me, nodded to Boris Petrovich and was gone: the waxed cloth of the flap hit the pillars a couple of times, then all was silent. I swallowed and tasted the salt of my rising tears.

Sheremetev shrugged and sighed. 'So be it then, Marta. He truly is the most powerful, after our Tsar. If he wants you, I can lay no claim to you. Let's have you bathed and find some clothes that might fit you, shall we?'

If even a Russian marshal and battlefield victor could not stand up to Menshikov, what could I hope for? I buried myself in his cloak like a stubborn child, clenching its seams and trying hard not to cry 'No. I don't want to. I am not a toy.'

I saw understanding in Sheremetev's eyes. 'Being born a woman is a punishment sometimes. Look, Marta, I am not saying I like it, but if Menshikov orders you to his tent, let me tell you, many other women would give an arm and a leg for the opportunity. Use life's surprises to your own advantage. See your power over men like a hand of cards; play them to trump other people.' He laughed before he added, 'And, by the way, Menshikov can be all words and no deeds. If his mistress cottons on that he is interested in you, she'll scratch his eyes out. Try to be careful of her.'

'Who is his mistress?' I asked, my skin prickling with fear. Had I dropped into a wasps' nest?

'Daria Arsenjeva. She is a daughter of an old Russian boyar family; be sure to stay on her good side or you'll need a very strong protector indeed. She's been with Menshikov for years. Although she looks the other way as expected when she has to, you can never be sure how she'll react. At some point he'll do the honourable thing and marry her, I suppose.'

The general took the map over to his desk and sat down, leaning his head on his hands to study it closely. The guard led in a maid. She curtseyed to me, which almost made me choke, and then led me to a tub in a curtained-off corner of the tent. While I waited, she filled it with bucket after bucket of hot water. The poor thing had to run endless times between the fire and the tent as I asked her to splash more and more hot water over me until I had cleansed myself of my old life and its memories.

When Menshikov's scribe arrived with his arms full of maps, I was sitting on the bed, ready and waiting for him. The borrowed clothes were a bit tight around my chest and hips, but my wet hair was pleated in braids and my skin burned from scrubbing. I felt like a new woman. The guard lifted the tent's waxed flap aside for me. I thanked him with a nod and turned one last time to Sheremetev, who feigned not to have noticed me leaving.

'General Marshal Sheremetev,' I said. He looked up.

'What is it, Marta?'

'You have saved my life and you have been very kind to me. I shall not forget that. If it's ever possible, I will pay you back.'

If the legendary general found those words strange coming from a penniless girl, he did not let on. He bowed his head and answered me solemnly, 'Gratitude is a rare virtue these days. I am sure we'll meet again and I am looking forward to it.'

23

The stench of sweat and latrines, dysentery and gangrene, pus, blood, dirty clothes, cabbage soup, bean stew, cold gunpowder and swathes of smoke lay like a bell jar over the wide field where Sheremetev's army was encamped. The smell stuck to my skin like nettles to a shirt. The Russian tents met the horizon, housing tens of thousands of men. It was an unforgettable sight; the Tsar's army truly stunned and shocked by its sheer size. While I walked, the sun set upon the camp and soldiers lay around the first campfires in their torn and dirty uniforms, stirring heavy cauldrons and playing cards and dice, as the Tsar had forbidden all other games of chance. Men cleaned their weapons, checked minor wounds, spooned up thick brews or downed litres of beer and *kvass*, which had been given to them every evening since the siege had ended in their favour: to the victor, the spoils.

I thought I saw a familiar face moving through the crowds, though I couldn't be sure. I squinted and then ducked behind Menshikov's scribe: it was *matushka* Sonia and her sorry band of girls, offering themselves. She was, if possible, even more portly than before, and spoke with the Russian soldiers as she had done with the Swedish dragoons, before pushing the little Tatar girl forward. Her gums were toothless, angry pustules bloomed on her neck and her dirty, ragged dress hung on her skinny frame. I was far from safe but I felt pity still for their wretchedness. How easily I could have ended up just like them. I noticed that even the camp washerwomen, their arms heavy with linen, made a detour to avoid them. I lowered my head until I had passed by. I had enough to deal with.

All around us the fields had been crudely harvested to feed the Tsar's hordes. In the vicinity of Marienburg there wasn't a sheaf of wheat left to grind, no livestock to slaughter, no chicken to pluck, no orchards with cherries, pears and apples to be picked. From the remnants of the town wall fresh smoke rose into the wide sky, and despite the late hour a steady stream of people moved out of the city, into the white night and an uncertain future. The Russians took off them whatever they pleased, sharing it amongst themselves there and then, ridding the wealthier burghers' carts of everything they liked, be it a jar of pickles, a rolled rug, a fine piece of furniture, a last plump chicken or a wailing girl, maids and burghers' daughters alike. Only the crippled and the beggars plodded on unmolested, as what they had to offer was too lousy even for the least of Sheremetev's soldiers.

I scanned the people who had made it safely out of Marienburg: were the Glucks among them? If they were alive, where would they hide from the Russians? We were like ants crushed under the Tsar's feet. It was horrible: things had turned out as Ernst Gluck had predicted. I felt like a swimmer caught in the rapids after the *ottepel*, the current almost swallowing me and just a branch to hold on to. If I so much as tried to come up for air and to think, I would drown for sure. So I looked ahead as that was the only way I could go.

I closed my ears to the crude jokes and the catcalling of the men; every step still hurt me and I hoped that my rapists had died under the knout. Nobody survived fifty lashes, I knew that as well as Sheremetev did. When we arrived at Menshikov's tent, I braced myself and weighed the general's words, which I had soaked up like one of his sponges had the bathwater just a few hours earlier. Tar dripped from torches stuck to pillars on both sides of the entrance where guards stood, bayonets slotted onto their muskets. Lanterns glowed warmly in the pale dusk.

'Wait here,' the scribe said, and went into a side room off the main reception area of the tent, which was more like a house made of canvas, with its formal entrance and several distinct rooms. I was stunned: there was no sign of war or hardship before me now. These were the most beautiful things I'd ever seen, beggaring even the wonders of Vassily's home. I saw daybeds carved from black shiny wood, standing on curved, elegant legs that ended in animals' heads. The beasts' mouths were wide open and wooden manes flamed around their heads. What on earth were they meant to be? Richly embroidered cushions and fur-lined velvet blankets lay carelessly piled up on these beds, and my naked feet – which were dirty once more after crossing the camp – sank into the deep, silky pile of the colourful rugs on the floor. On Menshikov's desk two high candelabra shed their flickering light over bowls of nuts, candied fruit, biscuits, fresh cherries and apples. I also spotted piles of maps on a campaign table. We had kept similar ones in the Glucks' schoolroom. When war had begun, the pastor had followed the campaign by sticking Caroline's sewing pins into the thick paper, trying to guess both Swedish and Russian strategies. The memory made me smile, but also feel a twinge of sadness.

Across the maps lay a freshly sharpened quill in a heavy golden penholder. I picked it up and twisted it in my fingers before sniffing at it. Mmm, fresh ink – what else smelt so beautifully of learning? I weighed the penholder; its value would have freed and fed my family a hundred times over. I calmly put it back where I had found it. Just then, the skin on my neck prickled. Was somebody watching me? I looked up and met a man's implacable gaze, fixed in oil on canvas. I shrank back in horror: he didn't look like our icon of Saint Nicholas or like the Holy Trinity above the Glucks' altar. His face seemed so real with that fine, pale skin and rosy cheeks; his dark, curly hair seemed shiny enough to touch; and his blue eyes gazed at me, sparkling and bright. His eyebrows reminded me of a raven's wings, high and dashing, while the fine moustache he wore led my gaze to his well-cut mouth. His breastplate of gold and silver, his white coat and the bright blue sash across his chest, turned him into a warrior; one elbow rested on his helmet, which was topped with a bunch of red feathers; the other hand pointed far ahead, to the West. In the lower right-hand corner, the double-headed eagle swooped, as I had seen it a thousandfold on Russian flags during the siege of Marienburg. Perhaps this was Alexander

Nevsky, the only Russian saint I knew next to St Nicholas. There was something about the man's eyes though, that didn't look very saintly.

'What are you doing, girl, ogling our Tsar like that?' a woman's voice asked me sharply from behind. I blushed deeply. I didn't want to look nosy: the sin of curiosity, as Caroline had called it, and I surely didn't want to be caught staring at a man. Turning, I was almost stunned by the woman's beauty. I shoved one mud-encrusted foot underneath the other and hitched my too-tight, coarse linen skirt higher, trying somehow to look more in keeping with this place, though it was hopeless.

Her blonde mane fell loose to her shoulders like shimmering fur and the tightly laced deep-blue silk dress she wore matched her eyes, which reminded me of violets. It was very low-cut and showed off the top half of her firm white breasts. Close to one nipple, a tiny beauty mark rose and fell each time she breathed. She circled me like a hawk does a mouse and I didn't dare move. Each of her steps doused the air with rosewater and a heavier, headier scent. But with the flick of a wrist she broke the spell by pulling a lacy handkerchief from her tight sleeve and pressing it in front of her tiny, upturned nose. 'God, you reek, girl. Don't you ever bathe? And it's you Menshikov wanted in his tent? I was worried when I heard about you, but now that I see you ...' She giggled, which felt like a slap to me. 'I suppose he just wanted to get one up on Sheremetev, which is just as well. I can do with another maid. Or did you flirt with him?' she asked, grabbing my wrist and digging her nails into my flesh. I met her eyes calmly, freed my wrist and shook my head.

'I did not,' I said. For some reason I was not afraid of Daria – for that's who this woman must be – in spite of Sheremetev's warning. The way she carried herself, so sure of her beauty, reminded me of my little Christina, wherever she was now.

'Are you Daria Arsenjeva?' I asked.

'How do you know?' she hissed.

'Well, General Sheremetev said that you were very beautiful and very witty – and that Count Menshikov is utterly besotted with you.'

Her smile was catlike. 'Well and wisely spoken, my girl, even though Sheremetev would never say anything like that. He despises me and thinks I am a whore for living with Alexander Danilovich. But who cares what that uptight ass thinks?' she said, smiling as she sank onto one of the daybeds, spreading her wide skirt, which was embroidered with pearls and gemstones and lined with lace. Small, silky slippers matched the colour of her dress. She patted the seat next to her. 'Sit down with me. How did you come to be here? It must be quite a story and I love a good yarn!'

I told her, skipping the worst details of the attack. But by the way she looked at me, I understood that she knew anyway. I was a prisoner-of-war: what else could have happened to me? Daria Arsenjeva listened to me while nibbling on some cherries in a way that made me blush. Then the curtain to a side room was torn aside and Menshikov entered the main tent. I sat up but Daria stayed as she was, half lying among the cushions, sucking on a cherry, the mark near her nipple reeling in Menshikov's gaze like bait to a big fish. She lowered her long, dark lashes, but her eyes never left him. He patted my head and tousled my hair.

'Ah, Sheremetev's little find. How do you like her, my darling Daria?'

She poked me with her sharp elbow. 'Not bad. She's a bit buxom for my taste, but we have had a bit of a laugh already.'

'I like a bit of buxom. What shall we do with her?' He took an apple from the bowl on the desk, threw it in the air, caught it again and bit into it, chewing and crunching it as loudly as a horse, every bite an explosion of spit and apple flecks. Daria moved as swift as a squirrel, slapping Menshikov's mouth with her lacy handkerchief. I held my breath as his face reddened with anger, but Daria casually said: 'She can work as a washerwoman. More hands truly make for lighter work. In the evenings she can be with us. If I catch you near her otherwise, I'll kill you both, and I am not joking.'

I curtseyed, grateful for Daria's jealousy. We'd get along just fine: if Menshikov was all she wanted, God, she could have him. Daria pulled him into a side room, yanking the heavy velvet curtain with gold tassels closed after them while she smiled at me around its advance: 'The guard will show you the washing place. You can sleep in a corner here; take all the cushions and blankets you need. My maid will bring you some of my dresses that she can alter for you. Those rags you wear are an eyesore.'

Somebody else should alter my dresses? I curtseyed once more and kept a straight face. Daria's scent lingered long after she was gone.

24

As a washerwoman, by day I scrubbed, rinsed, dried and pressed the general's shirts and those of the many other nobles camped around Marienburg. The Tsar had drafted the sons of the Russian nobility into military service, and young men of the realm's best families now stretched their long limbs under the Baltic sun in a well-deserved break from warfare. Most of them had seen neither their families nor their lands for years, as the huge distances involved did not allow short absences.

In the evenings I frequented Menshikov's tent and watched Daria very closely: her way of dressing, of moving, of treating people and speaking to them. She'd chat to men in a low voice, so they'd have to lean in in order to listen. She seemed to keep Menshikov on his toes with a mix of crude humour, servility and flashes of naughtiness. Her moodiness kept him in thrall, as he was never entirely sure what she would do next. Thankfully, that kept him too busy to pay me more attention than was necessary, or healthy. I could get on with the business of surviving. If life in the Russian camp was like quicksand, my friendship of sorts with Daria was a rope that a merciful God had thrown me.

'Your lips are chapped. Here, smooth them with this paste of beeswax and honey. Before you go to sleep, put some sour cream on your skin. There's nothing like a bit of *smetana*. And just look at your hands! They're as red and callused as a serf's,' Daria chatted on, handing out advice, bottles and jars. 'Keep your hair shiny by rinsing it with beer after each wash.' In our *izba*, Father had only had sips of beer on high holidays; if we spilt a drop he'd wallop us. Daria herself rinsed her hair in a chamomile brew before bleaching it strand by strand with the juice of a fruit I had never seen before, shiny yellow and egg-shaped. 'Have a bite,' she said, watching me when I bit into the waxy skin and then pulled a face: the taste was sour and acidic. Daria laughed so much she had to hold on to her chair; she liked a practical joke.

What she didn't share with me was a smelly grey paste she ordered from Venice, which kept her face pallid. 'It's so expensive you could live for a decade on the price of one jar, but believe me, it's no good,' Daria's maid told me while cleaning the tub. 'The Moscow *damy* who use it are always sick with headaches. And, you know, after a while, it looks like their skin's been eaten by maggots – and just when the Tsar has forbidden them to wear veils in public. So you know what they do?' she chuckled. I shook my head. 'They smear even more of it on. Beats me.' Daria's skin looked fine to me; the maid was probably telling tall tales.

Life in Menshikov's palace in Moscow sounded like a never-ending feast day, filled with light and laughter. If the court calendar with the many royal birthdays and saints' names days didn't give good reason to celebrate, they'd meet for a forbidden game of cards, a big dinner or a dance.

'With whom do the *damy* feast if the men are all in the field?' I wondered aloud, but Daria only laughed.

'That makes them all the merrier, silly. The Tsar has freed them from the prison of the *terem*. He *wants* us to live and laugh and gamble with the men.'

'What an idea,' I said. 'What next – should we all light up pipes?'

'He has seen court life like this in a palace called Versailles, in France, which he visited during his Grand Embassy. I tell you, the ideas he brought home! We women were not *bojaryni* – the boyars' wives and daughters – any longer, but *damy* in our own right. Our families were scandalised, but the Tsar threatened us all – my father as well! – with hard labour should he dress in the old way, refuse to send my brothers to school or lock my sister Varvara and me up until we were married off.'

'I hope I'll see Moscow soon, Daria,' I said.

'Oh, me too, Marta. I can't wait to go home! The sight of Moscow takes your breath away: a thousand spires and cupolas glitter in the sun and the mightiest houses sit right next to huts of mud and clay. It's the mix that makes it so special. But the Moscow of my childhood is no more. Moscow was once the centre of a world, the meeting point of East and West. Never mess with a Muscovite. We are full of tradition and custom and yet so wonderfully wild, for at heart, Marta, we are all Tatars.' She pulled at her eyes until they slanted.

I giggled, then asked: 'Why is the Moscow of your childhood long gone, Daria?'

'Well, what will happen if Peter really builds his new city, here in the West?'

'A new city? Impossible. How would he do that, just hack it out of the ground? Where, and how, and when? In the middle of a war?'

Daria shrugged sullenly. 'The Tsar can do anything. Whatever Russia has is his.'

I fell silent. If a noblewoman like this, who was so close to the almighty Tsar, felt helpless, what then did the merchant, the farmer and the serf in the field think?

Everything but boredom was welcome in Menshikov's tent. Mornings might start with Mass for the generals and nobles, while a second service was held under the open sky for the tens of thousands of soldiers: Alexander Danilovich and his friends would pray, bow and cross themselves with three fingers as custom demanded, and they'd kiss the icons and ask for God's protection. But in the evening an unbridled joy in life reigned; a haunted merriment, which was the other side of war's terror. Live today because you'd meet God and Saint Nicholas soon enough for the day of reckoning. The Tsar was said to have given new marching orders, so the brief respite in Marienburg would soon to be over. What would happen to me then? I'd be looking for a roof over my head yet again and the thought filled me with dread as well as a deep fatigue. So all I could do was smile sweetly when Menshikov tugged my hair and drawled, 'You never sleep, are radiant with beauty and drink every soldier under the table. Where do they bake girls like you? I'll order ten of your sort.'

As Daria's friend I was one of theirs by night, even if I washed shirts by day. The endless evenings were fuelled by wine, vodka and beer. No one here would drink *kvass.* I had never laughed and never drunk so much in my life.

'Hurry, Marta,' Daria would call, clapping her hands. 'Alexander Danilovich offers us a world of wonders tonight.' She'd squash my flesh into my bodice and lace me up brutally, to save time.

'A world of wonders?' That sounded like Master Lampert's tent.

'Yes, he has ordered in a group of Tatar acrobats who cartwheel and somersault, and dwarves who leap through rings on fire,' she said. 'I also asked for storytellers. Nothing like a good yarn, don't you think?'

'Indeed,' I said smoothly, but she pinched me.

'I know you are one for a story or two. I just love how you ran away from that merchant's house after he died of smallpox and then refused the lusty priest's son. I am sure you have so many more tales to tell me. With you, I am never bored.'

'And never will be, I promise. And if I run out of stories, I shall make up some more. Just for you.'

No, we were never bored: the evening before, a Ukrainian magician had baffled us, and for tomorrow's masquerade, Daria had some men's clothes altered for us as well as some old gowns that had been 'specially let out. 'Stunning,' I exclaimed when I saw her dressed up as a man. 'You look so much better than I do,' I said, though I knew that the tight knee-length breeches showed off my long, slender legs as well as my round hips. The men were less lucky, their broad shoulders bursting out of dresses' bodices, chest hair showing and big, clumsy feet tearing hemlines. Still, the sight of them left us in stitches.

Anyone who didn't drink enough for Menshikov's liking was forced to do so; he'd pick out his unfortunate victim and order, 'You, over there, hold him down. Marta, force his mouth open — yes, grab his jaws. Daria, fill that boot with vodka and pour it into his mouth. A true Russian needs nine days' drinking to put them in a proper stupor.' Menshikov downed a huge cup himself to keep the poor, gargling and writhing man on his tent floor company, before he shouted: 'Nine days. Three to get drunk, three to be drunk, three to get sober again.'

We roared, 'Nine! Nine! Nine!' and it seemed like the world's best word until Menshikov's guest passed out and was dragged from the tent to revive himself for further fun. Everybody who could, feasted with us: boyars' young sons who had hardly grown moustaches yet, as well as old, dignified princes who shouldn't have left their hearths. Peter hounded them all into his war. Apart from *matushka* Sonia's whores, and the washerwomen – most of them girls taken prisoner at sieges such as Marienburg – Daria and I were the only women in the camp. I was lucky to be protected by Menshikov. Most of the girls, bless their souls, were easy meat for any soldier who cared to reach out. Still, sometimes while I was soaking and scrubbing the clothes in the buckets, a man would sneak up from behind and grab both my breasts with his grubby paws: 'Lovely! They jiggle like an udder but are as firm as Crimean melons.' Or they'd smack my bottom: 'God, I could crack a nut on that one!' and I would slosh them with a bucket of dirty water. If someone made a rude joke, I came back with a quick, jesty answer that left them red-faced.

So I found my place in the camp and stored up whatever I saw and heard in my mind like a farmer would his grain: my life was linked to those of my Russian captors. Then, in late autumn, word reached us that Daria's sister Varvara and Menshikov's sister Rasia were to visit. I was excited, but also a bit wary. Would they treat me with the same ease as Daria did? To her, I was neither a maid nor a prisoner-of-war, but a friend.

25

Rasia Menshikova was no beauty, though like Daria she covered her face in the fashion of Moscow in a thick layer of chalk-white paste and powder, whilst crimson paint enhanced her lips and cheeks. Her eyebrows and lashes were tinted black. But she had a kind word for everyone, listened more than she spoke and held herself straight, so that her bodice would push up what little cleavage she had. She was a wise woman.

It was the end of October when I joined Daria, her sister Varvara and Rasia in Menshikov's crowded tent after my day's work. 'Come, Marta,' Daria said and patted an empty cushion next to hers. I saw Varvara, beautiful in a way that was all white skin and dark red hair, raise her eyebrows and shoot Rasia Menshikova a look of surprise. I sat comfortably with them anyway as Daria's guest, as if equal to the most powerful of the powerful. How had this come to pass? Life these days left me no time to marvel at its miracles. All I could do was run along with it and try not to lose my breath. I spotted Sheremetev amongst the guests, which was rare. He was sitting with the other generals so I waved to him and he raised his glass to me, smiling. The camp was buzzing, like bees ready to swarm. Were the marching orders well and truly given?

The evening's entertainment hadn't yet begun. People were sitting drinking and eating. Rasia Menshikova nibbled on a pastry filled with goose liver pâté, sipping some beer. She leant in. 'Have you heard about the Tsar and Anna Mons?'

Daria and her sister shot each other a quick glance. 'No. What is it, Rasia? Is Peter finally fed up with her?'

I felt a wave of Rasia's heavy Persian perfume engulf me when she shook with giggles. 'Yes! He's finally accepted she won't give him a child. My brother says that the Tsar is looking for a husband for her, which is quite generous of him really. She could just as easily have ended up in a nunnery like Evdokia.'

'She isn't in the least like a nun,' Varvara pouted.

Rasia said, 'She's lucky, but whoever marries her isn't. Anna Mons is as barren as a tundra bush. I have smuggled a loyal maid into her household who knows all her potions, so I am sure of it. It's about time she stopped whoring on her father's behalf, like all her siblings do.'

'Anna Mons has siblings?' I asked.

'The Mons are worse than rabbits, there are so many of them, and each more beautiful than the one before.'

The Mons family, too, seemed to belong in that tent of wonders. The pace of the evening was different, though. By this stage in the festivities there were usually magicians performing with trained dogs and jugglers. Tonight would be different.

Menshikov clapped his hands. I looked around but Daria and Varvara recognised their cue. Rising, they sashayed towards him. He took them one on each knee and pulled their dresses off their shoulders, stripping them half-naked. They didn't seem surprised in the slightest. A stillness settled over the gathering. The musicians sounded louder over the hush. Menshikov swayed to the rhythm with the girls; he roared out a song and started to fondle their full dangling breasts while his guests watched with hungry eyes. Rasia was hawk-eyed as the sisters started to kiss and caress each other: the flames of countless candelabras made their bare skin shimmer and their jewellery sparkle. They moved slowly, deliberately exaggerating their movements and their pleasure for the joy of those staring, licking each other's lips, throats and breasts, lacing tongues, showing off their loveliness. Daria closed her moist lips over her sister's nipple, sucking it, while she teased the other breast with her fingertips. Varvara arched backwards, sighing and moaning. Lust burnt in the surrounding men's eyes and even Menshikov held his knees still, watching with intent.

'But, Rasia, they are sisters!' I whispered, shocked.

She shrugged. 'The Arsenjevas are wild things, and there is nothing they haven't done. Rumour has it that they have even slept with their brothers and their father! Perhaps that is why my brother and the Tsar like them so much. Our boundaries are lost; we live in new times. Perhaps we need that,' she said, never taking her eyes off her brother and the Arsenjevas.

'The Tsar likes the Arsenjevas as well?' I asked carefully. Had Daria set her aim higher even than I had thought?

'Well done, Marta. Chatting like a woman and listening like a man. Daria and Varvara hope to marry my brother and the Tsar, while sleeping with both. If Anna Mons's reign is well and truly over, then of course this is their moment. Perhaps we'll see the sisters fight? What fun,' Rasia said, a sparkle in her eyes. Daria hitched up Varvara's skirt and spread her sister's naked thighs. 'Any of them could be the next Tsaritsa.'

She rose and left. I sat alone next to the tent's entrance, watching her go. Why was Rasia Menshikova herself here – on her brother's orders? Was she also meaning to make use of the moment that Anna Mons left his friend available? It could certainly fulfil Menshikov's – or anyone's – wildest dreams.

26

The half-naked Arsenjevas were enlaced in Menshikov's arms, Daria's head buried between her sister's thighs and Varvara sighing and moving her hips. Watching them made my mouth go dry. When I finally turned my head away, I spotted Sheremetev alone by a tent post. Both his plate of food and his jug of vodka were left untouched. What did he think of all this? His face was calm and unreadable as he watched the crowd. I dare say he didn't approve.

I was about to join him when there was the sound of hooves thundering outside in the camp. It was long after midnight. Only a madman would travel at such an hour, I thought. But, yes: horses neighed and snorted and men called out, cheering and clapping. Before I could step aside, the tent's waxed flap was flung open and hit me so hard that I stumbled and almost fell, but a man grabbed me by the upper arm. He was so tall that I saw nothing but his chest in a dark green uniform jacket and bright sash adorned with an order of sparkling diamonds. I looked up to check. It was the man from the painting.

Peter, Tsar of All the Russias, stood seven feet tall in his boots and his powerful body blocked out the candlelight, its flickering flame lengthening his shadow even further. His hand, which held me firmly, looked too dainty for his mighty frame. Still, when I tried to curtsey, he steadied me with ease and smiled: 'Stop bobbing about, girl, that's a waste of time. Can I let go of you now? Don't fall.

You might still be needed later on tonight.' He winked and let go of me, stepping further into the tent, trailing scruffy, laughing men in his wake.

Silence fell when the Tsar stood amongst his soldiers and raised his arms. Then, all hell broke loose: I heard shouting, laughing, cheering and whistling. The princes and generals leapt to their feet, bowing and running to greet him; some of them sobbed and even hugged him, getting a pat on the back or kisses in return. Corks flew from bottles, the cup-bearers shouted, the cook and his helpers dragged in more food, servants raced around and the musicians played a wild tune. Menshikov's merry court had found its true master.

I moved away from the entrance, settling down next to Sheremetev on my haunches. The Tsar greeted some of his childhood friends before he stepped up to Menshikov, who had set the Arsenjeva sisters down. They watched the Tsar like a mouse does a cat while Menshikov opened his arms wide.

'Brother of my heart! I have missed you so much. Without you there is no joy,' the Tsar called out in German. German! I was startled. Was that their secret language, ever since they had travelled together in the West? Well, if so, I, a serf, shared their knowledge – the thought stunned me.

Menshikov sobbed, speaking German as well. 'My beloved! A day without you is a day wasted.'

The two men embraced, laughed, cried and swayed to their own secret rhythm, kissing each other's cheeks again and again. Menshikov's tall, muscular body was dwarfed by the Tsar's powerful frame. How could a man of his build exist? Jugs were raised and voices cheered: 'To our Tsar, the victor of the Great Northern War! To the battle of Marienburg – death and destruction to all Swedish worms!'

Daria, as always a quick thinker, clapped her hands. 'Long live the Tsar! To the victor of Marienburg!'

Sheremetev almost choked on his beer and I gently patted his back to ease his cough. 'No worries, Boris Petrovich,' I said, 'we all know who the true victor of Marienburg is.'

He pulled a face. 'I could win a thousand battles, and give my life for Peter, but his heart will still always belong to Menshikov. Such a love cannot be forced. On the contrary, you go looking for it and it flees from you.' His words gave me goose-bumps, and he took off his cloak with a rueful little smile and covered my shoulders against the night chill. 'There you are. That's better. No, Menshikov alone is the brother of his heart.'

'Where do they know each other from?' I asked, clutching the cloak that once before had warmed me so wonderfully. How could I ever forget what this man had done for me? I moved a bit closer and took a piece of cold lamb from his plate, nibbling on it.

'Nobody knows where Menshikov stems from. Perhaps he sold *pierogi* in the streets Peter grew up in, or possibly his father was employed to drill Peter's toy army – your guess is as good as mine. The higher Menshikov rises, the cleaner he sweeps his traces.'

'How could he ever win the Tsar's heart, behaving the way he does?'

The general watched the two men. 'They were young together, Marta. Sharing the days of our youth is a stronger link than most. Soon, the Tsar himself might marry one of those Arsenjeva whores, and Menshikov the other. Then they'd finally be family,' he said, shuddering. I looked up: Peter and Menshikov were kissing the Arsenjevas. Menshikov took Daria's breast in his mouth, the pressure of his lips making her moan. I lowered my eyes, cheeks burning, as it reminded me of the lust I had felt in Anton's arms. The Tsar swung the half-naked Varvara over his shoulder like a sack of flour – fox-red locks flowing and her dress torn. Her laughter rang out like a silver bell as all four of them disappeared into the tent's side room.

Well, at least we now have time and some calm in which to talk, I thought, and poured more vodka into both our jugs. Sheremetev smiled at me. 'You are quite astonishing, Marta. Look at you: sitting here, laughing and drinking with the nobles of the Russian realm. Just some weeks ago things were very different for you.' I blushed: he had neither forgotten my torn clothes nor my bare flesh. No man would. In the dusky tent, the look in his eyes was unreadable. I lowered my gaze.

'What were we talking of?' he asked, clearing his throat. 'Menshikov,' I helped him. I wanted to hear as much about the man as I could. 'Menshikov is a mystery. Last week he had Prince Lopukin flogged, the brother of Peter's wife, because he had joked about Menshikov's low birth. He does what he likes and Peter allows it. The two of them are always, always together.' Sheremetev's voice sounded bitter.

'I have even heard that …' I began, but the general raised his eyebrows at me.

'Mind your pretty ears or they'll be cut off. Who has spoken out of turn? Menshikov and the Tsar are close, but I'll dare anyone to speak ill of my ruler.'

I sipped some beer, feeling ashamed, but he squeezed my shoulder, pulling me a bit closer. 'I am not surprised if people think such nonsense. They share everything, be it a plate at dinner, a tent or their women. Menshikov went with Peter on his Grand Embassy and studied with him in Holland. Well, kept him company at least, as Menshikov can't even read. It was the uprising of the Streltsy guard that confirmed his standing. It was he who chased home and put it down mercilessly, by beheading one Streltsy after the next, hundreds of them, until his arms ached, his shoulders froze and he waded in blood. That's just one more reason why Peter loves him so much …'

'Who were the Streltsy soldiers? And why should Peter love Menshikov for executing them?' I nicked a piece of roast pheasant from Sheremetev's plate. Its skin was hot, crispy and tasted a bit sweet, as it had been marinated in mustard and honey. I licked my fingers, listening to Sheremetev.

'The Streltsy guard was once the most respected regiment in Russia. When Peter was born, they feared the hold that his mother had over old Tsar Alexis, especially after she had given him a healthy son. On Alexis's death, they stormed the Kremlin and at the Regent Sophia's order killed Peter's uncles and foster father and made the boy watch: both men took two days to die, spiked on halberds.' I closed my eyes in horror. Ernst Gluck's words came back to me: 'Sophia kept him in the Kremlin, at least until he set fire to it …' Sheremetev's voice continued: 'The Streltsy called Peter a son-of-a-bitch and spat in his mother's face, letting them live, just about, and hailing the Regent Sophia. So when Menshikov beheaded them after that second uprising, he was in truth exorcising Peter's demons – or some of them at least.'

'What do you mean by that?'

'There are others and they make him ill, torment him with fits and seizures,' Sheremetev said. His face was very close to mine. 'But, you know, I could never have done what Menshikov did. Killing on the battlefield is one thing, but executing a man with my own hands? Never.'

I huddled deeper into the cloak. How strange the Russians were, forever caught between a zest for life and seeking penance for their sins; filled with deep religious belief, yet capable of heathen violence and full of disdain for common decency, swaying between hair-raising cruelty and deep, tearful regret that might haunt them for years. A Russian soul knew no calm, no balance and no peace, ever.

I touched Sheremetev's arm: 'No, Boris Petrovich. You are too good a man for that. You save girls who are being raped. Who knows? Menshikov might have joined in with those loafers.'

'Who knows indeed?' he said and downed his vodka.

27

Sheremetev and I spoke until the morning hours of that early-autumn night. Eventually we were alone in the main tent, the other guests having staggered away, grateful for some rare hours of rest before sunrise.

'God, girl, all of this is just the beginning,' Sheremetev told me. 'The Tsar says that travelling has opened his eyes to how backward Russia and its people are. Ever since his return from Europe he is a man possessed, as if time is running out for him to achieve everything he has planned. Nothing is safe from his meddling, be it matters of pleasure, agriculture, education, religion, administration, marriage and heritage, the army, food – just about anything that touches a Russian's everyday life, he will pounce upon. Russia is Peter's dough, yet the yeast doesn't quite want to rise ...'

'But does he really need to do all this? It's such an effort, the war and all ...'

'This war is a struggle for the life or death of Peter's realm. It forces us into the future, but the Tsar lacks the money, men and equipment to pursue his plans, which were needed at best yesterday or rather last week. War is terrible but it also brings progress,' Sheremetev said, and gently prodded me when my eyes closed. 'Stay awake and drink some more, Marta. I love talking to you. You listen so well to an old man's chatter.'

The beer did refresh me and I licked the foam off my lips, keeping them moist and shiny. Sheremetev's gaze lingered on them, before he averted his eyes.

'I see no old man. Go on, tell me more.'

'You flatter me.' He smiled at me warmly. 'Russia is like an old mill wheel, rotting away in a backwater, until a new young miller takes over, wanting to grind more grain or sell more sacks, and makes the water rise. The wheel spins faster and faster, until the blades break and even the millstone cracks.'

I chuckled. He had a way of putting things that even I understood.

'You laugh, but Peter won't stop at anything. The country is not up to his demands. His orders can't even reach the people – we have the *voivody*, the councils and the tax collectors, but since Peter keeps on asking for more of everything – men, money, planning, leadership and support – they can't keep up. He is looking for new sources of wealth at the same time as kicking the existing fields of manufacture into new shape. Every family, be it a serf's or a nobleman's, has to give him their sons, either as workers or to travel abroad and study, learning for Russia and bringing their knowledge back home. Have you heard that the Tsar is building a fleet? A fleet! Fifteen years ago nobody here had so much as seen a ship. All a Russian knew of them was from using a ferry to cross a swollen river or, possibly, a fishing boat. His will is our fate, even if it might take a hundred years for us to thank him for his efforts,' the general said bitterly.

'But the war is over, isn't it? You have beaten the Swedes?'

He rubbed his eyes and I felt his tiredness. 'Marienburg was just the beginning. The Tsar wants a harbour that is navigable throughout the year and not hampered by ice in winter. He wants the conquest of the West, a pact with other European powers. As long as both Charles and Peter live, they'll go on fighting, even if the war lasts twenty years. We count for nothing in this. Do you know what Peter did after the trouble with the bad cannon at the Battle of Narva?'

'No.'

'He had all the church bells melted down in order to cast bigger, better weapons.' I gasped – a man who touched the sacred possessions of the Church? Sheremetev saw my shock and said: 'Yes. I, too, wonder what is still sacred to him.' He lowered his voice. 'And then this idea of his to build a new city in the middle of the swamps of the Bay of Finland . . .'

He stopped mid-sentence. The curtain to the side room was torn aside and Peter swayed into the main tent, belting his breeches and tucking his sweaty shirt into the waistband. Did he see us sitting so close, side by side in the shadow of the tent post, or didn't he care? A man like him was never truly alone, I thought, and to acknowledge people or not was surely a matter for him to choose. The last of the candlelight drew shadows on his face, making it look gaunt and tired. His bright blue eyes lay deep in their sockets; he rubbed them, his forehead glistening with sweat.

Sheremetev and I sat still as though watching a shy animal. The Tsar slumped into a chair, which buckled under his weight, and stretched out his legs before grabbing a jug from the table next to him and drinking deeply. He closed his eyes, let his head tilt forward and hummed a little song, then fell silent and started breathing heavily. Was he asleep?

Sheremetev and I looked at each other: it was time to retire, he to his tent and I to whichever corner I might roll out my bedding in, as Daria's room was busy. I was about to get up when Sheremetev grabbed my arm. Peter had started from his slumber and sat bolt upright, his eyes unblinking and wide open. He flung the clay jug at a tent post. It smashed, splashing beer onto the rugs and cushions below. Peter bent over and buried his head in his hands, moaning and whimpering, then rose, roaring like an angry bear. His eyes rolled until I saw only their whites, and he leant heavily on the table, which gave way and broke. In a clatter, plates, glasses and bottles fell to the floor. He stared and then his knees buckled; he cradled his head in his hands and sobbed, foam bubbling on his lips, before he reared up, thrashing about, hitting the furniture and writhing in his fit.

Sheremetev held my arm and pulled me back.

Peter groaned, 'What have I done, Mother? What have we done?'

The mighty man bent double, tongue protruding between his lips and teeth. I thought of Grigori and felt no more fear: there was no time to lose, we had to help him.

'Hold his legs, I'll take care of the rest,' I said, and stepped away from Sheremetev, who had shrunk back in horror. I was not afraid. To me at this moment Peter was not the mighty Tsar who had ravaged my homeland and destroyed my life. He was just a helpless man who was suffering. If I hadn't been able to help Grigori, I could at least help Peter.

He lay curled at my feet, slavering and foaming, his eyes wide and rolling. Sheremetev grabbed his boots and weighed him down, but the Tsar instantly jackknifed and lashed out at his much smaller general, smacking him so hard that he groaned but didn't let go. I took a deep breath and lunged between those thrashing, bulky arms, grabbed the Tsar's twitching head, pulled him close and forced his forehead between my breasts, holding his ears and neck so tightly that he couldn't move away. We sank to the ground and his breath rattled, his body cramping up a couple of times before he lay still. His breath was hot on my skin and he sucked in my scent before he grabbed me around the waist, so that I could hardly breathe. After a long time he lay still and his breathing steadied. I dared to look at his face: he had fallen peacefully asleep. I rocked him like I would a baby.

'This was bound to happen,' Sheremetev sighed, slowly taking his weight off Peter's feet. 'The long ride, the girls and all this drink. Peter likes to see himself as a Titan, but he is just a man.'

I had no idea what a Titan might be but put one finger to my lips in warning. Peter's face was drenched in sweat and his hair smelt of dust, smoke, leather and the love he had made to the Arsenjevas. His curls stuck to his temples when I tenderly stroked his head, blowing some air against his face. He sighed and burrowed himself closer into me; his breathing grew heavier again and he held me even tighter than before. I never stopped caressing him and perhaps even kissed his forehead without thinking. Peter started to cry.

When Sheremetev got up, I saw the Tsar's feet: like his hands, they looked too dainty for his huge body.

'Don't let go of him, Marta, will you? Everything rests on him,' Sheremetev said before he slipped out into the darkness, which was still alive with fires and songs from all over the vast Russian realm: melodies that started slow and sullen, before gathering speed and culminating in clapping and chanting. Peter's arrival had rallied the men's spirits; they took fresh courage from it and gained new strength. Voices asked Sheremetev questions before all fell quiet.

My back hurt from holding the Tsar so steadily, but only when he seemed truly asleep did I dare to reach for some cushions. Yet when I shifted, he grabbed my waist so hard that I gasped for air. 'Stay,' he murmured. 'Stay with me. Hold me tight, *matka*.'

'I will, *starik*,' I answered in German, with a little smile. If I was his old girl, he'd be my old man: that seemed only fair. His eyelids fluttered and he looked at me in surprise but then fell back asleep, this time deeply and calmly. I grabbed all the cushions I could reach, stuffing them behind my back and under my bottom and thighs. The darkness in the tent had paled with the dawn when I, too, fell asleep, holding the Tsar of All the Russias in my arms as if he were a baby. Just before my eyelids closed I remembered a supper from days long gone by, and Agneta Gluck's high-pitched voice asking, 'Is it true that the Tsar of Russia is a two-headed giant who eats children for supper?'

I woke on my own, feeling drowsy after the all-too-short and uncomfortable hours of sleep. There was no sign of the Tsar anywhere, but the tent was swarming with people clearing up after the night's feast and packing things away, with chests open and everything piled topsy-turvy inside. For a moment I wondered if I had dreamt all that had happened. Neither Menshikov nor the Arsenjevas were anywhere to be seen. All the flaps were fastened open and a fresh breeze swept the tent: when I stepped outside I shivered, the blue, cold morning light blinding me. The camp was in upheaval and Daria and Varvara watched hawk-eyed as their maids loaded all their treasures onto carts, even though we'd need sledges soon. I tried not to look at Varvara's throat, where she wore her love bites as proudly as trophies of war.

She arched her eyebrows when I approached. 'Ah, Marta, too, is finally awake. What a lazy little thing you have found for us, Daria.' My friend looked up, surprised. Varvara had not been exactly friendly to me before this, but not outright hostile either. What had got into her? 'You really are unlucky, missing out on everything like that: the Tsar is long gone, without taking his leave from anyone. When I awoke, he had already left my bed,' Varvara added. With her shining auburn hair and glittering eyes she looked like the cruel, cunning vixens in the forests of my childhood. 'You'd better be off now, Marta. A maid like you has her hands full when the camp is being packed up,' she chirped, and reached out her fingers for me to kiss.

Daria was embarrassed, not knowing which side to take: 'No, Varvara, Marta, really, please don't ...'

I kissed Varvara's fingers. I might be in Daria's favour, I might have spent the night with the Tsar, but it would serve me well to remember that I was a maid here and everything could go horribly wrong for me in the blink of an eye.

I met Varvara's grey gaze. She knew about Peter, I could tell. I didn't know how, but she knew. Who would protect me from her?

Peter's new marching orders were a surprise to everybody. The Russians had to take the fortress of Nöteborg on the shores of Lake Ladoga, which was surrounded by vast, empty marshland. 'Must we?' wailed Daria while her dresses were folded away into oak chests. 'I swear, nothing good comes from there. In summer, countless gnats eat you alive, while in winter the River Neva rises and the whole place becomes a revolting swamp. What fun!'

But the fortress's dank walls and high turrets were key to controlling the estuary. The siege took Menshikov two weeks, until it fell after a skirmish at sea. Peter, I heard, was bursting with pride: he had won his first naval confrontation. Menshikov was made Governor of the strait – *Obergshathalter* – and the Tsar changed the fortress's name to the Schlusselburg as it was key to the future as he saw it. Menshikov had Peter's letter to him read aloud at dinner every evening for days on end following the victory: '*By God, this nut was hard to crack, but you have done it, my beloved brother.*'

When the first snowflakes fell, Daria's steady complaining about the wet and the cold – it snowed and snowed – paid off and Menshikov gave in to her nagging. He sent her, Varvara, his sister Rasia and me back to Moscow to get ready for Yuletide. While I helped Daria to pack, I wondered if the Tsar, too, would return to Moscow then, which was foolish, of course. What was I to him?

INTERREGNUM, 1725

The snow fell like a curtain, slanted and silent, shrouding streets, quays and prospects, up to the axles of the carts already making their way into town for the morning market despite the awful weather. Outside the city walls, beyond the reach of the lantern-light, paths and roads had disappeared. It was awhile still until the late and heavy dawn that wedged a brief day between the hours of darkness, its arrival marred by the steady snowfall and the dullness of the black ice on the river and the roads.

Your city knows, Peter. Your death is our secret. The high houses with their flat façades mourn their master's passing in silence; the waters flowing underneath the three hundred bridges murmur their loss. Only the winter winds, untameable as ever, chase down the Nevsky Prospect and defy my orders; carrying the news with them to the utmost corners of the realm. The vast, endless plains of your empire always have had to endure the whims of *batjuschka* Tsar; your people followed orders they could not hope to understand. The Tsar was as God-given as day and night, winter and summer, the sun and the moon; there was no questioning him.

In the wan morning light, all the bells of Russia will toll. Your people will drop whatever they are doing and kneel, cap in hand, tears streaming down their faces, praying for your soul, crossing themselves with three fingers. It would make you happy to see how Europe, too, will pay you, and your city, its respect. This is what you always wanted, isn't it, for St Petersburg, your paradise?

Thanks to Feofan Prokopovich there is no lack of legends about how you chose the spot for it. Was it true that Saint Alexander Nevsky had beaten the Teutonic hordes in battle here? Or were you hunting, my love, when an eagle circled above your head, settling on your shoulder, showing you the way with its beady eyes and its hoarse cries? Might you have wandered through the swamps of Lust Eland – as one would never do, really – when the bird guided you to the island's heart and you cut a cross from beech branches, marking a spot and shouting, 'In the name of Christ the Almighty, I shall build a church and a fortress here to honour the Saints Peter and Paul.'

None of this happened, of course. The truth was much simpler and much grander: to strengthen his hold over the Neva strait, Peter built a Russian fortress. The hard-fought-for new lands should never be lost again. The Tsar chose Lust Eland as the driest spot in all the Ladoga swamps. When Peter had the bones of Saint Alexander Nevsky re-entombed there, clouds of gnats set upon us. During the endless hours of the ceremony we went on swatting and cursing the useless serfs who were told to kill them before they bit us and flew off, their bellies heavy with our blood. Peter alone stood without blinking, never moving, watching stone-faced as the saint's coffin was lowered into its new tomb. For him, this marked the beginning of a new Russia.

In the evening, I treated my many bites with *kefir* and Peter went on talking about the paradise he'd build. By then I was ready to take every step along the way with him, even though I was only one of many girls to whom he'd toss a coin or two after a night of merriment. I smiled and urged him on; his first wife Evdokia's sour face and her unwillingness to follow him in his flights of fancy had been her downfall.

Prokopovich's claims that the Tsar's chosen land was empty, waiting for his blessed touch, is untrue as well: Swedes had settled all around the shores of Lake Ladoga in big, well-to-do farmsteads and I spotted many *mir* like my own. The first real house in St

Petersburg was a hut, Peter's and my cosy home. He left the fort one morning, walking all alone into the forest, his axe on his shoulder. Menshikov had sent out guards to follow him, as bands of marauding Swedish mercenaries had been sighted, but Peter threw stones at them, cursed and even kicked them when the men came too close.

Peter chose the trees he deemed right and chopped their trunks to the length he needed, before building our hut with his own hands, sweating, laughing and loving every moment of it. I held the nails as well as other bits and bobs and played pranks on him by hiding his hammer and chisel. Once finished, the little house was barely wider than it was long, comprising a small hall, a kitchen, a living room and bedroom. The hearth was fired up throughout the year, as Peter hated the cold, and I cooked our *kasha* and *chai* on the open fire, stacking our bowls as I had done as a child in our *izba*. Peter made our wooden furniture himself: a table, two benches and our bed, as well as a lockable chest. When working with wood he had his best ideas, he claimed. The only sign of Peter's wealth and rank was an icon of heavy gold, studded with pearls, rubies, sapphires and emeralds, which hung on our bedroom wall, right next to a map of Europe.

This hut was the root from which Peter's paradise was to grow and blossom; his New Jerusalem, glowing in all the colours of the rainbow. If he himself was content with his hut, he drove his architects and stone masons mercilessly to build bigger and better, a city such as the world had never seen. The glory of Russia was at stake.

Peter ordered orange and lemon trees to be brought from Persia, and had roses, mint and camphor planted in the gardens to scent and sweeten the air. He was beside himself when a messenger brought a sample of the first-ever blossom from the Summer Palace's gardens out to the field, as we stood once more in battle. The gardener had soaked the flower in olive oil to keep it fresh, but it had made the petals rotten and slimy. The Tsar knouted the messenger and ordered his gardeners to send him proof of the next blossom with the flowers wrapped one by one in tobacco leaves instead.

The first streets and prospects were lit by lanterns with candles and oil – their glass of course made in Menshikov's workshops – such as had never been seen in Russia. Heavily guarded barriers – *shlag-baumy* – were put up on the main roads and the bridges linking the forty islands. Nobody but doctors, or people whose visit was expected, was allowed through without a pass. When I looked out of the window after Peter's death, I knew that just behind the splendour of the palaces lay the first modest wooden houses, and before them row upon row of *izby* made of straw, clay and moss, and before that squalid, ragged tents. This city mirrors your world, Peter, whether you want it to or not.

St Petersburg grew quickly in the first twenty years of the new century. I remembered our senseless joy when the first Dutch frigate, bobbing on the already icy waters, weighed anchor. It delivered salt and wine for the long winter ahead and its arrival was reason enough for a feast so wild that it stunned even Menshikov, not to mention the visiting Dutchmen. Peter had the men drink mercilessly, before asking us all to go out for a sail on stormy waters in the morning. The rolling waves sobered us up fast and the Dutch were happy to leave with a present of five hundred gold ducats in their pockets. Peter promised each ship anchoring in the bay within the year the same generous gift.

I cooled my forehead on the windowpane. My thoughts were racing and I was laughing and chatting with Peter as if he was still alive; as if I could place my feet on his thighs and he'd squeeze and rub them, making my little bones crack, warming my muscles, and tickle me until I squealed. He'd do that until I had the fire in my thighs that he liked.

The glass mirrored my feverish face. I gathered myself for the long wait that still lay ahead, before Russia could begin praying for the soul of its new ruler.

For the time being Menshikov snored like a bear. His heavy body sprawled somehow in that small chair, head lolling to the side and his mouth open. The fire had burnt down and a chill crept through the thin pane. I still waited for the Privy Council, Ostermann, Tolstoy and Jagushinsky. Why were they not in the palace at their dying Tsar's side? Were they avoiding my call? I had saved them all countless times from Peter's anger, but people forget so easily when it comes to saving their own skin.

Had it been safe to entrust my secret message to the young servant? The Winter Palace looked so welcoming and gay during the day, its stunning shades of blue and green mirroring the Neva in springtime. Yet at night it had its own life of countless dark corners and secret passageways that led to the dark, icy waters of the river. The rats didn't even scuttle when a body splashed into those floes. Fishermen would find the corpse, or what was left of it, in their nets much later, once the *ottepel* had been and gone. How stupid of me. I chewed my wrist with anger. If my messenger had been caught, questioned and killed, then the Dolgorukis knew about my plan and, even worse, I'd have lost valuable hours. I should have sent Menshikov and the Imperial Guard. Menshikov coughed and sat up, shook himself awake like a dog casting off water, and then stretched the sleep from his tall body. A short slumber refreshed him as much as a whole night's rest, as I knew from the many times I had been in the field with him.

When he stepped up to me, the vodka, sweat and tiredness of his long wake at Peter's deathbed blended with his perfume of musk and sandalwood. His hair was messy, his full lace collar had slipped, and a red wine stain shone brightly on his crumpled shirt. I smiled and tenderly straightened his collar: he kissed my hand, surprised. This was the man I had shared everything with, even my husband's love, and now we shared a common fate.

Menshikov tore the window open and rubbed his face with some snow. 'Brrr! Cold. Looks as if we are in for a storm, don't you think?' he asked, eyeing the sky. 'Winter in these swamps is always to be relied upon.' Now wide awake, he shivered, closed the window again and stoked the fire with logs from the basket. The flames licked over the wood, burning brightly and spreading a dry scent, like a walk in a summer forest. He raised his eyebrows.

'Where is the Privy Council? I thought you had sent for them?' I gnawed my lips. 'By God, Catherine. How much time do we have left? Say something.' The tone of his voice angered me: at least I had done something. 'If you hadn't been so drunk I wouldn't have needed to rely on a little soldier, would I? Perhaps the lad has had his throat cut. I might as well shave my head for the nunnery, I suppose.' I heard the fear in my voice when Menshikov placed his hand on my mouth to silence me.

'Psst,' he whispered. 'Do you hear that?' He looked at the little door that led over to Peter's bedroom. I frowned. He was right: somebody was sobbing in there. Menshikov stayed by the fire when I tiptoed to the door and opened it soundlessly. Peter's chamber was bathed in candlelight: he looked as if he was asleep, even if death already spread its sickly-sweet shroud over the room. In front of the bed knelt a girl wearing a dark, hooded velvet cloak. Her shoulders heaved as she kissed his fingers, which were beginning to stiffen.

Doctors Blumentrost and Paulsen started when they saw me and cowered in the corner: they had failed to obey my strict order to protect the Tsar's corpse. I felt cold anger, but grabbed the girl, pulling her to her feet and forcing her to face me. Then I let go of her in surprise when she looked at me fearlessly and stubbornly, as had ever been her way, her pretty face and her light blue eyes – Peter's eyes – swollen with tears.

'Elizabeth!' I said. 'What are you doing here? Why are you not in bed, like your sisters?'

The dark cloak made her look regal: I still saw her as being as harmless as one of her own dolls, yet she had grown into a woman long since.

'How did you get in here?' I asked. If she had managed it, others could too.

'Easy,' she said. She licked her lips, her eyes as lively as a young bird's despite her sorrow. 'The corridor was as good as empty and Madame de la Tour was minding little Natalya. The poor thing is coughing like death itself and so the French locust stayed away from me. And Anna ...' Her voice trailed off. I knew that my eldest daughter was busy dreaming of her wedding with the German Duke Charles Frederic of Holstein. With his narrow shoulders and terrible stammer, he wasn't the most physically appealing prospect, but his family did rule most of Northern Europe. At first, he had asked for

Elizabeth's hand in marriage, but Peter gave him our eldest daughter instead. Their wedding day was close and Anna could speak of nothing else.

Elizabeth was hell-bent on angering me. 'There was only a young and handsome guard outside my father's door and I have my ways …' she said, showing her small, sharp teeth like the cat that got the cream. My heart sank. My daughter, Tsarevna of All the Russias, was only fifteen – a year younger than I had been when I had been sold to Vassily – but she already had the worst reputation of all the royal Princesses of Europe. Being born out of wedlock to a former serf and washerwoman didn't help. Peter had sent her portrait to every court with an eligible crown prince, and the painters didn't even need to flatter my daughter. Elizabeth was a beauty with no cleft lip and no pockmarks for a gifted brush on canvas to have to hide. Peter was puzzled when no engagement came to pass; why did Versailles keep on delaying their answer in such an insulting way? Who else could the young King of France be happy to marry than Peter's Lizenka, lively and beautiful as she was? Yet in the end, young Louis settled on the daughter of the deposed King of Poland, a dull girl with no dowry. Peter saw in Elizabeth what he wanted to see: his strength and his zest for life, his ruthlessness and his sensuality. Unlike all her brothers she had simply refused to die, neither at birth nor throughout the many illnesses that blighted a child's early life.

Her birth had been the most difficult of the thirteen times I had been brought to bed: she was born with her feet first, the very day that Peter celebrated his biggest victory of the Great Northern War. The midwife had crossed herself with three fingers, pale with fright, when she spotted Elizabeth's tiny soles where her head should have been. 'Holy Mother of God,' she had called, her face smeared with blood and sweat. 'Born feet first under the December stars. She'll be a wolverine.'

'What will happen now?' Elizabeth asked. 'Who will the next Tsar be? Did Father settle on little Petrushka after all? He's not even the Tsarevich.'

He decided nothing, I thought, but said, 'Yes, but he is Alexey's son. And soon, he will be a man. That's enough of a claim.'

'A man!' Elizabeth said gaily. 'Do you know what the dark cells of the Trubetzkoi bastion or the dank cellars of the Schlusselburg can do to a *man*'s body and mind?'

It seemed Peter's soul had slipped into his daughter's body. She'd make love standing up to a soldier outside this door, she'd sob her eyes out at her father's deathbed and she'd banish her little nephew to a musty dark cell. She was a true Russian and a stranger to me.

'Whatever happens, Elizabeth, nothing is to befall Petrushka. Whoever hurts him will be a murderer in the eyes of all other European courts. Do you want to start a reign like that?'

She shook her head, albeit gingerly, and said, 'Well, if Petrushka is not even the Tsarevich, and if my elder sister marries Holstein, and all my other brothers have passed away, then ...'

'Then?' I asked icily.

She shrugged and smiled brightly. 'Then I should be Tsarina next! Father loved me and he made me Crown Princess two years ago, together with Anna. Why shouldn't I rule?'

I felt like crying, thinking of Peter's vast realm with its millions of people. Their fate, be it war or peace, hanging on her playful finger-tips, which men liked to kiss after a masterfully danced minuet or a quadrille? Her little head that had so far mainly been used to show off the latest fashionable hairstyle, concerning itself with politics?

'Elizabeth!' I giggled instead, then laughed so hard that the doctors looked worried. She lunged at me like one of the small monkeys she kept in Peterhof Palace, battering me with her fists. Menshikov hurried into the room.

'What's this din?' he hissed, grabbing her arms. 'We are not in a *kabak*.' She winced, but he held her around her plump waist and lifted her up, carrying her into the other room. She wriggled and kicked; her red-hot anger left me speechless, yet I remembered a ball where Elizabeth had slapped another girl and torn a bushel of her hair out in front of the whole court, because both of them wore pink dresses and the other one looked prettier in hers. Peter had laughed himself to tears at it, but I had had the fight stopped and married the other girl off well, topping up her dowry. Perhaps I was a better mother to my dead sons than to my living daughters.

Elizabeth's squirming wound down. 'Will you behave now, Tsarevna?' Menshikov asked, lifting his hand off her mouth. She smoothed her cloak and raised her chin, which made her heavy diamond earrings sparkle. I closed the door to the other room, glowering at the doctors. My order was to be upheld and no one was to see the dead Tsar's body. They nodded, pale with dread.

Menshikov, Elizabeth and I were alone.

The new fire had warmed the small library. When Menshikov served us wine, Elizabeth downed hers in one go, smacking her pink lips.

'You drink like a peasant,' I scolded her.

'Well, *you* should know,' she said tartly.

'Stop it,' Menshikov cut in. 'Tsarina. Elizabeth. We don't have time for this.'

She spun around and stared at him, her eyes icy. '*What* did you say? *Tsarina?*' She lengthened the word to its full size and power, before turning to me. 'But of course. That's it. Now I understand: you want it all for yourself. Was that your plan from the beginning?'

I slapped her so hard, her lip split open. She gave a muffled scream and touched the wound.

'Don't,' Menshikov pleaded, and handed her his lacy handkerchief. We sat in silence while some logs crashed in the fireplace, making embers fly. Elizabeth dabbed her lip, looked at me darkly and slipped off her cloak, stuffing the handkerchief into the seam of her tight sleeve. Against her richly embroidered emerald-green silk dress and the foaming lace of her bodice, her shoulders looked like polished alabaster. Following the fashion of Versailles, the dress was so deeply cut that I could almost see her nipples; diamonds rained down from her neck into her cleavage. Countless peasant families could survive for centuries on these jewels alone. Was she on her way to a feast? I had long since lost track of her comings and goings. How did I lose interest in the strongest and merriest of my children?

Elizabeth moved her chair closer to the fire, kicked off her silk slippers and warmed her feet in their sheer silk stockings. She seemed happy to be here, in the middle of things, and asked, 'So, tell me, Menshikov. What is it that you want to do? You are never short of an idea or a plan, are you? Do you want to rule together with my mother, or do you want to seize power all by yourself? Shame on both of you: this palace still breathes with my father's soul. The water on the windowpane is not dew, but the sweat of your fear. Do you sleep with each other, now and then?' She smiled and I wanted to slap her once more.

Menshikov stayed calm. 'One day, Tsarevna Elizabeth, you will understand how hurtful and stupid those words were,' he said.

'No, Alexander Danilovich. I shall always sleep with any man who takes my fancy. I shouldn't hesitate if you wanted to be the lucky one?' she teased him.

I held my breath. Did she truly just offer him her bed, her birthright, in return for his support? How would he resist that? A ruler's world was made up of only friends and foes, even among their blood relatives. I looked beseechingly towards the door, begging the Privy Council to come. Ostermann, Tolstoy and Jagushinsky – I needed them all. I forced myself to sip some more wine and said, 'Prince Menshikov is right. One day you'll learn that it might be better not to sleep with a man just to secure his loyalty.'

'One day? When I am old and no one wants me anymore?'

I didn't want to have heard her; she knew how to wound. The flames danced, soothing my spirit and making me tired. 'The Dolgorukys will try to enthrone Petrushka. If that happens, we are all done for,' I said curtly.

'But Vassily Dolgoruki is my godfather. He would never ...' she started.

'He would, though, wouldn't he? For Alexey's sake.'

'Yes,' she said, eyeing Menshikov, who twisted and turned the colourful Venetian goblet in his hand as if he had nothing to do with all this. But Elizabeth wasn't finished. 'Oh, yes. For Alexey's sake. My brother. Oh, Alexander Danilovich, your sled to Siberia won't even have a cushion or a blanket. You'll burrow in straw like a pig in winter. Perhaps, just perhaps, you'll get enough kopeks to buy an axe once you make it there. If not, just chew the wood off a tree, as a beaver would. Build a hut, and get on with it. But you'll have to wait until summer, when the ice melts.'

Her laughter rang out like the silver bells she tied around her dwarves' necks so as to be able to find them in the darkness of the palace corridors. Menshikov let the joints crack in his fingers, tweaking them. He, too, I was certain, felt like hitting her.

'If Petrushka gets to be Tsar, I will be nothing but your father's whore and you, Elizabeth, will be a bastard born out of wedlock. Petrushka might still have to fear your bloodline and your birthright, but he will leave St Petersburg forever ...'

'No!' She shot to her feet. 'Never! That would be a betrayal of everything Father lived for,' she gasped. 'It would be like a second death for him. That's horrid.'

What a strange girl she was: to her, betraying her father's dream was worse than being buried alive in a nunnery.

'Well, then, you will have to sit and wait with us,' I said.

'Wait? What for?' She sat down again, eyeing me over the rim of her glass.

'The Privy Council,' Menshikov said.

She laughed. 'Those old fools? Ostermann has the gout whenever he sees fit, Tolstoy is so fat he needs two or three chairs to support his big bottom, and Jagushinsky stinks as if he's rotting from the inside. Which one of them will share your hut in Siberia, Menshikov?' She dug her toes into his thighs.

'Stop it!' I scolded. The Privy Council had been the wisest heads in Peter's empire. God protect Russia from Elizabeth, I thought. She shrugged her bare shoulders and hummed a tune before getting bored with that as well, looking sullenly into the flames.

I glanced at the window, trying to guess the time. The inky night was putting up a struggle against the morning hour with its wan blue shine and the day's short hours of sparsely measured grey light. The city lay in wait, shining in its cloak of sparkling white; ice crystals adorned the windows of the palaces and houses. As children we'd suck on icicles, surprised to find that they tasted of dust. Elizabeth asked, 'Did you ever love my father?'

And I didn't know the answer to that anymore.

28

My first journey to the heart of the Russian realm seemed endless: how could a country be so vast? The winter was severe and our train of sleighs and sledges was stuck right in its merciless cold. Birds froze in mid-flight, falling like stones from the sky, and travellers perished in sudden snowstorms, never reaching shelter. The wolves lost all fear of man and came right up to the *izby* doorsteps, snatching children and small livestock, crazed with hunger. How my family could have survived this, I did not know, having to shake the thought out of my head lest it eat me up. My Baltic fatherland was no more; from Reval to Riga, everything had fallen prey to the war's terror. At the end of our time in Marienburg, Sheremetev was said to be clueless as to what to do with all his loot, and prices for either a sheep or a child sank to a *denga* apiece. Half a kopek for a human being! There was no time to think as impatience drove the sisters Arsenjeva on. They'd have the drivers whip the small spotted ponies mercilessly to win *verst* upon *verst*, until the animals' mouths foamed and their backs were covered in weals. At every postal station we changed ponies, taking our pick from the innkeeper's and other travellers' stables, without ever paying for them. What belonged to any Russian belonged first and foremost to the Tsar and his friends, and Menshikov took full advantage of that.

When I had first heard about travelling to Moscow, I had pictured a modest number of sledges and sleighs, with possibly a guard in attendance, making their way through Russia. All I knew of travel, after all, was the drive with Vassily to Walk and then the smelly cart to Marienburg. Instead, we left in a train with hundreds of other people. Menshikov sent ahead everything he deemed necessary for the Yuletide festivities in the capital. I did not know where to look first, stunned by the splendour and also by his being so self-indulgent. Behind our sleigh travelled a good hundred other vehicles laden with luggage, food and people, such as Menshikov's political and military advisers, as well as two chamberlains and three pageboys, a cauldron-maker and two trombonists, a Moor and a family of dwarves, three scribes, a dozen castrati, a priest and two cooks with their chubby kitchen boys. When I asked Daria about it, she just shrugged: 'Alexander Danilovich needs what Alexander Danilovich needs.'

The closer we came to Moscow, the more handsome became the houses and inns, where all life centred around a big hearth, its mantelpiece made of stone or tiles. The kitchen served hearty cabbage stews, chicken broth with dumplings made of offal and *blinchiki*, little pancakes filled with molten cheese or salted and smoked meat. Pigs and poultry were locked in sties and coops and would no longer stray amongst the guests in the main room.

When we stepped into the cosy warmth our dank furs steamed up the small windows. The heat and the stench of the many people eating and drinking and sleeping hit me like a slap, but it took only a couple of glasses of vodka to get used to it all. At night, the men of our train burrowed in the straw like pigs, whilst I relished having a room in the inn, where I joined the Arsenjevas. If Varvara minded – 'Shouldn't Marta sleep in the stable with the other serfs?' – Daria's friendship protected me. The maid first warmed our bed with her body, before curling up on the threshold of our door for the night. Before I fell asleep I would pray to the god who wanted to listen, thanking him for my fate such as it was, even if my future hung on Daria's mood and goodwill. What if Varvara started to talk even more against me? Already, no day passed without a stinging word or two.

The seven hundred and seventeen *versty* from the Schlusselburg to Moscow could take anything from six days' to four weeks' travel:

we got into the sleighs in the early-morning darkness and stepped out of them long after sunset. They were like small, colourful houses on skids, painted gaily on the outside and stuffed with cushions and fur blankets, where we lay and chatted the day away, relishing the warmth of the copper pans full of smouldering coals that the maids had placed there as their first duty of the day.

The sun only showed in the leaden sky in the late morning and we craned our necks towards it from the windows of the sleigh, longing for its first rays. My belly was filled with hot, sweet and salty *kasha* and the bitter *chai* we'd had for breakfast in the inn. This was so different from the cold and lonely trip from Walk to Marienburg of just a few years ago, and I relished the comfort, the good food and all the laughter and the stories the sisters had to tell. Depending on whether Rasia Menshikova felt like company or not, she shared our sleigh or kept to herself, though I was sure that nothing escaped her attention. She guarded herself from joining in with Varvara's needling, but wasn't as close to me as Daria.

The landscape flying by the small barred windows looked alike from one day to the next. Forests, hills and plains were shrouded in snow, and only adventures and mishaps marked time's passing, such as the heavy snowstorm that forced the driver to sit with us – the sisters plied the man with vodka and told jokes to make his ears burn – or the wolves that attacked our vehicle, circling it one afternoon well before we'd reach the safety of an inn. When Varvara heard the first long, dragging howl that made my blood chill, she shouted at the coachman, 'Whip those beasts away! They are the Tsaritsa Evdokia's faithful servants and she has sent them to eat us up. She's a witch and they are of the Devil.'

The poor man thrashed as hard as he could, but there were just too many of them, so, the Arsenjevas and I, too, seized the whips that were stored underneath our seats and started lashing, taking turns to stand in the open door of the sleigh. By the light of the full moon rising I saw the wolves' eyes shine with madness and hunger; icicles hung in their fur and around their salivating mouths. The other sleighs caught up with us and the men started to shoot at the beasts, who turned into a howling, bloody muddle of fur, teeth and bodies. In the evening Menshikov's men boasted about their great bravery, the wolves growing stronger, bigger and more ferocious with each glass of vodka, until I snatched Daria's sable coat and pretended to be a big wolf. She chased me round the room with a whip, which made the men howl with laughter. Even Varvara was in stitches.

The same evening, Daria asked me: 'Marta, would you like to be my lady-in-waiting? Like that we can be always together and have all sorts of fun. Varvara can be such a spoilsport with her constant nagging. You'll have a room in Menshikov's palace and a salary.' I felt like throwing myself at her feet and kissing her toes, but instead embraced her warmly as a sister would, and answered: 'That would be a joy and an honour. I especially can't wait to dress you up as Menshikov's bride.' Daria smiled and kissed me back.

Yet the closer we came to Moscow, the less I wanted to think further ahead than Yuletide. What if Daria's mood changed or Varvara managed to sway her? Even a lady-in-waiting could very quickly be cast aside for some clumsiness or other and find herself alone, poor and homeless. Daria found me amusing, but I had been surer of my future at the Glucks. I tried to do as the Russians did and live for the moment. I did have one substantial asset, though.

Just before we left the Schusselburg, Menshikov had given me a purse heavy with coins. When I had opened it, it was filled with gold that blinked in the grey morning light.

'What is this for?' I gasped. Never in my life had I seen such riches, nor held them in my hand. What could I buy with that? My old life, ten thousand times over.

He shrugged. 'That's for you to decide. Go shopping if you like and get some dresses and a sable coat or two. Daria knows all the best places in Moscow.'

'But why are you giving it to me?' I stared at the open purse, trying to estimate the amount inside. It was too much. 'I mean, thank you –'

'Oh, the gold is not from me. I'd never just give things away, you know that.' Menshikov winked at me and folded my fingers around the purse. 'Close it, girl, and keep it out of other people's sight. Some secrets are best not shared.' He grinned at me. 'But no worries, I'll find out exactly what happened and what that money is for. Until then, spend it wisely.'

'Is it from Boris Petrovich Sheremetev?' I called after him, as he gathered his cloak and pulled his fur hat deeper over his forehead, before fighting his way back to the fortress through the thigh-high snow. Menshikov turned and pulled a face; the two men's rivalry was far from over. I smiled. Of course, that was well guessed. Dear Sheremetev didn't want me entirely at Daria's mercy. After the night when I had held Peter, Sheremetev had left at once on the Tsar's orders. I couldn't think of anyone else who would make me such a present. I weighed the purse again. If I knew where my family was, I could change everything for them. But life was never that easy.

One morning, after about two weeks in the sleigh, Daria craned her neck, lifted the curtain, looked out of the window and ignored our pleas against the cold and the wind. She'd often poke Varvara and point at the forest that lay like a dark line beyond the fields, or at a certain hill in the far distance. She knew the landscape around Moscow like I knew every field and road around my *mir*.

'Stop!' she called and knocked on the sleigh's side. The driver obeyed. Her cheeks were aflame and eyes shining as she pulled my hand up from under the warmth of the fur blanket. 'Come with me, Marta. I'll show you something your poor eyes have never seen before.'

When she hopped out, she sank up to her knees in the snow, which made her laugh and push on, forcing me to follow, until the driver ploughed a way for us up the hill.

'Come on, don't dawdle,' she called over her shoulder, stumbling over the dragging hem of her cloak and straightening up again, her hands red and sore and covered in snow. Up on the hilltop, she embraced me and pointed to the plain beneath us.

'Look,' she called, gasping for air. 'We are on the Sparrow Hills. And this, Marta, is the world's most wonderful city: Moscow!'

I held my breath: the heart of Muscovy stretched across the whole horizon and offered itself proudly to my eyes. Countless spires and cupolas sent their own golden light into the hours of the early dusk.

The Taiga's fresh evening breeze blew in from far beyond the city, but it carried sounds and smells with it: Moscow had a life of its own; a life so strong that I felt it as far away as the Sparrow Hills, closing my eyes and imagining it.

Whips cracked, women laughed, children bawled and men in the *kabaki* shouted. Animals brayed, water ran over mill wheels and hooves thundered on cobblestone streets and squares. I sensed the food in the kitchens, the sewage in the alleyways, the oils and perfumes in the shops and stalls – all the splendour and squalor. Moscow wasn't built like Riga or Marienburg, all orderly and laid out around a market square. While I saw high city gates, there was no city wall as even Walk had had, but houses of all sizes stood jumbled together, spreading out randomly in every direction. All around lay a belt of smaller settlements and fields that fed on the Moskva and its side rivers. Yet coiling like a snake around the city's very heart, a group of dark, large houses formed a palace with heavy, high roofs and even more spires and cupolas.

'It doesn't look at all like Marienburg!' I said

Daria laughed as if I had suggested something ridiculous. 'These are the *posady*,' she said, pointing, 'they're outer settlements, where you'll find the most shopkeepers and handymen, artists and gardeners, that the Tsar has lured to Russia; carpenters, rope-makers, blacksmiths, painters, welders and sculptors. Next to them are the mills and the fields that the Moskva floods to give the best fruit and vegetables. But you'll also find the trappers there, the fishermen and the breeders of falcons, horses and hounds. Next to them the beekeepers have settled. Wait until you taste Moscow honey.'

'Who lives further out?' I asked, squinting my eyes.

She shrugged. 'Serfs and peasants.'

Perhaps my family was there if they had been lucky enough to survive. If so, I'd find them, I thought, but Daria pointed to three shiny spires in the heart of the city. 'That is the Kremlin, the palace of all palaces,' she said in awe. Her pretty face looked like a rosebud cupped in the fur of her collar. 'And not far from it, over there, is the *gostiny dvor*. We'll go as soon as we can.'

'Why is that?' I asked. 'Is it like a market?'

'A market,' she snorted. 'You really have a lot to learn. It's a place of wonder for a girl with a purse full of gold,' she said, her eyes locking with mine. I thought it best to be honest and nodded, touching the purse that Menshikov had given me. Daria pressed my hand. 'Don't worry. I know about the money. In the *gostiny dvor* you'll find the most beautiful things a girl could wish for; stalls with gold and silver, Belgian lace, French fabrics, gemstones, fine leather, felts, feathers, studding, embroidery and so on.' She took my elbow. 'Let's go and feast. I want to get properly drunk to forget this hell of a trip. Tomorrow, there will be many people to greet. Come.'

We stumbled back to our sleigh where Varvara sulked as her copper pan had gone cold. Rasia Menshikova gave the signal for our departure and in the evening we feasted our near arrival in Moscow with freshly baked bread, fat salmon, smoked strips of venison, pungent cheese, pastries filled with mushrooms and offal as well as pickled radishes, sour gherkins and eggs marinated in mustard and cream. The innkeeper's pantry, not to mention his cellar, was empty when we moved on and as usual I didn't see Rasia Menshikova pay.

Our group was like a swarm of bees getting close to its hive. The next day we arrived in Moscow.

29

Menshikov's palace was the most splendid in Moscow and built of stone at a time when much of the city was still made of timber. The Muscovites only spoke of a fire if a couple of hundred houses were properly ablaze. The Tsar, I heard, adored the sight as much as he did fighting it with his own hands, and a new *ukaz* had ordered any burnt-down house must be rebuilt in stone; those who were unable to afford that had to sell their land.

Inside Menshikov's palace, the walls were clad in painted leather or covered by huge, heavy tapestries that he had bought in Holland. The corridors were lined with honey-coloured parquet and high, tiled stoves heated each of the hundred rooms, whether they were in use or not. Daria still called her quarters the *terem* and had made them cosy with plush-piled rugs from Persia, velvet cushions and fur throws, and old-fashioned icons on the walls as well as smaller tapestries that told stories neither of us had ever heard. We wondered together who that beautiful young girl, riding away from her clamouring friends on a bull, might be: 'It can't be comfortable with that spiky hair at her naked bottom?' I said, making Daria laugh. And why did the young man on another tapestry hold out a golden apple to three beautiful women? 'Just eat it yourself, boy, if they don't want it,' was Daria's comment, before I chased her – screeching, laughing and pleading with me to stop – galloping down the palace's corridors, pretending to be the misfit, half man, half horse, that we had spotted in a painting.

My room lay between Daria's and Varvara's: yes, my own room, no poky maid's chamber. It was bigger than our whole *izba* had been and I luxuriated in the rugs on the flagstones under my bare feet and brushed the icons' golden frames with my fingertips. My mattress was stuffed with horsehair and the bedlinen was scented. Daria gave me my very own oak chest and watched me fold my clothes inside it: her hand-me-downs as well as looted dresses that had been shared between us in Marienburg.

She frowned at them. 'They're no good. You need proper clothes if you want to feast at Yuletide. Give me that purse.' She weighed it in her palm after I had fished it out from behind my bedstead. 'Good Lord. That's more than I thought. And you really don't know who gave it to you? Alexander Danilovich just would not say?' she said, her eyes narrowing. As long as she was not his wife, she could never be sure of his feelings. So far, he showed no sign of wanting to step underneath the bridal crown with her.

'My guess is Sheremetev. He is kind and generous, but would not want to shame me. Just as Alexander Danilovich doesn't want your ladies-in-waiting to shame you,' I said smoothly.

Varvara joined us. She never left Daria and me alone together for too long, if she could help it. 'Sheremetev, you say? Everybody knows that he has a hedgehog in his pocket. Just look at his shabby house and his old hag of a wife who wears last year's fashion. What should a Russian count like him give you gold for?' She, too, weighed the purse. 'A maid should never be more beautiful than her mistress,' she said with a catty smile. 'Men always have second thoughts. Daria, you might have befriended your own undoing. Menshikov has a roving eye.'

I bit my lip, as I did not dare to be rude to Varvara. Still, I looked her straight in the eye. Nobody loved me more if I tried to please them. If Varvara didn't like me, she should at least know her limits as well as mine.

'Let's go, Marta,' Daria said, after passing a long look from her sister to me. 'We'll need quite some time to kit you out.'

Daria had made no empty promises: the *gostiny dvor* was a heaven on earth for a woman with a purse full of gold. So far, I had only bartered for things at the Spring Fair in my village, and in the marketplaces in Walk and Marienburg had watched wealthy, free-born people buy trinkets from travelling merchants. Those stalls were there one day and gone the next, whilst tailors, cobblers and carpenters would have their own shops, but those were not for the likes of me. From Menshikov's house our sleigh crossed the Red, or Beautiful, Square, snaked its way through icy, busy alleyways and then stopped outside the *gostiny dvor*. 'You can go into a *kabak*, but don't you dare get too drunk,' Daria warned the coachman and pulled me with her.

The *gostiny dvor* was no jumble of stalls covered in canvas. It was carefully planned and laid out two storeys high, built in brick, just for shopping, every day and all the year around. The entrance and space around it were as busy as a beehive. I craned my neck: arcade after arcade housed different shops and tradesmen flitted in and out carrying boxes and bales. Servants shouted at messenger boys, happy with their little show of authority, and maids followed their ladies, eyes lowered, yet casting discreet glances at the waiting foot-men and burly porters, who hung about at the building's entrance, wolf whistling and chewing and spitting tobacco-stained saliva.

'Come,' Daria said to me, walking with all the pride that her birth and rank as Menshikov's mistress gave her, head held high, knowing exactly where to go. I followed after, but soon trailed behind for all my looking and touching. The shops sold things I hadn't known existed: ivory and ebony, tortoiseshell and mother-of-pearl, enamel, porcelain and more pearls, gemstones, silk and velvet, leather and feathers. More treasures than I had thought possible. I tried to carry myself as Daria did, but poverty – its scent, posture and fears – clings to you like leeches in a pond. When spotting me on my own, the shopkeepers guarded their bales of silk with their body or busied themselves in front of their drawers and shelves of lace and ribbons, lest I nick a roll or two.

I hurried on towards where Daria was standing with a lithe man. I tried to summon haughtiness to my features but it wasn't necessary – the man's eyes shone like wet gravel, while the ends of his thin black moustache curved in a second smile. His eyes took measure of me and then he kissed my fingers, as if I was a lady.

'Mistress Marta. What a pleasure. I am Maître Duval. Do come in, I have exactly what you need,' he said in Russian that sounded even funnier than mine, ushering us towards his shop. He'd made no empty promise. His tailors measured me and in turn whispered with the apprentices. The boys unrolled yard upon yard of silks at my feet and held them to my face while I checked their effect in a plate of polished metal. Daria and I sipped *chai* with fresh, thick *smetana* and nibbled on pistachio biscuits dripping in honey while Maître Duval helped me make a choice that flattered me.

'The colours of spring are best left to Mistress Daria,' he said, squinting at her rosy, fair beauty. 'Your skin is like dark gold and your hair like polished ebony. Let's try jewel shades, shall we?' He held swathes of ruby-red velvet and bales of sapphire blue and burnt orange silk to my cheeks, before searching in his stockroom for an emerald-green wool cloak. 'Another lady's loss is your gain. This is just wonderful for you, as it matches your eyes,' he decided, and clapped his hands in joy when I tried it on. I could not help but turn and turn, until the heavy folds of fabric swirled all around me. Once all the orders were placed, he clicked his tongue. 'What a lady wears underneath is as important as her gowns,' he said, lowering his voice a bit, while holding yards of gossamer-thin and finely patterned lace up against the shop's lights.

Daria giggled: 'Go for it, Marta. You might still teach old Sheremetev a thing or two?'

When I had paid Duval what he asked – and certainly far more than seemed necessary – and we finally got to leave his shop after his many bows to us, walking backwards, kisses to fingers and demands for further visits, we dropped in at the furrier's to choose fox skins to line my cloak. The man asked me to return the next day to see better stock, but for that he generously offered me a matching cap there and then. I wore it as a young lady of good family would: proudly, perched to the left with my hair hidden underneath, and felt more giddy and light-hearted than I had when pinching some of my father's chewing tobacco as a child.

164

In my thoughts I sent thanks and kisses to Sheremetev. Perhaps I should have spent less, but having my own money to spend at will was simply too much for me. After all, if I wanted to live the good life, I had to look the part. How Christina would have loved this, I thought with a pang, as the coachman swayed towards us, of course legless after his visit to the *kabak*. Daria and I pelted him with snowballs to sober him up. As our sleigh slid through the darkness, the bells of the Archangel Cathedral – Moscow's highest spire – tolled into the lively night. Fresh snowflakes froze on the slush and made the streets and squares slippery: we saw many people fall, which made us laugh even more. The joy of Yuletide was upon us.

In the courtyard of Menshikov's house the groom bowed when helping me out of the sleigh. Only then did he recognise me and stared hard while taking the reins from the coachman. Both men led the horses away, looking back at me over their shoulders, smiling, until the dark of the stables swallowed them. Up the stairs, at the threshold of the door, two maids curtseyed to us and then did a double take on noticing me. Jealous expressions marred their young faces as they started to whisper, but I decided not to care. Daria and I linked arms, giggling and joking, as we entered the house.

As I bent down to wipe the snow off the hem of my new cloak, Varvara approached, hearing our voices. She came up to greet us as she would her equals, with a wide smile and outstretched arms, the offer of food and drink on her lips. Only at the last moment, when I straightened up, did she recognise me and stop, taking in my new look. Her face clouded and she dropped her arms, turned on her heel and went back to her rooms, even though Daria called after her light-heartedly: 'Don't be such a spoilsport, Varvara. Stay with us!'

That night I slept with my fox cap on as it made me happy to wear it even in my sleep.

In my childhood the Russian monks reckoned the dawn of time from God's creation of the world, but Peter changed even that. Henceforth the years were to be numbered from the birth of Christ; New Year now fell on the first of January instead of in early September. The festivities, though, lasted from the beginning of December right through to Epiphany in early January: every night there were dinners, parades, games, masquerades, fireworks and balls.

*

'The Tsar is in town soon,' Daria said to me one morning, holding a scroll. 'Menshikov sent word.' Varvara left for the *gostiny dvor* to buy more dresses and jewellery. I mustered my own gowns, which had been delivered by Duval's boys. I touched the fabric, the stitching and the lace again and again. Would they be suitable to wear while meeting the Tsar and make me look like a lady? I had to trust Daria's judgment. The thought of seeing Peter again unsettled me: would he remember the night when I had held him so close, chasing away his demons and giving him peace? Of course not, I scolded myself: the Tsar had countless arms to hold him, be he in battle or at home.

Still, I remembered the feeling of his hot breath on my breasts and how he had calmed in my embrace, like a fractious child. But of course only I remembered; he would not.

It was clear what was at stake for Varvara in meeting the Tsar again; she was catty and cruel. When a young maid burnt one of her dresses while ironing it, Varvara had her strung upside down until her face turned blue, before herself driving sharp splinters of wood underneath the girl's fingernails. The poor thing survived, but barely. I felt sorry for her, but kept out of it, as I didn't want to share her fate. I thought of Olga's words: *Don't help me. You can't. Help yourself.*

Two days before Yuletide, Moscow reared like a horse under the lashing of a whip: the Tsar, his son the Tsarevich Alexey and his thousands of men galloped into the city, unleashing a storm of festivities. The city threw itself at its master as a puppy might, clumsy and overjoyed, knowing it would be abandoned again soon.

30

Our sleigh moved as soundlessly as in a dream along narrow alley-ways and the streets leading to the Red Square. The Yuletide feast was held in the Kremlin's main hall with hundreds of people invited. To me, the Arsenjevas looked impossibly beautiful, even though foreign envoys were said to laugh at the Muscovite women, calling them provincial and grotesque. On Daria's advice I wore a dress of flame-coloured silk and her maid had braided some strings of her pearls into my loose curls; other than that I wore no jewellery, but was proud of a little golden lace running around my shoulders. 'Sheremetev should like you,' Varvara said, mustering me. 'The man has no taste anyway.'

The Kremlin towered above the Red Square in all its regal power. It was bathed in torchlight and the warm shine of lanterns as the shops in the three-storey houses all around were still busy. In the coffee houses, which Daria said had opened in Moscow only a few years before, every table was taken and the windows were steamed up. Servants ran last errands, girls of easy virtue shivered while waiting for customers and beggars searched, mostly in vain, for a warm, dry spot for the night. In the morning their frozen corpses would be thrown outside the city walls into clay pits, from where wolves dragged them into the forest.

Daria pointed to the highest of the neighbouring St Basil's Cathedral's towers: 'This is the bell tower that Ivan the Terrible built after he killed his son.'

'He killed his own son?' I repeated in disbelief and crossed myself with three fingers: what a terrible sin.

'Yes. He killed thousands and thousands of people. The whole populace of Novgorod was forced under the ice and drowned. His son he killed in a fit of anger. The tower was built so that he could do penance. Whenever his demons haunted him, he'd run up and toll the bell for hours on end.'

Varvara giggled at the story, but I looked outside. The Kremlin rose like a dark wall all along the Red Square, a defiant, gloomy fortress clashing with the gaiety of the cupolas of St Basil's Cathedral right next to it. When we crossed the lowered drawbridge, my heart beat faster and I clasped my fan and my purse tightly. I was spellbound and wanted to keep this moment – the moon, the snowflakes, the guards, the torchlight and the other sleighs full of gay, beautiful people – forever in my heart. Couldn't I make time stop?

'What happens now?' I whispered to Daria.

She opened her fan and I peered at it: on its silk fabric a picture showed a rosy, chubby blonde girl being mounted by a man with a ram's horns and feet. I thought of the lust I had felt in Anton's arms so long ago.

'Now, Marta, the world turns upside down. You wouldn't believe it if you hadn't seen it.'

Shadows gathered in the endless corridors of the Kremlin. They smelt of tallow and smoke as well as the frankincense and herbs smouldering in the corners. Every stone spoke of the Tsar's glory and power. Our steps echoed on the flagstones as we followed a servant to the great hall. The eyes of countless icons hanging on the sooty walls followed me in cold mockery: what was a soul like me doing in the heart of the realm? The courtiers looked like children playing dress-up, moving about gingerly in their Western-style breeches and embellished, knee-length coats. A group of priests in long black robes, each adorned with a golden *panagia*, eyed us with disdain. I could not care less if looked like a foreign whore to them. Yet the rooms made me shiver: was it here that the boy Peter had watched his family being hacked to death; where the Streltsy had dragged him by his hair, calling his mother a whore? Surely, nobody would want to go on living in a place filled with such memories. But suddenly a pair of doors flew open and we stepped forward into light and merriment, and heard music, shouting and singing as well as a steady, upbeat drum roll. I squinted my eyes at the dazzling brightness of the long hall before us.

Daria told me: 'Eat, drink, laugh, Marta, and be grateful to be here.'

Richly dressed people stood grouped around small tables. The music I could hear wasn't heavy with longing like Russian melodies but tinkled like water. Servants carried platters groaning with food: whole boar roasted in beer and honey, the snouts stuffed with apples and chestnuts; pies of fish and vegetables in a thick golden crust; bowls of creamy soup; huge salmon surrounded by walls of caviar and towers of *blini*, pots of *smetana* and slices of lemon. Waiters filled jugs full to the brim: the goblets we drank from reached from my fingertips to my elbow. People drank like horses, vodka dripping from their mouths, carelessly soiling their beautiful clothes. I heaped some caviar on a *blin*; it was so delicious that I had a second and then a third one straight away. Who knew how long my luck would last?

Daria and Varvara whispered and I strained my ears. What was going on?

'Look, there is the Tsarevich. Alexey has grown up ...'

I craned my neck with curiosity: Alexey was a boy of perhaps twelve or thirteen years of age and didn't seem grown up at all to me, still very much a child in his simple, dark clothes, with his pale face and dark eyes.

'And over there is the widowed Tsaritsa Praskovia with her three daughters. She so wants to marry them well, though everybody knows that Ivan the Idiot, Peter's half-brother, didn't sire them,' Daria said.

Varvara giggled: 'She lives surrounded by loafers and beggars, soothsayers and palm readers, like courts used to be once. When I last visited, a gypsy girl danced for us, naked. Her breasts dangled like the balls of an oxen and her bush spread over her thighs.'

I had no idea what courts used to be like, but after Menshikov's parties, absolutely nothing surprised me.

The drum roll grew stronger, until a kettle drum took the lead: everyone was silenced, even the Tsarevich stood to attention. The musicians rose in a wave, the doors of the hall flew open, and a group of men stormed in, shouting and cheering, carrying a sedan chair on their shoulders. The man sitting on it wore a clumsily wrapped white sheet and a crude copy of the Tsar's crown. I stared open-mouthed as the procession paraded past me, the men throwing rose petals and paper balls, hooting, blowing on pipes and spinning rattles, inviting everybody to join in. People bowed to the shockingly ugly, virtually deformed man on the throne. I looked around, wondering what was happening and who the imposter was.

When I saw the real Peter my heart leapt up into my throat. He was taller than everybody else by a good head or two and dressed like a sailor in narrow, side-buttoned breeches, tight yellow leggings and a short navy jacket with gold buttons over his white shirt and red neckerchief. What was going on? Menshikov smiled and waved to him. I spotted other faces I knew, too: princes and boyars who had fought alongside Sheremetev at Marienburg. I could not see the general himself and felt strangely relieved at that.

When the sedan chair was lowered, Peter bowed mockingly to the throne. 'Hail, Prince-Caesar!' he shouted, and the crowd repeated his words, the call rising and falling like the tide. 'We beg you, let the Drunken Synod begin!' Whoever the toad on the throne might be, the guests knew how to tell the game from reality and obeyed when Peter commanded them, 'Drink, all of you, and as much as you can!' He forced a young woman's jaws open and poured a whole jug of vodka down her throat. She swayed, glassy-eyed, pale and gasping, until Peter kissed her on her lips, smacked her bottom and let her go.

'Why is another man sitting on the throne?' I asked Daria.

'I told you, tonight the world is turned upside down. The Tsar is but a Friesian sailor and one of his friends, the so-called Prince-Caesar, rules.' The crowd roared a bawdy song and Peter clapped while they cheered, 'The Drunken Synod! Let's start the Drunken Synod!'

I looked for the Tsarevich: he was standing by Menshikov, not cheering or singing. Menshikov was nudging him, to get him to join in. Daria approached them, smiling at her lover, who greeted

170

her warmly and then smacked the Crown Prince. The boy's eyes filled with tears and he retreated deeper into the hall where I couldn't see him.

'Silly man.' Daria smiled tenderly in Menshikov's direction when she'd settled back next to me. 'Will he ever propose?' she asked, sounding a bit too casual, while opening her fan.

'Of course,' I soothed her.

'I would love to be at home, raising our children and being a good wife to him. But living like this, I have to play by his rules ...'

'Nobody leaves this room anymore under pain of hard labour,' Peter shouted. 'Also, there is no more Rhine wine to drink, only Tokay and vodka. Whosoever cheats has to drink double the measure.'

The fake Prince-Caesar now climbed onto a donkey; his sheet had slipped down to reveal a loincloth. Oblivious, his worshippers followed him. I almost choked with laughter, seeing the procession of half-naked whores, their faces gaily painted and *panagias* dangling between their naked breasts; blond angel-faced boys with laurel wreaths in their hair skipped after them, playing flutes and waving flags on which two tobacco pipes formed a cross.

'Patriarch Bacchus, give us your holy juice,' the crowd howled, reaching out to the rider, the whores and the boys. It was so funny that I laughed tears: that served the ugly priests with their stinky garlic breath right – too often had I felt their bony fingers pinching my bottom at the monastery. The Prince-Caesar sprayed the crowd with vodka; people caught the blessing with their tongues, pushing and shoving each other to receive it. Some younger princes wanted to kiss the donkey but he bucked and kicked, so they pulled his tail until he brayed in pain.

The Arsenjevas sat with Menshikov, but just when I was about to join them, a slender hand grabbed me around my waist and played with the ribbons of my bodice. Peter pressed me against his broad chest, whispering in my ear, 'How do you like my party, *matka?*' My heart somersaulted. He remembered me and once more was calling me his old girl. I looked up at him: his face was flushed from vodka, the heat in the room and the revelry all around us. He swayed as he held me. The Prince-Caesar rode past and splashed me with vodka. 'A special blessing for you, my girl,' he roared, trotting on.

My cheeks and forehead were sticky with alcohol: 'Ha! That calls for vengeance. Hold the donkey's head, *starik!*' I called.

Peter smiled at the nickname and grabbed the braying and bucking beast, almost throwing its rider off: 'Stop it, the two of you! This is a holy donkey, hands off,' the Prince-Caesar squealed. He tried to hit us with his censer, but both Peter and I dodged him, chasing round the donkey who shat on the golden parquet. We held on to each other in wild laughter until I could grab the donkey's head, forcing its mouth deep into one of the huge jugs. It drank greedily and then farted, which left Peter in stitches. 'Ahoy, there is donkey wind! Let's all set sail.' He ripped off his neckerchief and held it like a sail behind the donkey's bottom, but the animal staggered off through the hall, crashing into tables, toppling jugs, bottles and glasses and making people scream. The Prince-Caesar whipped the poor beast while downing the last of the holy vodka.

Peter touched my silk dress. 'What a lovely colour. You look as if you are engulfed in flames. But I hope that is not all you get for a purse of gold in the *gostiny dvor* these days?'

'Oh, no. There are lovely things such as ...' I stared at him: the purse that Menshikov had given me was not Sheremetev's gift!

Peter grinned and gave me a peck on the cheek. 'It's a small price for the best night of sleep I have had for as long as I can remember. I hope you spent it wisely,' he said, his fingers fondling my bodice and searching out my breasts without further ado.

I felt heat rise from my belly, but slapped his hands away. 'Careful! Wandering hands get caught in a wolf trap.'

He looked at me with shining eyes. 'Are you hungry?' he asked.

I followed Peter to Menshikov's table, where I saw the Arsenjevas, Pavel Jagushinsky, master of the Tsar's household, and Rasia Menshikova, who sat much too close to a handsome olive-skinned stranger: beneath the large silk cushions they held hands. Varvara reared to her feet when she saw Peter holding my hand, pulling me with him. Her face was pure threat that I tried to ignore. Tonight or never! Around us settled a motley crew – 'Meet Louis Bourgeois from Paris!' Peter said, slapping a giant of a man on his back – two dwarves and a Moor. My head spun: had my life had turned into Master Lampert's Tent of Wonders?

Peter pulled me down next to him while filling up our big cups again. 'These are eagle cups,' he said proudly. 'I had them made especially, as all the others were too small to cause a real stupor.' He clapped his hands. 'Let's play a drinking game. I had lost *matka*, but now I have found her again and she wears a pretty dress made of flames. Let's toast to that with Tokay. Be warned, I'll whip anyone who drinks Rhine wine!'

'To *matka* and her dress of flames,' Menshikov said and everybody drank, even if Varvara's eyes stabbed me from over the rim of her cup, a threatening, dark look that chilled my heart. But I pushed down my fear: tonight I wanted to be merry. The dwarf somersaulted, which made his face turn green. He fled away to be sick. Peter's dogs joined us, licking his face until the Tsar hid under the cushions, laughing and begging for mercy. The giant from Paris spoke with Rasia Menshikova's lover in a strange, foreign language, and I met Daria's questioning glance: I had never told her about that night in Marienburg. Yet now I sat on Peter's lap, feeding him sweet morsels and throwing food at passing courtiers. He whooped and cheered when I hit a target well, and Daria raised her cup in a toast to me. Thank God, I had inherited my father's steadfast approach to drinking. But when even I had started seeing double, the Tsar leapt up and grabbed Menshikov by the collar.

'Traitor! What are you hiding under that cushion?' he shouted, tugging out a bottle of Rhine wine. 'I knew it! That light plonk. You are such a cheat, Menshikov. Sorry, I must punish you. But as you are not an utter dog, you shouldn't drink alone.' His eyes locked on Daria and Varvara. 'The Arsenjevas will join you. Three eagle cups of Tokay will do for each of you.'

Daria passed out and Varvara was sick into her cupped hands before collapsing on the floor. All her finery was destroyed; she had lost one earring, her hair had come undone and the feathers in it were mere stalks when a servant hoisted her onto his back like a sack of barley. Menshikov drank obediently, before rising, saluting his Tsar, and then throwing his cup at the wall, where it broke into dozens of pieces. His eyes turned glassy and he crashed over like a felled tree. Peter skipped in circles around his friend, eager for more, more, more. He was about to grab me when a cushion hit his chest.

'Hey! What's going on?' he shouted, and was hit by a second cushion that came flying through the hall.

'Look, Peter,' I said, to distract him from the cushion fight. Rasia Menshikova lay with her thighs parted among the cushions and the dark-skinned stranger's buttocks heaving above her, his breeches around his knees. Peter whooped and grabbed the man's hips, spurring him on. 'Devier, you rascal. Do I have to teach you everything? Don't they even know how to fuck in your country? Rhythm, man!' Rasia Menshikova covered her face in shame when Peter fondled her tiny breasts, pushing them to the right and then left. 'Starboard! Larboard! All hands on deck,' he shouted.

Feeling sorry for Rasia, I grabbed one of the cushions and hit Peter straight over the head, once and then twice. The cushion burst and rained feathers, which stuck to his sweaty forehead and hair. I held my breath – had I gone too far? I had whacked the master of life and death, and there he stood, covered in vodka and down. I went for it: 'It's snowing!' I laughed, delighted, shaking my locks and spreading my arms, which almost made my bodice burst. 'Look, finally some snow and ice for you, and you are their king.'

'Just you wait! You'll be no better off than Menshikov's skinny sister when I catch you.' Peter lunged at me, but I ducked and ran, shouting, 'Well, catch me if you can, *starik*!'

I skipped around the Prince-Caesar who was kissing a laurel-wreathed boy; a courtier smeared caviar over the naked breasts of one of the whores, then sucked her full white flesh. The drunken donkey shat some more, swaying pitifully in the midst of the music, the writhing bodies and steaming heat. Soldiers watched stone-faced as Peter towered over me and I halted, hiccupping with laughter, panting, my cheeks burning and my blood rushing through my veins, waiting for his next move. He seized me and threw me on to some cushions; it rained more and more feathers, food flew through the air and the Prince-Caesar hung limp in his saddle.

I felt nothing but Peter's hands, lips and then his heavy body on mine. He spread my thighs and was inside me before I could even catch my breath: how could I refuse the Tsar of All the Russias?

31

I woke when a sunbeam tickled my nose. I stretched like a cat and looked around. Where was I? This was neither my bedroom nor Menshikov's palace. Furs and heavy covers kept me warm in a wide bed. A fire crackled somewhere. I opened the embroidered hangings around the bed: the Tsar sat at a table next to the open fire, his back turned to me, clearly visible in the white light coming from the window. His feet in their felt slippers tapped on the flagstones while he twirled a quill in his fingers.

I was naked and my clothes were nowhere to be seen, so I wrapped the sheet around me and slid out of the bed. The flagstones in the gaps between the furs and rugs were cold as I tiptoed my way to Peter and looked over his shoulder. The icy winter light fell on a pile of papers, unfurled or still in scrolls. Peter hummed to himself and lowered the quill onto the paper in front of him. I peered at it: he sketched something like a large arc. I touched his shoulder and asked quietly, 'What is that?'

He started and jumped to his feet.

'It's only me!' I said. '*Matka.*' He calmed; his eyes a bright and, given the short hours of rest, surprisingly clear blue. He stuck one hand into a fur-lined pocket of his green belted dressing-gown while waving the other breezily over the pile of papers, then rummaged in the scrolls, making paper rustle and fall. 'Oh, it's everything and nothing! Just some ideas I have, really, some for ships, some for buildings. Letters to write, to friends, soldiers and other rulers in the West, and drafts of laws that may or may not be introduced,' he said, laughing. 'Who can tell with the Russians? I also have to find new taxes!' He smiled and scratched his head like a boy.

'True. I have heard you will be taxing the winking of an eye next,' I said earnestly.

He looked at me, astonished. 'Who says so? Where did you hear that?' Realising it was a joke, he chuckled and stroked my shoulders.

'Everywhere. On the streets. In the coffee houses.'

'You've been in coffee houses? Oh! You could be my spy.'

'I could,' I said teasingly. 'But my services don't come cheap.'

He arched an eyebrow, before he asked: 'What are they saying there? Don't they love me? If you say yes, I'll abolish that tax on the winking of the eye just for you.'

'Well –' I began, but he would not let me talk, growing impatient.

'Do you know how expensive a war is? Giving my people places to live, to train soldiers and to turn Russians into thinking human beings, comes at a cost. And all they do is hate me for it! I almost have to beat their children into the schools I've founded for them. But wait …' He pulled out a closely written sheet of paper, which was signed and sealed with the gleaming double-headed Russian eagle. A little drying sand still stuck to the scarlet wax. 'Here is my last *ukaz*: any child of the boyars and free citizens who has not attended school is forbidden to marry. That's a fine rule, isn't it? No schooling, no wedding. I want my people to be educated. I want them to …' He hesitated.

'To … ?' I prodded him, thinking of Sheremetev's words: *Ever since his return from Europe, he is a man possessed.*

'I want them to think. To think for Russia.'

'But will they still follow you when their thoughts are so free?' I asked.

Peter caressed my tousled curls. 'Well, I never! *Matka* thinks and says wise words. Or did you overhear that at one of my parties?'

Without further ado he lifted me off the floor and the sheet slipped from my shoulders. In two long strides he reached the bed and fell upon me. It all happened as fast as the night before, when I had put his haste down to drunkenness. He gave my full breasts a quick squeeze before he cast off his sleeping gown and made short work of opening my thighs and thrusting into me. As he pushed inside, he sucked noisily at my neck and breasts like a child. After a few hurried movements he shuddered and fell on top of me with a contented sigh.

I lay still, feeling raw, unfulfilled and disappointed, his breath hot and unsteady on my aching breasts, and to my surprise mirth took over. Was *this* the kind of love he had learnt from Anna Mons? Was *this* the passion that the Arsenjeva sisters whispered about behind their hands? I so longed for the fire that Anton had lit in my veins. Peter had slipped off me, all spent, just when I felt the embers of lust stirring. He was almost asleep when I playfully grabbed his hair and asked hoarsely, 'What about me?'

He raised his head, looking at me with heavy eyelids and half a smile. 'What? What about you?'

I gave him a little push and he rolled onto his back. Sweat glistened in the thick hair of his chest, a sight that filled me with a sudden tenderness. I sat astride him.

'Caress my breasts!' I whispered. 'Tenderly, and don't stop.' My heavy breasts grew even fuller under his touch and my wide pink nipples hardened, just as my warm wetness found him. He was now limp and moist, but lay just beneath my secret spot. I gently slid up and down on him. My hair fell across his face as I found my own rhythm and began to moan. Peter grabbed my waist, holding it with both hands, just when starlight shot through my veins like a hot golden rain. I rose with a short scream and then curled up on his chest, panting, and with a satisfied sigh.

He held me tight for a moment, mutely, before he kissed my damp forehead. 'My kitten. Are you hungry?'

'I'm starving. I don't know about you, but there was this big man yesterday evening who kept me so busy I could hardly eat.' I winked at him.

He pulled a cord and a chamber boy entered through a door hidden in the wood panelling, yawning and rubbing his eyes. He must have fallen asleep standing up. I pulled the sheets over my nakedness. Peter laughed. 'No need for false modesty. I can't live without my chamber boys. They know everything about me and you had better get used to them.'

My heart skipped a beat: *You had better get used to them.*

The boy returned shortly with a tray. A dish was placed in front of me: *pierogi* – pastries filled with chicken and molten cheese – as well as cherries soaked in wine and raisin biscuits baked in honey. The chamber boy poured me a dark, steaming drink into a bowl. It smelt of sugar, milk and smoke and had a thick, bitter-sweet taste. It was heavenly and stoked all my senses. I felt like dipping my fingers into the gooey brew and licking them clean. Instead, I sipped it as a lady would.

'What is this?' I asked as Peter returned to his desk.

'Chocolate,' he answered, taking a gulp of cognac from a small flagon before stuffing and lighting his pipe. This was how he broke his fast.

'What is chocolate?' I asked, breathing in the scent of it again. It was wonderful; I wanted more and more of it.

'The Queen of France brought it with her from Spain, her homeland. Chocolate and the dwarves in her entourage are her only comfort as her husband, the Great Louis, carries on with his mistress who costs him so dearly. Really, the Sun King could fill his stables with whores instead of horses with what he spends on Madame de Montespan.' Peter carried on with his drawing and I silently sipped the hot, sweet brew. Who would have thought that I could have it better than this poor Queen of France? I bit into a sweet biscuit, before dipping it into my bowl.

Since Peter had taken me back with him, I hadn't been to Menshikov's house. The Tsar asked for my few dresses and under-garments to be brought to me. The messenger also carried friendly greetings to Daria, which I dictated to Peter's scribe. To my relief her response, read out to me, was quick and warm. She had done me nothing but good.

The church Masses leading into the New Year were strange, dark and endless. After the unbridled joy and wild blasphemy of the Drunken Synod, I was struck by the piety with which Peter bowed his head in prayer. I did likewise to please him though my heart was untouched. The priceless icons encrusted with gold and silver, the singing, the prayer-books bound in leather and velvet, the sparkling vessels and splendid robes heavy with gold that showed off the wealth of the Russian Church and intimidated believers, could not compare in my estimation to the cheerful ease of the Glucks' church at Marienburg. What had become of them?

Peter sent fireworks into a sky still heavy with sleep to welcome in the New Year. The display was his own idea and he cheered at each bright explosion, each glittering, starry tail. I stood close to him by the open windows of the Kremlin, as did his son. But Alexey averted his eyes and looked as if he wanted to stick his fingers in his ears to block out the noise. Peter shoved him and the boy stumbled.

'And you want to be my heir, join my recruits and one day lead my armies, Tsarevich?' Peter barked. 'Each cannon blast has you almost wetting yourself. When I think that I celebrated the occasion of your birth with a firework display!' He spat at Alexey's feet.

The prince regained his balance. 'Yes, and a Prince Dolgoruki was killed when a heavy firework cask fell on his head,' he dared to answer.

'There are enough of them around, God knows! But if it had hit you instead, I'd have one less worry,' Peter said and turned his mighty back on the slender boy. The courtiers tittered. I saw Alexey fighting back tears. In the short spell of darkness between two balls of fire, I squeezed his arm. He looked surprised to receive kindness from any of his father's friends and smiled at me shyly.

That same evening, the Tsar made me the gift of a pair of earrings.

'Take them, Marta,' he said, fiddling with the catch against my earlobe. 'They suit you, as they suited my mother.'

My eyes widened and I caught his fingers. 'Your mother? She, who shielded you with her own body against the Streltsy soldiers when they hacked the rest of her family to death?'

'You know the story?' He fixed his gaze on the earring. 'Stupid thing,' he said, unable to manoeuvre an object of such delicacy.

I touched the earrings, which were fashioned into crescent moons and studded with precious stones. They swung with each movement of my head.

'This is too valuable a gift, my Tsar,' I said, and feigned taking them off.

'They are very dainty. There is hardly any gold in them,' he said. 'Keep them, please.'

'I am not talking about the value of the gold.'

There was a brief silence and I only let go of the earring when he stepped behind me and embraced me. I felt his hands on my shoulders: 'They are yours. That is an order. Do you like them?'

'Yes,' I said hoarsely. 'I like them very much. No man has ever given me such a present.'

'You must have known the wrong men. They are to bring luck to a girl who warms my body and my heart.'

I turned to face him; Peter was awaited at a Synod, for men only this time. Afterwards Menshikov, with the help of two servants, dragged him back to his chamber. Peter kissed me and when I softly opened my lips to taste his tongue, I felt him grow and press against my belly. My hand slid over his brightly embroidered waistcoat to the soft deer leather of his breeches; I loosened the belt and wrapped my fingers around his warm flesh. He sighed and closed his eyes when I sank to my knees, the silk of my robe rustling, and placed my lips around him. He swelled even more and gasped when I took him fully. Peter began to move in my warm, wet mouth, where I sucked him deeper and deeper, tasting his lust and his desire for me. It didn't take long until he dug his fingers into my shoulders and cried out. My hair had come loose and he stroked it back tenderly.

'Where did you learn that?' He tightened his belt and smoothed his waistcoat.

I laughed. 'Well, I was a soldier's wife, after all.'

He rummaged in the little pocket of his waistcoat and fished out a coin.

'In that case …' He tossed the coin into my lap. I held my breath. Should I feel hurt? Peter was grinning away, looking terribly pleased with himself. I wasn't delighted but a coin was a coin: I picked it up and bit into it. The smile fell from Peter's face.

'Did you think the Tsar of all the Russias would give you coun-
terfeit money?' he asked, his voice low with anger. I did not flinch.

'You never know. Who can you trust these days?'

I could hear him laughing all the way down the hall. Smiling, I
dressed for a late dinner, one held for the *damy* of the Russian court.
A dwarf wrapped in bright ribbons jumped out of a pie in the early
hours of the morning. We all pulled him this way and that, making
him spin like a top, until he finally stumbled around the room stark
naked. He was every bit as adorable as the Princess Cherkassy's little
drunken lapdog, which was given bowl upon bowl of the sparkling
wine the Tsar had ordered especially from France.

Come Epiphany and the blessing of the waters of the Moskva,
the magic of the Yuletide festivities was over. Peter hopped impatiently from one foot to the other while the priests had a hole sawn
into the Moskva ice and boys, their cheeks pink with cold, swung
golden censers back and forth, lacing the cold winter air with
myrrh and frankincense. The scents hung in heavy clouds over the
ice as the court gathered round the Tsar one last time, still wearied
and still half-drunk, but in all its New Year splendour of gowns
and coats of silk and velvet, embroidered with gold and silver, and
furs of sable and mink. Many of the men still wore flat fur hats,
and some ladies pulled veils of gold-embroidered muslin over the
chalk-white and red of their sleepy painted faces. The Tsar looked
at them through smouldering eyes: not even this bitter cold that
touched the marrow was any excuse for wearing the loathed and
forbidden Old Russian style of dress. As the first courtiers stripped
off and dived into the hole for a swift dip in the icy waters to
bless the year ahead of them, Peter was already back in the stables,
checking on his men and horses. Everything was ready for him to
leave for the field again.

Peter ordered me back to Menshikov's house without the slightest hesitation: 'I want you to be safe until we meet again,' he said.
He had no idea.

32

Varvara came for me on my second afternoon back at Alexander Danilovich's house. I was sitting near the fire in Daria's rooms, embroidering a scarf of mustard-yellow wool that I planned to give to her as a present. The wool's soft down grew in between the thick, wiry hair of Persian mountain goats; it was so fine that I could draw the scarf through a ring, and worth its weight in gold in the *gostiny dvor*, as my now almost empty purse testified.

A flurry of steps echoed in the hall, the door smashed open against the wall behind. I shrank in my seat: Varvara's hair flamed around her head and shoulders. She held a whip in her hand. In her fury and self-righteousness she reminded me of Vassily; how often had he, too, tried to humiliate me? Now the moment had come for her to do me serious harm. At first I froze with fear, as I had done that night in my former master's kitchen. But I was not a nameless serf or a maid anymore who had to duck and seek cover, hoping for the best. I had slept in the Tsar's arms, however far away that moment felt now – almost as far away as Peter himself was. Who could protect me? No one but myself. She walked over to me, her bare feet soundless on the tiled floor between rugs and furs, and raised my chin with the end of her whip. 'So you're back after your little stay in the Kremlin!' she said, with a nasty smile.

I smiled back at her and took up my embroidery again, which made her furious, as I'd expected it would. She screamed: 'That's the thanks one gets for picking up dirt like you from the street – trying to take my place in Peter's life?'

The whip snapped through the air. God knows, I'd mastered the art of dodging blows as a child when my stepmother came for me and I was off the sofa in a flash. The whip tore into the silk cushion, making it rip, and Varvara stared at the damage, as if surprised not to have hurt me instead. I used this short respite to tackle her around the thighs and knees and she tumbled to the floor with me. Her hands closed about my neck, where her fingers and nails dug into my flesh. I gasped for air as she squeezed my throat tighter; I frantically scrabbled for the whip, but her nails seemed to be everywhere at once. I felt a smarting scratch at my cleavage and yelped with pain. In my despair, I grabbed her hair, twisted it around my fingers and tore out a clump. She howled and lashed at me, but I spun away.

'I didn't take Peter from you. The Tsar isn't interested in some tart who humps anything on legs. I bet you go down a treat in Menshikov's stables!' I spat the words in her face. She screamed and swung at my head, pushing me backwards into the edge of the mantelpiece, banging my head into it. She raised her whip again and took aim. I tried to duck away, and lunged from the fireplace towards the door, but she was quicker, grabbing me by my hair and pulling me backwards. I screamed as a red-hot pain seared through my scalp and neck. My head was yanked around and my body followed, as helpless as a rag doll.

'Look at me before I kill you,' she said, her words ringing with triumph. *Look at me before I kill you.* Vassily had said the same thing to me on that terrible night in the kitchen. In despair, my hands shot up, nails aiming for Varvara's face. I hit her straight in the eyes and dug in as hard as I could. She screamed and let go and I gave her a desperate kick in the stomach, which made her double over with pain. *Now!* I thought, but when I tried to get to my feet, I felt so dizzy I sank down again. Varvara stumbled towards me, looking deadly: her skin ashen, mouth snarling. She placed one foot on the hem of my dress. 'Stay still, Marta. So I can take better aim,' she said. 'I'll slice you to pieces and feed you to the dogs. What shall we start with? Ah, yes, your face …' I curled up, raising my arms and folding them over my head, trembling and crying – no, finally sobbing properly, openly, without shame. I had gambled and lost. But the blow never came.

'What the Devil is going on here? Can't you womenfolk be left alone for a minute?'

I only just dared a glance, for I couldn't believe my ears: Peter, whom I had imagined far beyond the Sparrow Hills, dragged Varvara backwards by her hair. She was whimpering with pain and crying.

'You, Fury, away with you to your rooms,' he ordered, snatching at the whip. Back to her room? So she could finish me off the moment he left for real? My heart stalled; I had to do something, anything! In my despair, I tore free one of his mother's earrings. As the catch snapped, blood dripped from my earlobe onto my dress.

'Oh, Peter, look what she has done!' I cried. Tears streamed down my face, as the shock and the pain were real enough. Blood trickled down my neck and there was an angry red weal on my bosom from Varvara's attack. 'She hates me,' I sobbed. 'She wants to kill me, just because I adore you. Look what she's done to your mother's earring.' My eyes briefly locked with Varvara's, who had gone ashen.

'No,' she gasped. 'It's not true! I didn't touch the earring.'

'My *matka*,' Peter murmured, his finger tenderly trailing over my cheek, down to my chest where blood blended with my tears. But as I'd hoped, it was the sight of his mother's broken earring that pushed him over the edge. Wielding the whip aloft, it seemed for a moment as though he would hit Varvara, who stumbled backwards, pressing her hand to her mouth.

Peter's face twitched with rage. 'I never want to see you again, witch! Off to the spinning mills with you.' The whip sliced through the air, narrowly missing Varvara's head, and she took to her heels. I sent a little prayer of thanks to whichever god might be listening: they richly deserved it. Peter knelt by my side, stroked my forehead and cupped my face, which was shiny with tears.

'My girl. *Matka*. That happened on my account,' he whispered, and I shivered while he rocked me gently back and forth. I threw my arms around his neck and wept and wept and wept, dampening his uniform. I felt him melting towards me: Sheremetev's feeling for my utter helplessness had been my salvation in Marienburg.

Now Peter's pity and my show of loyalty and love for him should save me twice over!

'Hush now ... shh, shh,' he said awkwardly, not letting go of me.

The door opened and Menshikov and Daria returned, her arms laden with small parcels from the *gostiny dvor*. She cried out and rushed over when she saw the state of me; Peter made sure I could stand, kissing my forehead once more. Then he took some gold coins from a pouch and held them out to Menshikov.

'Here, take them, Alekasha,' Peter commanded.

'For what?' Menshikov asked, hooking his thumbs into the loops of his belt. What had got into him? Menshikov hesitating before an offer of gold was something none of us had seen before.

'For the girl, of course.' Peter pointed at me. My heart was pounding. Did that mean he'd be taking me with him, that I would be his?

But Menshikov would not take the coins: I dared not breathe. What was he playing at? I'd got the better of Varvara this time round, but if she got a chance before leaving, she would kill me. Alexander Danilovich shook his head. 'Marta isn't for sale, my lord and master.' In the silence that followed his statement, I trembled in Daria's arms. What did Menshikov want?

Peter frowned and rummaged for more money. 'There you go, you greedy dog. Sometimes I've a mind to take a whip to *you*!'

Menshikov knelt and took Peter's hand in his, kissing the Tsar's fingers. 'I kiss the hand that blesses Russia. My Tsar's hand, to whom his underling, Alexander Danilovich Menshikov, can sell nothing, but only make a present to His Majesty of his heart's desire.'

It took me a moment to understand his words, but Daria embraced me. 'You belong to the Tsar now, lucky girl. Make something of it, Marta,' she whispered.

Menshikov beamed. '*Mijnheer* Peter, allow me to give you the girl Marta as a gift!'

'So be it,' Peter shouted as he flung an arm round Menshikov's shoulders, blew me a kiss and drew his friend out into the hall. 'We're going to celebrate,' he called over his shoulder to me. 'Celebrate properly. Pack your things, Marta, and have them taken to the Kremlin. I'll see you tonight.'

Daria and I held each other for a few moments more. When she let go of me, I still trembled, but she cupped my face and steadied me. 'You must fall pregnant soon, Marta,' she urged me. 'Anna Mons never had a child. It cost her her power and his love. Nothing brings such joy to a man, and a Tsar, as a son. Nothing will bind him more strongly to you.' I wiped my tears away and kissed her on both cheeks.

'Your advice will be forever in my heart.'

Then I turned to the door. To my surprise, Varvara had dared come out of her quarters again, pale and crying with rage, fingers pressed to one damaged eye. I weighed my options carefully. True, she was Daria's sister and I did not wish to hurt my friend by causing even more trouble. At the same time, I knew Varvara could easily bribe a maid who knew her potions, as she had done with Anna Mons, and then I would be left as barren as Peter's mistress had been. I stretched out one hand, holding my torn dress to me with the other, with as much dignity as I could muster. 'Kiss my fingers, Varvara, and I shall ask the Tsar for mercy, for your sister's sake. Not the spinning mills for you, but a fine, far-flung convent, where you can praise the Lord every morning for the rest of your life.'

Varvara, bubbling snot and water at the bleak turn her life had taken, choking back anger and with her teeth audibly gnashing, took my fingers and kissed their tips.

I spent Peter's last two nights in Moscow with him in his bed. The evening before he left for the field he fell asleep on my breast like a sated child, and in the morning tenderly kissed me farewell. 'You are a free woman, Marta. Should anything happen to me, the master of my household, Pavel Jagushinsky, will give you fifty gold ducats. You'll be able to build a new life with that.'

I opened my mouth to thank him, then stopped myself. 'Nothing will happen to you, ever,' I said tenderly. 'My love will protect you, always.'

He laughed as though it were a joke and nuzzled my chilly fingertips. 'That is good, *matka!*'

When the Tsar and his men rode out of the Kremlin gates, the whole city lay frozen, floating in a bubble of ice. The chill reached my heart: had I been left behind, ready to be forgotten and moved on from, as he did with Moscow? I could not allow that to happen.

33

The nobles' palaces on the streets around the Kremlin and the Red Square were bereft of masters, who were once more in the field with their Tsar. In the *gostiny dvor* womenfolk were serving, and the Moscow *damy* employed Swedish prisoners-of-war as tutors for their sons. Soon these men spoke Russian with an endearing accent and had mastered our latest dances as well as other kinds of games. The following year some of the oldest Russian families would be blessed with athletic, blond, blue-eyed offspring. My days in Moscow were comfortable, bright and full of life, my needs tended to by Pavel Jagushinsky. Yet I felt restless. I had heard nothing from the Tsar, who had moved back towards the West to keep the Swedes at bay. Was he simply too busy to write or had he forgotten me? Oh, I knew about the whores and washerwomen in the camps, and that Peter slept well only with skin against his, warming him and keeping the nightmares at bay. Or, worse still, was he ill or had he been wounded? The thought made my heart race. No, I would have heard about that. If my fate was proving elusive, I must seek it out.

It was one of the first days of spring. The wan sunshine was still grappling for the strength it would need to rule the night. Rays crept through the small windowpanes of the Kremlin and made the dust dance on the stack of papers on the desk in the cabinet secretary's office.

The young scribe looked at me uneasily when I held out the Imperial double seal. Makarov, the cabinet secretary, who had left with Peter, kept it in Moscow in case of an emergency and for *ukazy* issued during the Tsar's travels and campaigns. 'No, Marta. Do you know the punishment for misuse of the Tsar's seal? Death by suffocation. They don't just strangle you, they pour molten metal down your throat. Why not simply ask the Tsar if you so wish to join his camp?'

'Because I can't write and because he will not grant it. He doesn't want any women in the encampment – beyond what is necessary,' I added, blushing.

'Well, that's that, then,' the scribe said, his arms folded. As stubborn as a mule, this one, I thought, and pushed the seal towards him once more. 'You'll come to no harm,' I coaxed. 'On the contrary.'

He got up and looked out of the window onto the busy Red Square: merchants touted their wares; lepers rang the bells on their wrists to clear their way; children ran races; the sedan chairs of the *damy* passed one another, servants obediently stopping for their mistresses' quick exchanges; priests kept one hand on their head coverings in the blustery wind; people took a break from their daily business in the coffee houses.

'No,' he said, his hands dug into his pockets. My heart sank. In a moment he'd ask me to leave so that he could get on with his work. I thought quickly: the scribe was a young man from a simple background, just like Makarov himself. Hadn't he recently married the daughter of Peter's second stable-master? Yes, I had seen her; she was heavy with child. The needs of a young family were many. I reached into my money pouch, but all I found there was an *altyn*. The coin, worth three kopeks, was the last of my funds. No matter. It would be well spent, I hoped, and would buy the baby some fine lacy linen.

'Prepare the pass and let the Tsar's seal be my concern,' I whispered.

He looked at the *altyn*, gleaming brightly against the dark wood of his desk, and then slipped it out of sight. The ink dripped thick and black onto a small sponge from the sharpened tip of the quill. He filled a sheet of paper with long, graceful curves. When he was finished, he stretched, winked at me and said, 'I'll just nip into the hallway to see whether the messenger from the West has arrived.'

Before he left, he pushed a lump of wax as well as the candle towards me. He didn't want to be in the room to see this done in case it cost him his neck. I worked as swiftly as I could with trembling fingers, his fear contagious. Was I sealing my own death warrant? The hot wax dripped onto the paper at the very place where the words stopped. Once the layer was thick enough, I reached for the forbidden seal and pressed it down firmly, so that the crimson double-eagle both rose and sank on the thick, oozing mass, proud and threatening.

'You are mad,' Daria said while she watched me go through my clothes. 'What can I do to hold you back?' she asked.

'Nothing.' I smiled at her. 'You know me, I have to go. What if he forgets me, or meets someone else to replace me?'

'True. Then do me a favour at least and let these be,' she said, taking the lacy underwear and fine gowns from my arms.

'But –'

'No ifs and buts. I'll get you some men's clothes from Menshikov's staff. Though their bosoms are not quite as big as yours,' she said, giggling. 'We also have to cut your hair …'

'No!' I said in horror, touching my beloved locks. 'I will pin it up and that will do, together with a flat Polish hat that I can pull low over my forehead.'

'As you wish. But promise me: breasts in, belly out, Marta. And keep that cloak closed.'

I promised and she gave me not only a little money, but better still, a companion who was a good shot: Peter Andreyevich Tolstoy. He was on his way to Peter's camp, from where he was to be sent as an envoy to Constantinople. If he was less than keen on taking a young woman with him through the wild vastness of Russia, he didn't let on.

We left Moscow in late March. When we reached the Sparrow Hills, I halted my horse and looked back, remembering my arrival some months earlier. Smoke rose out of countless chimneys, and domes and spires reached proudly into the dense spring sky. I'd miss Moscow, whatever Peter decided to do.

The snow had thawed and we made slow progress with the muddy roads being torn open by the sheer force of the *ottepel*. Tolstoy had to wake the ferrymen from their stupor and kick them down to the river, where the haggard men struggled to keep their flat barges on course under our weight. Waves rolled and splashed against the sides of the vessel and last slabs of ice crashed into it. After passing half of the post-stations, Tolstoy, his men and I left the coach route. The rides were long and arduous, but I loved the feeling of the wind on my face as well as the crushing tiredness at the end of a day, weighing my muscles down and making me sleep dreamlessly. I felt strong and made sure not to hinder the men's progress.

The once fertile and lush country had turned into a barren strip: as in every war, the simple folk suffered most. The *izby* made of mud and straw were ransacked, houses of wood had been burnt down and stone buildings plundered and set alight, their walls blackened by flames.

Almost three weeks later, at one day's ride from the Tsar's encampment, Tolstoy pitched camp for the night near the ruins of a church. All that was left of its *mir* were the foundations of the razed houses and the graveyard, but even the gravestones had been knocked over and desecrated. War knew no respect, not even, or perhaps least of all, for death.

While Tolstoy and two of his men were hunting for our supper, I wandered through the burnt-out nave. The chapel's roof was gone and charred, broken beams reached into the sky like bony fingers, and the pews that had not been used for firewood lay toppled and smashed. First green shoots pushed through the cracked flagstones and I spread out my woollen cloak in front of the altar. It was uncomfortable to kneel down in my high riding boots, but I took off my gloves and folded my hands like a little girl. There, underneath the wide open sky, I prayed to the god who had done so much for me: I placed myself in his hands once more. When I stepped outside, the bushes and tall grass dripped with dew and the white moon was full and high in the sky.

The men and I shared a sinewy winter rabbit for dinner. When we lay down to sleep we used our Cossack saddlebags as cushions and our cloaks as blankets. The night was clear and Tolstoy and I gazed up at the stars and spoke quietly about our lives until our eyes shut. A soldier whose face had been disfigured by wolves kept guard that night. Ever since the attack he'd hated the beasts, hunting and killing them, then sewing their tails to his cloak. There was hardly any cloth left to cover.

Before we set off the next morning, I cleaned myself as best I could. Behind the church ran a brook where I washed the dust and the dirt off my face and fingers, before scrubbing my teeth with the roughed-up end of a twig and some sharp blades of grass. Finally, I tamed my curls into a Dutch braid. Neatness was more admired on the field than any lace and finery. I kept my pass at the ready in my belt, as we had to show it to one patrol after the other, the closer we came to Peter's camp. Tolstoy raised his eyebrows when he saw the paper's Imperial seal, but didn't comment, and I was grateful for that.

We easily found the Tsar's encampment on the shores of Lake Ladoga from the trail of destruction all around it. The small farms in the region had been plundered, the winter crops crudely plucked and entire forests felled for the building of the Tsar's flotilla. As we climbed the slope ahead of the camp our horses' breath steamed in the cold air. A light rain fell as we surveyed the plain stretching beneath us. I had forgotten the sight, the sounds and the stench of tens of thousands of people living side-by-side in one encampment. Behind the veil of drizzle, the first fires were being lit in the early dusk. Through the dying light of the day we could see part of Peter's fleet rolling gently on the water.

Tolstoy sighed. 'They'll never change.'

'Who? What?' I had been trying to spot the Tsar's tent, but in vain. No wonder: he'd sleep in as small and shabby a tent as all the rest.

'The Russian army,' he answered. 'They are savages, Marta. Just look at them. Half of them don't even have a uniform, and if they do get one the cost is docked from their pay. Their training consists of eating bad or little food, sleeping on the bare earth and having their ears boxed by their officers. They have to fight before they know how to hold their weapons properly. No wonder they scarper like rabbits given half a chance. Peter's soldiers are deserting in droves, didn't you know that?'

We rode slowly through the encampment. Several generals sat by the fires next to simple soldiers, talking, laughing and eating with them. Some of them recognised and greeted me and I spotted a crowd that had formed into a circle: at its centre, Sheremetev was prowling, breaking up a fist fight between a Tatar and a Russian with a snap of his whip. He lowered it, stunned to see me. I bit my lip: of course, he had heard about my finding favour with the Tsar. I was feeling less and less comfortable about my decision to seek out Peter. Maybe the scribe had been right and forging the pass would end up being a fatal mistake. Maybe Peter would send me right back, or I'd find another girl in my place and be cruelly punished? I saw some other women coming out of the washing tent, their day's work done. I warily eyed their low-cut dresses, knowing their hopes and ambitions all too well. One of the women smacked her lips and swayed her hips as we rode by. Tolstoy grinned and nodded at her.

The entrance flap to the Tsar's tent was fixed back and I could see the guards playing dice close by. My heart raced: there he was! Peter sat inside at a table with Menshikov and two other generals. Their loud calls and laughter told me that they were in the middle of a game of cards.

When I got down from my horse my legs were trembling in their tight riding breeches. Tolstoy watched in silence as the soldiers checked my pass; they couldn't read, of course, but the seal was all they needed to see. I took a deep breath and stepped into the tent. The men stopped their game and looked up. Silence fell before Menshikov grinned, dropped his cards on the table and cried out, 'Queen of Hearts, trumps.' Then he opened his arms wide: 'Marta, you are always good for a surprise. And that's my highest praise for a woman.'

The other men, too, relaxed and laughed. All of them apart from Peter. I trembled inside but stood firm as the Tsar jumped up, so that his low wooden stool toppled over. His eyes were dark with anger as he strode towards me. I felt like bolting back to Moscow there and then.

'How did you get here, girl?' he thundered, towering over me.

Menshikov rolled his eyes as I searched Peter's face. His mouth was thin with anger, but somewhere in his eyes was a glint of light. I pushed my luck and shrugged. 'I rode. I came on horseback, more than twenty long days of riding from Moscow to Lake Ladoga.'

'On horseback. And how, may I ask, did you get past the guards and the controls?'

I drew the pass from my belt and gave it to him, my heart pounding. This was the moment of truth. Peter unfolded it, studied it with a frown, and then turned and bellowed, 'Makarov, come here. Now!'

Sweat trickled down my neck. The cabinet secretary came at a run. Behind him, at the back of the tent, I spotted the Tsarevich. Alexey was looking glazed with boredom, standing in front of an outspread map.

'Is that your seal, Makarov?' the Tsar asked. The secretary blanched, turning the paper this way and that. He finally said, 'Yes, sire. The seal is mine, but I didn't issue the pass.'

The Tsar weighed Makarov's words before he looked back at me. I smiled and tucked away a strand of hair. 'Well, then, let us forget we have ever seen this paper.' Peter chuckled as he held the pass up to a torch and the paper caught fire with a crackle. 'Otherwise it could mean the wheel or the cotton mills for you, Marta. And that would be a shame.'

I made to curtsey, but Peter caught my elbow. 'Stop. It's such a waste of time. Do you think I have nothing better to do than to watch people bob up and down?' The smouldering pass dropped into the sand at his feet, where it fell to ashes. Peter stamped out the embers. 'Go now, Makarov. And try not to despair – it's not you at fault, it's Alexey. The Tsarevich is as dumb as an ass,' he said. 'But together we'll break him in.'

Makarov bowed and left. The other men settled down to their cards again and the Tsar and I stood alone by the entrance to his tent.

'You came on horseback?'

'Yes.' My cheeks were aflame.

'Alone?' He casually twisted a stray lock of my hair around his finger.

'No, I came with Tolstoy. It was a beautiful journey. Unforgettable, really.'

'A beautiful journey!' Peter snorted. 'It is madness for a young woman to do that in these times. Foolish and headstrong, that's what you are, Marta. Do you have any idea what might have happened to you?'

'Nothing that has not already happened in my life,' I said. 'Taking this risk is part of my duty to the Tsar.'

His eyes swept over me, taking in my tight-fitting men's clothes. My breasts, now even fuller than before, showed clearly beneath my waistcoat. I had undone the top button of my shirt so that there was a hint of flesh. He seemed to like what he saw.

'And why did you come here? Is life in Moscow so dull for a young woman?' His fingertip followed the line of my throat to my collarbone. My skin prickled with desire.

'I came,' I said, 'because I wanted to be with you.'

'Is that all?' He arched his eyebrows and cupped my face, ready to kiss me.

'No. I also came because I am pregnant with the son of the Tsar of All the Russias.'

The lights in the Tsar's tent burnt brightly all through that night.

34

The full moon took my wonder and surprise like a prince might: coolly and haughtily, as his due. Through the long, dark tube of the telescope it seemed impossibly close to us. What were those blurred shapes on its surface: towns and cities like ours, or plains and high mountains? Was the moon a mirror of our life on earth, and why did it shine only at night?

I asked Peter all these questions and many more when he set up his telescope for me, after rummaging in the chest that his servants had carried up a hill above the camp at nightfall. He kept all his treasured tools and instruments in it: one of his friends and helpers, General James Bruce, bought them for him in England for outlandish sums. Nothing excited Peter more than gazing into the sky: 'See what a book of God's marvels opens up before your eyes,' he'd whispered and tried to answer me as well as he could, but finally he said, 'Planets are like humans, Marta. There is always a dark side that we do not see. A side made of want and hidden desires.'

'Even the Tsar does not see it? Don't you know all and everything?' The moonlight seemed to change his face, even if the clear night sky was also sprinkled with stars.

'I wish! No. The Tsar above all others will never see that other side, as it is so carefully hidden from him. Perhaps it is for the better, though,' he said.

'Well. There's an exception.'

'And what would that be?'

'Love. To love is to know the dark side of the other and still want him or her. You are my planet and I see all of you, even without peering through a pipe into the sky.'

He touched my softly bulging belly. 'I like you in all your curves.'

I gave in to his embrace.

It was a raucous and cheerful group that had gathered for dinner in the Schlusselburg. The kitchen served five whole roasted oxen and the servants could scarcely keep up with refilling cups with beer and brandy. Only Alexey crossed his arms in mute protest: he refused to drink his measure. Peter watched the Tsarevich and banged his eagle cup hard on the table. 'Drink, Alexey!' he ordered.

Silence fell and all faces turned to the pale boy. Peter's dwarf Jakim tried to lessen the tension by pulling an angry face. 'Drink! Drink!' he mimicked in a shrill voice, but Menshikov smacked him so hard on the head that he howled and hid away in the shadows.

Alexey pleaded with his father. 'Please, sir, do not force me to. If I drink so much, I feel weak and terrible in the morning.'

'I bet you do. Pull your pants down so we can see you're not really a girl! But look at Marta here: she drinks me under the table before she carries me back to my bed. Our unborn son starts off as he should carry on.' He patted my belly and then glowered at the boy. 'Drink! Or I'll have you beaten.'

Alexey struggled for courage to speak up against his father: 'I am your son as well. I am your heir. You should worry about my health instead of harassing me.'

From the corner of my eye I saw Jakim crouching against the wall, pressing his small, fat fists to his eyes and shaking his head in silent despair. I held my breath.

'My heir?' Peter's voice echoed under the vaulted ceiling. Alexey reeled in his chair. Peter drew breath again, the veins bulging on his forehead: 'Listen to me. I might die tomorrow, Alexey Petrovich, but you will have little joy in your heritage if you do not follow my example. You must love what makes your country stronger and forsake everything that holds it back. Stop hiding behind stinking priests' robes, like a girl would.' Peter's grabbed his *dubina*: the knout had so far been lying peacefully beside him, but now he raised it in his hand. 'My heir you will be when you have listened to wise counsellors who will lighten the burden of your duty. My heir you will be if you spare no effort to secure the happiness of every Russian. But my breath, and my advice, are wasted on you.'

The *dubina* lashed through the air; Alexey shrank back, sobbing and folding his arms over his head. But Peter was not finished with him. 'Nobody is my heir because he was born between his mother's thighs. The Tsar suffers most amongst all Russians. I live for Russia, and one day, I will die for Russia.' Peter refilled his cup to the brim and held it out to Alexey and said, calmly but threateningly, 'Drink, or you'll be sorry.'

Alexey still hesitated, but Menshikov leant over, forced his jaw open and Peter poured the contents of the cup down Alexey's throat. The Tsarevich spat, gargled and coughed, but when Peter wanted to do it once more, I gave him a light shove.

'What?' he asked, the empty and dripping eagle cup in his hand. I raised my own, as if toasting him. 'You have spoken well, my Tsar. May the day of your death be as far from us as the stars in the sky.'

Alexander Danilovich was still waiting to carry on torturing Alexey, but Peter hesitated and said, 'Leave him. He has already wet himself with fear.'

Menshikov wiped his hands on his breeches in disgust and I glanced at the Tsarevich. A wet trace led from the crotch to the knees of Alexey's leather breeches and the boy wept openly, tears streaming down his face.

'Out of my sight with you,' Peter ordered, and Alexey fled. The diners roared with laughter, glasses were raised, the music played again and the feast continued.

'Marta the merciful,' Menshikov said, glancing at me sidelong as if to caution me. I knew what he meant: I had just convinced Peter to allow Rasia Menshikova's wedding to Antonio Devier, the dark stranger from the riotous party, against Alexander Danilovich's wishes. Four times Devier had proposed, four times Menshikov had had him brutally beaten up by his thugs, but Rasia had her heart set on the Portuguese. I raised my glass to Menshikov and he returned the toast.

After our love-making the next morning, I held Peter tight. I felt so close to him that it hurt – close enough to ask a question that pained and puzzled me.

'Why do you treat Alexey so harshly? He is just a boy. Don't you love him?'

In a serf's hostile and precarious world, everybody outside our *izba* was a possible threat or even enemy. Trust could only be placed in the family. We held together wherever we could. Whom to love, whom to trust, if not a father his child? Serfs had a saying, 'Other people's tears are only water.' It was brutal, but true.

Peter looked at me, amazed, and then shook his head. 'I don't treat him harshly. I prepare him for his life as Tsar. That's a life without real love.'

I frowned. 'What are you saying? I love you. And I don't want our child to turn out like Alexey.'

He kissed me tenderly, stroking a dark curl from my forehead. 'Don't worry. It won't. Alexey was not made with love, but only from duty and boredom. I never wanted to be with Evdokia.'

'Don't make Alexey pay for that.'

'He even looks like her!' Peter shuddered. 'Everything – his sallow skin, the dark eyes and high forehead, the thin hair, that moody, pinched mouth. God, even the way he walks, that slow gait, is Evdokia's. It drives me crazy. How did she make him so like herself?'

'That is not his fault,' I said. 'He can be like you in other ways. I suppose you have him always with you?'

'It might be too late for me to teach him. In former times, he wasn't with me at all. He was with the Lopukins and their priests too much as a child while I was travelling, learning. See what they have made of him. Only half a man!'

I bit my lip. I felt for Alexey, but this was not my battle. Furthermore, I bore Peter's next child. I leant on my elbow for some more pillow talk: 'So you never loved her? Evdokia, I mean? Never, ever?' I felt a ridiculous pang of jealousy of the wretched woman. Yes, she had been Peter's wife, but it was I who lay in his bed, while her flesh rotted from her bones in the convent she had been forced into.

'No, never,' Peter answered without hesitation. 'The thought of her and our life together makes me shudder and feel sick. My mother chose her for me, as she seemed to fit the bill. Of a lesser family than the Romanovs, fair of face, pious and seemingly docile ...'

'Seemingly?' I asked.

'Every time I came home from visiting girls in the German Quarter, she moped and nagged. Once I even brought her a present to appease her. It was a vase that she smashed at my feet, shouting at me, instead of greeting me with a smile and thanking me. And as stubborn as a mule! I spoke for four hours to her, to convince her to take the veil, and she refused. Now she is a prisoner in the convent, where her mind can turn as dusty and moth-eaten as her robes.'

I kissed his forehead. 'Well, if you ever come home to me from other women, I will whip you.'

Peter, though, would not smile. 'Nonsense! She was my wife, my Tsaritsa. It was her goddamned duty to smile at me and be gracious, whatever I did. That and to bear me many healthy sons. I did not expect anything else from her.'

To this there was no answer, but I took great care to remember his words.

After his victory over the Swedes in the first full-scale naval battle of the Great Northern War, Peter was in high spirits. He himself had fought in the thick of it, under the name of Captain Mikhailov. Sheremetev rewarded him with the Order of St Andrew. At bedtime, Peter tied the blue sash around his chest with childish pride and pinned the diamond-studded order to the threadbare linen of his nightshirt, before he slipped under the blanket. The celebrations that were to follow frightened even his battle-hardened cronies and the next day Tolstoy left for the Golden Gate in Constantinople, his face pale and drawn. For his own safety, we had to tie him to his saddle.

In truth, a day had not enough hours in it for Peter. No Russian toiled harder than his ruler as, in Peter's opinion, next to death, only wasted time could not be made up for. By four o'clock in the morning, he had already written, signed and sealed a dozen *ukazy*, making Makarov smile with the steady use of words such as '*immediately*', '*now*', '*without delay*', '*also do not forget . . . !*'

Less than two weeks after the battle, the first wooden huts of St Petersburg sprouted like mushrooms. Peter gave the conquered Swedish settlements in the marshy Neva plains to his officers. The souls who toiled in the fields hardly cared if a Russian or a Swede gave the orders; their misery just went on and on.

We failed to grasp what these huts meant to the Tsar, thinking it would be one of those passing fancies he took, before dropping it for something more promising. But to him, nothing was ever more promising than this new city of his. 'What do you think?' he asked. 'Isn't this just perfect?', while himself laying out the first wooden beams for the Peter and Paul Fortress, moving them around this way and that, until he was happy. He had but one thought: to hang on to this spot of earth. If it cost him his realm or even his life, never again should it be separated from Russia.

'Why are you founding a new city right here?' I asked him on the evening of the day we had given the remains of St Alexander Nevsky a new resting place on Lust Eland, the so-called 'happy isle' in the soggy marshland all around us, where St Petersburg was now founded. I lay in his arms, drowsy with vodka; logs crackled in the fireplace and the flames cast a warm light on my naked skin, which was rosy with pregnancy. I felt strong and safe as never before in my life, with Peter, and our son. 'Don't you have enough cities already – do you really need another one here?' I said teasingly.

'Everything I do is for Russia. My people will only understand much later what I am doing for them here.' He sighed. 'Moscow is dead and belongs to the past. It's part of the East, Marta.'

'Daria loves it for that reason.'

'Daria did not suffer in Moscow what I have suffered there. I hate the Kremlin, Marta.' I felt a tremor run through his body and held him tightly until he had calmed down.

'I will never sleep there again. When I have to be in Moscow, I'll be living in Preobrazenskoje where I grew up,' he said, caressing me distractedly. 'My new Russia needs a new landmark. I have not chosen this place at random: I fought for it and I will offer my subjects here a paradise, a New Jerusalem, on the water, dominated by a fortress as powerful as the city's spirit.'

'But how will you build a new city? When, and by what means, in the midst of war?'

'You find time and means for what needs to be done, Marta. Such as for love, for example!' He laughed and rolled on top of me.

Out in the field, I was fully part of Peter's world, even if I was not the only girl to share his bed. But he took the others the way he ate his *kasha* in the morning or peed against a tree. It was me he drank with. I was the one who made him roar with laughter when I smeared resin and fresh sap on his chair so that he stuck to it, or half-filled his boots with water before he got into them in the morning. I was the one who'd hold him tight when the fits came, or his mad rage, or when the blood-soaked horror of his memories overcame him. In my arms, the Tsar of All the Russias slept as deeply as a child; I guarded his slumber against nightmares. When he felt for the hands or feet of the child in my stomach, then no other woman was dangerous to me.

I was the one who carried his son.

35

I sewed infant clothes, slept as much as my body commanded me and happily gave in to any craving I had: sucking on fresh honeycomb or eating pickled gherkins from the Schlusselburg's larders. What I liked most, though, was the salty sweetness of Baltic herring: Peter's cook Felten bought the fish in the market near our budding city and marinated them in cream, apples and onions.

This market was only a row of ragged booths and stalls, but it drew a huge crowd of people. I followed Felten there one morning in June. The short, stout Dane was in a bad mood, as Peter had roughed him up the evening before: a big round of Limburger cheese had been stolen from the kitchen just when the Tsar had asked for it. It made me giggle, but Felten still smarted from the beating he had received at Peter's hands.

The Bay of Finland sparkled in the bright sunlight, the first grain stood in the fields and the earth shone with promise. Our low, strong horses thudded along the paths, torn open by the Russian army's carts, and the ruts and potholes baked hard by the June sun. I carefully steered my horse around the deepest furrows while Felten moped. 'When will we finally return to Moscow, where I have a real kitchen and proper supplies? Just to think of my spices and my vats of stock there makes me cry. How should one cook in this wilderness? It's like asking a donkey to play the harp.'

I led my horse around the thick stump of an oak tree, a remnant from Peter's clearing operation to claim wood for his fleet. 'You'd better prepare for a long, long stay here, and the Tsar wants to eat well in his new paradise. We need you for that, Felten,' I said.

'Paradise!' He spat out the word and then slapped at a bold gnat, which was sucking lazily on his cheek. Looking angry like that, he reminded me of the piglets he lathered in beer, mustard and honey before roasting them on a small flame. Once on the table, their slightly surprised expression, apple in snout, never failed to make us laugh. 'More like hell, I'd say. Is it true that the Tsar has ordered forced labourers, prisoners and souls, to build this city, next to the new recruits he has already drafted for that?'

I was shooing away a swarm of flies when my horse stumbled in a deep furrow. I held on, just about, but felt a jolt of sudden pain. The saddle's pommel had dug into my belly. I kept my voice steady. 'Yes. The first fifteen thousand men are to arrive next spring and a second load in August.' I stopped and drew a wheezing, painful breath. 'For this year, it is already too late for large building works.'

Felten sniffed, oblivious to my distress. 'If I had known that in Holland when I met the Tsar on the dockyards, never, ever would I have followed his summons. If only I had stayed at home.'

I laughed at his despair. 'Cheer up! You don't have to cook for all fifteen thousand workers. In life there can always be a worse option. Always. Believe me.'

He glanced at me, but said nothing. I clenched my teeth, belly still aching from where the saddle had ground into it. It felt as though I had been stabbed.

The wind carried the market's noise and smells to us. The first fruits and vegetables of the season, pies, cakes, earthenware pots and jars for meat, cheese and bread, bales of plain, coarse cloth, bundles of roughly spun and uncoloured wool, as well as roots and herbs that promised to heal all kinds of diseases and ailments, were laid out on the bare earth.

Felten checked the flashing blades of newly made knives at the blacksmith's and looked into the pens for pigs and calves – horses were traded somewhere else – bargaining hard for two fattened piglets. The guards bound them by the hooves before hoisting them with sticks onto their shoulders. I went ahead, walking with no aim in mind, when I heard a woman's voice above all the rest: 'This is usury! You should be put to the pillory, you scoundrel.'

I stopped in my tracks, heart racing: could it be? Felten had caught up with me and began, 'Mistress –' but I followed the lure of that voice.

'That's what you call filling a pastry? My pigs get more to eat than that and they are as skinny as they can get,' the woman said, her back to me. The baker defended himself meekly against the weight of her words: no trader sought that kind of attention on market day. I touched the woman's shoulder and she spun around, scowling. Seeing me, her pinched mouth broke into a wide, disbelieving smile and I threw my arms open: it was her, it was really Caroline Gluck.

'Marta!' she gasped, dropping her basket and embracing me there and then. For joy, I tried not to think about my aching belly or the sharp twinge of fear I felt. I leant into her: her cloak and her braided hair smelled of camphor and mint, the scents of their Marienburg home. She finally let go of me, or rather I finally let her.

'Marta! My God, you're alive. What are you doing here?'

'Is Ernst here as well? And Agneta? Frederic?'

We talked so fast and so much that we didn't even hear each other to begin with. I asked after the rest of her family. They lived together in a small wooden house, she said, where the wind whistled through the cracks and crevices of the hastily piled together logs and Ernst Gluck was working as a teacher. Eventually she noticed my belly. 'My goodness, family life becomes you. Poor Johann, God bless his soul. So who ... ?' Caroline spotted Felten, who stood behind me with his soldiers. Her voice trailed off as he moodily blew out his cheeks; I understood very clearly what he thought of me for making him wait but didn't give a damn. Caroline frowned and I bit my lip. Oh, until the end of her days, she'd be a righteous, dutiful pastor's wife!

'Well, are you married? Why are you here with soldiers? Have you done something bad?' she demanded.

'Well, no. Not at all. It's not that easy to explain …' I searched for words, as there were truly none for what had happened to me. When we had met last, I had been pregnant by her son and married to a simple Swedish dragoon. I took a deep breath. There would be time for the whole story later. Better stick to the truth for now. 'This child has a father,' I said. 'It is Peter, Tsar of All the Russias.'

Caroline dropped one of the *pierogi* over which she had fought so bitterly.

'Peter? The Tsar! Good God in Heaven!' she said, all pale with surprise, her eyes as big as saucers. 'But how … I mean, when … this is incredible.'

'Milady,' Felten interrupted, red-faced from holding a new, enormous wheel of cheese, which he wanted to offer to Peter in apology for his carelessness.

I embraced Caroline once more. 'Why don't you come for dinner tonight? Felten can roast one of the piglets to celebrate. I will send a guard to pick you up.'

Caroline hesitated but couldn't turn down my invitation: her curiosity wouldn't allow it.

All the way back, Felten complained about using one of the piglets, until I spurred my pony into a trot. My cheeks were flushed from the sun, the wind and the happiness of having found the Glucks again. Next to Daria and Peter, they were all I had in this world. I wanted to help and thank them for all the good they had done to me. I didn't ask about Anton and I couldn't care less about him. All I thought of was the joy of meeting Caroline – and not the nagging fear of what might have happened earlier on, when my horse had stumbled.

Our hut was cosy and warm, the tiled stove burning there even in early summer. Before sunrise Peter had already visited the docks, sorted out a quarrel between his generals and finally dictated a long, angry letter to Alexey. Then he had ordered orange trees, camphor bushes and mint plants from Persia, before drafting and signing a *ukaz* about the general education of Russian youth. As I pushed the door open he was bent over the ever-changing plans for his city, twirling a quill in grubby fingers and eating a spoonful of cold *kasha*. In the wooden cup, which he had carved himself, an oily layer floated on the now-bitter residue of *kvass*. His feet tapped and kicked underneath the table and his face and shoulders twitched, but when I entered the room he looked up and smiled, welcoming the sunshine and fresh air. I shook off my dusty cloak and slipped my swollen feet out of my leather sandals. Their straps had cut deeply into my flesh.

'God, this is good,' I sighed, sitting on Peter's lap. When I kissed him, his hand searched for our child.

'What is our young recruit doing? Is he standing to attention?' He nuzzled my throat, which made me laugh. 'Hmm, you smell good, like fresh air. Has Felten found something in the market? I'm as hungry as a wolf.'

'The recruit is swimming,' I said lightly. 'I think he's going to be a sailor.' I grabbed the half-finished *ukaz*. The sight of the heavy rolls of paper covered with thick black ink and shining, bright red seals, where Peter placed his sign, never ceased to amaze me. 'Why don't you carry on writing?'

He rested his head on my shoulder and I took in his scent of smoke and leather. 'Oh, *matka*. I can command as much as I like, it just does not work. Whatever I say is marred by the stupidity and unwillingness of the Russians. I cannot do this on my own. I need help.'

'Help you? Who could do that?' I asked.

'Someone who is well educated and can speak several languages. Someone who can be an example to them.'

My heart beat hard in my chest as a thought struck me. 'I think I may know someone,' I said. 'I think I do.' My heart leapt. I had found a way to help the Glucks without offending them by offering charity.

'Who?' Peter asked, amazed.

But before I could answer a wave of pain washed over me as if a giant had got hold of my body, squeezing and wringing all the life out of me. Fear and agony strangled me; I gasped for air, but my lungs failed me. I felt I was suffocating.

'No!' I panted as my skirt turned scarlet with blood. Within seconds its cloth was soaked and a crimson puddle had formed at my feet. The pain blotted out every other feeling and all strength and all life seeped from my body. Peter caught me with a terrified shout. Sobbing, he held me tight when our son was stillborn in the sixth month of my pregnancy.

The following months blur in my memory and disappear behind a veil dense with grief and deep sadness. It was as if everything I'd had no time to mull over before now caught up with me when I was forced to lie back and rest. The dark thoughts lost no time but swarmed my soul like locusts, devouring all joy and leaving nothing but bare, barren soil behind. It felt like birds of sorrow swooping down on me, dulling the light of my mind with their sombre wings. Their plumage was as black as soot, and they dug their sharp claws into my heart, breeding in my spirit, laying their rotten, stinking eggs in nests woven from my despair.

When Caroline caught me crying, she embraced me. 'Oh, Marta. How harsh this sounds but only you can rid yourself of this sadness.' She was right: no one except the person in whom the birds of sorrow settle can ever drive them out.

Caroline was always by my side: the Glucks had come into the camp after I miscarried and Caroline had taken over my care, pushing even Peter out of the room at first: 'Out! Nothing worse than men in such a situation, gawping like cattle and making the room dirty!'

Peter had given the Glucks a Swedish officer's former house to live in. Caroline said that the Tsar had cried when he tenderly touched the already perfectly formed little finger- and toenails of his stillborn son.

I felt cold with fear. This was my second miscarriage. What if I could never give him a healthy child, let alone a son? The birds of sorrow shrieked, and their shrill call made a terrible mockery of Daria's words in the void of my soul. *Nothing brings such joy to a man as a son.* Caroline fed me hot, thick stews made of bacon and beans, warm bread rolls stuffed with blood sausage, omelettes with fresh herbs, and dried sweet fruits she had soaked overnight in warm wine. Even Felten asked her for the recipe, she told me with a certain pride, when she laid hot stones on my feet and folded my blanket over the tiled stove before wrapping me in it. Strength slowly returned to my body, but my soul remained listless. I lay on my bed, staring up at the ceiling and counting the beetles crawling there amongst the dried tar and the boiled moss.

When I was strong enough, Peter sent me back to Moscow. All my resistance, pleading and tears would not help; if anything, they annoyed him.

'Please, let me stay with you,' I pleaded, despite knowing the answer.

'You're too weak. In Moscow the court doctors can take better care of you. We want you up and running again soon, don't we?'

I could only hope that was the real reason.

So I travelled in comfort on a litter, and accompanied by a train of coaches and carts, but when we rolled out of the camp I saw a group of young, healthy washerwomen swimming in the river. They showed their bodies without false shame, and their bare, pale skin glowed in the summer sunshine. Which of them would be with Peter, this very night? In a few weeks any of them could be pregnant with his son. I pulled the curtains shut and sank back into the cushions, sobbing uncontrollably and biting my fists until I tasted blood. Peter's favourite dogs, Lenka and Lenta, accompanied me in my litter; he had taken leave of them with tears in his eyes. Lenta was pregnant. I stroked her belly silently and steadily, like a lucky charm.

I was hardly ever left alone on my return as the Glucks had feared I might harm myself. The Lutheran priest and the Tsar had understood each other immediately, and Ernst Gluck, being still the upright, learned and kind man he had always been in Marienburg, on the Tsar's orders established the first grammar school in Moscow, which taught philosophy, ethics, politics, Latin, several languages, arithmetic and physical education. Agneta, the once frail and pale child I had looked after, had turned into a pretty young girl who made heads turn in the German Quarter. When Ernst died of a fever two years later, I took Agneta into my household while Caroline stayed on in the suburb of Moscow.

36

I knew from Peter's letters that he had left behind the pain and
sorrow of the summer. Did he expect the same from me? Just the
thought of it hurt so much, like betraying our stillborn child, but
it would be dangerous for me to forget how Peter had been bored
by Evdokia's moping and complaining. I painted crimson onto my
numb lips, practised being merry until my cheeks hurt and wore a
new dress of dark green velvet with golden embroidery. As careless
and neglectful as Peter was about his own appearance, it wouldn't
do for me not to look my best.

He sent for me on arrival. His leather breeches were stained, his
shirt reeked of sweat, and he was still wearing the boots he had
bought as a young man from his first pay at a Dutch shipyard.
When he took them off, his stockings were torn and he happily
wiggled his naked toes. 'You see, *matka*, even my socks miss you.
Nobody is darning them anymore. Their holes are as big as the ones
in my heart when you are not with me.'

'Have you missed me?' I laughed, my heart beating so hard it
almost hurt.

He pulled me close and I felt his breath hot on my throat. 'Very
much.'

'How much?' I sighed.

'Well, let me show you how much.' He lifted my heavy skirt and
played with the colourful silk ribbons that held my stockings to a
lacy silk bodice. I had feared this moment these last few weeks, more

sharply since his arrival was announced. Would I still feel desire? But heat rose through my stomach when Peter kissed me and lifted me onto the table in his living room. He opened my thighs and let his fingertips slide into my wetness, before finding my secret spot and gently caressing me until I moaned and opened myself further for him. 'It's time we made another child,' he said, between kisses.

In the New Year, Charles of Sweden and Louis of France chased away Augustus the Strong and placed their own protégé, Stanisław Leszczyński, on the Polish throne. Peter was consumed with anger, which was not helped by Turkey readying itself to join the Swedish–Polish alliance and fall onto Russia's back. The country, already exhausted by the Tsar's efforts, now had enemies on all fronts. Was this not his worst fear? How would we survive?

I travelled together with Daria back to Peter's young city. The Peter and Paul Fortress had risen on the shore of the Neva since my last visit. There were many more houses being built, too, even though all building materials had to be brought in from far away. The Tsar wanted his city built of stone, and for it to be as different as he could make it from the disorder of Moscow; its houses were to boast high, regular façades and line straight, long streets like pearls on a string, such as he had seen in Europe. Hundreds of thousands of men toiled with bent backs and gnat-bitten flesh, their ankles swelling in the brackish marsh water, fighting to dry out the swamps and force the swelling Neva into canals. Guards did not take their eyes off them as they laboured: attempts to flee this place were common.

Our coach had to slow down when passing them and a suffocating stench gathered in the hot summer air. I examined those hopeless, gaunt faces. Was my father here? Did my brother work among them? But I never recognised anyone. I listened to the men sing to forget their misery. Hammers and hatchets fell against stones and logs to the rhythm of Russian songs full of sadness and longing.

I was back in Moscow, pregnant once again. Caroline allowed me neither to go out nor to drink wine or vodka: 'You will give birth to this child in perfect health or you will have to deal with me.'

She'd forbidden one more thing, but even her zeal paled in the face of Peter's passion for me: 'You are so warm. If it was possible to get enough of you, I surely would try.'

That summer the Red Square sizzled with heat. Even the air in Peter's house in Preobrazenskoje was stifling. Flies swarmed in its rooms and the beams crackled with cockroaches. Peter was so disgusted that he had all the walls and roofs lathered with fresh boiling tar, which made breathing even harder.

I was pacing the corridors when the front door was pushed open: a welcome draught of air cooled my sticky forehead. It was followed by two soldiers who as good as carried in an exhausted messenger. The man staggered more than walked. Both Caroline and I retreated into the shadows of the hallway.

The men knocked at Peter's door and when he opened it, I saw the impatience on his face. Caroline and I listened keenly; news could be of triumph or defeat. But not a sound was to be heard from Peter's room. I felt faint – what could that mean? Just then, the men came out again, their eyes lowered and their faces flushed, and I caught sight of Peter looking forlornly out of the window, his shoulders hunched. My heart went out to him.

'Show them the stables and the trough. They can wash themselves and then eat in the kitchen,' I told Caroline before I slipped inside Peter's room. He didn't hear me and I held my breath, my hand hovering in mid-air. He was crying. When I embraced him from behind, his heavy body stiffened before he gave in to my embrace.

'*Batjuschka*. You cry. What has happened?' I softly kissed his shoulder and he leant backwards on me; I grasped the windowsill so that my knees did not buckle under his weight.

'Sophia is dead.'

'Your half-sister? The Regent?'

'Yes. She died two days ago in her convent. Finally.'

I buried my face in his back mutely. Sophia, who had relegated her brothers to the shadows of the Kremlin and had ordered both Streltsy revolts – she, the first woman ever to rule Russia. Peter turned and rested his face in my neck. His tears soaked my skin. His whole body was shaken by deep, desperate sobs. But I also felt another, dangerous tremor going through his limbs. Was this a fit? I sank to the ground and pulled him with me. 'Shhh. Come, sit down. Here, with me. Calm down, just calm down. I'm here ...' I held his head between my breasts and rocked him like a child, to and fro. It was a long while before he looked up at me and said, 'She is to be buried in the convent.'

'If we can find a coffin big enough for her ...' I muttered, risking a joke.

He chuckled while crying. 'Indeed! She got even fatter in that convent. I wonder who she bribed to bring her more food. And how did her lover ever mount her? But she was shrewd; so fast and so funny. A ruler, through and through. I feared her, always. Before I had her imprisoned, I met her alone in the great hall of the Kremlin. She stood before me. I had not expected her to curtsey. When I asked her, "Why did you not kill me back then when I was a boy?", do you know what she answered?'

'No,' I whispered.

'"Stupid boy, Peter," she said. "All that counts is Russia. Do you think I had not seen that our brother Ivan was an idiot? Who else but you should have ruled Russia after me?" Stability. Continuity –' He wiped his snotty nose with his sleeve, like a boy would. 'Yes, let's give her a grave with neither name nor date on the headstone. She is not to be mourned and no one shall ever worship her.'

I kissed him. 'Make that a very deep grave. Deep enough to swallow all the dread and all the demons she raised in you.'

He held me so tightly that the child in my body moved. 'Oh, *matka*, why do I have to be so lonely? Why do I always have to be Tsar? When Menshikov executed the Streltsy soldiers right outside Sophia's convent cell, decapitating them, or stringing them up by their feet until their heads exploded, leaving their bodies to rot so that vultures circled the square for weeks on end, Sophia just waved at us, smiling. She never had nightmares. Why me, then? Why do I always have to pay?'

I kissed his tears away. 'You're not alone. You have us, me –' I placed his hand firmly on my body '– and our son.'

Peter's generals spent the next two years roaming restlessly through the Baltics, taking crucial strongholds and preventing further Swedish attacks. After they narrowly avoided an offensive from the sea on the still-fragile St Petersburg, Peter spent the whole night on his knees giving thanks.

37

Fortune in the Great Northern War swung from the Swedes to the Russians and back, like the pendulum on a clock. Today the Red Square was alive with spectators when the Tsar prepared to celebrate a recent victory: thick, wet snowflakes fell and clung to my lashes and my sable cloak. A thousand torch-bearers lined the square, which had been strewn with sand and gravel, steeping the ground in hues of gold. Cannon fired salutes, fireworks lit up the sky in a rainbow of colours and a steady drum roll almost swallowed up the sound of the thundering steps of Peter's regiments, which marched underneath hastily erected wooden triumphal arches on to the square, swinging captured Swedish flags, the blue-and-gold cloth torn and burnt. In the evening ten thousand men formed a single body, calling out in hoarse voices for their *batjuschka* Tsar. Yet Peter himself was in the thick of it all the time, mingling with his soldiers, standing in the stirrups of his German saddle that lay on a blanket of leopard fur and red velvet. He waved to the adoring, cheering crowd and I, too, shouted until my voice was hoarse, but just as Peter had finished his first round of the square, our son decided to be born.

The first pangs of labour almost tore me to pieces; the cramps didn't build up gradually but hit me like a cart. I gasped for air as the pain cut like a knife into my lower body. Once I was brought to bed – the hastily summoned guards had to carry me – Caroline was with me, forcing me to rise and pace between the worst pains, and encouraging me: 'Go on, Marta. He will live. It's a strong and healthy son for the Tsar.'

Her words rang in my ears like the rattle of a prayer-mill while I bit on a piece of sandalwood that Daria had shoved between my teeth. The physician Blumentrost wanted to force me to lie down, but I knew how the women in my *mir* had given birth healthily, and it was not by lying on their backs. When only an iron band of suffering held me together, I crouched and then followed Caroline's orders. 'Push. Breathe. Press. Once again. And again. Breathe. Hold on. Steady ...' But still the baby wouldn't come. Daria and Caroline held me firmly by my armpits, made me sniff camphor when I threatened to faint and gently stroked my belly, easing the baby out. I soaked bundles of linen with my blood, and the midwife carried bucket upon bucket of hot water into the room.

By now Blumentrost was not to be held back any longer. 'Let me do my work or the Tsar will have my skin as a rug,' he said. 'Hold her. Firmer! Push! I can feel his head. He's close. Push – stop now ...'

Somebody screamed like an animal. Lights flashed behind my eyelids and the stench of sweat and blood was unbearable when Blumentrost reached into my body. I wanted to kick him, writhing with agony and rage at my own helplessness. He urged me on: 'Push once more. Yes! A boy. It's a boy!' The physician sounded as triumphant as if he was the father: he held the infant up into the fading light of the afternoon, spun him around and slapped him on his bottom, where his skin was still covered with white slime and blood. My son's first cry was strong and hoarse before a merciful darkness closed in on me.

The room was scented with camphor, sage and myrrh; hot water steamed in the bathtub, and Caroline made my bed with fresh, starched linen and fur blankets, before she opened the window wide, pushing the protesting midwife aside. 'What a stench! How is one supposed to breathe in here?'

Peter and I endlessly admired the small, perfectly formed fingers and rosy skin of our son. He had strong, straight limbs and a loud voice; last but not least, he drank like a field marshal. Soon, though,

Daria handed the little one to a wet-nurse and bound my breasts to keep their firmness and their shape: I belonged back in Peter's bed.

My son was baptised in the Kremlin chapel and Peter, who sobbed throughout the ceremony, ordered Makarov to enter his name into the yearbook of the Moscow court. Alexey congratulated me in measured words and Peter made me the gift of Kolomenskoye Palace outside Moscow. It was my very own house, the first I had ever owned, a palace with hundreds of rooms and as many windows that sparkled in the sun. Built for Tsar Alexis, Peter's father, its hunting grounds were vast – much more land than the monks in our *mir* had ever owned. The thought gave me great pleasure.

That Yuletide was the happiest ever: sometimes I'd change my fancy dress three times a night, appearing first as a Friesian maid, then as an Amazon, then a Greek goddess. When the festivities ended – normally an hour at which inky darkness still hid the Moscow rooftops from my sight – I'd slip through the dark corridors to my son's room, where he slept guarded by his wet-nurse. I'd lean over his cradle and listen to his breathing, entirely content.

At the thaw, I accompanied Peter into the field. It broke my heart to leave my little boy behind, but there were too many other women who were only too happy to follow the Tsar into his tent. I would not have one calm moment in Moscow. My little boy was to join us as soon as possible, but for the time being I left my four-month-old son in Menshikov's palace under Daria's care. I dictated long letters to her along the way and from Peter's camp, begging her not to forget him in all the disorder of Alexander Danilovich's household. *'Do not leave my Petrushka alone in the darkness, as he gets scared. Also, have some warm clothes made, Peter will pay for it. If you need to travel, please make sure my son has enough to eat and drink.'*

My little boy died suddenly before Easter of the year following his birth. He had just begun to smile when death took him. 'We must have another one soon,' were Peter's only words. I nodded, fighting to keep the birds of sorrow at bay.

The following year, I gave birth again. My son was small, yet healthy, but barely outlived his brother. The birds of sorrow nested in my soul: whenever I saw how the Tsarevich Alexey grew and prospered, I wondered whether my sons' deaths were a punishment from God for what the Tsar's wife Evdokia had to endure.

Daria, who was still unmarried and a maiden by name, gave me some advice. 'Only love a child once it can walk, talk and is strong enough to overcome the first fever.'

My beautiful daughter Ekaterina Petrovna was stronger than her brothers. Born in spite of Peter chasing warfare all over his realm, she lived past the sad little milestones of their brief lives. She was a dear child, with blonde curls and dimples in her chubby elbows, who walked and spoke early and had an easy, endearing smile. Between battles, Peter dictated loving letters, which his messenger read to me. *"Menshikov, too, is not here, and I sorely miss the two faces I love the most in this world. Let our Ekaterina be strong and healthy, so the two of you may join me soon. Yesterday a drunk soldier climbed on a rooftop and fell down: you would have laughed even more than I did at the sight of it. So, yes, I do have fun, but not as much as when you are with me ..."*

We joined him as soon as we could. While he sat with his men in the evening, sharing his worries about the war and the country with them, Ekaterina hid under the table, spinning the spurs on his boots and humming a song, until he lifted her on his lap and fed her from his plate. She took her first steps on the banks of the Neva and Peter was as proud of her progress as he was of the rise of his new city. In the nights, however, worry about Russia's future plagued him: he spoke in his dreams, shouting orders, or shot up from a light slumber, standing as stiff as a rod, and tried to slip on his dirty, crumpled uniform. I had to force him back into the pillows, soothing him with songs and kisses, so that he could gather strength for the next day, which again would weigh so heavily on him.

Charles of Sweden marched his troops southwards, where his trusted General Rehnskjöld defeated both the Saxons and the Russians. At first, the Saxons had been ready to welcome their Lutheran Swedish brothers. But word of the true nature of the occupation shocked even the Russians: Charles executed all prisoners on the spot, as he could not feed them. Whole villages were purged; men, women and children dangled from trees, head down and their bellies slit open. The crows pecked their eyes, and the wolves chewed their way up from the neck to the guts. Charles's men heated cow's piss and poured it into their bound, helpless victim's throat until the person burst, or gave no other sign of life, whichever came first. A stream of letters came from Saxony, pleading for help. Peter and his generals were desperate: was the war finally lost? They talked until late in the night, every night. Once when I came to see Peter, bringing him hot milk with cognac and honey, he crumpled up a letter, his face dark with rage.

'What's this?' I asked, picking the paper up from the floor and smoothing it. It looked important.

'It's a letter from England, written by His Grace the Duke of Marlborough,' he replied, gnashing his teeth.

'You wanted him to mediate between Charles and you, didn't you?'

'Yes. But he declined. Declined! And do you know what I had offered him in exchange?'

I shook my head.

'I gave him the choice between the titles of Prince of Kiev or Siberia. But that was not all.' Peter wagged his finger, to emphasise his generosity. 'So, we top that up with fifty thousand Reichstaler for every year of his life, as well as the largest ruby ever found, for his duchess loves jewellery and Marlborough is a gambler with huge debts. But that's still not enough for an English duke, so let's also add the Order of St Andrew – but His Grace rejects it all.' He shredded the letter. 'Of course he refuses. It is much better to know the Swedes are kept busy here rather than meddling in the Spanish Succession. Russia and I are to be sacrificed to serve as a useful diversion.'

The Swedes settled in Saxony, where Charles waited for his moment. He had more cards up his sleeve: we all knew that. Peter, more worried than I'd ever known him, made reinforcements at the Russian borders, and for the first time in a century the Kremlin, too, was fortified. Though when Peter signed the *ukaz* enabling that, he murmured, 'It shall go to hell, this abode of the Devil!'

Only a few months later Charles stood in Minsk, which had not seen foreign fiends since the Kingdom of Rus had taken it, six hundred years before. Were Russia and we lost?

38

We made our field quarters in Kiev, where Peter wanted Ekaterina and me to be comfortable, so I dictated long lists of necessary supplies to Makarov, who sent them first to Arkhangelsk and then west by ship. Patiently, the secretary repeated to my companion Daria and me the Tsar's own orders: 'A full English porcelain service, hand-painted with rural scenes, in blue, to serve forty-eight people. Thirteen bales of striped taffeta and several bales of Indian fabrics with various woven floral and square patterns. Twelve barrels of olives and two barrels of anchovies ...'

I snapped my fingers. 'I want stockings! The Polish ones run after the first ride. And when I am with Peter I need warm feet, otherwise I am in a bad mood. That's the last thing he needs now. And you, Daria? What do you order for yourself?'

She didn't hesitate. 'Italian balm for my hands, pickled lemons, silk from Amsterdam and rolls of Brussels lace.'

'And a golden wedding ring,' I said with a giggle, but instead of laughing Daria looked as if she might cry. I was ashamed to have hurt her, and immediately embraced her. 'Forgive me. You've been by Menshikov's side for almost nine years. Surely you are as good as married?'

'You have no idea what's been happening,' she sobbed. 'Menshikov has decided to marry, but not me. He has fallen in love with a Princess Saltykova. The slut is only fifteen years old and last night he told me he wanted to marry her and sire a dozen children, whilst I should retire to my family estate and await further orders.'

'What? This beggars belief.'

Makarov hastily stashed his papers and bowed his way out; Daria was so furious that she grabbed a small silver candlestick and threw it after the fleeing cabinet secretary. 'Just run away, coward! You men are all the same.' Then she flung herself at me. 'Oh, Marta. She is young, beautiful and of a much better family than mine. I've given him my best years. Who will want me now?' She pressed her fists against her swollen eyes. 'He's only crazy about her because he cannot have her! Her family does not allow him a single second alone with her and he scribbles one horrible love poem after the next to her, war or no war, battle or no battle. While I am always available. How interesting is that?'

I listened in silence and picked up Ekaterina, kissing her hair. Daria's tears had smudged her white face paint, which made her look even more careworn. She was almost twenty-three years old, like me. If she still wanted children, she had better get on with it. I kissed her, then pulled her to her feet. 'We will find a way, Daria,' I said, as reassuringly as I could. 'Go home, have a hot bath and then drink some warm milk with honey, so you can sleep. Trust me, and do not worry.'

I hoped it comforted her because I certainly didn't believe it myself. Peter and I laughed and drank and carried on so much in Kiev's bright nights that I was sure to be pregnant again soon. But what if he thought of marrying a young princess, for Russia's sake? I could imagine my fate then, as well as Ekaterina's. The thought chilled me like an icy wind.

When Daria's litter left, Ekaterina played at my feet with one of Peter's old pipe stumps and sucked on a carved Russian double eagle. Her sweet saliva changed it into a bulky, formless clot. Sunlight made her silky blonde head shine; she looked like an angel. I picked her up. 'Come. Let's go and see your father,' I whispered, and she smiled.

'What do I care about Menshikov and his trouble with women?' Peter looked up from a map he was studying. To the west, the Swedes held Saxony; to the east, the Don Cossacks and their Ataman Bulavin were staging a revolt, while the Porte in Istanbul was also readying itself to pounce. Russia was utterly beleaguered, ready to be sliced up by her enemies in a peerless, hitherto unimaginable feast. Had Peter pushed our luck too far?

'Women,' he snorted, before continuing to scribble his notes, which he sent out every evening in all directions. He had already forgotten my presence, but I would not give up so easily.

'What do you mean by that? Daria has given him her best years. Should she now watch him marry a younger woman?'

Peter shrugged. 'But of course. What else do you imagine? Daria has the worst reputation. I myself have chosen the Princess Saltykova for Menshikov. She's a juicy little thing, but horribly well guarded. He must put a ring on her finger to get her, which is as it should be with a girl of good family. I shall stand godfather to each and every son she bears him.' He smiled and fingered the ribbons on my dress. 'Perhaps we, too, should get on with having more children than just our sweet Ekaterina?'

I pushed him away.

'What are you thinking, woman?' he hissed, but I stood firm. Was I really only fighting for Daria? No, I was not.

Peter sighed. 'All right. Listen. So far, I did not want an ambitious marriage for Menshikov, for he shouldn't get too above himself and too greedy. But he has proved himself in battle as well as in life. I can now reward him without any eyebrows being raised. My love for him can no longer be labelled blind and unjust. When the times are better, I will also make him a Prince of Russia. For this, he needs the right woman by his side.'

I was stunned: besides the members of the Tsar's family, no one had ever been a Prince of Russia. Nobody was born to that rank, even a Tsarevich had to earn the title. Peter leant in to embrace me while I trembled with rage. 'I see. The Princess Saltykova is a "juicy little thing", is she? Well, just to be clear: for as long as Menshikov does not marry Daria, you are no longer welcome in my bed. He is to keep his word. His bloody, bloody word!' I sobbed as I spoke for I had just put everything I had gained at risk: for Daria, for Ekaterina and, last but not least, for myself.

Peter grabbed his chair so hard that his knuckles turned white. I backed away. 'It's my bed, not yours, Marta. Nothing in this

world belongs to you. Nothing! You are as poor as the Baltics.'
In all the years we had been together we had never quarrelled; no
raised voices, no long, ghastly silence. And now this! It hit me like
a cudgel. I could hardly breathe and my chest tightened as if under
an iron band. I held Ekaterina, who wept and clung to my neck,
tightly. I felt her heart race and buried my face in her hair, which
smelled of honey and sunlight. Peter avoided my eyes but looked at
his little daughter, pain in his face.

'That is not true, Peter. I do own something. I have my pride
and my freedom, which you gave me. If you think like that about
Daria, what then do you think about me? If Menshikov will not
be held to his word, will you? What is to happen to me … to us
… if you meet some other princess who is a "juicy little thing"? I
prefer to leave before I am driven away,' I said as calmly as I could,
swallowed my tears and turned to leave.

He crossed his arms. 'Where will you go? What will you live
on?'

I gave no answer but left the room.

'Marta! Stay here. Stay. That is an order!' he shouted, but I closed
the door behind me. Once I was in the corridor all the strength
drained out of me, like water from one of Felten's sieves. I sank
onto my heels, leant against the wall and hugged my child to me. I
gasped and tried to suppress sobs, but then like a dam burst I cried
so much that I had to wipe the snot from my face. Ekaterina touched
me with her little hands, eyes dark with worry, and muttered the
few half-words she could say.

Inside Peter's room, I heard wood splinter. That would be his
chair, I thought, or the desk. He shouted with rage. I steadied
myself, picked up Ekaterina with trembling hands and went to my
room. 'Pack my things,' I ordered my maidservant, wiping my face.
Crying would not help me. What had I done? I might have to give
Kolomenskoye back, but the jewellery and the gowns belonged to
me. I could sell those. And then? I'd have to learn how to read,
write and count. But lesser minds than mine had managed that.
In the *gostiny dvor* there was certainly room for another shop. I
could become a merchant and afford an education for Ekaterina.
She should enter into a proper marriage; a bond in which she was

loved and honoured. No one was to treat my daughter as I had been treated.

For two days and nights I heard nothing from Peter. I paced the house while he turned all his thoughts to the threat of the approaching Swedes. By day, he drew up plans for his army; at night, he whored his way through Kiev, striking fear in the heart of the most battle-hardened girls. I swallowed more laudanum than I should in order to be able to sleep. Sometimes I woke drowsily and listened. Did I hear footsteps halting in front of my door? Maybe. I knew that in his anger he could throw bolts of lightning then feel sorry for the blaze he had caused, doing all he could to extinguish its flames. But not this time. Had we both gone too far? Peter never came into my room – if he had been there in the passageway at all – and I slipped back into an unhealthy, intoxicated slumber. I suffered like an animal, as despite his words, I still loved him and it hurt me to see him suffer. Normally, I would have stood by him and Russia in this difficult hour. But now was not a normal time. My pain at the harsh words we had exchanged mounted. Of course I had known about his temper, but so far I had only witnessed his rage against others and sought to mellow it, never been at the receiving end of it myself. I had to do what I had to do, for how could I live with him if he did not respect me?

Finally, there was no reason left to delay my departure. My chests were packed and tightly chained and locked, as I was to cross the war-torn countryside from Kiev to Moscow. When I asked Peter for an armed escort, he had Makarov reply that he could not spare a single man at the moment.

It was a sunny morning in late August. The golden roofs of Kiev were damp and glistening with dew when I stepped into the courtyard of our low, dark house. In my arms, Ekaterina looked around in surprise: we were leaving the only home she knew. There was no turning back, even if I had to force myself forward, step by step.

Makarov and Felten were standing in the doorway, looking so downtrodden that I embraced both of them and pressed small medals embossed with the image of St Nicholas into their palms, folding their fingers around the charms. 'You have been my loyal friends. Please be the Tsar's faithful servants in this hour of need. And when you come to Moscow, come and see me in my shop.'

Makarov shuffled his feet and Felten wiped his eyes with his for once clean apron, before he handed me a bag of warm, freshly made fudge for Ekaterina. I swallowed and tasted salt. Was I throwing my whole life away? There ought to be another way forward, as there had always been in my life so far. Servants lifted my boxes onto the carts; I climbed into the carriage and reached out for Ekaterina, who would travel on my lap. *Don't cry*, I ordered myself through gritted teeth: *do not cry!* I had ample time for that once we had passed the city gates. I waved to the men again and Felten sobbed like a child.

The coachman clicked his tongue and raised his whip, flicking it over the back of the horses. I was ready to settle into the cushion when I was flung forward: the wagon jerked to a sudden halt and the horses dug in their hooves, for the Tsar's hand gripped the reins with all its might.

39

Daria's wedding to Alexander Danilovich Menshikov was a quiet but joyful event. Peter had ordered that we celebrate it in the European way. Daria just shrugged her shoulders. When the morning before the ceremony, I scrubbed her skin rosy and glowing with a pumice stone, she told me, 'I'd marry him wrapped in a net. That he becomes mine is all that matters.'

Menshikov glowered when he stepped under his groom's crown with a representation of Christ embossed along its golden rim; but Daria was radiant in her dress made of ivory silk and silver-thread embroidery. Her bridal crown depicted Our Lady. The light of the hundreds of candles that Peter had provided made her shimmer like the moon itself as she stepped into the dusky little church in Kiev. I wept with happiness.

After the wedding not even the proximity of Swedish troops hindered us from celebrating as we should, with drinking games and dancing. Just before the ashen morning hour, we stepped out into a balmy summer night and I felt the dewy grass as fresh as a promise under my naked soles, for I had left my embroidered slippers under the festive table. The afternoon I had swum naked in the Dvina had never felt further away. I shrank back when the first firework burst suddenly above our heads: Peter's very special surprise for Menshikov. He embraced me from behind and whispered the words that glowed in the sky: '*Vivant*. That means: may they live – and long and happily. Look now, the next display will spell out: *Connected by their love!*' I marvelled at the light and glory of it, and clapped my hands with joy, before we all coughed and wiped the soot from our faces.

That morning, after making love, my breasts were wet with Peter's tears. He raised his head, looking bewildered. I combed his dark curls away from his lined forehead. 'You must never leave me, Marta,' he pleaded. 'I am only a human being when you are with me. If you ever leave or forsake me, I am but an animal.'

Marriage was not too bad for Menshikov: only three months later Daria was pregnant and he pranced about as proudly as the peacocks he had ordered from Persia for his St Petersburg palace on the Vassilyev Island. Peter stood godfather to Daria's baby boy the following May, offering the child several villages with thousands of souls and a bale of fine Amsterdam cloth for his christening robe. But the little one died before he began teething and then Daria and I were linked by a different bond.

By autumn, when the still-supple summer earth was preparing for the first great frost, Peter was merely trying to avoid open battle with the Swedes for as long as possible: he lacked the means to win. But then he found an ally to strike fear into the bravest soldier's heart. An ally who had always been by his side, silently and almighty: Russia herself.

When I heard the words for the first time, they chilled the blood in my veins: *scorched earth*. I remembered my own hunger during the short siege of Marienburg. And the Swedes were to endure a whole winter of it? There could be no crueller plan.

Charles was about to march on Moscow, boasting he would dethrone Peter and shatter the Russian Empire into small Swedish provinces. Was this to be our end?

Peter stood in his study in Kiev, looking at maps of the Ukraine. Deep furrows lined his forehead, and for the first time I noticed sharp lines at the corners of his mouth. Dark shadows lay under his eyes and his cheeks were gaunt. When had he last had a square meal? I seemed to have breakfasted, lunched and dined with Daria all the time in recent weeks.

General Major Nikolai Iflant ran his finger over a chart and explained: 'Charles will move his men along here, but the country is hardly cultivated. There are few villages, and the forests are so dense that men and livestock can easily hide in them for months, if necessary. Scorched earth is a Cossack tactic, my Tsar. When an enemy approaches, they set fire to everything ...'

'Everything?' Peter asked, his eyebrows arched.

'Everything. The Swedes will be left with nothing to eat. Winter is coming. Charles marches into frost and famine. I tell you, no army conquers as well as scorched earth and the Russian winter working together.'

I paused at my embroidery: Peter looked pale, but as keen as an unsheathed blade. His blue eyes were gleaming as he laid his hand heavily on Iflant's shoulder. 'That's it, Nikolai. Scorched earth. Give the order.'

I knew what this meant to the little *izby*. As soon as the enemy set foot in the Ukraine, millstones would be smashed to gravel and all food, be it growing in the fields, waiting in the threshing houses or stored in the grain-chambers, and which was not necessary for the survival of our own army, was to be burnt. Fire would devour all houses, all churches and all stables; bridges would be tumbled into rivers, their rocks and stones damming up the water. Forests and embankments would be turned into walls of flames. People who refused to follow orders would have to watch their whole village being torched before they were killed by their own side, Peter's soldiers.

'What will happen to the people who live there?' I dared to ask, my voice husky.

Iflant shrugged. 'They will be sent into the remaining forests, along with their cattle and everything they can carry. It sounds cruel, but it's for the sake of Russia. We all pay.'

Peter paced the room like a captive animal. His old uniform jacket hung on his too tall, too bony body. What did he live off? Brandy, some *kasha* in the morning, and a few bites of whatever he found in the evening.

'And when the Russian winter comes?' I whispered.

Peter smiled for the first time in a long, long while. 'Oh, *matka*. I can't wait to greet him, the Russian winter, this most loyal friend who does my every bidding. For if we Russians think the winter cruel, what will the Swedes feel? They shall be culled like cattle.'

The following night Ekaterina fell ill. She had been coughing for a while, but now she gasped for air, wheezing and crying, holding her little ear, which was as red as fire inside. We tried everything to lower her fever; Blumentrost bled her several times and, oh, how bravely my little girl held up when the hot glasses were placed on her tender back. She sobbed, but bit her lip and pressed my fingers, which I clenched. The doctors bathed her in ice water and I felt like hitting Blumentrost but was about to allow her treatment with mercury when our little daughter died.

Peter was numb with pain but threw himself into the preparations for scorched earth, disappearing night and day into his study with his generals and advisers. His spirit and his soul were caught up in the struggle for Russia's survival. Though I failed to understand his distance from my mourning in those days, I heard him dictate a letter to a friend who had lost his son: '*I am so very sorry about your loss of a fine boy, but it is better to let go of the irretrievable rather than recall it; we have a path laid before us, which is known only to God. The child is now in heaven, the place we all want to be, disdaining this inconstant life.*'

And so, when he clung to me at night, tormented by nightmares, his words reached me, even though he could only speak them to others and not to me. But if I had been devastated by the death of my little sons, then my mourning for Ekaterina, our daughter who was talking and learning and giving us both so much joy, was like falling into a deep, dark well that had no bottom and from which I thought I could never emerge. Soon, I was pregnant again, but where the love for Ekaterina had burnt so warm and bright, a dark chasm of bitterness stayed within me, which I believed nothing would ever close.

40

St Petersburg grew with every month that my belly swelled. Despite the burdens of war, Peter insisted on being kept up-to-date with the progress of his city. The wooden Peter and Paul Fortress had been replaced by a star-shaped structure in stone, ready to brave any attack, and its bastions were named after Peter's best and most trusted men: Menshikov, Sotov, Golovkin, Trubetzkoi and Naryshkin.

The pregnancy weighed on me and I almost feared the moment of birth, not because of the long hours of pain, but because I would start loving the child so helplessly, and once more be open to sorrow and pain should I lose it. Mostly it was Daria who embroidered soft cashmere blankets and sent gifts of rattles and dolls. 'Don't give up, Marta. You will have a strong, healthy son that will bind Peter and you forever,' she encouraged me, forcing me to feel my child quickening. 'You must hope, and you must believe,' she urged. I was grateful for her support in something only another woman could understand. Peter was once more excited by the prospect of possibly having another son. He never mentioned our dead children.

Shortly before I was to leave for Moscow, I lay awake in my bedroom in the little Summer Palace, where the Fontanka Canal met the Neva. My body and limbs were so swollen that I could not even braid my long tresses and was too impatient to ask my maids to do it. My curls stuck to my face and neck, which were beaded with sweat. My chambermaid was curled up asleep on the threshold when I heard footsteps; the handle moved and Peter stepped into my room. His eyes were sunken in their sockets; he swayed a bit before climbing onto my raised bedstead. He bit me playfully in the neck and whispered, 'How are you, my beautiful Marta?'

'I'm feeling awful. Look! I can't even brush my hair,' I moaned, lifting my swollen hands and wriggling my fingers. He grabbed the silver brush from my bedside table, pulled me up from my bed and across the room to the dressing-table and its Venetian glass mirror.

'I'm quite good at brushing hair,' he offered, and helped me to lower myself onto the stool before he began to work his way through my thick tresses. My scalp tingled under the firm strokes. When he had finished, my hair framed my face in a shiny, dark cloud. He mutely rested his chin on my head and our eyes met in the mirror. We were both as pale as ghosts and the candle-light blurred the outlines of our faces but sharpened the bones beneath. I rose, wanting to lead him to the bed; perhaps I'd sleep better with him by my side, and the sheets of cool, starched linen looked inviting. 'Come,' I whispered, but to my surprise he held me back.

'No. Put on a cloak. Follow me.' His eyes were dark and unreadable.

'What kind of cloak?' I asked. 'Now? In the middle of the night?'

He pointed to my chest. 'Anything, just so you're not in a night-gown.' He paused and added, 'Something dignified.'

Something dignified! I chose a golden-yellow silk cloak which was lined with mink and embroidered with gold threads in a Persian pattern. It fell to my feet and its deep folds and the tie under my bosom covered my belly.

'That's good. Come now.' Peter easily lifted me over the sleeping chambermaid and, once in the hallway, placed a finger on his lips. He beamed now, his face as bright as a jewel. We were like children planning a prank. What on earth was he up to? We crept down the staircase then through the dark Summer Palace, which smelt dankly of the nearby Neva and of the bitter tar dripping off the torches. I felt the cold of the stone slabs beneath my naked feet, and my mirth and wonder mingled with sudden wariness. What had happened? Had the Swedes advanced so far that we must flee the city under cover of the night?

Ahead of me Peter pressed down the high, European-style curved handle to a small reception room. I squinted inside: the room was dark except for the amber glow in the fireplace. Peter's dogs snoozed on bearskins before it, wagging their tails weakly when they sensed us. Close by stood a priest, wearing a long, dark robe. His feet in their well-worn sandals were bare despite the October cold and dark hair straggled to his shoulders, though his beard was neatly trimmed. I bowed my head and he touched the *panagia* on his chest in a sign of respect. Peter laced his fingers through mine and drew me closer. 'Marta, may I present to you the greatest mind in the whole Russian Empire: Feofan Prokopovich.'

So this was Feofan, of whom Peter had so often spoken to me. He greatly admired this holy man even though he belonged to the old Moscow guard and had just returned from Rome; but Feofan's undisputed talents were reason enough to promote him. Prokopovich, Abbot of Kiev and head of the city's university, smiled at me: his worn face spoke of warmth and wisdom, and his shiny eyes of a joyful spirit.

'Now you must also tell me the name of your lady, my Tsar,' he teased, and Peter smiled. They were clearly at ease with each other. 'That is why we are here. Feofan, this is Marta. She is the sister of my soul.'

The priest's gaze weighed on me: I'd rather have this quiet little man as a friend than an enemy, I realised. 'And why have you summoned me in the middle of the night, my Tsar?' he enquired. He stroked his beard, while at the same time seeming much less puzzled than I was.

One of the dogs yawned and turned its belly towards the warmth of the flames. Peter chased it away and knelt down on the bearskin instead, pulling me down with him, despite my heavy body. 'Peter,' I moaned, but he raised his hand.

'Silence. I summoned you here to witness an oath, Feofan. Once happier days come for Russia, and once the greatest danger and the threat from the Swedes is turned away, then ...'

My heart pounded; the blood roared in my ears. Even the child in my body lay still while Peter searched for words to express the unbelievable thing he wanted to say.

'. . . I wish to make use of my freedom since my divorce from the Tsaritsa Evdokia Lopukina to marry Marta.'

I gasped. Marry me? It had always been on the cards for Daria, being from an old Russian family, even though she had lived in sin. Menshikov had needed to marry sooner or later, to sire rightful heirs. Yet Peter had Alexey, and we were happy together as we were. All the anger and doubt that I had felt in Kiev were long-gone, forgotten like an enemy in exile. I knew what Peter was doing for me now and what he would face as a result – the criticism of his family and the aristocracy as well as the scorn of the foreign powers by whom he so desperately wished to be accepted, almighty or not. Russia meanwhile feared all change that Peter brought about and revered all custom he did away with. He would be lonelier than ever thanks to this decision. He'd only have me, I thought, and the realisation made my heart hurt.

'Are you sure?' asked Feofan, emboldened by the power of his office and clearly sharing my thoughts.

'Yes,' Peter repeated firmly, 'I do not fear whatever this might entail.' My heart leapt and I squeezed his fingers. No, he would not fear, ever, and I was determined to join him in that. Peter spoke solemnly. 'Feofan Prokopovich, you shall here and now, this morning in October of the year 1707, witness my oath. Marta, when times are better, I shall welcome you into the Holy Russian Church and give you my son as a godfather. I shall marry you, and you shall be known by the name of Catherine Alexeyevna.'

I blinked my tears away. Feofan blessed us before he left, the sound of his footsteps fading away down the passageway. Peter and I were alone in the little room. It felt like a fairy tale; I would not have been surprised if the room had spun three times around us. We settled in front of the fire, holding on to each other, talking quietly for a long time until a late, leaden morning light crept through the half-closed shutters of the room. Just before I fell asleep, I murmured, 'You do not have to do this, *starik*, you know that? You are everything to me. But I certainly never expected marriage.'

'That's precisely why, *matka*, I want to give it to you. You have no expectations, which makes it wonderful to delight you. I do not know what the war will bring or what the future holds. But I want you to be sure of my love, and I want you to be safe. My family is a snakepit. The whole world must treat you and our children –' he felt for the child in my belly '– with the respect you deserve. We are, after all, two of a kind.' He smiled, nuzzling at my shoulder.

Later in the morning I woke up in his arms. The fire had burnt down and the pale sun was high in the sky. Peter breathed quietly and slept calmly, some of the hairs of his fine moustache fluttering as he breathed out. His smug expression reminded me of Daria's tomcat when it had drunk some cream, and I chuckled and tickled him. Peter woke and wrapped his arms around me.

'Do you know what you did last night?' I asked him softly.

He feigned surprise. 'No. What?'

'You proposed to me.' I grinned, hardly able to say those wondrous words.

He leant on one elbow, his eyes sparkling with mirth. 'Do you have any witnesses to this, Catherine Alexeyevna? No one will ever believe such nonsense, you know that, don't you?' *Catherine Alexeyevna*: it was the first time he'd called me by my new name. Peter's fingers slid over my swollen belly and between my thighs. 'I've often made love to Marta, but never to Catherine. I bet she's an utter vixen. I can't go into battle without finding out, can I?' he murmured.

The blood flowed faster through my veins and I felt myself going wet between my legs. 'Oh, no, Peter, I'm already much too heavy. Come and see me in two months, after the delivery,' I pleaded.

'Nonsense. We will find a way . . .'

He helped me onto my knees and his hands slid over my body, enjoying my full buttocks. I knelt naked, my swollen breasts lying on the rug, and my stomach stretched, yet stifled a scream of sudden pleasure when his tongue searched me from behind, hot and moist, finding my most tender spot with ease. 'Please,' I panted as he slowly began to lick me, spreading my legs further and pressing my hands to the ground. Peter tasted me with slow, sucking circles, and when I came with a short, joyous scream, he was already inside me, placing his hands ever so gently around my hips and stomach, feeling our child, as he searched and found his way.

When I left St Petersburg to give birth in Moscow, Peter gave me a long and loving letter and a sack of money to take with me, which Pavel Jagushinsky, master of the household, tucked into my sleigh at the very last minute.

'What is that?' I asked. Peter looked at me gloomily.

'Five thousand roubles, in case any Swede aims better than I hope they do. The money is for the child, Ekaterina and you, should I fall and not be able to keep the promise I gave you.'

'I do not want it. I want you to live,' I said, pushing the bag away from me.

'Good. That makes two of us,' Peter declared, forcing the sack back into my fingers. 'I, too, am in no hurry to appear before my maker.'

The Tsarevich Alexey met me in the first courtyard of the Kremlin. He kissed me on both cheeks and lovingly pressed my swollen fingers. 'Marta ... Your Grace. How was your journey?' His dark gaze checked my stomach. After the deaths of my sons, he had kindly sent one of his priests to console me – he had loved to play with his little brothers, whose godfather he had been – but Peter had forced the holy man to sing obscene songs before chasing him away, even throwing stones at him. Now, Alexey hopped nervously from one foot to the other as he spoke to me, his pale skin blotched with unsightly red patches.

'The Tsar writes me one angry letter after the other. Am I not doing a good job as Moscow's Governor? The city and the Kremlin are well fortified, in case the Swedes do make it here. Why is my noble father so very angry with me?' he asked.

'Do not worry too much,' I said, deciding to hide Peter's fury from him.

A good job as Governor? 'He does not know his arse from his elbow,' Peter would mumble, when he read the orders Alexey had given. 'Tons of building materials for the fortifications have been squandered, stolen and sold elsewhere. Has he sent the wagons I asked him for? Have the recruits been dispatched, as ordered? None of it. Oh, God. Why doesn't he just hand Charles the key to the city?' The harder Alexey tried, the more Peter found him wanting.

I leant heavily on the arm of Alexandra Tolstoya, Peter Andreyevich's sister, who had accompanied me on the journey as my new lady-in-waiting, trying to make it safely into the Kremlin across the slippery courtyard. Alexey padded around me like a young dog, coughing again and wheezing with excitement. 'Marta, tell me, did you put in a good word for me? Do you know what people at court say?'

I shook my head, biting my lip.

'If not for Marta, we'd suffer endlessly from the Tsar's whims.'

I took hold of Alexey's cold, red-raw hands: while I was wrapped in a thick sable coat, a matching hat and brightly embroidered gloves, he was dressed like a schoolboy in a simple dark knee-length Polish jacket and a crumpled and stained linen shirt. His hair fell to his shoulders, long and unkempt as a priest's, and his eyes had a feverish gloss. Did he not understand how risky his comments were?

'Yes, of course I put in a word for you, Alexey. Your father loves you dearly.' I crossed my fingers, now back inside the muff, so that God could forgive me this little white lie. The rift between father and son was already deep in those days; still, not I, not anyone, could ever have imagined what was to happen later. 'He will be so proud if you hold Moscow against the Swedes,' I added.

Alexey's German tutor Huyssen joined us then and reluctantly bowed his head to me, but I ignored him. In Huyssen's letters home, which Makarov of course had opened and read, the shrivelled old prune showed off about his work – making up half the subjects he said he taught the prince – and made fun of me, the washerwoman at the Tsar's side. Everything about me merited his scorn and apparently caused endless mirth in the German-speaking courts: my way of dressing, my style of make-up, the amount of jewellery I wore.

Alexey embraced me again, then immediately stepped back. 'I should not get too close to you. I have a bad cold and you are so close to delivery. I do not wish you to become ill before you give birth to my little sister.' He coughed again, this time into a handkerchief. When he raised his head, I spotted blood in the fine white cloth.

But I had no time to react to that as my last thought, just before my waters broke and the first, drawn-out pain of labour wracked my body, was: *Your sister, Alexey? Why ever not your little brother?*

Only hours later I held my beautiful, healthy daughter Anna Petrovna in my arms. The feeling of besotted love I had dreaded took me over almost instantly. How had I ever doubted I could feel that again? Fool that I was. She was too much of a miracle. Feofan Prokopovich sent me a copy of his book, *A First Doctrine of Youth*, which was full of ideas on how to educate a child. I had a few pages read to me, and at first laughed, before snorting in derision and flinging the book into the corner; such nonsense could only occur to a childless priest. Sheremetev offered me a beautiful pearl necklace: each smoky grey pearl was as big as a chickpea, and the locket's oval sapphire as large as a pigeon's egg. It was a surprisingly valuable gift: had he heard about the Tsar's secret promise to me?

As soon as I was strong enough and the *ottepel* was well past, I boarded a carriage together with Anna and two maids and headed for St Petersburg. I breastfed Anna on the journey and enjoyed my closeness to the little being, kissing and cuddling her at every possible moment. I was determined she would live and at every inn drank litres of the warm, almost black beer, so as to have enough milk for her. God willing, she'd soon have a brother.

41

But then fate struck again: we were busy with the preparations for Easter in St Petersburg when Peter returned from a trip to the Schlusselburg lying on a stretcher. His adviser Peter Shafirov, who had accompanied him on a visit to the planned Ladoga Canal and the oak forests there, which were to be cleared for the timber to build another fleet of ships, told me, ashen-faced: 'He suddenly felt faint and then stumbled and fell.' Even though Shafirov's grandparents had converted from Judaism to the Russian Orthodox faith, Peter called him 'my little Jew'. He now sat in the Privy Council, an unheard of rise in fortune for a member of the 'chosen race', as they called themselves. Shafirov's was an exceptional case, as Jews were the one people Peter did not generally welcome to his Empire, saying: 'I'd rather have Muslims and pagans in our midst than Jews. They are rogues and cheats. I want to eradicate evil, not to multiply it.'

On his stretcher Peter moaned with pain. I gave Shafirov my little Anna Petrovna to hold, which he did clumsily. I felt Peter's forehead, which seared my palm with fever. His eyelids fluttered and when I turned his hands in mine, I noticed red blotches on his skin. I chided Shafirov: 'That's what you get from all your wild feasting. Or has he been with a sick girl?' I dreaded the answer. Ships from Europe as well as traders from all over the East had brought many an unwelcome visitor to St Petersburg: new and fearsome diseases.

The whores did their utmost to spread them further and the courtiers were no better.

Shafirov avoided my eyes. I felt uneasy – was there something I ought to know about? There was no time for further questions: the physician Blumentrost immediately began to treat Peter with mercury pills, which was an atrocious business. The Tsar lay slack in my arms in his sick chamber whose thick drawn curtains dampened down the light and made the air stifling. The pills made him slobber with saliva like a dog and on his naked feet I spotted the same red sores as on his hands. Were these similar to the ulcers that had started to show on his loins? Rime covered my heart, yet I held his hands, instead of folding my fingers into prayer. I had seen these signs of illness many times in the streets of Moscow and St Petersburg, be it on princes or serfs. Spare us, I pleaded, as Peter was further weakened by each bleeding. Whatever his illness was, I wanted him healed and healthy. Two weeks later, he looked at me with a thin, sorry smile on his haggard face. 'Perhaps I can never keep my word, Catherine,' he whispered: 'My bloody, bloody word, as you call it. Maybe I will never be able to marry you properly.'

I knelt at his bedside and kissed his fingers. Tears welled in my eyes. 'Who cares? All I want is you here with me.' He nodded and tried to move towards me, but dropped back onto his pillows, faint and pale. I bit my lip: would he ever recover from this mystery illness?

I prayed for it, and my wish was granted: he recovered and rose from his bed, wearing his old green velvet dressing-gown and simple felt slippers, to look out of the window over St Petersburg, where thousands of forced labourers toiled like ants; eagerly, incessantly, giving shape to his dream. The plans for the Winter Palace were ready. As soon as he was strong enough, we visited the different building sites and met the German builders, the Italian sculptors, the French painters and Dutch carpenters whom Peter had lured to Russia in that spring with big promises and even bigger bags of gold. When all the snow had melted, a French expert in fountains and canals arrived, as Peter wanted to stage water games, like the ones he had heard happened at Versailles.

The number of forced labourers rose steadily. In any approach to the city they were visible like a dark river whose source was hidden somewhere on the horizon, where the sky met the earth, while its estuary was our city. Only at close range did the stream of humanity gain form and faces. Peter had them guarded ruthlessly, as labourers tried to flee at each stop along the way. Once captured, their leaders were executed and the rest of the group whipped. At a second attempt, their noses would be cut off. The sight of the many gaping holes in those gloomy, bony faces made me feel sick.

42

It was Shafirov who dared shake the Tsar from his sleep. Peter sat up with a jolt, which woke me as well. The milky summer night seeped into my mind, blending reality with the realm of dreams.

Peter held his head in both hands, eyes searching the room. 'What is it, Mother? The Streltsy soldiers?' He started twitching and kicking but Shafirov lunged forward and held him, dodging the Tsar's thrashing arms. 'It is I, my Tsar, Shafirov. I have news ...'

Peter's breathing calmed. 'Shafirov, you old Jew! Why are you sneaking through the palace at night? What is your news? Spit it out and then let me sleep as any honest man would.' He embraced me and I felt his tension.

'The Swedes ...' Shafirov began.

'Yes?' Peter's voice was alert. 'Where are they?'

Shafirov chuckled. 'The Swedes are moving south, as they should, marching directly into the scorched earth! Our Seventh Dragoons captured a food train and took thousands of prisoners. The Swedish general and six thousand of his men were able to flee, but several thousand carts of food and ammunition are ours.'

'So already they have nothing to eat and they are moving south?' Peter whispered, his eyes shining. 'They will die of hunger.'

He jumped out of bed, radiant with joy, embraced Shafirov and pulled him into a short, sharp dance, before kissing his cheeks and holding him at arm's length. 'Shafirov, my brother, this is the dawn of our new happiness.'

The men clapped each other's backs and chuckled, but in the dawn's dull light I felt their words crawl like a spiders over my skin.

'What do you think of her? She's a German princess: Charlotte Christine von Brunswick.'

'Quite a mouthful,' I said dryly.

'Is she pretty or not? Will she like Alexey? And, more importantly, will he like her?' Peter asked doubtfully, as he studied the portrait. It had been propped up close to the window and the morning light fell unforgivingly on the face of the young woman depicted. She wore a short, wavy and powdered wig, her cheeks glowed brightly, and she was unadorned with any jewellery. A heavy cloak of blue velvet and ermine covered her shoulders and half of her plain-cut dress of light yellow silk. One slender hand held a rose; she smiled with closed lips, but her round blue eyes looked at us blankly.

'She seems pleasant enough,' I said, for to me all these paintings looked the same. Was there a secret workshop somewhere, which made portraits of nubile princesses to order, following a pattern? 'Is it true that she suffered from smallpox as a child?'

'Who says that? Her skin looks as soft as Anna's bottom. And even if she did, good on her if she survived; scars cannot be passed on. She just has to powder herself more, that's all. But she is so thin! Will such skin and bone bear me a dozen healthy grandsons?' Peter wondered, before shrugging his shoulders. 'Her sister is married to the Crown Prince of Austria. With those relations, I can happily ignore a flat bosom and a bony bottom.'

'Good. It's not you who is supposed to touch that bosom and bottom anyway,' I said, but without any hint of jealousy. There is nothing like vinegar in a woman's voice to drive men away. Still, sometimes that strange night in the Summer Palace, as well as Peter's oath, seemed like a dream to me. Would he ever keep his promise? I'd rather slice my wrists than remind him of it. 'You heard that the Emperor in Vienna wishes to introduce the death penalty as punishment for adultery?' I teased him instead.

Peter laughed. 'My cousin on the Danube probably has more subjects than he thinks necessary. If I did that, I'd soon be without any Russians to rule.' He waved at Pavel Jagushinsky, who had been waiting patiently behind us. 'Take the painting to the Tsarevich's room, so he gets used to her face,' Peter said. 'She will be his wife. Until then he can go on mounting the thickest and ugliest chambermaids he can find, and drinking himself into a stupor every day. Marriage will be a kick in the pants for the useless sod.'

'Don't say that about your own son,' I scolded him, as Jagushinsky was listening. Peter shrugged. 'He can marry her and love elsewhere.'

'That is not what you do, I hope?' I asked, arching my eyebrows. He nuzzled my fingers.

'What other man is as lucky as I am, to be with the best of women?'

I smiled tenderly at him, already feeling pity for the slender young German princess. Alexey had been unhappy and restless ever since he couldn't prove himself against the Swedes. Perhaps he could appease Peter by fathering a strong son? I did not know what to believe any longer: the Tsarevich wrote me cordial and pleading letters, whilst at the same time I heard shocking stories about him that I refused to believe. True, he surrounded himself with flatterers, but wasn't that hard for any prince to avoid? Surely all that was said was malicious gossip, even if I had decided to talk to him about his drinking. It was fine to get into a stupor every night – only not if it rendered Alexey helpless and sick the next day. This was against Peter's rules: after every feast he was the first up and back at work, more eager than ever. Worst of all, Alexey was said to have bragged: 'When it happens, as it must, I'll put my father's friends and his washerwoman whore on the stake. Just you wait.' I kept the words – if indeed they were his – secret from Peter, as I feared for Alexey's safety if they were made known to his father.

Peter continued talking. 'But before I can think of grandchildren, I must marry off my nieces, the Tsaritsa Praskovia Saltykova's daughters.'

'Why?' I asked. Praskovia and her daughters lived outside Moscow in Ismailov Palace, where they had assembled an old-style court of loafers and jesters to whom she doled out her charity. When Peter and I visited, the courtiers fled in terror, hiding in the

Tsarevny Ivanovnas' chests and cupboards, as they knew just the sight of them made him angry.

'Those girls are pure politics. I want a foreign prince for each of them, in marriage. Alliances are the new way forward, Catherine. No one should live alone.' He leant in to me, burying his nose in my cleavage. 'Above all not me. You are my finest flesh, Catherine. I'm so glad to be back with you. I hate any time I have to leave you. Now my shirts are clean, my boots are polished and my stockings mended.' He purred like a cat while I played with the unruly little strands of hair on his neck, just above the collar. I relished the moment and we held each other close, until I heard feet shuffling: Pavel Jagushinsky had returned. With his deep-set eyes, strong cheekbones and sagging cheeks, he always reminded me of a sad old dog.

'My Tsar, Dr Blumentrost is here,' he said, and I was startled: was Peter's treatment not yet over? Was he still suffering from that same strange ailment that Blumentrost would not name, even though I badgered him about it at the same time as I feared his answer: was this Peter's reason for staying away from my bed? How should I give him a son if we never had a moment together or if he was ill? I scanned the Tsar's hands: the red blotches were still there, but had paled under the effects of the mercury ointment.

Peter pulled a face. 'Blumentrost may go to hell! But bring him in, Pavel. The quicker he starts, the sooner it's over and done with.' Then he held Jagushinsky back. 'Wait, wait, wait. What is this? Your cheek is swollen and I hadn't even noticed. Come here.' Jagushinsky did not dare to resist when Peter grabbed him by the hair and bent his head back: 'Open up, as far as possible. That's it.' He stared into Jagushinsky's mouth and wrinkled his nose. 'Your breath stinks like a donkey's arse. How does your wife bear your kisses? Or do you mount her when she is too drunk to notice? Never mind, I shall soon sort you out.'

He dragged the stumbling man over to the window and did not let go of him while he rummaged in the top drawer of a little desk, looking for a bulging bag and a long, thin pair of pliers. Jagushinsky gurgled, begging in vain for mercy. 'Open your mouth again ...'

Peter grabbed the tooth he thought to be the culprit with the pliers, and gave a good twist and an even better jerk. Pavel Jagushinsky spat out a stream of blood. Peter laughed, let go of him and proudly held the tooth to the light, turning it this way and that. 'Splendid. Into the bag with it.' Pavel's tooth fell into the little sack already filled with teeth: it bulged more than a miser's purse. When Peter and his friends roamed the streets, taverns and brothels of the city, both the bag and the pliers were always hanging from his belt. If he spotted a swollen cheek anywhere, he'd set to work. Pavel Jagushinsky held on to a chair, lest he collapse, but Peter stamped his foot impatiently. 'What are you waiting for, Jagushinsky? Let Blumentrost in.'

The physician pressed past me with muttered greetings. Peter opened his arms to him. 'Finally you come! I have ulcers all over my arse, my cock seeps pus and pissing burns like hell. What am I paying you for, man? Your cures simply do not help, and Russia needs many heirs. Will I ever be healthy again?' Before I could hear Blumentrost's reply, the door closed behind him. I wished I could press my ear against the timber door – I had to be able to tame my mounting fears – but Jagushinsky lingered in the corridor. He was bent double with pain, crying like a child that had hurt its knee. I gently placed my hand on his face. 'Ask my *damy* to send for my Cherkessk maid Jakovlena from the kitchen. She has many secret recipes and will surely mix you a soothing paste.'

'Yes, Your Grace,' he answered, but still lingered.

'What is it?' I asked. Something weighed on him. He cleared his throat and spoke.

'The Tsar has assigned a new chambermaid to your household.'

'Has he now. What is her name?' I made my voice sound even.

'The Tsar calls her Boi-Baba. She already has a couple of children and ...'

'And let me guess – she's pregnant again, isn't she? Do I happen to know the father of this child?' I tried hard not to sound shrewish.

Jagushinsky blushed with the shame Peter would not feel. I sighed. 'Leave it to me, I'll take care of her. It's not the first time this has happened, is it?'

He darted away, only too glad to obey me.

I took Boi-Baba in. She wore her thick dark red hair in a single braid and had so many freckles, you hardly saw her skin. Her wide mouth was always ready to smile, showing strong, healthy teeth. I scanned her waist, but her body was as vast and soft as a cushion, so her pregnancy wouldn't show. She gladly followed my orders and fulfilled her tasks without complaint.

I congratulated Peter laughingly on the strength of his loins, and he smiled, flattered, and bobbed his head; after several bottles of wine and beer he was in an indulgent mood. Before he fell asleep in my arms, he murmured, 'Whatever I do, old girl, my best belongs to you.' He dug his face into my hair like a sow in straw. Only a breath later, he was snoring heavily. I carefully slid away from under him and stared up at the dark ceiling.

What if this girl Boi-Baba meant something to him, and what if she gave birth to a healthy boy? I had not yet fallen pregnant again, and only little Anna Petrovna lived of my many children. I could not suppress my sobs, the pain ran too deep. Iron chains were tightening themselves around my heart and I wept and wept, my body heaving. Only after a long while did I, too, fall into a deep, exhausted sleep.

43

In winter, the Neva clenched its icy fist around St Petersburg. Our city froze into a single, glittering crystal, and on a sunny day, all life there was caught in a shiny, frosty bubble. Waves froze mid-tide, ships lay enclosed like the skeletons of huge, mysterious sea creatures, and skaters or sledges drew patterns on the uneven surface of the ice, pearly against the dense blue sky. On the other hand, it was now much easier to get from one place to another: as Peter still refused to build a bridge over the Neva, each noble family had to maintain boats and barges. In the summer there were public ferrymen as well, but only the poorest went for free. Russians of standing had to pay one kopek for the crossing, each way. Perhaps that was why St Petersburg grew much more slowly than Peter had hoped: work suffered from both the turmoil of the war as well as the silent, sullen resistance that both nature and man put up to his orders.

In the spring, during the *ottepel*, the ice floes broke with deafening roars and shocking force, tearing us from the sleep that the still-dark nights encouraged. The river flooded the paths and washed away the foundations of the new buildings, while the thaw cut us off from the rest of the country. The east wind could blow so violently that the Neva flowed back into the Bay of Finland, its waters swelling, rising and crashing down in a storm wave on the freshly laid out fortifications and quays of the young city. The city seemed like a boat lost at sea, ready to be swallowed in the maelstrom of Peter's dreams and desires.

But if the buildings scattered along the banks looked like oysters devoid of pearls, the cathedral of the Holy Trinity was almost finished next to the imposing Fortress of Peter and Paul with its bastions and church, while the former market of Nyenschantz with its motley assembly of shops and stalls had moved into a *gostiny dvor*. On Peter's orders, to satisfy the foreign sailors, a Lutheran church and guesthouse were built, even if no vessel was allowed into the harbour unless it carried a load of at least thirty blocks of stone and a ton of earth – a levy which made construction possible. Nowhere else in Russia was anyone allowed to build in stone, yet to move the masses of materials needed to our marshy lands was a horrible task. The building sites lacked everything: the forced labourers shovelled the soggy clay soil with their bare hands into aprons or shirts, because they had no proper buckets with which to carry the mud and brackish slush.

Despite the setbacks, Peter and I would hold on to each other, shaking with laughter, when we saw people wading up to their knees in water, carrying their belongings on their back or paddling on whatever they'd found, be it a door or an upside-down table. After every flood, Peter himself marked the high point of the receding water on the stone walls of the Peter and Paul Fortress, and then had barrels of beer and bottles of vodka cracked open: his city was still standing! Soon the stench of mould would hang over the streets and prospects, but before it even appeared Peter ordered both the forced labourers as well as the hired foreign artisans back to work. Rasia Menshikova's husband, Antonio Devier, the head of Peter's secret police, intercepted a letter written by the French Ambassador, Campredon. It was destined for Versailles and made Peter foam with rage: *'This city is built on bones. St Petersburg is no better than a rotting corpse.'*

'A corpse?' First he hit Campredon with the *dubina*, his ever-ready knout, tearing the French Ambassador's fancy new coat and making his cheek bleed. Then he crumpled up the letter and stamped on it in front of the whole court. 'You French fool! Building a city is like waging war. Neither can be done successfully without sacrificing human life.' He lashed out again at the Frenchman, who dared neither duck nor defend himself. I tried to calm Peter down with the help of Jagushinsky and Menshikov, but the Tsar drew his sword and injured both of them, cutting their cheeks and ears.

Campredon fled, holding his bleeding cheek and sobbing. 'It took me twenty-four days to move here on these godforsaken roads! I have paid twelve hundred roubles from my own pocket. Eight of my horses have died, and half of my luggage has disappeared without trace. And now this. *Mon Dieu*, what have I done to deserve this?'

'Keep your anger and your thoughts for the pages of your diary, Monsieur Campredon, where they are safe from discovery and betrayal,' I said dryly. He stared at me like a pig that had found truffles in his home country's forests. His hand patted a breast pocket, where he kept his secret little book. Was he truly surprised I knew of its existence? Surely he realised that Peter's police kept close watch on any strangers residing in Russia.

'Madame.' The ambassador bowed to me. 'My deepest respects.'

Peter found a kindred soul in the Italian architect Domenico Trezzini. Even if I did not like the tall man with his arrogant expression, aquiline nose and dark curly hair arranged so as to tumble over his shoulders, at least he did not complain about life in St Petersburg, like other craftsmen did. When we visited the building sites, there was nothing but moaning from them.

'How can I live and work in this dump? My mind needs space and beauty,' said the German painter.

'The food is disgusting. I would not expect my sows to eat that,' cried the French landscape designer.

'My delivery of marble and tools is still blocked by customs in the port: how shall I work without chisels and stone?' asked the Italian sculptor.

'My workers are nothing but clumsy fools. They can't tell their arses from their elbows,' sneered the Dutchman, who was to build the bridges over the Fontanka and Moika canals.

In the coming years, Trezzini dreamt and built restlessly, beginning with St Isaac's Church, the palaces for the ministers, the fortifications of Kronstadt, the St Alexander Nevsky monastery, the Senate, as well as simpler things such as plans for quays and a number of wooden bridges across the canals. When his tenure ended, other masters stepped in: the proud Alexander Le Blond of France, the quarrelsome German Schädel and Harebel from a town called Basel, who hated caviar with a vengeance – 'Such slippery, glibbery stuff!' he said – and instead wanted to dunk bread in molten cheese whenever things got festive! Well, each to their own.

When Peter ordered the first few hundred Moscow noble families to move to St Petersburg, any excuse was futile, and neither age nor serious illness was allowed to delay the move: old Prince Cherkassy, the richest man in Russia, begged for some leeway as his legs were swollen with gout. Peter's guards dragged the venerable man by his hair out of his palace near the Kremlin and placed him stark naked on the ice of the Moskva, mocking him and laughing. His staff started packing up with utmost haste. When a fire destroyed a large part of Moscow, Peter was overjoyed: the burnt houses were to stay rubble and ashes; if the homeless needed a place to stay, they were welcome in St Petersburg.

During a festive dinner I overheard Sheremetev say to Peter Shafirov, 'Do you know what Neva means in Finnish?'

He shook his head, and Sheremetev answered, 'It means dirt.'

44

On a clear morning in early November the guards declared the Neva's ice safe to bear the weight of sleighs and skaters. The sky was palest blue, the outline of the Peter and Paul Fortress looking sharp and almost unreal against it. Trees on the riverbanks were heavy with silvery rime. Every freezing breath was an assault on lungs and brain.

Eight steeds were tethered to the sleigh in which I sat together with Alexandra Tolstoya and Daria, who was pregnant once more. It was adorned with flags, bunting and silk banners in all the colours of the rainbow. The animals' breath steamed from their nostrils as they chewed on their bridles. Peter stood straight on a small, simple sled, his legs set wide to maintain his balance, holding the reins tight in his restless hands. Behind him, the whole court awaited his orders, their own colourful vehicles pulled by horses, deer, pigs, dogs, dwarves or souls.

'Are you ready?' the Tsar yelled.

'Yes!' a whole excited chorus of voices echoed across the ice and my pulse quickened. Peter raised his arm, face beaming with excitement, and we held our breath and strained our ears until a cannon shot from the Peter and Paul Fortress tore through the crisp air. Peter's arm fell and he lashed his horses. 'Come on, then. The Neva is open to traffic,' he cried, and the wind swept the words from his mouth, making away with them.

'Come on!' I drove my horses on with a short crop; Daria and Alexandra cheered and waved colourful handkerchiefs while our sleigh shot after Peter, and all the others followed us onto the virgin ice.

I slowed down and held my breath as Peter approached the other bank. What would he say when he saw what I'd had made for him? He stopped his sled with a sudden jerk and stared in silence at the glittering building, rising like a dream before his eyes: walls, towers and battlements glistened, all made of ice and sparkling like a fairy-tale castle. It had taken workmen an entire night to chisel the pavilion from giant ice blocks: its roofs, domes and spires sparkled like shards of blue glass in the sun, and to right and left of the entrance to the snow palace stood Peter's Moors. The oiled black skin of their bare chests was a splendid sight against the purity of the palace, as were their silk pantaloons and boots cut from blue and red leather. I caught up with Peter and he turned to face me, slowly, his eyes moist and full of wonder and disbelief. It touched me deeply: he looked like a child at its first Easter. I smiled at him tenderly when he whispered, 'Did you do this?'

I blew him a kiss. 'Yes. It's a palace fit for the King of Snow and Ice, my Tsar. A gift from your most faithful, loving servant.'

He helped me from my sleigh. I carefully set down my feet on the slippery surface as Peter led me inside the Ice Palace, his face shining with joy. 'It is wondrous!' he said, his eyes taking it all in, his mouth open wide. Between pillars of ice stood two thrones made of packed snow, which were covered with leopard skins. Behind them, a red velvet flag embroidered with a golden Russian double-headed eagle was draped from the ceiling to the floor, several metres in all. Flames danced in a fireplace made of ice, so that our backs were warm and cosy, though the rest of the guests froze their buttocks firmly to their seats. Peter and I giggled so much, we almost fell from our thrones; but whoever got up without permission was ordered to drink a potent mix of champagne and brandy as punishment. The musicians had to move their hands all the time, otherwise their fingertips would have frozen to the instruments. Peter made them play a minuet to which our dwarves danced, slithering on the ice with their short, bulky limbs, and tumbling over each other.

I laughed so much that the inside of my stomach turned sour and I had to be brought to bed with a colic.

45

Despite the merry Yuletide, the difficult time for Russia was not yet over, even if the Swedes were starving and scorched earth killed them like flies. When I visited Sheremetev in his new St Petersburg house, he did not hold back any of his fears and reservations.

'For the New Year I wish you health and all the happiness in the world,' I said, and tried to kiss his hand, but he hastily withdrew his fingers.

'You should not do that anymore. I certainly do not wish to be seen having my hand kissed by you – Your Grace.'

It was the first time he had called me that, but I hid my surprise and linked elbows with him before settling in front of his fireplace. As always, I enjoyed being close to this man. I felt I had so much to thank him for. If he had ever hoped that we might be more than friends and comrades-in-arms, he never let on. The palatial house was still almost empty, bar a few well-chosen pieces of furniture. In the reception room, the walls were bare except for a life-sized portrait of the Tsar hanging above the mantelpiece. The servants had probably just got the fire going as I felt the chill and wrapped myself tighter in my cloak of dark red velvet and blond mink furs. A servant brought us steaming mulled wine and a tray full of crisp, freshly baked *blinchiki* stuffed with fat salmon and sour cream.

'Mmm, they're delicious,' I said, nibbling on a pastry and eyeing the next. 'Better than the food in your house usually is,' I teased him. 'Did you get a new cook?'

Sheremetev blushed. 'No, nothing of that sort,' he said. Why did my question embarrass him? I wondered, but changed the subject.

'How long will you stay in the city? Has the Tsar issued a new marching order?' I had not seen Peter for several nights. He consulted his generals and advisers ceaselessly, and afterwards his men still had to drink and make merry with him, to make him forget his troubles. Come the early-morning hours he'd be carried to his frigate that lay frozen in the water, where he'd sleep, cloaked in loneliness, in a narrow bunk.

Sheremetev weighed his answer. 'How long can we keep the Swedes at arm's length? The last open battle was several years ago now and Charles has itchy feet. Do you know how close he is to Moscow, despite scorched earth? Only twelve hundred *versty*. Never before has an enemy been so close to the city walls. There must be a battle this summer. A big, decisive battle, which will force either country to its knees for all eternity.' He looked warily into the flames. 'Who knows? By next year, we might all be Swedes.'

'Don't say that, Boris Petrovich. That is high treason,' I said, and took one of his rough, callused hands in mine. 'Promise me that you will not leave the Tsar, but will stay by his side, whatever happens. He always plunges himself into the thick of things, you know that.'

Sheremetev pressed my fingers. 'That's true. Yet if he didn't do that, he would not be our *batjuschka* Tsar. But you know that I'd gladly take any bullet that is aimed at him.'

Just then a door flew open and a small dog, covered with snow, scampered into the room, somersaulted towards Sheremetev and snapped at the general's ankles. A young girl chased after the lapdog, picked it up, kissed its head and then buried her pretty, glowing face in its fur. 'He's so naughty, Bobushka,' she said in German-sounding Russian. 'In town he went for the ladies' heels and the men's boots. Please make sure that your next gift to me is better behaved.' She spotted me and fell silent, while Sheremetev blushed deeply: who else in the world called this successful, hardy soldier Bobushka? I was happy to see his little secret, though, whoever this girl was.

'*You* should be better behaved, Alice. Curtsey, please. This is Marta, the faithful, generous and warm-hearted companion of our Tsar,' Sheremetev scolded her, but winked at the same time.

She curtseyed gracefully to me, the wide skirt of her simple blue wool dress opening like a flower's petals, and eyed me from beneath her very long, very dense lashes. Her ash-blonde hair was loosely braided in a crown across her head and freckles sprinkled her tiny nose. In stunning contrast to her fairness, the eyebrows and eyelashes framing her amazingly bright, blue eyes were almost black.

'I am Alice Kramer, Your Grace,' she muttered. How old was she? Fourteen or fifteen years old perhaps, certainly no older, I thought with a pang of jealousy. Her body seemed as slim and supple as the branch of a strong, young beech.

'I found Alice, lost and hungry and hiding in the smouldering ruins of a burnt-out city in the Baltics. Back then she was still a little girl, but now she's always with me. Have you not seen her before?' Sheremetev asked me.

Now it was Alice's turn to blush. I knew the terror she must have felt: hiding in burnt-out ruins, fearing discovery at any minute. And finally, most probably, changing hands between men as a gift. How alike our destinies were, yet how different. No, I had not seen her before, ever, and glanced at Sheremetev curiously: how well do we really know our friends?

'Does the Tsar know her?' I asked casually toying with my glass.

'Of course.' Boris Petrovich looked into the flames, his face expressionless.

'Of course,' I said gently. Peter knew every pretty face in town. I tried to imagine this slight girl in the Tsar's arms, but felt no anger. How could she, or anyone, refuse him?

Alice curtseyed again. 'Your Grace, allow me to retreat,' she said, and I held out my hand for her to kiss. When she had left and we had settled once more, Sheremetev held my hand without looking at me. He said almost inaudibly, 'We are on the verge of a great battle. But for the first time in my life, I am afraid to die. For the first time in my life, I really want to live.'

'My friend,' I whispered, tears welling in my eyes, 'take heart. Love is a reason to live. Actually, there is none better.'

*

Before it came to an open battle, Peter's old friend and devoted subject, the Russian winter, weakened the Swedes further. As predicted, Charles fled with his troops into a little-cultivated area, where his men either collapsed dead from their exertions or else dragged themselves on, famished and frozen. They had eaten their horses long since and carried the saddles on their shoulders, sucking and chewing the leather straps. Their hands were covered in chilblains and poorly wrapped in rags. There was no means of numbing the pain of the sick and wounded, if they received any treatment at all; frost-bitten limbs were amputated from fully conscious men. At night Cossacks crept out of the thickets from which they had watched the enemy, harrying them under cover of darkness, just as wild animals might. They tiptoed through the deserted villages, knowing every corner, and sliced the sleeping Swedes' throats. The wolves grew fat that winter.

An Ambassador from the Cossack Ataman laughed during a meal we shared in St Petersburg and told us, 'The Swedes hope for only three things: brandy, garlic or death.' He gargled and spat vodka to warm his throat for further feasting.

'What does Charles want to do?' Peter asked

'The Swede will go to Poltava. He is foolish or desperate enough to think that if he seizes that, he might well seize Moscow. As if there was a training ground for the prize of prizes.' The wiry little Cossack wiped his mouth with the back of his hand and smacked his lips for more. Peter grabbed the fattest chicken he could find on the table, sniffed at it, tore a thigh off and plunked the rest on the Cossack's plate. 'Eat, brother. The best food my table has to offer, just for you. Open another barrel of vodka! Are we celebrating, or are we celebrating? Poltava, eh? Well, then, it will be in Poltava that we meet. Charles shall eat gravel, earth and horse-shit, take my word for it.'

The Cossack shrieked with contentment, shrill and piercing like a war cry. The sound gave me goose-bumps. He tore apart the chicken, which was dripping with grease and sauce, and buried his face in it.

I raised my glass to him, inwardly full of fear: Poltava it was.

46

In April, when the first flowers blossomed on the dewy green of the meadows, the surviving Swedes camped outside Poltava's city walls. A stray bullet winged King Charles in the foot during the siege. Nevertheless, he continued forcing his men on in insane anger, rendering impossible their hopes of any return to normal life. Peter's regiments intercepted a bag of letters sent by Swedes: *'We are desperate and the king closes his ears to even the best advice. He thinks only of one thing: war, war and war once more.' 'Nothing matters to him, not even victory.'* Peter waited for the right moment, knowing the power of patience. With Russia at his back, he was stronger than ever.

'No. Do you think I'll sit and embroider clothes in front of the fireplace in Kiev when you are out in the field? Of course I'll come with you.' I placed my hands on my hips. 'No one will stop me from doing my duty; and my duty is to follow you, wherever you go. Especially now – just look at yourself!'

Peter glowered at me: it was shortly after Easter and we had travelled to Azov on the shores of the Black Sea, to oversee the building of his new fleet. While the air was filled with the scalding heat of the tar that sealed the timber, the shrill singing of the saws and the steady, dull beating of hammers on countless anvils, Peter was bedridden once more after a first walk on the docks: all the strength had simply seeped out of him, his eyes were bloodshot and his face ashen. The cure

Blumentrost still gave him did not help; the illness returned when least expected. Peter sweated acid, peed pus and faltered in my arms. He suffered, but so did I. I found myself battling a faceless enemy. Would my worst fears be confirmed? What did the illness mean for the child carried? I was pregnant once more. Peter reeked of putrefaction and sweat, although every day I washed his whole body with tepid water. Still, Blumentrost refused to discuss the disease with me.

Now Peter closed his eyes, tired of our discussion. 'Damn stubborn woman! Can't you ever let go? And what if I order you to stay away from the battlefield?'

I gently pushed him back onto his bedstead. 'I will not be on the battlefield, silly. I shall pray for you back in the camp. And I shall be the first to congratulate you upon your victory. Please, don't make me stay in Kiev. You *need* me. I am your lucky charm.'

His waxy fingers searched for mine. 'All right, for God's sake. But I do not want to hear any complaints.' He sighed.

'Have you ever heard me complain?' I asked, kissing his fingers. When he smiled, his lips pulled back from the gums, like a corpse's. I forced the dread I felt back into a dark corner of my heart, like a wild animal that needed taming. Surely this was a terrible omen for the all-decisive battle?

'No,' Peter murmured, and I held his hand until he fell into a light slumber. The air in the room was stifling: despite the sticky weather he would insist that the fortress be heated, as he always felt cold. But just when I rose to open the window, I heard a sound behind me and spun around: Peter's principal physician Blumentrost rose from the sofa next to the fireplace. Had he been sleeping there? He looked like a ragged old bird, his frizzy hair pointing in all directions and his silk neckerchief and waistcoat awry.

'Your Grace,' he said, straightening his round glasses and bowing.

'Blumentrost – when will the Tsar be well enough to get back on his horse? Poltava is waiting,' I said cheerfully while remaining inwardly determined not to let this man depart without telling me what was going on.

He ever so slightly shook his head. My smile froze and I cleared my throat. 'What's happening? Share the bad news, Blumentrost. It makes it easier to bear.'

The doctor chewed on the long ends of his moustache. 'I don't know what to say to you. Please.' He pointed to the chair next to the sofa, as if I were the guest here and not him. Still, I sat down. The heat from the flames made my skin tingle. Gamely I folded my hands and waited.

'His Majesty is very, very ill. He suffers from –' Blumentrost seemed to search for words.

'From what?' I held my breath: finally, an answer! And surely not the one I feared most. No, the Tsar was to be spared, as he always had been so far. He was no ordinary man. Soon enough, he would be healthy and so would our child. I'd give Peter what he wanted most in this world: many, many more sons.

'He is suffering from a venereal disease.' Blumentrost nervously flexed his fingers; I heard the bones crack.

'A venereal disease?' I repeated the words, lengthening them. 'Blumentrost, I am a peasant girl and speak neither Latin nor Greek,' I snapped, feeling fear rise in me nevertheless. I had known all along, but had refused to acknowledge the truth. By not naming the monster, I'd hoped to prevent it from raising its ugly head.

He sighed. 'All right then. If I must spell it out: the Tsar has syphilis. I'm trying to treat him to the best of my knowledge, but there's no cure.'

'Syphilis.' I sat rigid, unable to move. *It won't happen to me*, Peter had always reassured me when I'd dared to mention other cases in court circles, as though for entertainment's sake. A direct warning would not have been tolerated. But had he not seen his own court-iers suffering from the French Disease, their skin covered by ulcers, feverish madness clouding their minds before they died like dogs? He had and had not, always believing himself to be beyond its reach. Fear swallowed me, holding me captive as surely as the dark cells in the Trubetzkoi Bastion.

'Should we not have known earlier?' I asked.

'We did,' the physician said sheepishly. 'I was not allowed to speak of it to you.'

'How did the disease made itself known in the Tsar?'

'Well, to start with, a burning feeling when urinating, blood in the excrement, pus in the –'

I raised my hand, stopping him short. 'Has Peter caught the illness from me? Am I to blame?'

'No, Your Grace. When I examined you after the last birth, you were perfectly healthy. You are as strong as a horse, it's a miracle. No. The Tsar has caught the illness from a certain Boi-Baba.'

'Boi-Baba? But she is one of my maids and pregnant with the Tsar's child.'

'Not anymore. The Tsar had her whipped after the delivery of a daughter, before banning them both to Siberia.'

'He had her whipped?' I asked in disbelief, feeling faint. 'After giving birth?'

'Yes. As punishment for having given him the illness. Her husband and her other seven children, too, have been exiled to Siberia.'

This had happened in my court, right under my nose. I read sadness and pity in Blumentrost's eyes.

I straightened my back. 'Can the Tsar be treated with a different cure? Surely there must be something other than mercury you could try? A new discovery, possibly?'

The physician shrugged. 'There is no cure. One can only slow the course of the disease, no more. It is in God's hands. As for yet unconceived children –'

'Yes?' I asked, my voice hoarse. He avoided my gaze.

'If Your Grace falls pregnant at all, and if there is no miscarriage in the early stages or a stillbirth, it would be miraculous if any surviving children were strong and viable. But we ought to believe in miracles, oughtn't we?' he added quickly.

I felt myself drifting deep under icy winter water and drowning: the surface above me lured me to light and life, but I was doomed, incapable of ever getting there. I saw sorrow and compassion in Blumentrost's eyes, which made his words even more unbearable. I leapt to my feet and rushed to the window, tearing it open. The spring air flooded my lungs and the blue sky arched far above the dark Sea of Azov. Yet on the horizon, storm clouds gathered and smaller boats took down their sails so as not to have them shredded by the wind. The seagulls surfed in the strong easterly, piercing the air with their shrieks, mocking me with their beady eyes.

I skimmed my belly with my hands: Blumentrost did not yet know that I was pregnant again, for the sixth time. I closed my eyes and cooled my feverish forehead on the glass pane, clenching my fists: I would give the Tsar a healthy son. This was perhaps my last chance to do so.

'Yes, Blumentrost,' I said, turning to him, smiling and gathering my dignity. 'One should never cease to believe in miracles.'

'Your Grace –' he began to say. I merely raised my hand and wiped a tear from my cheek. He bowed and retreated; I heard the door being gently pulled shut. Good. No one should ever again see tears running down my face.

47

The truth about the Battle of Poltava is simpler and sadder, but also much more glorious and grander, than any of the folklore surrounding it.

I stood in the entrance to our tent on that morning in June 1709 and watched as Peter mounted his Arabian steed Finette, a gift from the Scotsman James Bruce. Clouds hung stubbornly and potbellied in the sky; not even the wind that bent the tree-tops could drive them away. Menshikov held the Tsar's stirrups and then kissed Peter's hand; the Tsar embraced Alexander Danilovich in turn. I saw them whisper: 'For God and for Russia, today!'

When Peter straightened and raised his arm, all of the Tsar's generals as well as forty thousand soldiers knelt like a single body. His silent gaze scanned the sea of faithful men; a gust of wind caught the red feathers of his hat before the breeze settled in the folds of his mantle, just when the cloud tore open and a single ray of sunshine touched the Tsar's head. I held my breath: God had blessed him. A stunned, reverent murmur rose from the rows of kneeling men, many of whom made the Sign of the Cross.

Finette pranced and Peter drew breath. Only I knew that he had sat together with Feofan Prokopovich until late last night, writing this speech, polishing every word, until it was shiny and perfect.

'God in Heaven,' Peter cried, the wind carrying his words to the very last of his men. The hairs on my neck rose and my skin prickled as I felt destiny close in.

'The fate of Mother Russia is in your hands: doom or glory – men! You decide whether our country shall be free forever, or forever enslaved by the Swedish devil. Today, you're not taking up arms for me. Neither my vanity nor my quest for personal glory send you into battle. No. God in His grace has entrusted Russia to me, Peter Alexeyevich Romanov. But a decisive moment has come, and that decision rests in your hands, not mine.'

Peter steadied Finette for a moment before his voice echoed over the battlefield once more. 'Do not be fooled or scared witless. The Swedish soldiers have no miraculous powers. Their hearts beat, their blood flows, their bodies die. Everything else is a lie and there is only one truth: God is with Russia. And if I know only one thing for sure, it is this.' He stopped short, and forty thousand pairs of eyes sought out him alone. 'I shall give every drop of my blood for the greatness, the glory and the fear of God of All the Russias!'

Finette reared, the wide eyes in her delicate head rolling, and Peter spurred her on. He raced ahead, crouching in the saddle, galloping past his men, who crossed themselves with three fingers. A hoarse cry rose to the sullen sky, and the mass of people as well as the wide horizon swallowed up Peter's retreating figure; a vision in a flowing red cloak, sparks flying from Finette's pounding hooves. I knew that if he was to fall today, I had witnessed his finest hour.

The Generals Sheremetev, Ronne, Menshikov and Bruce followed suit and their troops fell into formation, taking up their positions against the Swedes. Only Peter, or so I later heard, was everywhere at the same time, hounding Finette across the battlefield, shouting orders, encouragement and insults into the foaming mass of fighting men. The Tsar was to be seen always, and everywhere: I am sure that only my prayers led the three bullets intended for him astray. One tore the felt of his hat; the second dug itself deep into Peter's pectoral cross made of solid gold, rubies and emeralds, a gift from the monks of Mount Athos, and the third bullet stuck in his saddle's wooden frame. Peter himself was unharmed, as if by a miracle.

I know nothing of the battle itself, as when the first wounded soldiers were brought into the camp, I was kept too busy with tending to wounds, ladling out dulling vodka to deal with the horror, or holding hands and drying tears of sorrow. Only once I had the

Tsar's letter, which he had hastily sent to me, read aloud, did I understand: '*Catherine Alexeyevna:* matka! *God, in His grace, has given us the victory over the King of the Swedes. We have kicked the enemy into the dust; all I want now are your kisses to congratulate me. Come immediately! In the camp, 28 June 1709, Peter Alexeyevich Romanov.*'

I wept and downed a goblet of Hungarian wine, offering one to the messenger as well, before I neatened my plaits, washed the blood, pus and sweat from my hands and face, took off my dirty apron, slipped into my boots and had my horse saddled.

My mount flew over the plains in the amber light of the afternoon and I felt the child in my body stirring, strong and healthy. My son, too, was celebrating this victory of his father: *Yes, you should always believe in miracles, Blumentrost.* I laughed into the wind and spurred my horse on further.

I shall never forget my horror at first sight of the battlefield of Poltava. The plains outside the fortress walls were covered with corpses or the maimed remains of what had once been human beings. Vultures already circled in the sky and crows cowered in the trees, waiting patiently for their turn. Wild dogs dragged body parts away, fighting over limbs. I slowed my mare, afraid to trample any still-living, but wounded soldiers. Bloodstained hands reached out to me and men begged for a kind word or pleaded for a sip of water, a doctor, a last sight of their beloved or their mother.

One man managed to get hold of my skirt; he lay on his stomach and his breath was heavy and strangled. 'Please, milady. Water,' he whispered, and I got off my horse. The sight of his wounds was so sickening that I had to fight down the bile in my throat before searching for the water in my saddlebags. When I turned to him again, the man had died.

A bitter cloud of gun smoke gathered sluggishly over the windless plain, soaking up the sweet, sickening battlefield smells like a sponge. I wrapped my braids over my mouth and nose so as not to breathe in the odour of death a thousandfold. My eyes were fixed on the way ahead lest I would either weep or be well and truly sick. Peter, at this moment of his greatest victory, should find me nothing but beautiful, proud and radiant: his greatest prize.

The Swedish soldiers who lay nearest to my path, bloodied, starved and dying, looked to be no better than skeletons. Scorched earth and the two Russian winters had finished their gruesome work, I thought, choking on tears: I knew that Peter had done what a Tsar had to do to save Russia. Still, nearly seven thousand of Charles's men had fallen that day, and three thousand more went into Russian captivity. Ten thousand men for whom, somewhere, a woman such as I waited and mourned; a daughter like mine, or a son like Alexey, were orphaned; never to know what had happened, never to receive word again. Still, at least for those prisoners the war was over, as opposed to their comrades who had fled alongside King Charles, the haunted man whom God had punished them with as a ruler. The horse carrying the wounded king had been shot dead underneath him, but he had succeeded in getting away unscathed.

I spotted Peter from far away, standing tall and proud outside Poltava's walls, surrounded by his generals. A mass of prisoners knelt around him, their faces empty and exhausted, with gazes dull as animals'. There were soldiers as well the retinue of the Swedish King: servants, musicians, scribes, cooks, doctors, priests and pharmacists. Captured Swedish flags were stuck crookedly in the ground, their proud blue and gold cloth hanging dirty and torn in the slowly settling dusk.

Peter spotted me and waved, excited as a child: his hair was dishevelled, his mantle torn, and the blue sash around his chest, with the diamond-adorned Order of St Andrew still attached to it, sullied by blood and smoke. His face, too, was blackened by soot and mud, but his blue eyes beamed with pride and joy as he embraced me, before pulling me over to the Swedish troops.

'Come, and look at this, *matka*. What a haul of prisoners, eh? A marshal, ten general majors, fifty-nine senior officers and eleven hundred juniors. And to top it all off, the king's chief adviser, Minister Piper himself.' He seized a small, bald man by the scruff of the neck and forced him to his feet. Minister Piper barely came to Peter's elbow. He kept his eyes squeezed shut and trembled with the fear of imminent death. 'Well, Piper, we'll find something to do for a smart man like you. Many streets have to be paved in St Petersburg, don't they, Catherinushka? Or shall we send him to the mines in Siberia?' Peter kissed me and I tasted leather, sweat and gunpowder. The Swedish officers averted their eyes; they themselves had been separated for so many years from their families and loved ones, but Peter cried, 'Look, you damn Swedes. This is the kind of woman who will bring victory to a man.'

Then his gaze fell on the Swedish marshal who knelt among all the others. Peter frowned. 'Are you Marshal Rehnskjöld?'

The man understood only his name. He nodded, seeming hesitant and confused.

'Get up,' Peter shouted at him. 'On your feet, Swedish swine!'

The Swede looked confused as he stumbled to his feet. Silence fell. All eyes turned towards the Tsar and the Swedish marshal, who had fooled Peter for so many years and made him suffer throughout the drawn-out campaign, defeating his army left, right and centre. Sheremetev and Bruce exchanged a worried glance and I folded my hands in silent prayer. Please, God, let Peter not sully his glory, his joy and his victory through a vile, capricious crime. The battle was over; killing Rehnskjöld now would be heinous murder. The marshal met Peter's eyes calmly.

'Now kneel again,' the Tsar snarled.

Goose-bumps formed on my arms as Rehnskjöld obeyed, disdain on his face. He was ready to meet his maker, having always fulfilled his duty, however high the price he had to pay.

I dared not breathe: even the wind had all but ceased and clouds drifted slowly in front of the setting sun. First campfires were being lit on the hills around the city and the air reeked even more strongly of smoke and death. Peter slowly drew his bloodstained sword from its sheath, which I myself had embroidered for him in Kiev. The last rays of sunshine caught on the steel, making it sparkle, as he raised the weapon high above his head.

Rehnskjöld had his eyes closed and his lips moved. I recognised the Lord's Prayer, which I had so often recited in the Glucks' house.

Peter! I wanted to plead, but bit my tongue. The Tsar lifted the marshal's head by the hair, forcing his eyes open. 'Rehnskjöld. Do you know how much you have made Russia suffer? A warrior like you is rarely born. In Narva one of your bullets narrowly missed me,' he growled.

I wiped my moist hands on my skirt. When the marshal replied, his eyes were as blue as the skies over St Petersburg. He spoke quietly in the language of Johann: 'I ask God for forgiveness for my sins. I'm ready for death, Tsar Peter.'

His voice was full of fatigue and Sheremetev closed his eyes, ashen-faced. Menshikov crossed himself with three fingers. Rehnskjöld turned and said some last, encouraging words to his men, then lowered his head. Some of the Swedes sobbed, burying their faces in their hands.

Peter raised his sword high and higher, then paused and took one of the marshal's limp hands, closing his fingers around the sword's pommel. 'Take my sword as a sign of my respect, Marshal Rehnskjöld. You are a true soldier.'

Marshal Rehnskjöld, the fearless hero of countless battles, sank to the ground, dropped the sword, buried his face in the damp, dewy grass and cried like a child, his shoulders heaving. None of his men dared to touch him, but looked on in mute shock. Menshikov, Bruce and Sheremetev relaxed, and I laced my fingers through Peter's.

He shrugged and shook his head. 'Really. The Swedes are softer than I thought. What is his problem?'

48

We rode slowly back to the camp. The surviving men followed us in the dying light of the day in a more or less orderly train, together with thousands of ragged, limping and starving Swedish prisoners. As I took a last look back at Poltava, people poured out of the besieged city's gates to plunder the corpses and the mortally wounded, even breaking the gold teeth out of dead men's mouths.

Our camp was lit and people were singing, dancing, clapping and celebrating the victory. Peter had barrel upon barrel opened, serving wine, beer and vodka to his men, and Felten robbed the cellars of the town and the barns of the surrounding villages to roast enough oxen, lambs, pigs and chickens, and find enough salt fish, cabbage and flour. At the table, Peter threw away his cutlery and grabbed my greasy hands, holding them up for all to see. 'Tonight we shall eat only with our hands. If I catch one of you carving with his knife, he will be in trouble. Have I made myself clear?' Then he kissed me and served me a crackling piece of pork, dripping with gravy and stuffed with fruit.

The Swedes sat in our midst like islands in a raging sea: they reminded me of Johann's gentle manners. None of them farted or burped while they ate, nor did they spit on the ground, but politely turned to one side to pick food out of their teeth. I had Felten, who hated the Swedes, play the role of the Swedish King that evening. The humiliation drove tears of anger into his eyes. Peter laughed so much that he fell off his chair, pulling everything from the table in an enormous racket – cloth, cutlery and crockery.

In the early-morning hours, when the soldiers and generals clung exhaustedly to their chairs, Peter handed out the spoils to the victors: Sheremetev got more land and souls around Kiev. Shafirov – 'my favourite little Jew' – was made Vice-chancellor, a count, and each of his daughters was to marry a prince. Shafirov kissed the Tsar's knees, which made Menshikov even more jealous than he already was, but I calmed him, winking at him and saying: 'Alexander Danilovich, surely the light of Peter's grace shines brightly enough for all of us?' Though the more Menshikov got, the more he wanted; such was his nature. Peter himself was promoted as well, and he kissed me. 'Now you are the companion of a Vice-admiral. Are you proud of me?'

In the morning, the child in my body lay quiet. I thought of Blumentrost's words and clenched my fists: the infant was my Prince of Poltava, a miracle in himself. We left two days later, as the surrounding land and villages could no longer feed our army, and the stench of death and decay suffocated all merriment in our tents.

The victorious soldiers of Poltava entered the Red Square in a whirl of thick snowflakes, the ice mirroring their triumph. I myself was not stand on the balcony of the Kremlin on that day as I was to give birth in Peter's house at Ismailov: 'Give me a healthy son to celebrate Poltava. Please!' he had whispered as he helped me from the sleigh, tears in his eyes. Moscow was alight with life and joy. Waiting for the hour of birth bored me to tears. I messed up my embroideries and drew figures in the ice crystals on the windows.

So I only heard about Peter riding into the Red Square on Finette, who was adorned with leopard skin, red velvet, shining leather and silver bridle. Behind him marched his regiments and his generals, followed by the endless stream of Swedish prisoners, half mad with fear, and the captured three hundred flags and thirty-six Swedish cannon. The crowds were beside themselves; boyars and wealthy merchants such as Peter's friend Count Stroganov invited the Tsar and his generals to their houses: Peter and his men never refused.

Seven thousand candles burnt, each of them seven foot high, and seven triumphal arches had been raised: once Peter had passed beneath them all, he reached the throne where his old crony, the fake Prince-Caesar sat, his hair and shoulders covered with snow.

Peter laid his hand upon his heart: 'With the help of God and the grace of Your Majesty, I have won the victory for Russia at Poltava.' The Swedish soldiers thought they had now become completely mad: who was the Tsar after all? The man in the rough, worn uniform whom they had met in Poltava, or the toad who sat painted and adorned on the throne, giving his court of fools and jesters a signal for the feast to begin?

Daria later told me that the Master of Ceremonies had to cross the hall on horseback, as there were so many guests, and the colour-ful ceiling of the Kremlin's festival hall was destroyed when the men shot into the air instead of having fireworks.

What she did not tell me, others did: Praskovia's daughter, Peter's pretty and nubile niece, the Tsarevna Jekaterina Ivanovna, would not leave the Tsar's side. Perhaps he was right. It was a good idea to marry those girls off sooner rather than later.

Only a few days after the victory celebrations a most violent labour began for me. During the long hours of pain I clung to the curtains of my bed or kicked the midwife who tried to soothe me. When I felt the delivery was close, Blumentrost shouted, 'Quick, my God, quick! He is lying the wrong way around. I can feel the feet.' The room went black: I fainted, which mercifully veiled the pain for a couple of seconds. When I came to, I saw Blumentrost's fat hands holding my child's perfect wriggling body to the dull light and frosty air of a Moscow winter day. A hoarse, strong scream tore through the exhausted, stifling silence of the room. I laughed, and stroked my damp, wet hair from my sweaty forehead. 'He is to be named Peter, like his father!'

Daria busied herself with bedlinen and Alexandra Tolstoya washed her bloodstained hands in a porcelain bowl full of warm water, avoiding my eyes. Blumentrost, the ass, turned to the window, checking the child, and then wrapped it in clean linen. He turned around and it looked at me, its eyes deep and blue.

'I'm afraid that's not possible, Your Grace. It's a girl. A wonderful, healthy little daughter for our Tsar.'

It took almost a week before I would hold Elizabeth in my arms. Peter, however, was beside himself with joy at her birth, calling her his little Princess of Poltava. She drained her wet-nurse, was soon strong as none of my other children had been and loudly refused to let herself be swaddled.

49

Things were looking up for Russia. After Poltava, Tolstoy not only negotiated a new peace treaty with the Turks, but also dismissed as nonsense rumours that the wounded Charles of Sweden was hiding at the Sultan's court.

I was in the storage rooms of the Kremlin together with Jagushinsky, choosing furniture for the new Winter Palace in St Petersburg, which was still bare, its rooms vast and our steps echoing in the endless corridors. Jagushinsky made careful note of every chest of drawers, chair and mirror that I liked, though there wasn't too much. Peter's hatred for the Kremlin as much as his love for all things new, shiny and European, made for the happiness of many a carpenter in France, Italy and Germany. Just before leaving, I spotted a painting, half covered with white linen, like a shroud.

I frowned. 'Is that not the portrait of the German princess the Tsarevich is to marry?'

'Indeed,' said Jagushinsky, all of a sudden eager to pack up his scroll and quill.

Not so fast, my friend, I thought and ordered him: 'Take off the cover. Why is it here and not in Alexey's apartment, as ordered? He must get used to her face, pretty as it is,' I added.

'The Tsarevich ordered it to be brought here,' the master of Peter's household said, sweat beading on his face despite the chill in the storage rooms. I waved at his helper, who with one sweeping gesture made the shroud drop. I gasped: someone had drawn a thick moustache above the princess's lovely lips and disfigured her rosy skin with black spots. Worst of all, the canvas was slashed all over.

'What has happened here?' I asked, stunned.

'The Tsarevich practised his knife-throwing skills on the portrait,' said Jagushinsky.

'Does the Tsar know?'

'No. Of course not.' Jagushinsky mopped away sweat, as would anyone who had hidden an event of this magnitude from Peter. It was enough to earn them a serious thrashing.

'Try to have it cleaned and mended. Then take it back to the Tsarevich's rooms. Talks about the match are in progress,' I ordered.

'Thank you, Your Grace,' said Jagushinsky, bowing out of the room backwards. What else, I wondered when I left, was going on that Peter and I knew nothing about?

At a feast for the name day of St Alexander Nevsky in Menshikov's new palace, it was apparent that Alexander Danilovich had spared no expense on his residence. Peter was delighted with its splendour, as well as glad that he needn't foot the bill for the extravagant celebration. The building on the Vassilyev Island was the most glorious in the city, adorned with Persian silk, Italian marble, Libyan cedars, Siberian gold, Chinese lacquerwork and wallpaper, Delft tiles, African ivory and English silver. In Menshikov's library three librarians took care of the thirteen thousand volumes, of which he himself could not read a single one, as well as of his unique collection of maps. The walls of the staircases, the corridors and the hundreds of private and public rooms and halls, were covered with tapestries, trophies, and countless paintings and portraits he had brought from abroad by the shipload, as well as the finest icons embellished with silver and gold.

Daria led me through the long mirrored passages before the banquet, chatting and giggling as if not a moment since Marienburg had passed, and I saw some flattering paintings of myself and countless others of Peter at every age. Finally, she stopped, showing me an almost hidden row of smaller paintings. 'This is the wall of my grief,' she said, and I saw the little faces of her deceased sons, Paul Samson and Peter Lukas. A third childhood picture showed the delicate, rosy face of her daughter, who was just then bedridden with a high fever. Daria hastily dried her tears, for Peter did not tolerate any display of grief or sadness on a public holiday. I had pleaded for her to be allowed to stay away, but in vain. So we walked on, looking absent-mindedly at the pictures, such as a painting of a naked, beautiful girl holding up a decapitated head and laughing triumphantly. With her round cheeks and dark braids she reminded me of the Tsarevny Ivanovna, whom I intended to study closely while we were at dinner.

Menshikov struck the floor with his diamond-studded cane and the first course was carried into the hall; Peter drank from his eagle cup and burped before openly eyeing his nieces, who seemed to wear just about everything they had been able to find in their wardrobes. No wonder the French and Spanish Ambassadors had had a good giggle upon seeing them! Still, I thought, as I rapidly moved my long fan made of grey ostrich feathers, ivory and mother-of-pearl, no one should laugh at a Russian Princess.

Peter smacked his sticky lips: 'Well, which of these girls shall we give to the young Duke of Courland? He is a nephew of the King of Prussia. Is there a better way to consolidate our conquest of the Baltics than by marriage into that royal family?'

Just then, Praskovia's eldest daughter Jekaterina rose as smoothly as a cat and came over to us, hips swaying and silk skirts rustling. She settled herself on Peter's lap and put his cup to her own lips. 'To a long and healthy life, my victorious uncle.' She smiled at him, her eyes as dark and shiny as sour cherries. She drank and Peter laughed, placing both his hands on her bosom and kissing her naked neck. She wriggled most invitingly, while I pretended to talk to Menshikov.

'By God, it's no wonder I forget too often that you are my niece,' Peter said huskily.

'Well, my father was only your half-brother,' Jekaterina gasped, as he sucked her swelling flesh above the low-cut dress. I moved my fan, feeling all eyes on me. Of course, Peter had other girls, but being so open with his favour, in my presence, was a novelty for him. I read the curiosity in people's eyes. Were my days of influence over? Would I join in? Was there a new mistress to be reckoned with here? I tried to keep calm, but Menshikov stroked the fine moustache he now sported and murmured, 'Watch that little bird. She'd love to be the Tsar's wife and order her mother and sisters around. It wouldn't be the first time that a Tsar married a so-called close relative. Who knows who really sired those girls – certainly not Ivan the Idiot.'

Jekaterina slipped her hand between Peter's legs. I leapt up and dug my nails into the flesh of her arm, pulling her hand away. 'We are not in a brothel but in Alexander Danilovich's palace. He was just wondering about a suitable bride for the Duke of Courland,' I said.

'Hmm, what?' asked Peter, breathing heavily.

Jekaterina eyed me coldly, but Menshikov obligingly bobbed his head under his heavy powdered wig. 'If we wish to prove the sincerity of our bond to the King of Prussia, we should give his nephew, the Duke of Courland, our most beautiful princess. That would be you then, Tsarevna Jekaterina Ivanovna,' he said, beaming at her.

Jekaterina was not fooled, but stuck out her tongue at Menshikov and pressed herself against Peter's chest. 'Dearest Father-Uncle, I only want to give children to Russia. Many, many sons. My mother has shown how fertile we are.' She shot me a triumphant look. 'I'll be unhappy all my life if I have to leave you, my Tsar,' she chirped, tousling Peter's hair.

I clenched my fists to stop myself from scratching the princess's pretty pink face to shreds. 'Fertile? Yes, my princess, your mother bore nothing but daughters,' I said cattily

Peter stopped our smouldering quarrel. 'You might be right, Menshikov. But I think we can do better for Jekaterina here,' he said, and embraced her while studying her mother and sisters: Praskovia had just smacked her second daughter Anna hard and pulled her by the hair. Peter grinned. 'Anna Ivanovna should go. She is to be Duchess of Courland. And lovely Jekaterina and I, Alekasha, will visit your galleries together,' he decided.

Menshikov laughed uneasily and I smiled serenely as Peter and Jekaterina left. The sounds coming from the hall's anteroom soon afterwards told me that Peter was not even waiting for the darkness of the corridors before he honoured Jekaterina Ivanovna with his attentions. I would not look.

The night in the Summer Palace when he had promised me his hand, and the closeness we had felt then, seemed like a distant dream.

The Tsarevna Anna Ivanovna was a proud young bride. The Duke of Courland had originally asked for portraits of all the Princesses Ivanovna, Peter's nieces, but was eventually satisfied with Peter's choice for him – Anna was a tall brunette with rosy cheeks and dark, radiant eyes – and even more so with his bride's dowry of two hundred thousand roubles. The duke immediately repaid his gambling debts.

On their wedding day, a first layer of thin ice glistened on the Neva and the air was crackling with the promise of snow. Peter and I visited Anna Ivanovna as she was being dressed by her sisters for the ceremony.

Jekaterina lifted her sister's hair away from the nape of her neck while beaming at Peter. 'My Tsar, what an honour for my sister: what more can any woman desire than to be a happy bride? May God give her many sons.' I felt like slapping the troublemaker. Oh, I would make sure that the eldest princess was married soon! She was like a bitch on heat, and Peter came ever more rarely, and only very half-heartedly, into my bed. What if she, a Tsarevna of royal blood, bore him a son?

Peter kissed Jekaterina on both cheeks before cupping her sister's face. 'Anna Ivanovna. You must honour Russia and your dead father, my beloved brother, Tsar Ivan, in your marriage. You marry for your country: keep faith, love your new home and obey your husband.'

'I shall, dearest Father-Uncle,' the bride sobbed.

Peter led her up the aisle of the Peter and Paul Cathedral. Our breath hung in clouds in the icy air as we prayed and chanted, but when the ceremony proper was about to begin, the priest held up his prayer-book and said in a trembling voice: 'I shall not carry out this marriage, for reasons of faith.'

'What is the matter?' The young duke looked nervously at the Prussian Ambassador, who rolled his eyes. Nothing here surprised him anymore, I felt.

Anna Ivanovna sobbed, bewildered, and Praskovia rushed to her. 'My dove, my little sunshine. Don't worry,' I heard her cooing.

Peter rose, grabbed the priest by the collar and drew his *dubina*. 'And why is that, you cursed little traitor?' he thundered.

The man bravely spoke up. 'In the name of the Holy Russian Church, I refuse to marry a Tsarevna to a disbeliever. This is blasphemy and against our law.'

'The law? *I* am the law!' Peter shouted, his voice echoing, as he beat the priest twice over the head. Blood dripped onto the colourful marble of the altar and Anna Ivanovna gasped. I crossed myself but Peter threw the priest towards his guards. 'Scourge him. Thirty lashes for insulting the Tsar of All the Russias in front of foreign dignitaries.' The Prussian Ambassador looked as if he wanted to speak up for the priest, then changed his mind, seeing Peter's anger. The bride was in shock: tears left ugly marks on her carefully painted, chalk-white face.

'Blood on the altar! What a horrid omen for my marriage,' she cried. I offered her smelling salts, but Praskovia scolded her, 'Pull yourself together.'

'Menshikov!' Peter roared. 'Bring me one of your priests. But warn him what will happen if he refuses to marry my niece to the German.'

All our Russian customs had disappeared from the very joyful wedding feast that followed: men and women mingled freely and instead of the traditional *kournik*, a multi-layered dome-shaped pie made of breadcrust stuffed with candied fruit, there was a giant cake fashioned to look like Peter's new Winter Palace. We danced through the night and splendid fireworks etched the flaming coats-of-arms of the Romanovs and the House of Courland into the sleeping skies. The young duke was too drunk to do his marital duty that night. Three days later the newly-weds climbed into their sleigh to travel to Courland, while the new duchess wailed and embraced her sisters and mother, with whom she had almost always fought. The hooves of the strong ponies tethered to their sleigh struck sparks off the hard ice of the Neva pier and colourful flags waved them goodbye in the fresh morning breeze.

Only three days later, Anna Ivanovna, the young Duchess of Courland, was back with us, a widow. Fifty miles away from St Petersburg her husband had felt unwell and had climbed out of the sleigh where he fell headfirst into the snow and suffocated on his own bile, to the accompaniment of the horrified screams of his helpless young wife.

50

'Tolstoy is certainly the most demanding of my ambassadors,' Peter snorted, crumpling up the latest letter. 'This is the third petition he has sent in a week. Is he not kept busy enough with shopping at the slave market of Constantinople?' Peter chucked the paper ball amongst other papers, plans and *ukazy*. 'He always wants more gold, more silver, more sables. Either the greed of the Sultan at the Golden Gate knows no bounds, or Peter Andreyevich fills his own pockets.'

I rolled onto my belly, nibbling on warm *pierogi* filled with *smetana*, nuts and honey. The cushions in front of the fireplace, where I kept myself busy looking at drawings of new dresses, were soft, but when the logs in the fire shifted and fell, my lapdog started. 'Silly,' I said, and kissed him on his damp muzzle. Peter circled me like an eagle in the sky; I watched his scruffy boots with their rundown heels and scraped tips coming and going. Suddenly he stood still and clenched his fists.

He sighed. 'I just can't do this on my own anymore. So be it then. The accursed French and English are right. I shall follow suit.'

'What are they right about? Come here to me,' I said, patting one of the cushions. Peter rested his head on my shoulder and my lips tasted the cold sweat on his forehead while I tousled his hair. He suffered and I felt like chasing that quack Blumentrost away to find a proper doctor, one who could heal the Tsar.

'I simply cannot rule Russia alone,' Peter sighed. 'This yoke crushes me.'

My fingers halted in their caress. 'What does that mean?' I asked, my voice unsteady. Peter had never said anything of this sort before. He certainly didn't mean that it was time for Alexey to ascend to the throne. Did the Tsar want to marry a foreign princess? A young woman who could give him sons and always have sound advice to offer? His niece Jekaterina's self-indulgence, as well as her steady demands for clothes and jewellery, had started to bore him, this much I knew. Peter gave gladly, but he would not be asked to do so. In the past few months he had returned to my bed, but at twenty-seven I would not fall pregnant so easily anymore.

'In former times, Russia was easy to rule. It was like a simple hut. But now my realm is a palace, with endless corridors, many storeys, stairs and towers. I feel like a boy who must clear the huge forest around it using a penknife.'

'What do you want to do?' If it was too much for Peter, who on earth could bear this burden?

He looked into the flames. 'I need a Senate. Russia needs many men to lead it, not just one.'

'A Senate? What is that?' That word sounded better to me than another princess's name. From a small Venetian phial I poured rose oil into my palms and gently rubbed Peter's temples. The fragrance, scented with the last of summer, filled the air. He sighed with pleasure. 'A group of men who will help me govern Russia; but not men who are chosen just because of their high birth.'

'Will they have real power? Isn't that dangerous for you?'

Peter laughed. 'My clever, cunning Catherinushka! Of course they will have only just as much power as I think fit. But they are to draft the new laws that are needed and enforce them. Complaints about greedy and unjust courts have been flooding in lately – they can overhaul those too.' He paused briefly, grinning at me. 'And the Senate is going to find me money. Lots of it: for new recruits, for new alliances, for St Petersburg. Whoever brings in the most money is the best senator.'

'Do we need more money?' I thought of the sheer magnificence with which Peter had furnished our Winter Palace. He twisted my curls around his fingers.

'The Tsar always needs money, though he is never short of it as long as he still has Russia and the Russians. What belongs to them, belongs to me, and I can use it as I see fit. But a Senate will be my eyes and ears.'

'And if the Senate agrees on something you do not want?' I asked.

'No senator will ever trust another. Only hungry bellies and free spirits make for rebellious hearts.' The muscles in his neck tensed again and he rubbed his head briefly on my shoulder. 'I'd really like to stay here. But I must write the *ukaz* right now.'

He was standing on the threshold of the concealed door in the wall, which allowed him to slip unseen to and from my apartments, when there was a soft knock. Peter raised his eyebrows. 'Do you expect a secret visitor, Catherinushka?' he teased me. I padded to the door and the rugs felt warm under my bare soles. Who could this be?

When I opened it, the guard helped the exhausted messenger outside to stay upright. His breath was still erratic from his long, hard ride, his cloak covered with mud and ice crystals. Grimy slush from his boots melted onto the shimmering marble floor of the Winter Palace. He hit his chest with his fist. 'My Tsar. An urgent message from the Golden Gate.'

'Does Tolstoy want even more gold and sables? Well, tell him that he can't search a naked man's pockets,' Peter barked.

The man looked at us, his eyes burning. 'It is too late for that. Charles of Sweden is at the High Porte. Tolstoy tried to win the Sultan's favour, but in vain. He did not have the means to do it.'

Peter pulled the messenger into the room, grabbing him by his collar. 'That is impossible: if Tolstoy did not have the means, what means did Charles have after fleeing Poltava as poor as a church mouse?'

The man almost cried. 'That is what we thought! But the king saved his war-chest: he is swimming in gold, and furthermore the brothers Cook of the English–Levantine Society have lent him money.'

'And?' Peter asked, his eyes dark and beady with anger.

'The Sultan fears the growing Russian influence in the Black Sea: you are much too close for his comfort in Azov. In the end, Tolstoy forced the Sultan to choose – Russia or Sweden.'

I bit my lip. Nothing good ever came of forcing someone to choose, and sure enough the messenger carried on, 'The Sultan replied to us with impossible conditions, such as handing back the Baltics and St Petersburg to the Swedes.'

Peter simmered with anger. 'This fat toad of Constantinople! I hope Tolstoy gave him the right answer?'

'He did,' the messenger confirmed.

'And?' Peter continued. 'What happened then?'

'The Sultan has locked him in the Castle of the Seven Towers.'

Peter cursed under his breath.

'What does that mean?' I whispered, looking from one man to the other.

Peter turned to me. 'That, Catherinushka, means war on two fronts, exactly what any leader should always avoid,' he groaned, then cheered up. 'But Russia will not be crushed. Never! Come to Turkey with me. I'll roast the Sultan over a low flame and give you the biggest emerald Constantinople has to offer.'

On the same day on which Russia created its Senate, it was also at war with the Golden Gate of Constantinople.

51

'And, of course, his whore of a washerwoman is going with him ... '
The timing of the Tsarevna Jekaterina Ivanovna's words was ill
chosen: they fell like stones into a well in the momentary silence
amongst the small circle of people meeting up in Praskovia's house.
The servants were just clearing the second course and the musicians returned to their instruments. The other guests, Peter's closest
friends and family, had been wiping their greasy fingers, leaning
back against the soft cushions. The princess blushed to the roots of
her hair when she realised that we had all heard her.

Peter, who had just been arguing with Shafirov and Sheremetev
about how to raise funds for the Turkish campaign, looked up. His
mood had not been the best in the past few days, as of all his allies
only Prince Dmitri Kantemir of Moldavia had agreed to follow
him south. Jekaterina must have felt his gaze as heavily as a galley
slave feels the whip; no one in the room dared to breathe; the air
crackled with fear.

Peter looked at me. I did nothing to hide the tears such a public
humiliation had caused me to shed. He gently took my hand. Our
daughters Anna and Elizabeth, too, were trying to comfort me with
hugs, praise and kisses.

Peter rose to his feet. 'Praskovia, widowed Tsaritsa of Russia,' he
said, and she knelt with difficulty on her cushion, adjusting her
abundant folds of flesh. 'My Tsar,' she murmured, her forehead
touching the artfully laid honey-coloured parquet.

'Yes. On your knees, all the Tsarevny Ivanovna including the Duchess of Courland,' Peter ordered. The three younger women obeyed, pale with fright.

Peter led me over to them. 'Tsaritsa Praskovia, my sister-in-law. Tsarevny of Russia, my nieces. You are the highest *damy* in my country. I have honoured you all my life. But the time has come ...' He paused. The princesses were scared witless, not knowing what to expect. What would Peter do next: shave their heads and commit them to a nunnery, or banish them to Siberia? The youngest Tsarevna Ivanovna, who was of a simple mind with a flat, pancake-like face, sobbed with fear.

Peter gave me a tender glance. 'The time has come to declare my beloved companion, Catherine Alexeyevna, mother of my daughters Anna and Elizabeth, the highest lady at court. Everyone – you, my family, as well as my people – should recognise her as such.' He raised his voice, so it echoed off the walls. 'Should I not find the time to marry her before the Turkish campaign, or should I fall there, know this: Catherine Alexeyevna is henceforward Tsaritsa of Russia. To insult her is to insult me. Makarov, write that down,' he ordered the scribe, who had already chased one of his men away for paper and pen.

I could hardly breathe when Peter blessed me. Before he could prevent it, I fell to my knees before him. 'By God,' I whispered, holding his gaze and his fingers, 'I will do justice to this honour.'

'You'd better.' Peter grinned before he pulled me to my feet. 'Music!' he commanded. 'Is this a betrothal or a funeral? Lazy buggers. Bring the sparkling wine from France. And woe to the one who tries to leave the room before he is allowed to.'

The musicians played a merry tune and Peter bowed. 'May I have this dance?' he asked, unusually gallantly, before dabbing my cheeks with a not-so-clean lace handkerchief. 'Please stop crying, *matka*. You should be nothing but happy when the Tsar declares you his companion and the highest lady in Russia.'

That, though, only made me cry more, and I would not calm down all evening.

When I had my chests for the Turkish campaign packed, Anna and Elizabeth were playing hide and seek in my rooms. Both girls were tall and strong for their ages, but the younger Elizabeth always bullied Anna in one way or the other and I heard her maid of honour cry: 'Lizenka! Stop pulling Anoushka by the hair, will you?'

The choice between being with them or with their father was, as always, terrible to me. Despite the honours Peter had heaped on me, life with him was forever like a walk on the first brittle ice of the Neva in the early winter. It might carry me on to shining joy and glory; it might also break, and the black, icy water swallow me forever.

Russian troops had to reach the Danube before the Turks invaded Moldavia and Poland. Peter urged Sheremetev and his troops on. When we left St Petersburg in March, a banner decorated with the sign of the Holy Cross and the words of St Constantine blazed above our heads: *In this sign you shall conquer.* Alongside us rode Prince Dmitri Kantemir of Moldavia and his five thousand men, who were battle-hardened by the challenging conditions in their mountains.

Next to the prince, a little girl sat on her pony: I had never seen such a beautiful child, with hair like honeycomb and skin like hewn gold. Her eyes were of a curious amber colour, as bright as those of a sledge dog, and she held herself as upright as a princess. Peter, too, stared at her, who might have been eight or nine years old.

'Who is that, Prince Dmitri? War is no place for children. Even grown women have a hard time convincing me of the necessity of their presence in the field.' He winked at me.

Prince Dmitri Kantemir smiled. 'This is my daughter, Princess Maria Kantemir. There is no one in Moldavia I could trust enough with her care.'

'How beautiful she is.' Peter stared at the girl and his expression was that of a man appreciating a woman. Maria Kantemir spurred her pony and left the Tsar of All the Russias to swallow her dust. His gaze followed her until she had disappeared from view.

*

The early-spring sun was burning up the meagre seeds on the otherwise fertile fields, which worsened the famine after the failed harvests of the previous year. Furthermore, the Ukraine had still not recovered from a plague of locusts and the wars. The anger of the people, from whom we took what little they had left, followed us like a curse, but we had to save Russia, even if that meant feeding thousands of men and horses in a famished country. When we reached the Dniester, our wagons were stuck in the torrents or washed away; many horses drowned, and whole charges of gunpowder were soaked and rendered useless. On the other side, the landscape changed to a sea of blistering hot sand. Its utter desolation confounded us: our soldiers suffered from sunstroke; hunger and thirst caused hallucinations and nosebleeds. Our troops were beaten by the terrain before they had even seen the enemy.

We placed all our hopes on the fertile valley of the River Pruth, which we reached in early summer. Here we could recover from the arduous march, we thought, and the evening on which we celebrated the memory of Poltava on the banks of the Pruth was one of the rare happy moments of the Turkish campaign. Peter and I emptied a barrel of sweet Tokay and rolled in the dunes, laughing and gasping in the sun and sand. My skin was tanned; my dark hair streaked with lighter strands. I was as lean and supple as before my pregnancies. In spite of the hardships of the journey, I still took the trouble to dress, groom and adorn myself carefully for Peter: as always, I had taken all my jewellery along.

We tried in vain to locate the Turkish army. Had those cowards even left Constantinople? Our spies and messengers did not return and we grew giddy and light-hearted. Ha! The cowardly Turk had crawled back into the hole in which he belonged.

'A pity about the emerald I wanted to cut off the fat Sultan's neck for you,' Peter sighed.

'Oh? And who says you can't still give it to me?' I teased him.

We fell asleep at the table that night, blissfully unaware of what lay ahead of us.

Instead of the first rays of sunlight, the shrill sound of trumpets, the hooting of war horns and Sheremetev's voice in our tent woke us: 'The Turks! We are surrounded. There are thousands and thousands of them, strong and well-armed,' he cried.

Peter tucked his dirty shirt into his breeches, stumbling out of the tent, while I blinked in disbelief at the blinding brightness of the morning and the turmoil in our camp. Everywhere men were running and screaming. I held my breath: was the sight terrible or glorious? We were not so much surrounded as overwhelmed. Our forty thousand men, who had seemed so mighty in St Petersburg, faced almost three times as many Turks and Tatars: a sea of soldiers foaming with hostility. The crescent moon blazed on thousands of red flags, dancing like devils in the hot wind. As far as the horizon I saw nothing but enemy soldiers, who looked terrifying, brandishing their heavy cutlasses. I could make out the shining metal of their breastplates and the rough animal skins tied around their shoulders and calves. In their midst, on an elevated litter strewn with pillows and carpets, an incredibly fat man sat under a canopy, as still as an idol. He was covered with jewels, sparkling like a statue in the sun. This must be the Grand Vizier.

'Holy Mother. What shall we do?' Peter breathed.

Sheremetev shrugged helplessly. Peter gathered himself. 'To arms,' he shouted, and shoved Sheremetev. 'Take position! Go, go, go! Do you think we have all the time in the world? The Tsar is not a sitting duck. I am the Russian bear who fights and strikes back, until defeat and death.' He ran into the tent, calling for his sword, for his armour, for Finette to be saddled.

I embraced Sheremetev, whose lean body was shaking with dry sobs. In the past two years he had known neither rest nor respite. 'Be brave, Boris Petrovich,' I whispered. 'Fight! Russia depends on it.' I owed him my life at Peter's side. If I saw him today for the very last time, I had to give him strength. 'Thank you for everything,' I said. 'May God protect you.' My heart ached: how very small and helpless the Field Marshal looked before that wall of Ottomans, running off for his horse and sword.

The Turks blew a call to arms from their long trumpets made of shiny metal and soldiers struck large drums: the rolling sound made my skin prickle with fear even before a concerted ferocious war cry rose to the sky.

In the tent, Peter dictated his last words while being clad in his armour.

'Write, Makarov! *"We, Peter Alexeyevich, by the grace of God Tsar of All the Russias, decide the following. Should I be taken prisoner by the Turks, I am no longer the Tsar. No rouble shall be paid and no drop of blood shall be shed to save me. If I should fall, give the throne to the most worthy of my descendants."'* He shook his head, considering his words. 'Even if that's just a damned useless sod like Alexey ...'

'*Batjuschka! Starik!* Don't even think of that!' I cried, and he cupped my face before kissing me, hard and passionately.

He looked at me with burning eyes: 'At least I have proved myself to you just before our departure. Thank you for all the strength you gave me, *matka*. Thank you, always.'

He left: the tent flap knocked against the posts and I was alone, kneeling, crumbling under my burden of fear and digging my hands into the hot desert beneath the rugs that covered the floor of our tent. Were the sands of the Pruth to fall upon our graves instead of good Russian earth?

The sounds of battle reached me but faintly in the following hours, for I had had a solid dose of laudanum dissolved in wine, but despite my dazed stupor, I clasped a dagger in readiness. If I had to, I would defend myself against any marauding Turk or go out and fight for Peter's life.

52

I woke in darkness. It was a cloudy night and the moon was new, so I needed to touch the pillow next to me to find out if Peter had returned. It was empty. Outside stretched a silence more threatening than any noise that had gone before. My heartbeat was still slow from sleep while my thoughts somersaulted. With unsteady fingers, I reached for the dagger on the rug beside my bed and sat up, still feeling dizzy from the laudanum: I had overdone it. How should I have fought in this state? I stumbled to my feet and heard murmurs coming from outside the tent. Was that Russian or Turkish? Had we lost or won?

I wrapped a warm scarf around my shoulders, stepped out into the frosty desert night and almost choked on the stench of despair, death and blood. My foot struck something that could only be a corpse. I cried out, but all of a sudden a hand was pressed over my mouth, almost suffocating me. I caught Peter's scent and dropped the dagger, feeling relieved. His grip loosened and I wanted to embrace him.

'Peter,' I whispered.

But he seized my wrists, telling me, 'We must flee, Catherinushka. Russia has been defeated. Our horses are ready and we have a local guide to help us cross the riverbed. Put on your boots and take your jewels with you. We'll need them to secure our way back,' he said hoarsely, just as the breeze stirred and carried the stench of the battlefield closer, thicker and even more sickening than before. It was as unbearable to me as the words Peter had just spoken. I squinted at him through the darkness: he was still in his dirty, torn uniform, booted and ready to mount. The Tsar of All the Russias wanted to flee like a boy who had lost a bet at a bear-baiting? What had happened to the brave words he had dictated to Makarov? This was a nightmare. Even Charles of Sweden, our fierce, deadly enemy, would always choose death above a shameful peace.

I glanced at our so-called guide, a small, wiry man who chewed on a betel nut. In the moonlight his Cossack eyes gleamed like the fires with which wreckers lured ships aground. I would not trust that man with a round of mouldy cheese, let alone my life, I decided, and crossed my arms.

'No,' I said.

Peter was stunned. 'What? Come on! We need the cover of darkness. Lucky that it is so cloudy. No one will see us!'

'Have we surrendered to the Grand Vizier?'

Peter nodded sullenly. 'We had no other choice.'

'So what?' I insisted. 'The Turks probably don't even understand what they did. What do they know about our supply route? General Ronne is already in Braila with his men. From there he'll easily cut off their retreat.'

'Woman,' hissed Peter, 'you have no idea.'

'Oh, yes, I do.' I gave one of his guards a sign. He thumped one fist between the guide's chest and belly, making the man double over with pain and groan. 'Good. Make sure nobody ever learns why he was here,' I ordered, handing the soldier my dagger. The man dragged the guide away, gagging him with one sooty hand.

'What are you doing?' Peter cried. 'Now we will never find our way back to Russia.'

I locked eyes with him. 'Nobody shall ever know that the Tsar of All the Russias wanted to run away like a common thief. You would become the laughing stock of all Europe and destroy everything you've ever built.'

After a moment of silence, he asked: 'What do you suggest instead, Catherine Alexeyevna?' How formal my name sounded all of a sudden.

'I am going to get my jewels, Peter. *All* my jewellery. Everything that you in your love and generosity have ever given me. More gems than the fat, greedy Sultan has ever seen. Sheremetev and Shafirov are to hand over the loot – as a gift, with my sincere respect to the ruler of the High Porte of Constantinople, the Prince of the Golden Gate. And then ...' I grabbed his wrist.

'And then?'

'Then we negotiate,' I said calmly, even though my heart pounded.

Wind chased away the clouds and the slim moonlight made Peter's face look gaunt and his eyes huge and shiny. He tenderly touched my cheek. 'At heart, you are a man. Perhaps you should rule Russia, not I. At least for tonight,' he quickly added.

I returned to our tent, where two large studded oak chests contained my most precious possessions. I draped several Persian scarves over the floor, dragged the chests to the middle of the tent and tipped them over, their sparkling contents cascading like a waterfall of wealth: pearls and beads, strings of sapphires, rubies and emeralds mounted on breast crosses, jewelled hairpins, rings, earrings, bracelets, brooches, tiaras, chokers and ropes of pearls.

I knelt to eye the treasure and my chest tightened: this was everything I had. Tokens of Peter's love, surely, but also my only security against his whims – such as the danger still that he would marry a European princess – as well as those of fate. What if he were to die tomorrow? I combed my fingers through the jewellery, untangling the strands of pearls from the other pieces. Peter had always spoilt me on my name-day, each Easter, at Christmas, and of course every time I had given birth. There was the tiara made of pearls, rose-quartz, tourmalines, blue topaz and thinly beaten gold, which I had worn a year ago in my hair, dressed up as a flower fairy, together with the matching necklace and bracelets.

I sifted through the jewels as if they were pebbles in the Dvina, letting diamonds run through my fingers like droplets of the river where I swam in my youth. They were magnificent and the finest stones Russia had to offer. To please me, Peter pushed his jewellers to use larger and more unusual gems, such as green or yellow diamonds, and to set them in new ways. I liked my necklaces to reach my breasts or even dip between them, a cascade of dazzling light and wealth. I gladly accepted the ache a tiara gave me in my head and neck – and held my chin even higher with pride. An earring had to brush my shoulder, competing with a chandelier's lustre, for me to consider it worth wearing. After a feast, I loved the cool feeling of the gems and precious metal against my heated skin and often Peter had made love to me when I wore nothing but these stones. Now the Sultan would break them apart.

I searched for and found the earrings that had once belonged to Peter's mother, his first gift to me. I hooked them into my earlobes. I also took a bracelet made up of tiny portraits of Peter, Anna and Elizabeth, and their faces smiled up at me from the diamond-studded miniatures when I snapped the clasp shut. Just then, I spotted the ring that Peter had given me in Kiev to mark our darling little Ekaterina's first birthday. It was a huge, heart-shaped yellow diamond set in a simple band of gold; the goldsmith had worked one of Ekaterina's blonde curls into the band. I slid it on my finger, got up and gathered the rest of the jewels into a couple of bulky bundles. Good riddance, I thought. When I looked up, Shafirov and Sheremetev's son were waiting in the doorway.

'Take it all,' I said, and soldiers hoisted the bundles on their shoulders.

A small group of men left the camp at the first sign of dawn, swiftly moving into the desert. I watched them leave. My throat burned with thirst, but my eyes remained dry. Peter stood silent beside me. When the men had disappeared, he pulled a ring set with a big, round ruby from his finger, placed it in my limp palm and closed my fingers around it.

'Let us never forget what you have done today, for me and for Russia. I shall pay back my debts to you, double and triple. Let us also never forget the bravery of Shafirov and Colonel Sheremetev. Who knows if they'll come back alive?'

I slipped the ring into the little pouch that hung on my belt. I wouldn't need it until much later.

*

The Grand Vizier accepted my gift for the Sultan with an appreciative clicking of his tongue. He graciously consented to peace negotiations in which Russia was robbed of all and everything. The Treaty of Pruth returned Azov to the Ottoman Empire, and all Russian fortresses along the Black Sea were to be razed. Peter Shafirov had to stay in Istanbul as hostage. He was to join Peter Tolstoy in the Seven Towers, a prison feared for its dank dark cells. I gave my word to look after his daughters and honour the Tsar's promise of marrying them to a prince each. It took us two years and a new peace treaty to regain his freedom, together with Tolstoy's.

When we were close to St Petersburg on our return, Peter stopped his horse on a hillside, seizing my reins and lacing his fingers with mine. 'Catherine Alexeyevna, marry me as soon as the ice on the Neva thinks about melting,' he asked solemnly.

The plains lay peacefully in the evening sun. The star-shaped walls of the Peter and Paul Fortress turned crimson in the dying light of the day, while the water of the Neva shimmered green and mysterious. How beautiful my home was; how glad I was finally to return here. We had lost the war, but I had triumphed.

'Did you hear me?' Peter asked, but still I had no answer for him. The evening mist rose from the marshes, hiding the city like a veil and spicing its dew with our dreams and desires.

53

My wedding to the Tsar of All the Russias took place almost ten years after the fall of Marienburg. It was a decade since I had entered Alexander Danilovich Menshikov's tent, when I'd had dirty feet, worn a hand-me-down tunic and slept wherever I could roll out my bedding.

In my bedroom in the Winter Palace I sat with my legs crossed, touching the soft soles of my feet; the feet of a woman whose skin was peeled and pampered every week in the *banja* before she was anointed with a paste of almond oil and lime juice. A woman who barely walked a step too far, and then only when wearing velvet slippers. How much would the pointed pebbles and sharp stones on the banks of the Dvina hurt my feet today? I thought, wiggling my pink toes with pleasure.

With a light knock, Alexandra Tolstoya and Daria slipped into the room: I peered at them from between my fingers when they curtseyed deeply. Oh, God, no! Daria was already wiping tears from her eyes. I scolded her for it. 'We will all cry so much today, do not start now.'

My chambermaid drew back the Chinese silk curtains from the window and morning light flooded the warm, cosy room, where the fire in the Delft-tiled stove had been alight throughout the night. I pushed aside my breakfast of pancakes and hot chocolate and opened my arms to my visitors. 'Very well then, let's weep together. I cannot believe it either,' I sobbed, and they both rushed across to embrace me.

'Come here.' I patted my sheets and they climbed onto my bed, giggling like girls, even though they were already dressed, coiffed and adorned for the celebration. Their new brooches with my intricately laced and diamond-studded initials sparkled as badges of honour on their breasts: Peter had made them my official ladies-in-waiting. Daria poked me and laughed. 'Get up, Tsaritsa! You cannot marry in bed.'

'Why not? In bed Peter has learnt to love me,' I replied

My chambermaid curtseyed to us. 'The *parikmacher*, Tsaritsa.' The hairdresser bowed and entered, carefully carrying the high powdered wig he had made for me; behind him I spotted the tailor with his two apprentices, and a footman, who carried my wedding dress.

'Eat and drink, the day will be long,' I told my ladies. I slid from the bed and skipped on my bare feet to the window like a girl would. Daria and Alexandra laughed with their mouths full: 'Dance, Tsaritsa, dance!' they chanted before eating more pancakes. Daria was now as chubby and soft as a cushion due to her weakness for good food.

On the shining ice of the Neva skaters slid and spun in circles; sleds decorated with cheerful bunting and wreaths and garlands of evergreen skidded along. The sky was a dense blue and the white winter sun gave the city a glossy, almost unreal look, with trees and bushes apparently wrought from silver and houses built of sheer crystal. It was a kingdom of ice, and I was to be its queen. Trumpets sounded and cannon salutes rang out. St Petersburg was about to celebrate our wedding with pride. The joy to be felt in this crisp morning seized me; I was not only part of it, but at its very heart. I gave a sob, but Daria chided me, 'I cannot do your make-up when you cry, Marta.'

'Catherine Alexeyevna,' I corrected her, which made me cry even more. That morning I heard my old name for the last time as before the mirror framed with silver and mother-of-pearl, Marta, the soul born out of wedlock, gifted with a desperate heart and a growling stomach, disappeared forever. Into her place stepped Catherine

Alexeyevna, who returned my amazed look with the proud gaze of a Tsaritsa. For weeks Peter's Italian barber had lathered my skin with potions of buttermilk, lemon and vodka, to make my shoulders look like the marble from his home country. My hair had been rinsed in a wash of chestnut, beer and eggs, to give my curls shine and colour after the merciless sun of the Pruth. Thanks to Daria's droplets of belladonna my eyes were big and bright.

Daria and Alexandra Tolstoya helped me into my wedding gown, woven from silver damask. I gasped when I felt the robe's full weight on my shoulders but admired its pearl and silver-thread embroidery of birds, butterflies and blossoms; thick, twisted cords of silver held a heavy cloak of blue velvet and ermine in place on top of it. I struggled for balance when I took my two faithful friends by their hands. 'Daria. Alexandra. Promise to help me never to forget who I am and where I come from.' Alexandra Tolstoya curtseyed in response and Daria nodded, her eyes as round as saucers.

In my salon, Peter, Menshikov and the Admirals Cruys and Botsis waited: Peter had asked his favourite Dutch sailors, who had helped him set up his fleet, to be his ushers. The Tsar looked so splendid in his uniform that my heart beat faster. He bowed and held out a velvet-covered casket to me.

'Open it, Catherine,' he said brightly. 'My mother wore this crown for her wedding. Now it shall be yours, *matka*, and our daughters after you.'

I gasped when I saw the delicate diadem with its pearls and yellow and pink diamonds. Peter smiled tenderly as he took it out of the case and everybody clapped. Only the *parikmacher* made a worried face: how on earth would he fix the crown to my hairstyle? But Peter was already holding out a second casket. 'You might wear far too many clothes for my taste, but your neck is decidedly too naked.'

I snapped it open and was speechless: on a ten-strand choker, each pearl was as large as a chickpea. It was secured by a clasp, to be displayed in front, depicting the Imperial double eagle in diamonds, rubies and sapphires. Peter placed it around my neck, kissing my shoulders as he did so. 'This is the foundation for your new collection.' He winked at me as the clasp snapped shut.

I touched the eagle, which covered my whole throat, and said, 'This beast is suffocating me.'

'Tell me about it,' he said, wrapping his arm around my waist and whispering, 'Really, when will I be able to tear all these heavy clothes off you?'

The doors to the wider palace were flung open and the sounds of trumpets and drums became deafening. Anna and Elizabeth flew towards us in silver dresses, taffeta trains and lace veils. Peter caught them before they could make me lose my balance. 'Hey, behave, you little witches, or I will have you thrashed.' Both of them giggled and Elizabeth tickled her father's chin and twisted his uniform buttons. She knew that Peter would never raise a hand against her. Oh, if only she were a son, I thought, but reined my thoughts in: not here, not today.

Feofan Prokopovich blessed our union before God and man in the small wooden church of St Isaac. Clouds of incense dulled my mind; sparks of gold and purple danced before my eyes just as they had done so long ago, on my way down to the Dvina, my arms heavy with dirty laundry. The chants and prayers rose and fell all around us. The bridal crown floated over my head. After my vows, Menshikov helped me stand up and steadied me.

After the ceremony, our sleigh flew across the frozen Neva to Alexander Danilovich's palace, which bloomed with flags and flowers that were brought in from greenhouses on the Krim. Menshikov himself struck the parquet with his diamond-studded staff to let the feast begin. The tall French mirrors on the long walls of the splendid hall reflected images of unbridled joy a hundredfold. When Peter had drunk three bottles of Moldavian wine, two eagle cups filled with Prague beer and a carafe of pear vodka, he swayed to his feet and called over towards my group of *damy*, 'Stand up, Anastasia Golizyna, I appoint you Her Majesty's jester!'

The old princess was still chewing her food and pleadingly raised her hands, but he seized her by the hair and dragged her off her seat: 'In the middle of the hall with you. Spin, *babushka*, spin!'

She turned awkwardly in the middle of the hall, more or less in tune with the music. Peter grabbed a piece of smoked salmon and threw it at her cheek, where it clung to her chalky, pasty make-up. Her high powdered wig started to slip. He shouted, 'Hit and sunk! Now you, Catherinushka, show the old frigate that you are a good shot.' I laughed myself to tears, took a sip of vodka and threw a chicken wing at Anastasia Golizyna, which hit her smack on the nose.

I whooped with pride and Peter shouted, 'A salute for the Tsaritsa, who is as good a shot as the best of my men!' They drew their pistols and fired into the ceiling; stucco and gold leaf rained down on us. At three o'clock in the afternoon the sun set and the fireworks lasted all night long, tinting the houses of St Petersburg in flaming hues of red, blue and gold. For three days afterwards, the smell of soot and gunpowder enveloped the city. In spite of the bitter cold, musicians played in all the squares and streets and people danced outside, wrapped in furs and coats, free wine and vodka warming their veins instead of blood.

The following morning, a procession of vehicles brought Peter and me to the Winter Palace. Menshikov staggered ahead of us to our rooms, shaking sleigh bells that he had nicked from a driver and still far too drunk to mind the din he was making. Shafirov and Peter were holding on to each other, and both Daria Menshikova and Alexandra Tolstoya made rude jokes about my wedding night. When Menshikov was about to throw back the bedcovers, Peter grabbed him by the scruff of his neck. 'Do not touch my bed with your sooty fingers, you scoundrel,' he cried, and shoved his old friend towards the door. 'Out, all of you. I must now fulfil my marital duties with my shy bride.'

Everyone linked arms, laughing and swaying, and it took awhile for their shrieks and singing to fade away down the long corridors of the Winter Palace. The room was warm, the curtains drawn to block out the winter day. My feet ached and my head spun; exhausted, I leant against the wall as Peter stepped up to me. 'How am I going to take you now, Tsaritsa?' he asked, his eyes sparkling.

'Well, how any good sailor would take his girl, Peter Alexeyevich,' I chuckled, toying with the collar of his uniform.

'You asked for it,' he said, loosening my skirt. The heavy fabric fell in folds around my ankles. My bloomers followed and I kicked them aside. He lifted me up as if I were a feather, cupping my buttocks. 'My wife has the best arse in Russia. If that is not a good reason to marry, I do not know what is,' he murmured, sucking my nipples, which burst from my half-undone corset. I wrapped my legs in their silk stockings around his hips, before playfully pushing him away, pleading, 'No, please don't! I am still a virgin.'

'Let me do something about that, so help me God!' Peter roared; I arched and he thrust inside me; I tightened my muscles around him and rubbed myself against him.

When I was close to coming, I held him back, whispering, 'Wait!' He paused and blew softly over my face as I slowly and lustfully satisfied myself.

When I sighed and placed my moist forehead to his neck, he laughed. 'My Tsaritsa. You are a soldier indeed.' I held him tightly as he came inside me. For a while we leant against the wall together, panting, before he let me slide to the ground. He stroked the sweaty hair from his forehead and his eyes were as bright as a boy's.

'What now?' he asked.

'Now?' I laughed. 'Now we're going to bed. I'm exhausted. And don't dare to wake me up before tomorrow evening.'

Peter held me while I slept, slipping dreamlessly into my new life as Tsaritsa of All the Russias. Nothing, or so I was convinced, could ever blight our happiness.

54

St Petersburg was expanding; the spring green of the trees lining the Nevsky Prospect filled me with as much pride as the stately buildings along the Fontanka and Moika shores. Could it really be only ten years ago that Swedes, souls and swine had dwelt here? When the Neva thawed, foreign frigates danced on the waves next to the boats of Russian noble families and merchants. Their houses gladly answered the midday cannon thunder from the Peter and Paul Fortress with pistol shots and volleys.

'Go ahead and leave me. There's business to be taken care of,' Peter said half mockingly, half sadly, when I left for the Neva pier in early May. A new bout of syphilis had left him bedridden for a week; the bloating of his body made him howl with pain. 'I expect this Mr Schlüter would rather deal with you than with me,' he murmured.

'Well, after the long trip from Berlin he will be glad to have firm ground under his feet, no matter who welcomes him.' In truth I was looking forward to the outing and to some fresh air as I was pregnant again. This child was more than a sign of our love; it celebrated the hopes we had for the new city and a new Russia. Would God finally grant me of His Grace a healthy son? I prayed for it every night before going to bed.

Peter placed his hand on my belly. 'Take good care of the Tsarevich,' he whispered, and I started: Tsarevich. To date, Alexey still held that title.

As if my thoughts had summoned him, a messenger handed a letter from Alexey into my litter just as I was about to leave. He wrote from Brunswick, where he was with his bride Charlotte. Agneta read the message aloud to me. ' *"Your Majesty, I am glad to hear that my father has raised you in rank to be his wife, and that you are with child again. Please always bless me with your grace. I do not dare to congratulate my father, as the Tsar has left me unaware of his decision and his happiness. Please commend me to him. I am in your hands –* Humbly, Alexey.*"'*

It was incredible: Peter had not told his own son about our wedding. Not that I would ever speak that thought aloud.

'Enough! I've heard enough. Give me the letter, Agneta.' Ernst Gluck's daughter had been my lady-in-waiting for several months. 'It reeks of stupor and fornication.' I grimaced, sniffing at the crushed paper, then pushed the scroll into my sleeve.

We rocked along to the Neva pier where Schlüter was due to arrive. The air in the litter was stuffy. I moved closer to the window to fight my rising nausea. When I fixed my eyes on a still point it usually helped, but the midday sun made the stench of the drying swamp around the city unbearable; gnats cruelly bombarded the labourers and our bearers skilfully avoided teams of workers, who were either carrying the stones needed for the construction of the Peter and Paul Cathedral or else loading the barges that sat low in the water. The architect Trezzini had carefully planned every one of the cathedral's details, from its pointed tower, which allowed a sighting of Finland, to the exquisite furnishings of its interior, where from now on all members of the Tsar's family would be buried. I looked across the construction site, which was teeming with workers: would my own grave, too, be there one day?

Just then, directly next to the window of my litter, I saw a man staggering under the weight of the rocks he carried. His arms had been scourged and scarred, dark holes gaped in his skull instead of his nose and ears: he had already twice tried to escape; at a third attempt he would be killed. My stomach turned, and

I drew the curtain in front of the window. I could not help him, even if I'd wanted to.

The quay was teeming with sailors, merchants and children, girls of easy virtue, tradesmen and people strolling by checking the wares newly arrived in the city, which was in need of everything. The sweet scent of hot pies and fresh beer drifted into the litter. *Babushky* bent low under the loads on their shoulders, the old women blocking our route as effectively as the herds of cattle and drays laden with barrels and chests. We reached the port just as the frigate from Rostock furled its sails and sailors cast the ropes ashore. Everywhere, galleons and smaller vessels rocked on the waves, and the air smelt of salt, pitch and smoke. The wind caught at the colourful flags and bunting displayed by ships creaking at their berths. Sailors climbed nimbly from one mast to another, swinging like monkeys on the rigging. Voices shouted in all known languages, and seagulls rode the wind under their widespread wings, gliding ahead before diving down into the spray and reappearing with fish glittering in their sharp beaks. Agneta gave me a hand before two guards stepped up to give me firmer support and I found my footing. How good it felt to escape the stuffiness of the Winter Palace and be here, amongst real, ordinary people. Since my wedding I had not been on my own for a moment, and I missed solitude.

'Who is this Andreas Schlüter?' Agneta asked, smoothing her skirt.

'A German master craftsman who is said to have built a room entirely from amber for the Prussian King. Peter lured him to St Petersburg by promising a huge sum.'

We were joined then by Domenico Trezzini, Peter's master builder. I made a few pleasantries, waiting to see how long it would take for his hot-headed Italian pride to get the better of him. 'Trezzini, what are you doing here instead of supervising things at the cathedral?' I asked ingenuously. 'Why, you are the man who has created the city of the Tsar with his own hands – how will they manage without the benefit of your expertise?'

I felt him seething. 'Oh, I'm here quite by chance,' he said, grim-faced, looking out over the waves with brows furrowed.

'What a lucky coincidence it is then,' I said amiably.

'Why did the Tsar bring Schlüter to St Petersburg?' he burst out.

'Jealous, Trezzini?' I said, feeling quite sorry for him despite myself. 'The Tsar admired Schlüter's work in Berlin and has invited him to help ornament St Petersburg.'

'Schlüter has squandered the King of Prussia's money. The foundations of his last tower wouldn't bear its weight. Nevertheless, the Tsar appoints him director of constructions here and pays him five thousand roubles a year. I have neither such a title nor such a salary!'

'The Tsar calls Schlüter a – genius.' I pronounced the word carefully.

Trezzini snorted, but I saw tears in his eyes. I tapped his shoulder lightly with my fan. 'The city is big enough for ten or even twenty talented builders such as you and the German. Do not worry.'

He bowed just as Andreas Schlüter appeared on deck, counting his belongings, since chests and bundles disappeared all too easily in the hubbub of the harbour. Compared to the men of St Petersburg, who after the long winter looked like maggots or whose faces were permanently reddened by vodka, he resembled a young god; his dark-blond hair was long and unpowdered. The open collar of his starched, pure white shirt showed off his strong neck, accentuating his fresh complexion and bright even teeth. Agneta stared at him so openly I was forced to shove her. 'Pull yourself together, Agneta! Close that pretty little mouth. You look like a trout, gawping like that,' I whispered.

'Forgive me, Tsaritsa. But I think that only a man of such beauty can create something as wonderful as a room made solely of amber . . .' she said dreamily.

'We have not seen it yet. It is highly unlikely it exists at all,' I replied.

The sailors dragged Schlüter's boxes from the ship, while he himself walked down the companionway and stepped onto the wharf. 'It's good to have solid ground under my feet again. So this is the Venice of the North, the paradise of the great Tsar?' he said to me in German and bowed.

I graciously extended my hand for him to kiss my fingers.

Trezzini wasn't jealous for long. Schlüter died that autumn of the fever that rose like mist from the marsh around St Petersburg. The same illness took my delicate newborn daughter Margarita. After only a few weeks of life, her name was recorded in the saddest of all the court's many lists: the roll call of my dead children. Peter mourned with me, but I knew that in his heart of hearts he was relieved it was but a daughter that we buried. A few weeks later, he came to me and say, 'Poor little Margarita. What is done is done and there is no way of questioning God's will. Still, it is time now for a healthy, strong son, a strapping recruit for my army.'

He smiled and kissed me, but his eyes were sad and serious.

I first met Charlotte two years after her wedding to Alexey, when she finally arrived in St Petersburg. I remember the strict parting in her thin blonde hair as she curtseyed: my ladies-in-waiting giggled at her as she truly was as flat as a boy and her face was badly scarred from the smallpox. But her eyes were friendly and mild, her smile came easily, and her voice sounded like a silver bell when she said to me in German, 'What a joy it is for me to meet you, Tsaritsa. I have heard so much of your grace and generosity that I pray to be your devoted and loyal friend.'

She eyed me closely while she spoke so politely. I knew that the whole of Europe gossiped about me. In Paris, Madame, sister-in-law of the Great Louis, openly mocked me: 'The Tsaritsa of Russia is mouse shit pretending to be poppy seed!' But I opened my arms to embrace my stepson's wife. 'Welcome to Russia, Tsarevna. May St Petersburg become your home, as it is mine. God bless you and your marriage.' The princess leant in to me like a bird that had fallen from its nest and I offered her a stool next to my throne. 'Sit down and tell me about your wedding. Was it splendid?'

She blushed. 'Oh, yes. Divine, in fact. We all deeply regretted that you could not keep the Tsar company back then.'

I hid a smile, for the one who had not regretted it at all was myself. On Alexey's wedding day, Peter had been obliged to drag him by his hair into the chapel of Torgau Castle. The evening before, the Tsarevich had clung to his confessor, shrieking shrilly: 'Never! I will never marry a heretic. As Tsar, I must defend our faith. How am I to do that with a Lutheran woman at my side? This is blasphemy.'

The priest had shielded the Crown Prince with his body until Peter knouted him; Alexey got the Tsar's fist between his eyes. The next morning he was wed to Charlotte, who was allowed to retain her Protestant faith and received twenty-five-thousand Reichstaler, a collection of extravagant tableware as well as carriages and horses from Peter – the dowry her impoverished father could not pay. Both men, Peter and the Duke of Brunswick, beamed with joy at the union. Menshikov, I heard, sent a watermelon as a present.

She chattered on breathlessly and a few scarlet spots bloomed on her pale, sunken cheeks. 'Well, at least the Tsar was with us. I cried like a fountain when my father led me up the aisle to the Tsarevich.'

Charlotte had been sold to Alexey just as I had been sold to Vassily, I thought with sadness, though for rather more money. 'On the morning after the wedding, the Tsar sat on our bed and chatted with us,' she said. The poor girl! Alexey had probably raped her more or less, and then she had to report to Peter on the consummation of the marriage. My eyes grazed her narrow waist and she blushed: there was no sign as yet of a pregnancy.

All the courtiers were seemingly engrossed in conversation, but I knew they were straining their ears. 'I'll give you Marie Hamilton as a lady-in-waiting. She will help you form your household,' I said. Charlotte kissed my fingers and Marie Hamilton curtseyed submissively. But by the look in her big green eyes I knew that she understood I was to be kept fully informed of everything that happened in Alexey's household and bed. Marie Hamilton would follow my orders just as she already fulfilled the Tsar's wishes.

55

The guest Peter most ardently wished to welcome to his new city –
peace – made itself scarce. For two years Menshikov and thirty
thousand soldiers roamed the northern German princedoms in
order to negotiate peace, but the governments were wary of having
to feed Menshikov and his men after the Swedes' long years of
occupation. The wounds of the Thirty Years War – which started
almost a century ago, the ruling European powers locked in a
murderous struggle for supremacy – were yet to heal in the heart of
Europe; so that even Peter was impressed when Menshikov pressed
further money from Lübeck and Hamburg, which had just been
ravaged by the Black Death. Despite all the German complaints,
Peter refused to call Menshikov back; one-third of the funds raised
paid for the construction of the new fleet.

In May, when the first sunshine warmed our souls and skin,
Peter went to Finland to wage war further. When Helsinki gave
itself up to the sixteen thousand Russian soldiers, he wrote to me
from Åbo in early September: *'Soon Finland will be purged of any
Swedes. The Finnish girls have rosy thighs, but I have not laughed for
days. Remain faithful to your* starik, *who loves you so dearly, and come
to me, Catherinushka, as soon as you can. Kiss our little daughters
goodnight.'*

I smiled when Agneta paused in her reading: after a short knock,
Charlotte's new lady-in-waiting hurried into the room. I waved

Agneta out and eyed Marie Hamilton, the beautiful Scotswoman who stemmed from the German Quarter in Moscow. She, too, was pregnant. Who was the child's father: Peter or the former Streltsy soldier Grigori Orlov? He had escaped the executions by sheer courage and cheek. When he mounted the scaffold, where Peter was waiting, axe in hand, Orlov kicked aside the head of the man who had been executed before him and shouted, 'By God: must I make room for myself?' Peter, always appreciative of bravery and wit, pardoned him there and then, and today Orlov blessed the *damy* of St Petersburg. I had heard he was hung like a horse.

'What's the matter, Marie? You seem out of breath?' I asked mockingly.

'It is about the Tsarevich,' she panted, laying her slender hand on her ample bosom, not at all embarrassed about her condition.

I sat up, excited. 'Is Charlotte finally pregnant?'

'On the contrary. Alexey has not slept with her since their wedding night.'

'What?' That was the last thing I had expected. Like his father, Alexey suffered from a surfeit of lust.

'Worse, just this afternoon he asked his confessor how he could rid himself of her and send Charlotte back to her parents,' Marie Hamilton cried.

'And what did the old fool answer?'

'Apparently this can easily be done if you are married to a woman of another faith who is barren. If she does not bear him a child in three years of marriage, he can expel her, the priest says. Otherwise he can baptise her, shave her head and send her to a convent. Charlotte does nothing but wail and when Alexey sees her, he throws whatever is to hand at her, be it a chair, a vase or crockery.'

Hearing this, I struggled to control my anger, rising so hastily from my stool that it toppled over. In my heart, I dearly wished to believe in Alexey – to me he was still the timid boy I had met so many years ago, who'd smiled at me shyly on the Kremlin's balcony. Peter had left him to Menshikov's guidance and to careless, often brutal tutors. It wasn't Alexey's fault that he had not an ounce of his father's strength of character. Still, he was the Tsarevich, and this was more serious than I had thought. 'Get my carriage and my cloak. I shall pay a visit to my stepson,' I ordered. A servant ran off, his metal-capped soles sounding on the wooden parquet.

'But …' Marie began, sounding worried.

'But what?' My Imperial green silk cloak was placed on my shoulders and I felt stronger and empowered to do whatever I had to do, stretching out my arms and raising my chin. 'Dress me up, Marie. I have to look like the Tsaritsa.'

She hung a necklace of multiple strands of turquoises and diamonds around my neck and hooked the matching pendants into my ears; bracelets snapped shut around my wrists. 'Alexey has guests in the Winter Palace tonight,' she said carefully, her eyes lowered.

'Whatever that means. Do you think I have not seen a feast before? Don't worry, I'm not easily shocked,' I said dryly, as I checked my appearance briefly in the mirror. Good. Marie curt-seyed to me as deeply as her swollen belly allowed.

The small staircase of the Summer Palace on the Fontanka Canal was still warm from the day's sunshine when we left. Our carriage shook on the gravel drive through the garden that Peter had carefully planned. Marie fought against nausea, but I felt no compassion for her and looked out of the window instead. Dusk drew a veil of blue light over the water, and in the balmy, bright summer's night lovers were sitting on the steps of the jetties along the river, talking and laughing. On the quayside, men taught their sons how to swing their fishing rods into the Neva, and the teal-coloured feathers of the ducks blended with the river's waves. St Petersburg evenings cast a spell like a net, in which we all were caught as helplessly as fish.

The carriage jerked to a halt outside the Winter Palace. Alexey and Charlotte had moved in to its cold splendour, whilst Peter and I preferred the simplicity of the Summer Palace with its Delft tiles, low ceilings and brightly painted wooden walls. It was a house, properly speaking – our house – and not a palace.

I looked up at the imposing façade, Trezzini's masterpiece: torches flickered behind the countless windows, whether the rooms were in use or not. Footmen hurried to my carriage, but otherwise the vast courtyard was empty. When I got out, I heard voices raised in rude songs in the upper reaches and laughter and shrieks from Alexey's banquet. Suddenly I had a premonition that made my skin tingle.

'Give me your whip,' I ordered the coachman, and he passed it to me with a look of surprise. I clenched the silver-mounted handle in my fist. 'Marie. Show me the way.'

Our steps echoed up the wide, empty staircase and then along the corridors of grey and white marble; our figures were reflected in the high gold-framed mirrors along the walls. Soldiers stood to attention at every corner we passed, but no courtiers were to be seen. They were either with Peter in the field or else had used his absence finally to spend some time with their families.

'Should we really do this?' Marie whispered, but I followed the sounds of voices and music until we reached the small black marble dining-room.

The guards outside the door crossed rifles with bayonets spiked on top. 'No passage, by order of the Tsarevich!' a soldier with spots as big as bulbs on his face barked; the other one had barely any teeth left and gave an empty grin.

'If you do not wish to go to Siberia tomorrow, boys, or be broken on the wheel, then make yourself scarce,' I said coolly.

'The Tsaritsa,' Marie snarled, and both men knelt, banged their foreheads on the floor and muttered reverences and apologies. I entered and the first person I spotted in the hall full of carousing, cavorting people was Charlotte herself. It was unbelievable. The wife of the Tsarevich of All the Russias was serving his drunkard friends beer! Just then, one of them smacked her meagre backside. 'Ouch! What a bony arse! But vodka is a magic potion: it makes any girl beautiful,' he howled, pinching her naked arm. The princess fought back tears and from the other end of the hall I heard hoots and claps. I felt cold to the pit of my stomach, to witness her humiliation.

'Take Charlotte to the Tsarevich's bedroom,' I ordered Marie, who fought her way through the crowd to the weeping and cowering Crown Princess.

I myself turned up the collar of my cloak, though nobody noticed me; they were all too drunk. When I reached the other end of the hall, a group of men stood gathered around a table, jeering. 'Yes! A toast to our Crown Prince!'

'He takes all hurdles like no other. That is what I call a rider.'

'Give her the spurs! Make her whinny!'

Alexey's hair hung loose to his shoulders; his shirt was half open and glued to his glistening, sweaty body. He wore riding boots, but his breeches hung around his knees and a girl was lying on the table in front of him, her fat white thighs spread wide. He grunted as he fondled her plump breasts and slapped her buttocks until her flesh turned as red as a cherry. 'Yes, my horsey. You must be broken in!' he cried. I felt dizzy; the sight was too awful. Despite all the rough games I had witnessed in the tents, in the field or in the Kremlin, seeing this girl made me feel like a maid in Vassily's house again on the first night he came for me.

Alexey's companions neighed, whinnied and imitated the sounds of horses' hooves, before howling with laughter. The girl herself screamed with joy. When I could see her face, her skin was very fair under thick red hair, but her tiny eyes and thick nose gave her a vicious look. I was about to leave when Alexey shouted, 'Now witness me making a son and heir for Russia. My father and his whore only manage daughters and I'm not going to do it with that scrawny German cat.' He rammed into the girl, who squealed and arched her back, her breasts bouncing, her nipples wide and light pink. Without thinking I lashed out, whipping the Tsarevich's naked back. He reared with pain and spun around, foaming with anger and disbelief that anyone would dare, but at the sight of me his cock went limp.

'Cover yourself, Tsarevich!' I hissed with barely hidden rage and contempt. The girl sat up, looking at me almost defiantly, while Alexey's friends fell to their knees, their heads bowed. I lifted the crop, ready to strike again.

'Do as I say.'

Alexey pulled up his breeches, pale with rage. His eyes popped and his lips were pressed together in a narrow line. 'Tsaritsa, what an unexpected honour. Why all this fuss? We are just having a little fun.' He bowed to me mockingly. 'What brings Your Majesty here?'

'The same thing as you: my wish for an heir to the Russian throne,' I said. 'Come with me.'

He went ahead, blushing with anger. Around us the silence was deafening.

'Where are we going?' he asked as I shoved him through another door.

'Charlotte is waiting for you in your bedroom. You know the way better than I do.' He shuffled his feet, walking as slowly as possible, but I thrust him in the back with the whip's handle. 'Move! We don't have all day.'

'I do not want to have anything to do with Charlotte. I love another!' he shrieked.

'Who is the lucky girl?' I asked sarcastically.

'You just saw her. Her name is Afrosinja. She was a washerwoman in the Finnish campaign.' He looked at me defiantly, but all I did was chuckle.

'And I suppose I'm meant to feel sympathetic to her on that account? You are mistaken about so many things. I love you, Alexey, and always have, so listen to me carefully. It would be far better for your health to love and impregnate your wife than some Finnish hussy.'

'You're just like my father!' He spat on the elaborate parquet of ebony, ivory and ash. 'I love Afrosinja and no one else.'

'Your father would have killed you and Afrosinja in his rage if he had just heard that.'

I drove the Tsarevich to his rooms like a shepherd his livestock. There was no one to be seen, but I knew that these walls had ears. 'After you,' I said curtly as we arrived at his bedroom door. Marie had stoked the embers in the fireplace and Charlotte sat up in bed, almost disappearing in the vast frame, the curtains and layers of sheets. Her naked shoulders trembled. Her hair was limp and straight, chest as flat as a boy's. I noticed a red bruise on her skinny arm marked the spot where the drunkard had pinched her.

'I don't want her. She disgusts me!' Alexey screeched, reeling away and trying to escape me, but I kept him in check with the whip. Angrily he tore his breeches open: his long, thick cock hung down as limp as a worm. More than ever before he reminded me of Vassily, and I fought my disgust.

'See how the German excites me? No wonder we have so many children,' he said, mocking me, but on the verge of tears. 'She reeks of beer and vodka, like a whore in a *kabak*.'

I laughed: 'Well, if your Afrosinja smells better …'

Charlotte sobbed, and I hesitated briefly. Was I doing the right thing? 'Stop crying. This is for Russia, and for your own good,' I said to her, and then called, 'Marie!'

The appearance of the pregnant courtier, her always full breasts now almost bursting out of her loosely laced silk dress, startled even me. With her auburn curls, moist pink lips and lively green eyes, she was a real beauty. No wonder she had shared Peter's bed for so many years.

'The Tsarevich needs to sire an heir. Help him,' I said curtly, to hide my shame and horror at what was happening. Marie smiled, showing her small, pointed teeth, and knelt before Alexey. From the doorway, I cast a glance back into the room. Marie Hamilton had pulled her dress from her shoulders, showing her full white breasts. Alexey gasped when she took him between her rosy lips, closing her mouth around him. The prince clawed his hands into her shoulders and I saw him growing hard again. Somehow, I felt this was not their first time together.

'Marie,' I reminded her, 'don't forget: the best belongs to the Crown Princess.'

Alexey groaned with anger and disappointment when Marie led him to his marital bed, where Charlotte cowered in one corner, ashen-faced and hiccupping with fear. I left them to it.

Out in the hall, I sank onto my heels like the peasant girl I had once been, and tears came. I heard Marie talking and laughing, Alexey shout briefly in protest and then Charlotte cry out, again and again. I trembled and twisted my fingers until my knuckles turned white. What I did was for the good of Russia: when Charlotte bore Alexey a son, I, too, could breathe easier.

Peter, I was sure, would not have acted differently in my place. The thought of that made me weep even more.

56

When I joined Peter in Finland, I told him neither about Alexey's problems with his wife nor about Afrosinja. I had better news to share: Charlotte was finally pregnant. The Tsarevich himself had told me, his face stony, before he, his retinue and Afrosinja left for Carlsbad to take the waters.

Peter shrugged and said, 'With what sort of son am I punished? Oh, why does his weak health not take him from me?' Then he ordered: 'Replace all the foreigners in Charlotte's court with Russians. Her ladies-in-waiting, her jesters, physicians, midwives: all of them. The child is not to be secretly swapped after its birth, be it boy or girl.'

Charlotte pleaded with him to change this cruel order; the ink of her dozens of letters to him was smeared with tears. No wonder she longed for her familiar ladies in this still so foreign court, but her pleas were in vain: she gave birth to her daughter surrounded by strangers whose language she still did not speak properly. It was clear that no one was willing to bet a kopek on the delicate princess's future. The news of her being brought to bed reached us at Hangö Bay and Peter stared across the harbour's grey waters. He looked once more like the young man I had met so many years ago in Marienburg: his skin tanned, his blue eyes sparkling, dark hair streaked handsomely by only a few grey strands, dishevelled by the wind.

'A daughter!' he spat, handing the letter to Makarov, who stuck it in his leather pouch. 'Wipe your arse with it, if you want to. Daughters I have enough of myself. If only Alexey wasn't so bloody useless.'

I laced my fingers over my stomach: I, too, was pregnant again. The morning light danced on the waves, and the coast of Finland was but a thin blue line on the horizon, where white clouds billowed like sails in the wind. A gull dived into the waves and did not reappear.

Two weeks later we surrounded the Swedish fleet in Hangö Bay. After the battle, the sad remnants of the enemy drifted on the waves: bloated bodies, tattered canvas and broken wooden planks. Back in St Petersburg I gave birth to my daughter Maria – '*I have a son called Maria,*' Peter wrote jokingly to Menshikov – but the little girl was too weak to survive the day of her birth. Peter kept her birth, as well as her death, out of the weekly bulletins that were sent to the European courts.

The young woman was in such a haste that she ran right into me; if I hadn't caught her, we would both have tumbled to the ground. I was deep in thought, for Peter had just shown me his Kunstkamera, which was newly founded in the Summer Palace and open for all the people of St Petersburg to visit. Peter had told me: 'Ever since my childhood, I have collected misfits of nature, rare weapons, animals of all kinds and souvenirs of my travels. Now everyone can see them, *matka*, and learn from them.' He pulled me with him between the rows and rows of shelves full of glasses and containers: I saw lambs with three heads, the legless torso of a baby with four arms, twins that were joined at the breast – they made me think of Master Lampert's Tent of Wonders so long ago! – as well as a child with a fish's tail and two young dogs that were said to have been born of a sixty-year-old virgin.

'Do you like it?' Peter asked me, full of pride. I nodded, but he frowned. 'What's wrong? Are you sad?'

'The Summer Palace was our home. We planned the house and the garden together; from here, we watched our city grow. Now everybody will take a walk in my garden, visit your collection in my salon, and get drunk on wine and vodka in my hall.'

'Ah. Don't worry. I'll build you a palace that is much bigger and more magnificent than you can ever imagine,' Peter promised before leaving me alone.

So I heard hurried steps on the gravel path, but only when the young woman pushed by me, and with a shout of 'Damn!', dropped her thickly filled pouch, did I pay any attention. My shoulder ached from our collision as she tried to gather up the dozens of scattered coins.

'What a lot of loot,' I commented, and she blushed.

'Tsaritsa! Mistress, forgive me!' She had refilled the pouch and was about to move off when I noticed her bright blue eyes and ash-blonde curls. I frowned.

'Have not we met before?'

'Yes, Tsaritsa. I'm Alice Kramer. We met at Boris Petrovich Sheremetev's house.'

'Of course! At Bobushka's,' I said jokingly. 'Are you still in his household?'

'No. His wife got so jealous, she forced him to give me as a gift to General Balk,' said Alice, her pretty face darkening. I felt for her: how easily that could have happened to me as well.

'But General Balk is married to Anna Mons's sister. She'll hardly tolerate you under her roof?'

Alice fought back tears. 'Indeed. The Balks owed Marie Hamilton a favour and now I belong to her, as her handmaiden.'

'I see,' I said carefully. 'Is that Marie's money? Are you running an errand for her?'

'Yes. I picked up money due to her from the jeweller Blumenthal. She has sold jewels to him.' Alice sounded hesitant, even if this was nothing new in St Petersburg where Peter's fondness for lavish, long-lasting festivals and amusements caused his courtiers a great deal of expense. Many *damy* shifted the family jewellery to pay for a seated dinner for three hundred or more guests.

'Is Marie Hamilton not pregnant again? Isn't this her second child?' I said casually, but Alice paled with dread.

'I know nothing about it, God help me!' she whispered, pressing the pouch to her chest. 'I must hurry, Tsaritsa, my mistress is a strict woman and I do not wish to be beaten and starved.' She curtseyed to me and then ran on, her skirts flying.

I walked on, for the last time enjoying the privacy of the Summer Palace's gardens before Peter gave them to the public. Marie Hamilton had been pregnant back when I'd forced the consummation of Alexey's marriage. Had she given that child to an orphanage or was it being raised in the country because, from Alice's reaction, I was sure her mistress was pregnant again. But why make a secret of it? I walked on, even deeper in thought.

57

Peter and I were sitting by the fireplace in his study while two foot-men tried to impose order on his desk.

'Let me show you the palace I will build for our summers together. You know that I never make empty promises, Catherine,' Peter said. He stroked Lenta – he gave all his dogs the same name – and the dog growled softly with pleasure. When Peter gave her an old leather glove to chew, she settled down on the worn toes of his boots. He had taught her all sorts of tricks – taking off a hat, rolling over, giving her paw, jumping over a stick – but now she was where she wanted to be, at his feet, warming her hide.

'Can we not simply live in the Summer Palace again?' I pleaded once more. 'Just us and the children? Perhaps we can house the Kunstkamera somewhere else?' I sipped some of the bitter *chai* and added a good shot of vodka to my cup, as I felt the cold of autumn to my bones. My last pregnancy had drained much of my strength.

'No. It is no longer just about us, *matka*. We must show Europe that Russia does not fear comparison to any other country; I am the peer of any ruler on Earth. Even the Winter Palace seems small and humble to me. But still, it can be my Louvre, and Peterhof my Versailles.'

'Peterhof? Versailles?' I looked at him, confused, but he caressed my hair.

'She who has never seen Paris and the court of the Great Louis cannot understand this. But the Tsar of All the Russias can do anything the King of France can do. On top of that, Menshikov is building his summer place of Oranienbaum. His palace on the Strelka is already the most beautiful in the city. That dog shall not trump me in the country, too!' Peter stood up. 'I have been working on my ideas for Peterhof for almost two years, whenever I had time.' He got up and searched his desk, before cursing and kicking the footmen. 'Damn it! If you make order here, I'll never find anything.'

Then he settled beside me on the carpet and dropped a dozen paper scrolls onto the floor. 'But there was just too much else going on. The new law of inheritance alone has cost me months, and still my nobles and peasants refuse to leave their possessions and property to only their eldest son.'

'No wonder. You're not doing anything different, after all.' I wanted to bite my lip from anger at my own stupidity then. How could I have said that?

Peter stayed silent but pulled at the glove in Lenta's mouth in a playful tug-of-war; she growled and snapped after her toy. Then he sought my gaze pleadingly. 'Give me a son, Catherinushka. Only then can I sleep in peace again. I need nothing so much as a son. Just one, please, so I am not completely dependent on Alexey. It's for my beautiful Russia: I beg you.' His eyes were dark with longing. My heart clenched.

'If it was up to me, I would give you ten strong sons, my Tsar,' I whispered, kissing his fingers.

'I know, I know,' he murmured. We heard a noise beyond the concealed door: 'The Tsar and the Tsaritsa are not be disturbed,' Makarov insisted, but between various male voices I could hear a woman's whimpering. What was happening?

'That's Shafirov!' Peter strode to the door and looked puzzled to see the guard holding back a ragged-looking old woman in shackles and a strange man, with Shafirov behind them. 'What is it, Shafirov? Can't you wait until suppertime?'

'May we speak to the Tsaritsa?' said Shafirov, who was pale with excitement, pushing his two companions ahead of him. Peter scratched his head, and I, too, was surprised. The woman reeked of sweat and vodka; her grey hair was all dirty and tangled, and her one good eye was hidden behind puffy bags of skin and wrinkles. The other was covered with a dark, dirty linen bandage. She wrung her hands in their shackles and her fingernails were long, filthy and curved. I pressed a perfumed handkerchief to my nose: 'Yes? What is it?'

Shafirov forced the woman to her knees. 'Lower your ugly face in front of the Tsaritsa!' he said.

I rose and the scrolls with the plans to Peterhof slid from my lap, rustling. 'Shafirov, who are these people?'

'Speak, Uncle Blumenthal,' he said to the old man, who wore the flat black hat, black cape and side-locks of the observant Jew. What had Shafirov called him – Blumenthal? I had heard that name before but could not remember where. The man bowed to me with quiet dignity then pulled a flat velvet box from his wide cloak. The old woman struggled for breath, too terrified to whimper, as Blumenthal opened the case. I came closer and had a look, without really understanding what I was seeing: in it lay the necklace of turquoises and diamonds I had worn when I had forced Alexey back to the path of marital virtue. By virtue of the unusual combination of stones, it was a unique piece.

Peter grasped the necklace in his fist. 'Where did you get this jewellery from, old man? I myself gave this set to the Tsaritsa.'

The goldsmith bowed. 'I recognised the noble origins of the piece and turned to my nephew Peter here.'

'Who sold him this, Shafirov? And who is this stinking woman?' Peter asked, pale with anger.

'The old witch is an angel-maker. She ends the unwanted pregnancies of the *damy* of St Petersburg,' replied Shafirov.

I looked at the disgusting fingers of the woman while she rocked back and forth in her shackles, on her knees, moaning. Her lips were trembling over toothless gums.

'And the jewellery?' Peter asked. My throat felt parched. Where was this leading?

'Well, the jewellery was stolen and sold by Marie Hamilton. She needed money to have a pregnancy ended. Or rather several pregnancies, if the witch is to be trusted.'

All was silent. I did not dare look at Peter.

'May I?' said Shafirov, ramming his knee into the woman's back. She fell forward, screaming. 'Speak! Maybe you can save your skin,' he hissed to her.

She looked up with her one good eye. 'Marie Hamilton is a bitch on heat. And now I, a poor *babushka*, should pay for her sins? She used to come and see me every four or five months, crying and lamenting that she could not have the child. God knows with whom she whored. The whole of the town, I'd say,' she shrieked. 'But my work doesn't come cheap.'

I avoided Peter's gaze when Shafirov said, 'Marie Hamilton has stolen from the Tsaritsa more than once and has sold the jewels to my Uncle Blumenthal. It was only this especially beautiful and rare piece that aroused his suspicion.'

'How many jewels did Marie Hamilton bring you, Blumenthal?' I asked haltingly. The implications of the whole story dawned on me only slowly.

He weighed his answer carefully. 'She usually sent her German servant, Alice Kramer. She came often. Sometimes with just a ring to sell, sometimes with chains, chokers, earrings or belts.' I no longer wanted to hear. Suddenly I realised how many of my belongings had gone missing in recent months. How careless I had grown about it, thinking a maid had mislaid a belt, or that my earrings had slipped off my lobes during a wild dance. I who used to own nothing in the whole wide world.

Peter tilted the woman's head up and stared into her one eye. 'Tell me, old hag, before I have your tongue torn out of your filthy mouth. What gender were the children you took from Marie's body?'

She looked at him coldly and chuckled, obviously not afraid of what fate had in store for her. 'If I am to die anyway, my Tsar, I might as well tell you. They were all boys – splendid, strapping sons. And how she sniggered, the Hamilton, when she saw the tiny, chopped up bodies. You know what she said, more than once?'

I wanted not to hear, but Peter nodded.

'I might be a whore, but I can do over and over again what the Tsaritsa can't do even once.' She toppled backwards, howling and bleeding from her nose as well as her mouth, as Shafirov struck her with his clenched fist.

58

It was a grey, overcast day when Marie Hamilton mounted the scaffold. Both the Crown Princess and I were pregnant again, but Peter had ordered us nevertheless to witness her execution. Waiting at the execution site outside the Peter and Paul Cathedral, we'd heard in the distance the jeering and whistling as Marie mounted a sledge at the Neva gate of the Peter and Paul Fortress. I had asked for her not to be tortured, for I had forgiven her both her thieving and her slight to me. Was she not to be punished harshly enough in any case? Peter would not be swayed from his judgment: Marie had spilt possible royal blood and she must pay for that.

Her sledge, which was strewn with rotten straw, drew nearer; snowflakes fell, and the sturdy ponies slipped on the icy cobblestones. The crowd, who had been waiting since before dawn, shouted obscenities and threw rotten vegetables, laughing and screaming. Marie neither ducked nor blinked when the first rotten cabbage leaf hit her face. Was she crying? I was too far away to tell, but thought I saw traces of ill treatment on her face as well as a burn mark on her shoulder. Crude hands had shorn off those tumbling auburn locks, which had aroused many a man's desire, and on her bald head cuts and bruises festered.

'God be merciful upon her poor soul,' muttered the Tsaritsa Praskovia, crossing herself with three fingers. She, too, had begged Peter in vain for mercy for Marie. Charlotte lowered her eyes and clasped her fingers, while next to her Alexey nonchalantly stretched out his legs and munched an apple. He spat out the seeds, hitting his wife's silk shoes.

The wardens lifted Marie from the sledge and took her shackles off; she held herself very straight, as if she was on her way to a ball. A woman pushed through the rows of soldiers and spat in her face. 'Whore! Child killer! Witch!' The saliva trickled down Marie's cheek, but she gracefully unfolded the wide skirt of the white silk dress that Peter had made her wear for her very last hour. Small black bows adorned the shoulders and waist, but it hung loose on her gaunt frame. Her gaze skimmed the crowds until it found me: she curtseyed very low and I saw her praying for forgiveness, before the prison wardens dragged her to the scaffold. Her knees and shoulders bumped on the steps up to the executioner's block, where they dropped her like a sack of barley. She tried to get on her hands and knees, looked up, and gasped: Peter awaited her there. She pressed a hand to her lips in horror and shrank back, but a soldier stopped her, laughing and saying,

'You did not expect that, my girl, did you? The Tsar fears he might fall out of practice.'

The crowd howled. I shifted restlessly on my throne. Peter gallantly offered her his arm and helped her stand. I saw hope flashing in her eyes: would he pardon her after all? No. The Tsar led her the couple of steps to the executioner's block and his hand on her shoulder pressed her down. Her knees buckled and I saw Peter's lips move. Marie sobbed, bowed her head and leant forward. Her white throat shone against the rough, dark wood of the block. Peter turned, raising his hand. The assembled crowd fell silent and his eyes sought out mine. I shivered and pulled my fur cloak tighter around my shoulders.

'I cannot mitigate this most severe of all judgments, for that would be against divine and human law. Marie Hamilton, may God forgive you,' he cried.

Tears streamed down Charlotte's face and Alexey looked sidelong at her, briefly and coldly. He was in a bad mood. Peter wrote him angry, threatening letters every day on just about every subject: his studies, beliefs, duty to become a fitting heir to the throne, and of course the state of his marriage. Marie's execution did not seem to touch him in the least. In his retinue I spotted the Finnish girl for whom he had professed his love, Afrosinja. She curtseyed to me but I looked back at the scaffold. It was too horrible and yet I could not help but watch.

The executioner adjusted his hood and then lifted his sword at Peter's nod. The blade caught the wan light and I heard the crowd gasp. With a single blow he beheaded Marie; a stream of blood was sent high up in the air and her head rolled into a basket filled with straw. The people cried out; the scent of roast meat reached me on my pedestal: the merchants of St Petersburg profited from the masses and their holiday mood to do good business.

Peter seized Marie's head from the basket and the crowd sighed when we saw her wide, terrified eyes. Very slowly and tenderly, the Tsar kissed Marie Hamilton's dead, open lips. Charlotte gagged, and I gave Alice Kramer, who had replaced Marie as my lady-in-waiting, a sign: she stooped and spoke calmly in German to the Crown Princess. Alexey watched Alice with a glint in his eye: was it desire or curiosity? Whatever, I slapped his arm with my fan made of ivory and silk, lest he had any ideas. I could have been Alice Kramer once and I was going to protect her if I could.

59

I was not far from the Tsar when he turned to Tolstoy during a feast in Menshikov's palace for the name-day of our daughter Elizabeth. 'You have always given me the right advice. Help me this time, too,' Peter said darkly, and Tolstoy moved closer.

'What is it, my Tsar? Has somebody wronged you?'

I leant back in my cushions. My hour was only weeks away, and all my limbs were heavy and swollen. 'Yes. My son Alexey. Everything he does. Merely by being, he wrongs me,' Peter spat. 'In England, a king once called into the ranks of his knights, *"Will no one rid me of this troublesome priest?"'*

'And? What happened to the troublesome priest?' Tolstoy asked with a lopsided smile, as Peter drank deeply of his Tokay.

'The knights went to the cathedral where the man was preaching and slew him in front of the altar.'

Tolstoy weighed his answer for a moment and warned, 'Do not act in haste, my Tsar. Both Alexey's wife and the Tsaritsa are with child. We might be lucky and then nothing need be done. Otherwise ...'

'But I can no longer bear it,' Peter cried, then lowered his voice as some of the foreign envoys had looked up. 'He is an insult to me, not a son.' He glowered. Even Elizabeth stopped playing with her little dog and looked questioningly at her father. I smiled at her soothingly, and then met the ambassadors' eyes until they lowered their gaze. For good measure, I sent them the cup-bearer and his two companions with a vat of liquor. Campredon, the French Ambassador, grimaced when his eagle cup was filled to the brim.

Peter groaned. 'The thought that Russia might pass to Alexey haunts me. Let's do something. Now!'

But Tolstoy was not to be swayed: 'Please, wait. For how demanding can Alexey be, if he has a son and a brother?'

Yes: if, I thought, and checked myself as I had done a hundred, thousand times before. Did I feel different during this pregnancy to when I had expected my daughters? Was my belly more pointed than round; was I more or less sick in the morning; more beautiful or uglier? Was I sad or jolly? Then I tried to chase out these old women's tales, the myths and all the laymen's advice, and meet all the questions and doubts in my heart with prayer.

The Tsar studied Charlotte, his brow furrowed. Neither marriage nor her blessed state had enhanced her looks. She hardly ate and always asked for fresh lemonade, which annoyed him. Wouldn't vodka and Tokay do? Her skin was grey and blemished with unsightly pimples; her hair had lost the last of its shine and body and would not stay in soft curls. I pitied her, thinking of her last letter, which, thanks to Peter's secret service, had never reached her father's court of Brunswick. *'I am a lamb, which is slaughtered senselessly on the altar of our house. I shall die a slow death, from sorrow and loneliness,'* she'd written. Makarov had read it aloud to me.

'Sister-in-law of the Emperor of Austria or not, I do not know how my stupid son has impregnated this grasshopper again. I would not get a hard-on with that bag of bones,' Peter muttered. and Tolstoy replied, 'Alexey is said to have been helped by his mistress.' He made an obscene gesture and the two men almost choked with laughter.

I turned around, looking for Alice Kramer. 'Where is the Tsarevich tonight?' I asked her under my breath.

'He dines alone with Afrosinja. Every evening. They are always together; the Tsarevich gave her a big apartment.'

Peter lifted his tankard and shouted, 'A toast to the welfare of my unborn son! And a toast to my unborn grandson!' Everyone rose; I smiled at Charlotte as she sipped the wine politely with pale lips. Then I, too, drank deeply, for wine drove my worries away.

I paced my little Chinese study, its walls covered in silk and dark red lacquer, to ease the last days of my pregnancy. Persian incense burnt in copper pans as it was a clammy, damp October day; even the flames in the fireplace cowered in the draught. For the first time ever, I feared giving birth. I was so big: was I expecting twins? Two sons for Peter, possibly? I forbade myself any sort of hope or daydream.

'Listen, *matka*,' he said, and read to me what he had just written to Alexey. '"*My son. It hurts me more and more to address a lowly being such as you. I have spared neither my life nor my strength for Russia and my people. So why should I spare your life, which is so unworthy? I'd rather give my throne to a worthy stranger than to an unworthy son.*"'

'Is not that a bit harsh? Don't send the letter just now. Think about it: let us wait for the birth of Charlotte's child. Perhaps he will improve ...' I said, against all reason. I still could not, and would not, give up on Alexey so easily. He had not become the way he was all by himself.

'Oh, you, with your heart of gold. No one can ever be so bad that even you might see the evil in him. If I so much as think of Marie Hamilton ... but if it had been left to you, she'd still be alive.' Peter tousled my hair in mock reproof.

I shrugged. 'Life is too short for us to be vindictive. Hatred and anger only burden the heart.'

There was a knock on the door then and Alice slipped in: 'Peter Andreyevich Tolstoy asks to be admitted. The Tsarevna Charlotte is in labour.'

'Is it not too soon for her?' I asked, but Peter ordered,

'Let him in. What are you waiting for, girl?'

Peter Tolstoy came in together with his handsome Moorish slave, Abraham, whom he had bought at the slave market in Constantinople. Tolstoy himself looked pale and drawn. 'I cannot stay long, my Tsar. The Crown Princess is in labour. Blumentrost says it's far too early, but –' His voice trailed off, and Alice shot me a worried glance.

'How can that old quack be so sure about it? Was he present at the moment of impregnation?' Peter laughed mockingly and kicked the logs in the fireplace. Sparks shot upwards before settling in the embers.

Tolstoy shuffled his feet uneasily. 'Rumours are going around the Crown Prince's household,' he began.

Peter looked up. 'What kind of rumours?'

'The Crown Princess is said to have fallen down the stairs. She has bruises all over her body and some of her ribs are broken, according to Blumentrost.'

I sat down, stuffed a pillow behind my back and put my feet on Peter's thighs. Charlotte fallen down the stairs? She hardly moved anymore. I feared the worst. Peter began to knead my swollen ankles. 'Spit it out, Tolstoy,' he ordered. 'What has really happened?'

Tolstoy looked browbeaten. 'If you so command: Alexey kicked and punched Charlotte so hard that she threw herself down the stairs. Now labour has set in, many weeks too early.'

'My God,' I gasped. 'That's impossible.' What had we all allowed to happen?

Peter pushed my feet aside, got up and went to the small desk. He pressed his seal into the soft lump of wax at the end of his letter to Alexey. When he looked up, his gaze settled on my belly in a silent plea. 'The prince must decide. Either he behaves as befits his rank or he retreats to a monastery.' Peter's voice sounded choked and hoarse. 'Or –' He broke off. Neither Tolstoy nor I dared to look at him. *Or* – ? I placed my hands on my stomach. The child hardly moved anymore and I had grown so big. My hour was close.

'Call the messenger,' Peter commanded, folding the letter.

I knew that this was Alexey's last chance.

60

On a rainy day at the end of October, Charlotte gave birth to a healthy boy. The Tsar was present at the birth and held his grandson up in the hazy light.

'Look at him: my heir. Petrushka!' he cheered, eyes shiny with tears as the child wriggled and clamoured for his first feed. He was well formed and in good health, I saw, stronger-looking than my sons had ever been at the moment of their birth. Peter bathed and swaddled Petrushka himself, laughing and cooing, before laying him in the arms of the buxom wet-nurse he had brought in from the German Quarter of Moscow. The little prince was to soak up the principles of the new, open Russia with his milk.

'Well, let's get on with it, shall, we, my little one?' she asked tenderly, and Petrushka snapped at her large red nipple.

The Tsar whooped: 'Wonderful! He's already as strong as a bear.'

Behind us, Charlotte stirred in her fever. Blumentrost wanted to bleed her and stood ready with his cursed heated glasses in his hands. 'Stop it. You are bleeding the life out of her. Serve her hot chicken broth with red wine instead,' I ordered, and knelt next to her as best I could despite my belly. 'Charlotte?' I asked softly. She turned her head. Her eyes were glassy, a veil of grey sweat dulled her skin, yet her cheeks glowed an unhealthy shade of crimson. Her fingers twitched briefly before going limp in mine. '*Mutter* . . .' she whispered. A maidservant spooned some of the broth I had ordered into her mouth, but the princess could not keep it down.

'See to it that she is not too tightly covered. Open the windows. Dried fruits soaked in warm wine and bowls of chicken broth will strengthen her. Burn camphor in the room. That cleans the air,' I told her bored retinue.

Charlotte did not stop bleeding; her fever rose and of the six doctors Peter had sent to her, each was as useless as the other, standing in the corner, muttering and shaking their heads. On his last visit to her apartment, when she was trembling and her teeth rattled, Peter had to be supported by two of his footmen, for he had celebrated the birth of his grandson in the past days a bit too thoroughly and could scarcely stand for flatulence. I myself did not see Charlotte again, so that no curse and no evil eye should lie on me when my own hour drew close.

'You go,' I said to Alice. 'Speak German to her in her last hour, will you?'

When she returned, her eyes were swollen and her face worn with grief. I told my reader to stop instructing me. 'And? Sit down. Drink from the hot wine and then tell me everything.'

'Her end is near. Charlotte is an angel. In her last confession, she forgave Alexey everything. She – ' Alice's voice broke. I stared into the flames in the fireplace. Our world was no place for angels.

'What exactly did she say?' I asked.

Alice swallowed hard. 'She could speak no more, but nodded her assent when her priest asked if Tsar Peter had been kindness himself and Alexey always a loving husband to her.' She slid closer to me, digging her fingers into my skirt and burying her face in the folds of my robes. 'Forgive me, Tsaritsa, but please, do not send me back there. I can't bear it.'

Her delicate body trembled and I stroked her hair. Alice was not yet twenty, yet a shadow of the merry girl I had encountered in Sheremetev's house. She raised her head and sobbed. 'The Tsarevna kissed the Tsar's hands. When Alexey came into the room, he threw himself at her feet, kissed her and fainted three times with grief – until the Tsar kicked him and dragged him out of the room by his hair.'

Just then, the bell of St Isaac's church began to toll, deeply and steadily, before the other bells in the city took up the call, carrying the sad news far out into Russia all through the long, dark night: the Tsarevna Charlotte was dead. I crossed myself with three fingers. 'May God give peace to her soul.' Alice sat motionless at my feet, face buried in her hands. The child in my body lay still, as if listening with us to the bells of St Petersburg.

Peter himself dissected Charlotte's corpse to put an end to the rumours that she had been poisoned, studying her organs with great interest. While the princess lay in the morgue, the Tsar held his grandson Peter Alexeyevich over the font. Like that, he chose the boy publicly as his successor, though he did not yet give him a title, neither Tsarevich nor Prince of Russia. I knew he was waiting and praying.

I did not attend Charlotte's funeral lest an evil spirit might strike and my caution was rewarded: I myself gave birth to a strong and healthy son. I wet his scalp with my tears and held him tight, counting and recounting his strong, rosy fingers and losing myself in the sweet smell of the nape of his neck. 'Peter Petrovich,' Peter shouted in triumph, holding him up into the light, tears streaming down his face, checking the boy's limbs again and again, kissing the little toes and fingers and gazing into the child's eyes of deep, dark blue just like his father's. He embraced the baby, sobbing, and holding him so tightly that the worried midwife had to prise him away. We kissed, tears of joy streaming down our faces, as cannon salvos echoed a hundred and twenty-one times through the St Petersburg night. The bells in church towers all over Russia danced with joy. The next morning Peter presented me with a suite of Siberian diamonds that took my breath away: necklace, bangles, brooch and earrings were shaped like ice crystals. It was the most beautiful thing I had ever seen. When I wanted to thank him, he waved my words away: 'Small fry for a woman who has given me everything. Everything.' He choked with emotion and we cried again, together.

That night, I gazed through the open window at the fireworks Peter had ordered. He himself was out and about in the streets, beating his drum and gladly accepting a myriad of invitations to drink to my and the little boy's health. The sky filled with rainbow showers of light. I had a son, I thought, before my eyes closed. Finally. My very own beautiful, strapping boy, and Russia had not one, not two, but three heirs.

' *"My father",* ' Pavel Jagushinsky read aloud, and frowned, looking down at Alexey's letter. Was he deciding to alter the words before he spoke?

It was the first time I'd returned to the Senate after giving birth to Peter Petrovich two months earlier. I sat next to Peter, gently steadying his kicking, twitching legs when he heard that salutation. Menshikov, wearing a red coat and a wig of silvery hair, his cheeks looking fresh from the morning visit of his barber, listened closely too.

' *"If Your Majesty wishes to exclude me from the succession to the Russian throne, your will shall be done. Please take this yoke from my shoulders. My inheritance crushes me, and my unsteady mind makes me unfit to rule. My body is too weak to steer the country with the iron hand it needs."* ' Peter snorted in derision, but I placed my hand on his: Alexey had been diagnosed with the Wasting Disease after all. He grunted and Jagushinsky went on reading. ' *"I pledge never to seek the crown of Russia. May God protect my brother and give you many more years to live and to reign. The well-being of my children is in your hands. For myself I ask only what I need to live."* '

Peter raised his hand, and Jagushinsky paused. Silence stretched in Senate. 'Give me this,' the Tsar ordered, scanning the letter. Menshikov watched him with burning eyes. What was going on: did Alexey really wish to give up his inheritance?

'I can wrap fish in that, nothing else. *"Your will shall be done",* ' Peter mimicked, crumpled up the letter and threw it at Makarov. 'For your archives. Empty promises and silly phrases.'

Makarov smoothed the paper and let it slip between his documents. The senators sat waiting in silence until Peter spoke in a dangerously low voice. 'The Tsaritsa Catherine Alexeyevna has given me a healthy son. The matter of the succession must be clarified. We are planning a long journey through Europe. Upon my return, it shall be determined. Until then –' he snarled, so loud that the veins on his forehead bulged and his face turned crimson. 'Until then, my useless son has to decide: either he shows himself worthy of the honour or he disappears forever into the darkness of a monastery.'

Peter's last words faded into a gargling sound; he fell from his chair, face distorted. I jumped up. 'My God, Menshikov, hold on to him. Hold his legs tight!'

The members of the council had shrunk back, pressing themselves against the wooden panelling or seeking cover behind their chairs. Menshikov weighed the Tsar's feet down while I dodged his beating arms. He swiped the tiara from my head, but I managed to press his face into my bosom where he calmed down.

'The council is over. The Tsar needs peace. You will be told how to proceed,' I said.

Menshikov and I stayed behind while they left. The only sound in the room was the Tsar's heavy, irregular breathing.

61

When Peter had set off on his first journey through Europe years earlier in search of knowledge and progress, the Western courts and their kings and queens had greeted him with curiosity rather than respect. This time he left to be welcomed as a European: Dutch and British ships now protected trade in the Baltic Sea. Poland, Saxony and Denmark formed a defensive wall against the Swedes. And another reason for Peter's departure to the West made me smile: his niece, the little vixen Tsarevna Jekaterina Ivanovna, was to marry the Duke of Mecklenburg in April.

Our sleighs were loaded with luggage and laid with skins, furs, cushions and blankets, while Peter strolled about in the courtyard, our little Peter Petrovich in his arms. The boy was three months old, strong and full of life, and the thought of leaving him for so long, after all the years I had waited for him, broke my heart. Snowflakes danced in the icy breeze and the sky was covered with thick clouds. It was late January in St Petersburg and so cold that our bodies left warm traces in the crystal air and our breath hung in icicles on our lips. Peter showed off his son proudly to the household while the child's nurse followed him, running around like a headless chicken.

'My Tsar, please, let the prince wear his fur cap. Otherwise he might catch a deadly cold,' she begged, but Peter pressed the little one to his chest and sniffed at his neck. 'Oh, rubbish. A Russian prince is hardy. Is that not so, my little one? Your mother and I are off, but not for long. Just to kick the Swedish King in the arse and to visit all his former friends. Remember, one must attend to one's enemies as much as to one's friends.' He kissed our son, and the little one cooed as Peter's moustache tickled him and freed his chubby hands from the sable blanket in which he was wrapped. 'You must not be offended that we leave you behind. I'll take you with me next time. Do not be angry with your *batjuschka* – I would never leave you alone if it was not necessary. Look, even your mother will only follow me a little later. We will find you a fine European princess for a bride.'

Peter nuzzled our son's pink fingers, then sniffed and wrinkled his nose. 'The prince has just relieved himself. On my uniform.' He handed him to the nurse, who hurried back to the palace with the infant. Peter slung his arm around my shoulders. 'It is right that you stay here until our angel has survived his first winter. Besides, I expect Jekaterina Ivanovna's wedding is a matter of little interest to you,' he teased.

'On the contrary. The Tsarevna wanted to marry so badly that I wish her all the luck in the world.' I smiled. 'Hopefully her husband will survive the wedding longer than her brother-in-law, the Duke of Courland, God be merciful upon his soul.'

Peter frowned. 'Soon we must also think of finding husbands for our daughters. Let me have a proper look at that young King of France.'

I fell silent because I was still hurt Peter did not want me to go to Paris with him. Instead, I had to remain in St Petersburg and then meet him later on in Hamburg.

'Why can't I go with you?' I had pleaded.

'Oh, Catherinushka, you would just be bored there! Besides, I do not have to worry about Russia if you are here as my Regent,' he had tried to flatter me.

'I'd be bored? In Paris?' I had stared at him blankly. I might not know Europe, but I knew that a woman could not be bored in Paris. I suspected the truth and it burnt like fire: Peter was ashamed of me. Like all the foreign envoys, Versailles mocked the way I presented myself. I just did what the other *damy* did, wore what we deemed fashionable here in St Petersburg, which was normally fine for Peter. But now he was eager to be received with all possible honours in

Paris: the Regent and the little King Louis XV should welcome him personally, and take him seriously. Whereas at first sight of me the whole of Versailles would be sent into fits of laughter, as we knew from the intercepted letters Campredon had sent to France. When he briefed Peter before the visit to his king's court, he'd said: 'French courtiers change their robes up to five times a day.'

Peter had been stunned to hear it. 'Five times? Really? How dissatisfied are these Frenchmen with their tailors?'

'Don't worry, Catherinushka,' he tried to placate me. 'I shall share my joy and my memories of the road and the city with you and write every day.'

'Isn't that very ambitious, seeking sons-in-law in Paris?' I asked, to hide my shame and pain. Peter took my hands out of my sable muff and held them: 'Little Louis is a sweet boy, with rather too much powder and make-up on his face. But once he grows into a man, he'll be just right for Elizabeth. Queen of France, our daughter! What do you think?' He spun me around in a circle, dancing wildly among the whirling snowflakes. 'I want a king!' he cried, his voice echoing from the smooth, high façades of the Winter Palace. 'The King of France for one of my daughters.' We slid over on the icy cobblestones and fell into the snow, where we lay on our backsides, holding on to each other, helpless with laughter.

Two weeks later fog and frost swallowed the Tsar's train of five hundred sleighs heading for the West. The last I saw of Peter was the royal standard, the crimson double-headed Imperial eagle, blazing in the pure white of the surrounding landscape.

Alexey's expression had been gloomy when he took his leave of his father. I could not read his thoughts any longer; those days were long gone. Did he really wish to retire to a monastery, or was he just trying to win himself time? A monastery was neither a prison nor a grave, and many a man had willingly swapped the royal mantle for a robe. However we all knew that Peter could and would not live forever. What was his eldest son playing at?

Shortly before he left, I had accompanied Peter to Alexey's apartment. A stupefied and drunken Afrosinja had been drowsing half-dressed in front of the fire. She jumped up on seeing us, curt-seying deeply yet sullenly. Peter's dwarf Jakim mimicked her clumsy movements and she kicked him, but he avoided her heel with a swift twist, cackling and shrieking like a monkey.

Peter ignored the girl and held the letter that had been read to the Senate towards Alexey. 'Are you serious about this? You wish to retire to a monastery?'

Alexey knelt and I noticed the bald spots on his head. 'Yes. Please believe me, my father!'

Peter shook his head and seemed to soften. 'You do not know what that means. You're still so young. Think about it again. Then write to me.'

Despite everything, he was ready to give Alexey another chance and I loved my husband for that. Somewhere, deep down, there was still good in Alexey. In spite of everything he had done, I could see the traces of the fearful child within him, a child that could be helped and educated.

'When do I need to answer by?' he asked, perhaps a little hastily.

Peter, who had already turned to go, hesitated. 'I shall give you six months, my son. I wish to receive an answer upon my return.'

I saw relief and triumph flicker over the Tsarevich's face as he exchanged a quick glance with Afrosinja. We all knew how much could happen in six months.

A few weeks before my own departure for the West, I heard a knock on the door of my study. When Alice opened it, I heard words in German being exchanged.

'Who is it, Alice?' I asked.

'It is Anna Mons. I mean, the Countess Keyserlingk,' she said. I rose from my desk where I was studying drawings of new robes to be made for me. What a surprise: what could Anna, Peter's first great love, possibly want with me? I shot a quick glance into the Venetian mirror that hung over a dainty console table. My eyes sparkled, my lips were full and rosy; my throat was covered with diamonds, which also dangled from my ears; and I wore a dress of burgundy velvet that flattered my golden skin. Yes, I felt ready to receive Anna Mons, the woman all the *damy* and whores of the realm had feared more than the smallpox.

She was still beautiful; her ash-blonde hair was silky and her deep blue cloak matched her eyes as well as her sapphire jewellery. She curtseyed to me deeply. 'Tsaritsa. Thank you for receiving me.' Her voice was hesitant and I sighed to myself. Ever since my marriage to Peter no one ever spoke to me in a straightforward manner but threw in my title whenever possible, like seed in freshly hoed soil, hoping for a harvest. Each sentence was as convoluted as its true meaning. I felt for Peter, having only ever known this. 'Countess, please sit down.' I patted the small sofa next to the hot Delft-tiled stove and belatedly spotted the young man standing behind her.

'Who is with you?' I asked.

'My younger brother, Wilhelm Mons. He has just returned from Europe and is now looking for a position at court. Is there any use in the Imperial household for him?' she asked.

The young man bowed: he was as impossibly handsome as the whole Mons family, all of them fresh-faced and with an air about them that spoke of walking barefoot in the grass and swimming naked in a river. His dark-blond hair was thick and wavy, and blue eyes, clear as the St Petersburg spring sky, were looking at me earnestly from beneath long, almost black eyelashes and eyebrows. He was tall and well built, which his tight breeches, long, shiny boots and fashionably narrow-cut jacket made clear to his advantage. He bowed deeply, looked up – and smiled. One of his front teeth was slightly chipped and on both suntanned cheeks, deep dimples formed. It was a smile such as I had never seen before, lighting up his already handsome face as well as the room. All and everything else disappeared for me – Alice Kramer as well as the Countess Keyserlingk – and I had to hold on to the back of a chair; that smile's promise of solace in times of suffering as well as unbridled, light-hearted joy was almost too much for me to bear.

I blushed, which made me angry. Was I the Tsaritsa or some silly handmaiden? He straightened and I looked at his long, slender fingers, where he wore four rings forged from different metals. He noticed my gaze and opened his palms towards me, as if making an offering. 'These are my lucky charms, Tsaritsa. A ring of lead to lend weight to my actions, copper for the warmth in my heart, iron for steadfastness, and . . .' He broke off.

'And?' I asked, somewhat tersely.

'And one of gold,' he answered, his eyes never leaving me.

'What does it stand for?'

'True love,' he said. 'It is as valuable and as indestructible as gold, I believe.'

A sudden silence hung in the room. I rose and the former Anna Mons curtseyed, worry and surprise in her face. Had they angered me? Had her brother not done well? 'Your brother may join my daughter Elizabeth Petrovna's household. If he proves himself there as her chamberlain, we can take things further,' I declared curtly. He bowed, his eyes full of gladness. His sister wanted to kiss my hand, but I turned away quickly. 'Good afternoon,' I said, and left the room, ignoring the mumbled expressions of gratitude from the siblings.

Alone in my bedroom, I leant against the wall and took deep breaths. My heart pounded, but my head was as light as a feather. I suppressed the urge to walk to the window and see them leave, see how this Wilhelm Mons moved, see if he turned in the courtyard to look up at my window. I would not. True love, he had said: as valuable and as indestructible as gold.

A few weeks later I left St Petersburg. Anna and Elizabeth as well as my little Peter Petrovich were left with Daria Menshikova. The city disappeared behind us under fresh snowfall, which eased the further west we moved. Reaching the Baltic provinces, I tried to recognise what I could, yet failed. How confusing I found Europe – and especially the German states – to be; the number of small duchies and principalities here was astonishing. Soon I no longer counted the customs and frontier barriers on which we were held and controlled; our purse emptied quickly in the face of all the tariffs and border taxes. We made swift progress, though, and the inns were clean and comfortable, so that I felt fresh and full of vigour when we arrived in Hamburg in late May. The King of Denmark, Frederick IV, together with Peter, awaited my train of five hundred coaches and wagons.

After the last Swedish attack, the city lay in ruins and its inhabitants lived in the still-smouldering ruins, feeding themselves on berries, roots and, it was said, stray dogs, cats and rats. We set up camp in lavish tents, their waxed linen adorned with gold tassels. My foldable furniture was forged from gilded metal. Peter sent me his barber every day, as he wanted me to shine next to the other ladies.

While he and Frederick tried to agree on a last joint strategy against the Swedes, I strolled through the city, well guarded, together with my three hundred *damy*. We visited the first opera house in any German state, which was still standing. What a difference from the Moscow theatre that Peter had tried to establish, where the audience laughed, cried, clapped, chanted or shouted and threw rotten vegetables, whenever it felt like it.

When we camped outside Copenhagen in the summer, I was pregnant again and praying for a healthy brother for Peter Petrovich. What more could I hope for? Things there dragged on until eventually we left for Mecklenburg, where we expected Jekaterina Ivanovna and her husband to lodge us, our troops and our entourage. But fearing the cost and effort involved, they fled as fast as they could, sailing or paddling across the Elbe to seek shelter in the free Hanse cities of Hamburg and Lübeck. At our first meeting since her marriage, Peter kissed Jekaterina on the mouth in front of her husband, which made the young duke blush with embarrassment. Peter poked him and then patted my belly.

'Look, Karl Leopold. My Tsaritsa is again in blessed circumstances. Aren't you young people stunned by what we old foxes can still do? Better get on with it, man. Let us drink a toast to that!' With a single gulp he emptied the glass a page held out to him.

We had not heard from Alexey since I had left St Petersburg. Why not? I wondered. It would have been wiser for him to keep in touch with Peter, proving his earnest wish to be a worthy heir. I remembered the look that had passed between Afrosinja and my stepson at our last encounter: a look of cunning and connivance.

Daria Menshikova wrote to me daily, telling me of little Peter Petrovich and his sisters, but also including news of the Tsarevich: Alexey had fallen back into his old ways, it seemed, and Afrosinja even wore the late Tsarevna Charlotte's jewellery at banquets and feasts. Didn't he know that he only had these few months to persuade his father that he could be trusted? I struggled to understand Alexey's impertinence and recklessness. Sure enough, just before the date of his decision loomed, he did write to us, though I wish he never had: his words were like a rock thrown from a cliff's edge that kept on rolling, gathering momentum, eventually crushing all and everything in its way.

I was getting dressed in the Castle of Mecklenburg when Peter came to me. The high windows were open and fresh air filled the room and made the delicate silk voile curtains billow in the autumn breeze. I felt homesick and lonely: in just a few days Peter Petrovich, my one and only surviving son, would celebrate his first birthday. Oh, to kiss his rosy cheeks, to see him stomp patterns with his little feet in the snowy park, or, even more fun, to throw snowballs at the unsuspecting servants and hide behind snow-capped statues, giggling and running back to the Palace, where hot chocolate awaited us. Here, the forests lazily turned golden, but their beauty left me untouched.

Peter's arrival in my room was like a fox's in a henhouse. My *damy* scattered and regrouped, all flustered and giggly, but he ignored them; his face had a high colour; his hair, which he had lost in patches after Blumentrost's mercury pills, was ruffled by the wind, and mud stuck to his boots from the military morning exercise. I could not read his face, but when he kissed me, I tasted beer. 'Peter, you drank without me. That's against the rules,' I laughed, but ignoring this he sat down next to me on the padded bench in front of my mirror and drew two letters from his worn-out coat. The wax of the seal had turned brittle; the paper had been opened, read and folded again many times. I laid down the silver-studded brush and my heart thumped.

'What is it?' I asked, alarmed. 'Is it word of our son?'

'Peter Petrovich is fine, thank God. But these two letters from St Petersburg arrived this morning and they make no sense.' Peter frowned. 'One is from Menshikov. The Tsarevich has borrowed a thousand ducats from him to join us here together with his Finnish whore. Just before that, he had borrowed two thousand roubles from the Senate, giving the same reason.'

'That's a lot of money for one short journey, even if one travels like Alexey,' I said. The Tsarevich easily trumped Menshikov's extravagance while on the road. 'And? Has he left St Petersburg already?'

Peter chewed on his lower lip. 'Apparently so. He is said to have left the city with Afrosinja, her brother and three servants.'

'Alexey travelling with such a small retinue? Normally he does not take a step without his priests, singers, cooks, scribes, barbers, tailors and jesters.'

'It sounded fishy to me, too. But listen to this: the other letter is from my half-sister Maria, who is a friend of both Alexey and his mother. She says she met the Tsarevich on her way back from Carlsbad, where he took the waters and was on his way to us.'

I held the brush out to Peter. 'Well, then, everything is in order, *starik*. Come, make yourself useful instead of moping about Alexey's travel costs.'

He brushed my hair nice and firm, so that my scalp tingled, chasing away my feelings of dark foreboding and fear. Then he stopped and frowned at his reflection in the mirror. 'There's something not quite right with that story. Carlsbad is not very far away. If he truly was there, he would have reached us long since. No. The Tsarevich, I'm sure, has fled.'

INTERREGNUM, 1725

Alexey. In my mind, the moody face of my stepson blended with the shadows of the dying night. A new day was creeping into the sky above St Petersburg; soon, dawn would drop its silver veil. No sound was to be heard outside the library. Where were the hundreds of courtiers who had spent the night on their feet? I was back at the windowsill: a frightened, tense silence lay over the Winter Palace, but on the forecourt, I spotted people gathering; carriages and sedan chairs were arriving. Were Ostermann and Tolstoy among them? From this distance I was as blind as the moles that as children we had smoked out of their holes, before bludgeoning and skinning them. Travelling traders paid us a good price for their soft, shiny furs, from which they sewed caps and collars, or lined the coats of rich people.

Cold air crept through the cracks in the window frames and made the room even chillier, for the fire had burnt down. Elizabeth had fallen asleep, tired of waiting for the Privy Council and their decision. Her head was tilted and her pink mouth a little open. I envied her calm. Well, she had decided to fold for this round of the gamble for power and survival. For me, however, this was the last chance to play my cards.

'What are you thinking about, Tsarina?' Menshikov used the salutation as easily as Feofan Prokopovich had only a few hours before. I turned. How strange: I had seen him countless times, and still could not really describe him. Throughout his steep rise from baker boy selling *pierogi* on the streets to the richest and most powerful man in Russia, the astonishing Alexander Danilovich Menshikov was forever changing his appearance, as the coarse features that had once reminded me of a wood carving reflected all his fresh sins and shortcomings. He ran his fingers through his hair that still had the colour of the wet sand on the shores of the Bay of Finland. I knew that Menshikov was capable of taking his time before he struck; I had better watch my back.

'I am thinking of the Tsarevich,' I said.

'Of your son Peter Petrovich?' Menshikov glanced at the painting hanging above the fireplace, and Elizabeth sighed in her sleep and then settled again. When my little prince was bedridden with high fever, I had offered God a despicable trade, asking him to take my living, healthy daughters instead. But the heavens had laughed at my despair and punished us with a cruel, swift hand: Peter, as well as myself.

'No, of Alexey. Was it not your duty to turn him into a Tsar?'

Elizabeth smacked her lips in her sleep. Menshikov looked at her thoughtfully. What did he see in her – the throne of Russia? Were his ambitions limitless?

'A Tsar! How should a man who is a fool, a coward and a drunkard be a Tsar?' he said. 'Do you remember when he came back from his studies in Dresden and Peter wanted to see if he had learnt how to draw maps?'

'Yes.'

'He was so afraid of his father's judgment that he shot himself in the hand. We heard the bang and then he staggered from his room, bleeding and sobbing like a child. A fool, a coward and a drunkard,' he repeated.

'Maybe he was just too trusting?' Menshikov shrugged, but I was not yet finished with him. 'Who could Alexey have trusted, if not you? Whose example might he have followed, if not yours? You left him to his weak, cruel tutors, and then an old Russian cleric was clever enough to offer him love, warmth and respect,' I said.

Menshikov narrowed his eyes. 'You speak of trust? Do you know where Charlotte fled to, when Alexey beat her up the first time and no one was to know, or no one chose to know? She came to me, wicked old Uncle Alexander Danilovich.' He slapped his chest. 'My doctor put a brace on her broken shoulder and healed her splintered ribs. By God, it is a miracle that her children were born healthy. Alexey beat her worse than he did his dogs. He kicked her into labour. Not once, but twice.'

I raised my hand. 'I do not wish to hear this. Not now, at least.'

Menshikov bowed his head. 'Very well, Tsarina. I am not telling you anything new really, am I? You know about the pathetic letters the poor child wrote home. How strange her parents never replied ... or rather, not so strange because those letters never reached Brunswick, did they? Charlotte hung around the corridors like a harbour girl waiting for her sweetheart, pacing up and down before the windows, looking out for the messenger from the West. But, alas, he never had an answer for her. And she trusted you!'

The gloves were off now. 'That was unavoidable,' I hissed. 'If a Crown Princess of Russia writes home to Brunswick about how horrid her life here is, it reflects badly on the entire realm. This cannot happen. The Tsarevich's wife is no daughter to any father and no sister to any brother, Menshikov. She belongs to Russia alone.'

'Of course. So be it, my Empress.' The bright light of morning blurred his features, and I could not tell his thoughts as he brooded by the window. Abruptly he wiped the clouded pane clear.

'Catherine Alexeyevna,' he called. 'Come and look!'

I hastened to join him: riders galloped into the courtyard of the Winter Palace. Their hats were pulled low over their faces and the fur collars of their cloaks turned up. The guard followed them; the Imperial green of the uniforms and the gold thread of their epaulettes and buttons gleamed in the sluggish morning light. The thunder of hoofbeats echoed off the façade of the palace. I suppressed a childish urge to press my fists against my ears.

'Who is this?' I whispered.

Menshikov said, 'Do you see little Petrushka amongst them? I don't.'

'Must he be with them to be named Tsar of All the Russias?'

Menshikov hesitated. 'No. Not strictly. But it's better to force everyone to swear their allegiance to the new Tsar to his face, there and then.' I took in those words before he added, 'But it's much more important that they get hold of us. Even in Siberia we are still far too dangerous to them. It will be the religious life for us, if they are merciful; the Trubetzkoi bastion and death, if not.'

The men got off their horses and threw the sweating animals' reins to the running stable boys. A guard looked up at Peter's room and crossed himself with three fingers. The breeze caught the red cloth of the Imperial flag with its double-headed eagle, which still danced at the top of its pole: to the rest of Russia, the Tsar was still alive. The wind played along with our lie, our love and our hope. One man broke loose from the others and motioned them to follow him. Was that Prince Dolgoruki, Petrushka's adviser? The blood rushed from my head. I ought not to faint; the moment of truth had come.

'I'm sorry,' I said.

Menshikov waved his hand. 'Don't be. You've done everything possible. Now we are in God's hand and can only pray for His mercy.'

Just one breath later, a fist hammered against the door. It echoed like gunshots in my ears, and someone shouted, 'Open, in the name of the Tsar!' *Which Tsar?* I was wondering when Elizabeth woke up, rubbed her eyes, stretched herself like a cat and looked questioningly at me and Menshikov.

'What happened?' she asked. 'Who is this?'

Menshikov straightened his shoulders and his coat and retied his lace jabot before running his fingers through his hair once more, smoothing it. At a glance from me, he shrugged. 'At least I will not look like the scoundrel I am when they arrest me.'

In a couple of strides he reached the door and unlocked it.

62

Peter was furious. He turned the envelope this way and that before snarling: 'The dog! He's fooled me. Who, I wonder, conveyed this letter for him? They'll pay for that. And where is Alexey now?'

I tried to take it back but he would have none of it, folding it up and hiding it in his pocket. 'The heir to the throne has fled my realm. He makes a fool of me in the eyes of the whole of Europe. Behold! The Tsar is so terrible that his own son must fear for his life and runs like a rabbit. Oh, how they will laugh in Paris, London, Vienna and Madrid! I hear their laughter here in Mecklenburg,' he said, biting his lip. Then he urged me, 'No one must know about this, Catherinushka. It's a secret between us. Oh, the shame. When I catch him, I shall cut him off like a gangrenous limb.'

'Don't say that,' I pleaded.

'Do you know what he wrote to his mother in her convent? Thank God Makarov catches every letter of importance. Alexey said that once he was in power, he would reverse everything I had done: raze St Petersburg, use my fleet for firewood and reinstall the old customs.'

I sat down, stunned at the madness of Alexey's words. Peter paced the room. 'Where can he be? Who gives a coward like him shelter?'

'I do not know, my Tsar. Friends or relatives?' I wondered.

'In Russia, Alexey is surrounded by nothing but flatterers. Who wants to call such a misfit his friend? And we have no family in Europe apart from Jekaterina, here in Mecklenburg.' He brooded by the window before looking back at me. 'Oh, Catherine. This is monstrous. Relatives, you say?' Patchy red blotches bloomed on his cheeks as he wrenched open the door to the hall. A servant, who had been leaning against it, struggled for balance. Peter shoved him aside. 'Move, man, if you want to keep your dumb head on your shoulders. Get me Peter Andreyevich Tolstoy. And then bring me quill, paper and ink. Quick, quick!'

Peter looked so cruelly determined that I dared not interfere. He paced while he waited, muttering to himself, kicking at the dainty furniture. Finally, he sat down in sullen silence.

'Why are you sending for Tolstoy?' I finally dared to ask.

'Because he is the best bloodhound in the realm, of course. No prey he chases continues to live.'

There was a knock at the door. Peter opened it and I recognised the familiar, broad figure of our visitor. 'Tolstoy, saddle your horse. You must find a traitor who has fled Russia. I will dictate to you a letter that gives you unlimited funds and free passage.'

Tolstoy thought the Tsar was joking. 'Unlimited funds and free passage? That sounds tremendous. Where has this quarry disappeared to, my Tsar?' he laughed.

'To Vienna, Tolstoy. Vienna,' Peter replied, before he pushed me out of my own dressing-room and shut the door in my face. I turned to see the look of horrified understanding on Tolstoy's face giving way to one of determination.

I took refuge in my bedroom. Raindrops drummed against the windowpanes. Strollers in the lush castle grounds hurriedly sought shelter from the gathering storm. Young trees bent in the gale and lightning flashed across the sky, making the roofs of Mecklenburg shine as brightly as on a summer's day. To Vienna, Peter had said. What was about to happen?

Peter abhorred the hunt. He did not own a pack of dogs and only used weapons in battle. But now he pursued the hunt for Alexey with shocking zeal and devotion. Tolstoy picked up the trail effortlessly. Under a false name, the Tsarevich had spent the night with his so-called wife and a servant in Frankfurt-on-the-Oder, where he bought Afrosinja men's clothes made of dark brown velvet. In

Prague, Tolstoy learnt, Alexey used the alias of a Polish trader. By the time he reached Vienna, Peter had marked out his route with a trail of small pins over a map of the European countries. He placed his tobacco-stained finger on Vienna. 'I knew it,' he said proudly. 'My son is so easy to second guess. What a shame I've begotten a fool.'

'How did Tolstoy find him so quickly?' I asked.

Peter laughed. 'Alexey gets so drunk wherever he goes that everyone remembers both the bill and his misdeeds. A blind man in the night could have traced this good-for-nothing.'

Vienna! Alexey had to be more desperate than I had thought. Was he really hoping for the grace of the Empress, who was a sister to poor Charlotte? Or did she not know what her little sister had suffered at his hands in St Petersburg? I would never have given shelter to a man who had beaten my sister to death. But the *izby* of Livonia were no preparation for the palaces of Europe.

Peter read to me a secret report about the arrival of the Crown Prince at night-time in Vienna. ' "*The Chancellor was torn from his sleep at midnight, as the Tsarevich begged for an audience. The Crown Prince of Russia threw himself on his knees, asking for protection for both himself and his companion.*" ' Here I had to hold Peter long and tight before he had calmed down enough to read on: the Tsarevich had bent his knee in front of a foreign chancellor! Peter was still shaking with anger as he read further: ' "*Alexey Petrovich Romanov asks the Emperor for the protection of his right to the throne and the rights of his children, but Charles VI also wishes for peace with Russia and prefers not to interfere in the Tsar's family quarrels. Vienna fears a Russian attack on Silesia and Bohemia, so he has asked Prince Alexey and his companions to stay near the city and await his decision.*" '

Peter's fist clenched so tightly around the letter that his knuckles turned white. 'The decision, my son, comes from St Petersburg and not from Vienna. Just you wait,' he groaned, and brought his *dubina* down on a chair, breaking its artfully carved back.

Winter came. I hoped that the child growing in my body would not be harmed by the bitterness and hatred all around. Peter's dilemma was clear: he wanted to be perceived as a worthy ruler of a Western empire, while he also wanted Alexey caught and punished. In my presence he sent his Christmas wishes to Vienna, and only on the last page, underneath Makarov's formal words, did he scrawl, *'Please send Our Son back to us. We will lead him back to the right path with a loving heart; the heart of a father. Your dearest cousin, Peter.'* Yet when he received a reply of sorts, I was astonished by the Austrian ruler's cockiness. At his New Year's reception, Emperor Charles said to the Russian envoy, 'As far as we are aware, the Tsarevich of Russia has never entered our Empire.' Peter was fuming and sent the Russian Ambassador to the country two bags of gold. The glare of the coins loosened a number of tongues in the Imperial household in Vienna, but Alexey had first been taken to a Tyrolean castle, which clung like an eagle's lair to the mountain, and then been spirited away from there in the night, together with Afrosinja. No one since had seen or heard a thing. Or perhaps did not want to say anything. But the Tsarevich could hardly have travelled north, towards his father, and so Tolstoy directed his horse towards Italy. He would hunt Alexey down and drag him back to Russia, even if he had to sweat blood to do it.

63

The wet and cold in Mecklenburg made me miss the dry, mysterious winter of St Petersburg and its crisp Baltic air. I wished myself on the Nevsky Prospect, sensing snow in the crystalline atmosphere and spotting patches of ice forming on the Neva. The short daylight hours of winter tinted the walls of the palaces and houses in richer hues than before, and people went about wrapped in furs, using the few hours of brightness to hurry through their business. Early dusk cast a spell over the city and its many sounds, from the shouts of the chestnut merchants and the ringing of the bells at the entrances to *kabaki*, to footsteps crunching in the snow and sleds tracing their way home with a shushing sound. Their sharp metal skids struck sparks on the ice, which froze in mid-air like crystal stars.

And, God, how I longed for my children. Little Peter Petrovich was growing from an infant into a toddler unseen by his parents. Anna and Elizabeth's most faithful playmate was loneliness; they could not have accompanied me to the fields and camps of the Great Northern War, where I had always been by Peter's side. Instead I made sure they were kept safe elsewhere, first in my own vast, dilapidated palace in Kolomenskoye and later with Praskovia's motley household. They lived, and their continued good health was a gift from God, I felt – I must have done something right. Now I must give birth to my next child while separated from the ones I loved.

*

On a wet January afternoon I was delivered of a son, Paul Petrovich Romanov. I had rested at an inn in a Northern German state. It was an easy and fast birth: after only two hours of pains, the strong little boy lay on the sheets between my thighs. A midwife bathed him and the prince fed at the breast of a hastily employed wet-nurse. The messenger with word of his birth left for Amsterdam, to which Peter had pressed on. He congratulated me by return, full of pride at the healthy birth of yet another recruit, while also announcing Paul's birth to the courts in London, Paris and Madrid. But before those letters had arrived, our son had already died in the disorder of too many people, luggage, wet cloaks, icy draughts and overheated stoves. The tender features of my little boy were still with me in memory months after his coffin lid had been nailed shut.

The Tsar wrote to me from Carlsbad while I recovered: *'This place is as funny as a prison; the hills are so high that I hardly see the sun, and the beer, if I find any at all, is warm, without foam, and tastes of cow piss. The worst thing is that they soak me every day like a horse with this filthy water.'* Upon our meeting again, we celebrated with a dinner and he beamed: 'You know, I'm glad we can return home soon. Let's not stay too long in Berlin. Otherwise, Peter Petrovich will grow up before we meet him again.' He shouted into the drunken round, 'Fill the cups. Three salutes for Peter Petrovich; a toast to the Tsarevich!'

Our guests all knew that the rightful Tsarevich Alexey – a grown, healthy and able-bodied man – was on the run from his own father, frightened out of his mind and threatened with death. Still, they drank obediently to the well-being of a child who had only just taken its first steps.

Did Alexey know which bloodhound his father had put on his heels? Did he taste the bitterness of Tolstoy's sweat; feel the pain in his limbs after weeks of tireless pursuit? Tolstoy's hatred, zeal and disdain ought to have pierced his dreams and poisoned the warm Italian wind when Alexey stood high on the battlements of St Elmo near

Naples. He and Afrosinja took shelter in the fortress with its shady garden, filled with the scents of almond and orange trees, and a view far over the Bay of Naples. Tolstoy heard that Afrosinja was with child and that Alexey himself was half mad with fear of his father.

'They have been found.' Peter's face was pale with tension, but he clenched his fists in triumph. 'The Emperor believes Alexey to be safe in St Elmo, but in truth he is trapped there, like the dirty rat he is. Let me write to Vienna at once. That shopkeeper on the Austrian throne wants to fool me, but I shall teach him a lesson. We'll pay Italy a visit, and I shall take forty thousand soldiers along, just to keep me company. Maybe then His Majesty will be a bit more talkative.' He opened the door and barked into the study opposite, where the cabinet secretary was reading the last dispatches from the Great Northern War, which dragged on into its second decade. The Swedes would not lightly abandon their supremacy in the Baltics and to the west of Peter's realm. 'Makarov, move your arse or I'll put it on a stake,' Peter called. Was he joking? No. These days, his voice lacked any trace of a jest. I wanted to leave, but he held me back: 'No, stay.'

Peter waved impatiently towards the desk when Makarov came in, a blank paper scroll in one hand, quill and ink in the other. For the first time I noticed the silvery hairs on the cabinet secretary's temples as well as the puffy bags under his dark eyes. Keeping up with Peter without having his physical strength was an impossibility.

He dictated, ' "*My cousin, it pains me to learn that my beloved son, who has left Russia without my permission, is in your realm. We ask Your Majesty to make an appropriate statement and for this we send Peter Andreyevich Tolstoy to you, who knows of the Tsarevich's whereabouts and will appreciate an encounter with him. We will not suffer any contradiction, as the laws of God and of nature are on our side. Russia's next step is in your hands. Your Majesty's most loving cousin – Peter.* "' He watched Makarov's quill flying over the paper, before sand was dusted over the ink and molten wax sealed the letter. 'Yes, that's good. The scoundrel will understand ...' Peter muttered.

'Which scoundrel?' I asked, astonished. 'Alexey?'

Peter smiled. 'No, silly. The Emperor of Austria, of course.'

The Emperor in Vienna did indeed understand. He weighed Alexey's well-being against a possible Russian attack on Silesia and Bohemia and soon Tolstoy again travelled south, but this time under the Imperial flag. The Emperor himself had begged him for mildness with the Tsarevich and during Tolstoy's ride to Naples, it rained for weeks, as though the heavens were crying for Alexey's soul.

He waited in Naples with a trembling heart and a brave face. Tolstoy had words of forgiveness on his lips and treason in his soul. He promised Alexey what he wanted to hear: yes, the Tsar loved his son and forgave him; yes, Alexey could hope for a free passage out of St Petersburg; he would be allowed to marry his mistress as soon as they arrived in Russia and then to live with her in peace and quiet, wherever he wanted. When Tolstoy wrote: *'It is astonishing how much true love and care the Crown Prince shows towards this girl,'* Peter just snorted in contempt. Yet I thought to myself that Alexey, too, was nothing but a human being.

64

We reached Berlin in August. The landscape was lush and fertile. Lakes sparkled between green meadows; cool, shady forests gave way to clean and tidy villages. Peter trotted his horse beside my carriage. From time to time he peered into the dim, steamy interior and blew me a kiss. 'How do you like it in Prussia? Everything is a bit too clean, huh?'

'Yes,' I replied. 'So much order would drive me mad, I believe!'

He chuckled. 'True. In Russia, such wealth and contentment would lead to a revolt.'

The farmers stopped their work in the fields when our train of over a thousand carriages passed them by in a cloud of dust and noise, followed by the same number of riders and then servants on foot. The land we left behind had been razed as if a plague of locusts had set upon it. Excited children and girls from the villages ran along with us, staring at the last group in our retinue, men who were so tall that their legs and feet hardly fitted into the stirrups. Peter had plucked them from all over Russia as a living, breathing gift to the Prussian King, who loved tall soldiers in his regiments. King Frederick William had had the wisdom to encourage into his country settlers such as Lutheran refugees from the Palatinate, Franconia, Thuringia and Austria, as well as many Huguenots from France. Peter was jealous. Berlin remained unmatched as a city, while he had to pay every gifted foreigner dearly to persuade them to come to St Petersburg.

Seeing Berlin, I could not help but remember handsome Andreas Schlüter, whom I had welcomed many years ago at the Neva pier. He had built tirelessly for Prussia until he failed to lay proper foundations for a tower that was to reach as high as the clouds, and fell into disfavour there before his early death. What could Schlüter have given St Petersburg, had he lived? The new city of Berlin had peeled itself away from the once dirty, stinking village it had been, like a butterfly from its cocoon. Tall lime trees cast cool puddles of shade over the strollers beneath; people met in coffee houses or examined the wares of travelling merchants. Stately homes rose along the Spree; both the city-castle and the Charlottenburg Palace were impressive in their splendour and size.

'Peter, my Russian cousin. At last!' the King roared as he greeted us.

The two big men embraced each other while the Queen and I exchanged gentle compliments. 'Sister, welcome to Berlin,' she greeted me. 'How does your niece like it in Mecklenburg? Did you bring a portrait of your lovely daughters? Our Frederick will soon be of marriageable age.'

She looked exhausted. Her husband was not called the Soldier King for nothing but favoured a spartan lifestyle, continually travelling to inspect and improve his standing army of fifty thousand men.

'Are these your ladies-in-waiting?' the Queen asked me cautiously, eyeing the women behind me. I blushed with shame: as a practical joke Peter had swapped my noble Russian ladies-in-waiting for some rough peasant girls without rank or manners. The sight of the wretched women in their blotchy make-up and slovenly clothes made him roar with laughter. My real ladies were probably at home with their children.

Just then, the young Princess Wilhelmine tugged at the countless icons sewn to the hem of my robe. 'Why do you have these colourful pictures dangling from your dress? *Les images font beaucoup de bruit,*' she noted.

'This is the fashion in St Petersburg, Wilhelmine. In different places, you dress differently,' the Queen scolded her daughter, but I stroked the child's head.

'These icons shall keep me from evil and misfortune, my Princess,' I told her. She could scarcely be older than Elizabeth, and seemed curious and intelligent.

The King spoke in a strangely abrupt way, as if he wanted to save himself time and breath. 'If we survive that damn' state dinner today, come to my chambers tomorrow. Simple fare ... pea soup and roast pork with crackling.' He poked the Tsar in the ribs. 'And our good German beer, of course. You will need that after visiting Holland. Can't even water your flowers with that brew. Tastes like piss.' Peter nodded, delighted, and Frederick William looked at me kindly. 'Do not know how the Tsaritsa feels about this, but any courtier who bows, I just want to kick in the arse. Nothing better than a straightforward, upright Junker I can trust.'

The Queen added, 'My son Frederick can play the flute beautifully. He might give us a little concert tomorrow night.'

'Flute!' spat the Prussian King. 'Crown Prince Frederick should exercise or study instead of playing the flute. I will whack all that fluffiness out of him.'

Wilhelmine looked at her father gloomily, but Peter chuckled. 'I know what you're talking about, my royal brother. I am already looking forward to our dinner together.'

Peter's gift, the tall Russian men, howled like dogs when they took leave of their fellow guards but Peter did not pay any attention after this first meeting with the Prussian royal couple. 'Prince Frederick plays the flute and my son flees, drunk, with his whore all over Europe. Well, what fun we'll have tomorrow night,' he observed when he got into the carriage and knocked the knob of his silver cane against the back window as a signal for it to depart. On the way to our guest quarters in the palace of Mon Bijou, a favourite house of the Queen's which she had offered for our use during the stay in Berlin, I tried to cheer Peter up, but he remained sullen and deep in thought. He uncorked a bottle of Rhine wine and emptied it to the last drop.

Wherever we were, it seemed, Alexey cast a long shadow upon us.

'By God, I've never seen anything so beautiful in my life. Has it really been created by human hands?' Peter's fingertips skimmed the walls of a chamber that glowed in shades of gold, rust and honey. 'How can you work something as brittle as this? Schlüter was truly a master,' he said in wonder. The whole room in the Berlin City Palace, the Stadtschloss, was panelled seamlessly with amber, and the candlelight brought the mosaic images to life, breaking the golden hue into dozens of facets. I, too, was in awe of its beauty and splendour.

The Queen laughed proudly. 'We too are stunned each time we see Schlüter's Amber Room. Nothing compares to it in the whole wide world.'

'Oh, really? Nothing?' Peter asked, eyeing the walls with newly awakened interest. I thought I could read his mind then but hoped to be proved wrong.

'Nowhere,' the Queen confirmed. 'This room is my joy and my pride. I originally wanted to put it into Mon Bijou, where I keep everything that is dear to me.'

We had eaten pea soup and bread, then strolled through the palace's state rooms until the roast pork was ready to be served, its flesh crackling and sweet, and afterwards young Prince Frederick was to play the flute for us.

'What is behind there?' Peter tugged at a curtain covering one wall. Frederick William chuckled and pulled a cord: 'The pride of my collection.' The curtain opened and the King held a candlestick high above his head. 'Look.'

I saw a statue placed on a pedestal. Peter cheered and the Queen giggled behind her fan, but I blushed deeply: it was a depiction of a disgustingly ugly man, half turned away from us, holding his stiff oversized cock between his hands.

'That must be a fertility god. Kiss him, Catherine Alexeyevna,' Peter said huskily.

'What?' I whispered, stunned.

'Kiss him. You heard what I said. With his help, we can have even more children. Sons, of course.'

'Really, I do not know if a kiss on a pagan statue will help with that,' the Queen said, embarrassed by the situation.

Frederick William hastily tried to close the curtain and said, 'Shall we return to table?'

But Peter seized his arm, stopping him. 'Kiss him, Catherine,' he ordered. Peter drew his flat hand over his throat. Our hosts went silent with shock, seeing his dark, serious expression while he threatened me with beheading. He would not countenance losing face, I knew, and so I bent forward and kissed the cold stone of the statue. 'There you go. Easy!' Peter slapped Frederick William on the shoulder. 'My brother, if this is your greatest treasure here in Berlin, I will gladly accept it as a gift and take it back with me to St Petersburg.'

The King was speechless and I feared what might happen next: in Denmark the King had denied Peter a rare mummified body from Africa as a keepsake. Peter had been so upset he had broken off the mummy's nose and turned to the King with a sunny smile, the nose in his hand, saying, 'Now you can keep your mummy!'

But courtesy forbade the Prussian King from refusing Peter's wish. 'Of course. Would you like another keepsake from Berlin?' Frederick William asked, with an attempt at humour. 'Porcelain maybe? Or some vats of pickled herring?'

'No, thanks, I have enough at home.' Peter looked at the Queen, his beady eyes glittering with both greed and joy. 'But since you ask, I'd like to have the Amber Room. I'll put it in my most beautiful castle as a sign of the blossoming Prussian–Russian alliance. Long may it last!'

'I am not sure ...' the Queen began, paling and looking around her glorious gold-tinted room, this unique wonder of craft and beauty.

'It would be damaged, my cousin, if dismantled. Also, it takes up a lot of space for transportation. At least forty crates or so,' the King added, steadying his wife by her elbow. She looked as if she was about to faint. I felt for her.

'Bah! Never mind. If it breaks, I shall have it replaced. After all, I have access to the finest amber once more, just north of Danzig. And do not worry about space in my train. I shall leave more people behind than merely the tall men I offered you. They were my most generous gift to you, after all.' Peter smiled, leaving neither the Queen nor King of Prussia any room for refusal.

*

We left Mon Bijou two days later. I felt sorry for the Queen of Prussia once again as I walked through her small palace's once perfectly presented rooms. Many of the high, polished windows had been shattered and shards of glass lay everywhere. The Persian rugs were trampled and I spotted burn holes from cigars or careless fire-laying. Belgian damask curtains hung in tatters and the gilded wall panelling in one room had been demolished. Chandeliers of Bohemian crystal and candlesticks of ivory had been smashed; Delft tiles lay broken while soot covered the fine parquet. On the furniture, carving skills had been practised. The faces in some of the gilt-framed portraits had been cut to pieces by countless blades. Oh, yes, Peter's men had felt at home in Berlin. I doubted we would be invited there again.

Our baggage train to Russia contained six more carts. The Amber Room was hastily peeled from the walls and packed into forty crates, just as the King had estimated. Peter had them opened twice so that he could check their contents and finally marked and numbered the panels himself before nailing the boxes shut, hammer in hand, nails squeezed between his lips. Back in Russia, he asked his craftsmen to look at Schlüter's masterpiece and better the room. It was impossible. Peter lost interest then and the crates were moved, nailed shut once more, to the storerooms of the Winter Palace, where they gathered dust. The disgusting pagan idol, however, had travelled in my coach at Peter's behest. I hung my cloak on its cock, but perhaps he worked his horrid magic after all, for when we reached St Petersburg with the first autumn storms, I was pregnant again.

Sometimes, when I lay awake at night, listening to Peter mumbling and cursing in his sleep, I thought of Wilhelm Mons and his ring of solid gold: as valuable and indestructible as true love.

65

Alexey returned to Moscow in the bleak midwinter. All along his way, Russian peasants threw themselves on their knees, calling him a saint and praying for his welfare. It had been impossible to keep his escape secret and for them the Tsarevich had become a symbol of hope. Someone had dared to rebel against the almighty and often incomprehensible ruler – and not just anyone: the Tsar's own son.

Peter paced the Kremlin's walls, scanning the Red Square: Alexey must cross it to come to him. The Tsar had sworn to treat his son with forgiveness and gentleness upon his return to Russia. He had sworn by God, the Christian faith and the Holy Spirit.

He had sworn by his very soul.

Icy Moscow frost glazed Alexey's heart when he finally crossed the city's boundaries; he was frozen with fear and had no idea what awaited him. Not knowing was a punishment in itself. Afrosinja had stayed back in Vienna, very pregnant, and constantly demanded consignments of food: fresh caviar, smoked salmon and sacks of cornmeal for *kasha*.

Four days after his arrival in Moscow, Peter called Alexey before a 'specially convened council. I myself was not allowed to attend, as he feared my softening influence. In truth, I was glad not to have to witness this farce.

On the evening of the trial, Alexandra Tolstoya came to my rooms, carrying a tray of hot wine and savoury pastries, but I had no appetite. 'What did the Tsar say?' I asked her.

'Say?' She touched her ear as if it hurt. 'You mean *shout*. All afternoon, all night, until nightfall. Until his voice deserted him. The council members are deafened by it, and the Tsarevich knelt before them for hours on end, listening to it all, crying and begging for his life.'

'What is Alexey accused of?'

'Just about everything,' Alexandra Tolstoya said plainly, sipping mulled wine and briefly closing her eyes. 'His poor education, his weak health, his cowardice, Charlotte's death, his fornication with Afrosinja, his choice of mother –'

'His choice of *mother*?' I asked, bewildered.

'Yes. Forgive me. Only my brother knows about this besides the council members, and now we too. And at least in your rooms the walls do not have ears.'

'Tell me,' I whispered. Tears of fear were shining in Alexandra's eyes when she said hoarsely, 'The witch-hunt has begun, Tsaritsa. Everyone who has ever been in contact with the Tsarevich, or his mother, must now fear for their lives.'

'But Evdokia has been locked up for years. She has taken the veil – finally! – and is known by the name of Sister Elena.'

'The Tsar doesn't care. He is already talking about the Suzdal conspiracy, after the name of her convent. Supposedly, the poor soul had a lover there, a Stepan Glebov. Alexey is said to have written to and visited her there. That makes Evdokia guilty of Alexey's attempt to flee the country. I think she will grow to regret ever having given him life.'

Wind rattled at the closed shutters; flames cowered under it in the fireplace. 'What else is Alexey accused of?'

'High treason.' Alexandra Tolstoya's dark eyes were big and sad.

'High treason?' I gasped. 'But that means ... He can't ...'

She crumbled and cried nervously, almost without a sound. 'His own son!'

I knelt down next to her and we embraced each other. 'Is there no hope for mercy?' I whispered.

The shadows swirling in the room made her delicate face drawn and aged when she said, 'The Tsar will forgive him on one condition.'

'Which one?'

'Alexey must tell him the names of all his allies. Each and every one, and he must spare no one. My brother says the Tsar will kill them all.'

Only a few days later, my young son Peter Petrovich, who was unwell with a cold and fever, was declared Tsarevich and the successor to the throne. I would not leave his side, now that I was finally back with him, but Peter presented him on the Red Square to his two regiments in spite of the bitter cold.

'Can't we wait?' I had pleaded, holding the boy and feeling his delicious weight, taking in his scent.

'No, we can't,' Peter replied simply. 'It's now or never. I'll strike Alexey with an iron hotter than anything he has ever known.'

The court flooded in all its finery from the Kremlin to the Cathedral of the Redeemer. In his additional capacity of Archbishop of Pskov, Feofan Prokopovich led the service. Alexey was ashen-faced as he kissed his half-brother's chubby hand and his knees trembled when he swore loyalty to my son. He kissed my cheeks three times as a sign of peace, but avoided my gaze. He must have thought that this was what I'd always wanted. In truth, I hoped that it would suffice for Peter. But Alexandra Tolstoya's warning haunted me: '*Tsaritsa, believe me, it has not yet begun.*' While orators shouted Alexey's sins from the four corners of the Red Square to the people: 'Even when his virtuous, loving wife was still alive, he was fornicating with a creature of the lowest descent' – what a mockery! What was Peter thinking? – I felt my child quicken: a brother for the Tsarevich, my son? Never before had I felt so secure, and at the same time so threatened, at Peter's side.

During my years with the Tsar I had witnessed many atrocities. Men had their caps nailed to their heads because they did not pull them off fast enough upon Peter's arrival. Monks and nuns had their guts slashed because they had dared to call his decisions blasphemous. Old-fashioned Muscovites who had questioned the direction Peter was taking the country in and were smothered with molten metal. But he imposed the cruellest of all capital judgments – dying on the stake – on one man alone.

Nothing had prepared me for what it meant to die on the stake. The man's screams tore apart the air of the cold Moscow day before they faded to a faint whimper at nightfall, after endless hours of pain. His dark blood kept on seeping over the stones of the Red Square, which was true to its name that day, and the stench of his dying drifted into the Kremlin, strangling my soul. Why did this man have to suffer so much? An officer of the guard whose name none of us had heard before: Stepan Glebov. The answer was almost a joke, if it hadn't been so sad.

In his witch-hunt, Peter learnt that his first wife Evdokia, despite her monastic seclusion, had not only seen Alexey in secret, but had also begun a harmless little love story. Stepan Glebov was told to guard the Tsaritsa, but had been moved by her pitiful plight. She responded to his pity with all the passion that had been kept locked up in her heart during her years of imprisonment in the convent. The fire in her had smouldered still, instead of being suffocated by cold, starvation and endless prayers. Glebov did not name anyone else under torture, but Peter found her tender letters to the man, calling him *lapuschka*, her rabbit's paw. Hadn't she whispered the same nickname in his ear, during the few nights they had spent together? Glebov must pay for that.

When all of his bones had been broken and flesh had been torn from his body with fiery tongs, Peter commanded him to be put on the stake. The pointed wood was driven through the poor man's guts up to his chest. Evdokia howled at the news until her voice broke. After that, she refused to speak, I heard, and her mind drifted off into a realm that lay between the horrible truth and a gracious veil of madness and forgetting. To ask for forgiveness was in vain, that much she knew. Her only sin ever had been to marry Peter and fail to satisfy him.

In those days, even I could not reach him. Afterwards he, too, was never the same again. No sleep was ever free from nightmares, and even his laughter was haunted and strained. Every feast, every drink, was a doomed effort to forget.

On the night Glebov's punishment started, I went to the locked door of Peter's study. He was still awake: the unsteady light of candle flames flickered in the gap beneath the door. I knocked and his steps approached, but he would not open up. Yet I sensed his heartbeat through the wood: steady and as cold as ice.

'What do you want?' he asked roughly.

I folded my hands in pleading, as if he could see me. 'Please, *batjuschka*! Let us put an end to this madness, my love. Why are you persecuting poor Evdokia? Hasn't she paid enough for the sin of giving birth to Alexey? You have me, and our children, and the love of your people. We are happy. Have mercy on her, love. What harm can she do to you, to us?'

Peter opened the door and I drew back in horror: there was an expression of sheer madness on his face.

'You ask for mercy for Evdokia? Well, if her lot means so much to you, then share it: I can have you shorn and carted off to a convent tomorrow. But it won't be Suzdal where she was, with its sweet air and warm sunshine, you can be sure of that.'

From somewhere far inside the palace, I heard footsteps approaching, halting, and then hastening away in the other direction. I pressed myself against the opposite wall. I could only pray for the souls of those who were near and dear to me. The Tsar had already sent his half-sister Maria to the dank cells of the Schlusselburg. Anyone could be next: myself, even my children.

'All she did was to have a harmless little love story. And he was moved by her plight. Please –'

Peter strode across the corridor and seized my elbow. He forced his face close to mine. I smelt his bitter breath but did not flinch away and met his eyes. There was no point in trying to escape.

'Ah. You ask for favour for the horny goat who fucked Evdokia? I'll tell you one thing and listen to me well – a Tsaritsa remains forever and ever the Tsar's wife, untouchable by any other man. And you wish me to reconsider my judgment on Glebov? He'll be alive for a good while, you know. I didn't have the stake greased.'

I swallowed hard, struggling for composure and courage. I had never seen him so threatening. 'Yes. Show mercy. Please,' I said.

Peter hesitated. He reeked of long nights spent in the torture chambers, their dampness and dread; I could also distinguish stale smoke and the scent of the strong, cheap vodka he drank by the barrel together with his companions. He grabbed me by the hair and bent my head back. I howled with pain and my heart raced: was this it? 'Catherinushka. Just to please you, my dove, I have thought again about my judgment on Glebov. Do you want to hear my decision?'

'Yes,' I gasped, as I knew I ought not to show any fear.

'Well, then. I'll have him wrapped in a fur coat, he'll get socks on his feet and a cap on his head,' Peter said, grinning.

'What on earth for?'

He forced me back against the wall, cupping my head in his hands. It felt as if he wanted to crush my skull.

'Silly! The warmer a man is on the stake, the longer he lives; the longer he suffers.' He laughed, shrill and sudden, and tried to kiss me, but I pushed him from me in disgust. He stood back, breathing heavily.

'What's wrong with you, my little Tsaritsa? You are not normally so squeamish, are you?' His voice was mocking while he reached for me.

I felt the fingers that had caressed me so often, that had chosen to hold me above all other women, against all the odds. What had I sworn to myself back then? I would not fear, even if it hurt. I would not fear, for his sake.

'You reek of the blood on your hands. Do not dare to touch me,' I said, almost in tears, and wiped his taste from my lips. 'Let go of me.' I pulled my hand from his. He stared at me. His silence frightened me more than his anger.

'Brave as ever, Catherine Alexeyevna.' In cold fury, he turned away, slamming the door to his study behind him.

It took a long while before I could move away from the support of the wall and stumble along the empty corridor to our son's room. He slept in his cradle, his nurse beside him, his little hand holding one of her fingers tightly. 'Go and sleep,' I said, gently shaking her and taking her place. 'It's my turn now.' Little Peter Petrovich's cheeks were rosy and round, and in his sleep his lashes cast shadows over them. At least he was spared the spectacle of this madness.

Alexey did not ponder very long over whom he could sacrifice to save his own skin. The names spewed from his mouth like water from a spring. The majority of them were shockingly familiar to me. Peter's oldest friends as well as his half-sister Maria; Evdokia's family and an Old Muscovite bishop: the latter confessed without hesitation to praying nightly for Peter's death. To him, Alexey was the only legitimate heir, born from a marriage blessed by God. I knew that he was not alone in this opinion in religious circles, but no voice from the Russian Church was raised to defend him. Better that Peter take the bishop's skin than theirs.

The following weeks and months swamped our lives, as icy and dark as the wintry Neva in their cruelty. I chose not to know, witness or remember the events of that time. When their bones were broken on the wheel, Peter's oldest friends spat at him: 'Despot! The mind needs freedom to evolve, it can't be dragged there in chains. You strangle us in captivity and terror.' He was stunned into silence and cold fury. Others were condemned to blows from the knout or forced to do heavy labour in mines or building canals.

The bishop still had the strength to curse Peter before his death on the wheel: 'Son of the Devil, you are a curse upon our country. If you lay a hand on your son, his blood shall come upon you and yours, to the very last Tsar. Fire and death upon your dynasty. God have mercy upon Russia: a curse upon the Romanovs!'

Alexey had to witness the torment of his loyal friends and could neither eat nor drink as a result. He had hardly slept since he'd been brought before the council. The heads of his allies were displayed on pikes in the Red Square; their empty, horrified eyes stared at the passing crowds. In their midst, on a scaffold, hung the corpse of Stepan Glebov, Evdokia's lover, still on his stake. Crows pecked at his eyes. Wild dogs tore the limbs off at night, dragging them away into the alleyways.

I resisted the dark lure of evil, but watched helplessly as it took hold of Peter, turning his heart to stone.

A few days after Glebov's death, I left my rooms together with a young pageboy. I still did not like the Kremlin's dark corridors; their shadows and the cold eyes of the icons on the walls scared me. I strained my ears: were those footsteps coming towards me? I halted, heard weapons clink. My heart raced. Was someone being arrested again? Had Menshikov set off on a bear hunt, or was it the guard patrolling as usual? In those days, every sound and every movement could signal death. I was trying to hear more when a detachment of guards came around the corner, led to my surprise by Antonio Devier, Rasia Menshikova's husband and the head of Peter's secret service. He bowed to me and the soldiers knelt in spite of their weapons. Only then did I notice the woman in their midst: a slight person dressed in black, her head veiled. She had to be a nun, as her long robe was woven of a rough, dark cloth.

'Tsaritsa,' Devier said, and she lifted her veil, eyeing me coolly.

'To whom are you talking?' she asked him, and then I recognised the tall, rounded forehead and the coal-dark eyes with their unhealthy shine. She had a long, narrow nose above her fine, bloodless lips. It was clear that her waxy skin never saw the sun and on her shaven head, boils and chilblains festered. Her fingers clenched the hem of the veil, as if she were about to grab something – or someone. I noticed her dirty, naked feet in worn leather sandals; her toenails were long, curved and discoloured. Yes, she did look like Alexey, or rather Alexey looked like her: Evdokia – or Sister Elena as she was now known. Her gaze scorched me as she took in everything about me: the grey pearls braided in my dark, glossy hair, my sable-lined, blue velvet cloak and warm boots made of embroidered leather. I felt ashamed: this woman should wear my clothes; this woman should have continued to bear Peter's children; this woman should see her son ascend to the throne.

The silence in the corridor became unbearable. I found it hard to breathe. Devier looked from her to me, unsure what to do. This was not God's will, I thought. I felt only compassion for a wasted life and so I bowed my head and said: 'Be blessed, Evdokia.' Her gaze drifted from me into the darkness of the empty corridor: there was no more life in her heart, no more fire in her mind.

Devier cleared his throat. 'Let us go.' Soon, Evdokia's footsteps were lost in the musty cold of the Kremlin and oblivion swallowed her. Peter moved her to a convent near Lake Ladoga. Conversation, even writing letters, was forbidden to her. She lived her life as a shadow and the punishment that Peter gave her was time: endless, empty, slow-dripping time, years and decades of it. I tried not to think of her; her fate scared me witless.

At least she had loved once more, truly loved. For what had happened to my own feelings for Peter? Had they also fallen victim to the witch-hunt for Alexey and his allies? I roasted in hellfire in those days, emerging feeling raw as never before. How was I to live by his side and to love him as I should?

I could only try.

66

We stayed in Moscow until Easter. Peter exchanged painted eggs and blessings with every courtier and the tables in the Kremlin were laden with *kulitsh*, a sweet milk-based Easter cake, and delicious *pashka*, a pudding made of fresh cheese and pickled fruits.

Alexey sat at the table but would not eat; his clothes hung loose on his thin body. He seemed to me like a man made of glass who'd shatter at a mere touch. Peter, I guessed, was far from done with him.

'When all the boring ceremonies are over, can I come to you tonight?' he asked me, unperturbed, eating his pudding. I agreed, trying to forget the horror of the past few weeks, and he slept tightly snuggled up to me, one hand resting on my swollen belly. In the morning he listened through a little tube to the heartbeat of my unborn child.

The feast ended the following day when Peter ordered all the guests to clear the paths in the Kremlin's park so that we two could walk there before another restful little sleep. We both laughed at the pale faces of our guests, struggling to shovel away the snow fast enough to keep up with our steps.

Anna, Elizabeth and my little Peter Petrovich threw snowballs at them, and whooped with joy when they hit my fool, the old Princess Anastasia Golizyna, straight in the face. 'Hit and sunk,' cheered Peter, spinning wildly with our son. 'Come, fly with me, my boy.' We clapped and cheered until they both fell down in the snow. They both started to make an eagle, until the little Tsar felt sick and vomited in the snow.

It rained on Easter Monday and the downpour washed away Glebov's blood together with the last of the snow from the stones of the Red Square. I thought the horror had ended.

The Great Northern War had been raging for almost twenty years. At last, Sweden seemed to give in and the struggle for supremacy in the Baltics was settling in Russia's favour. Everyone was tired: the generals, who had been criss-crossing Russia and Europe for years; the soldiers, who had forgotten the faces of their families; the nobles, who told their sons to flee instead of serving in the Tsar's army for life; the small landowners, who were burdened with high taxes; the souls, who could never hope to buy their freedom; Peter himself, who finally wanted to look from Peterhof over the Bay of Finland and say, 'This is forever Russia.' Above all Sweden, which no longer had a ducat in its treasury and was tired of the madness of a king who was a stranger to his own people. They all wanted an end to the war. In May 1718, Peter Shafirov, General James Bruce and Baron Ostermann were sent to the Åland islands to negotiate a peace. But the war had lasted so long that no one remembered its cause anymore, which made a settlement impossible. Shafirov and his companions came back to St Petersburg empty-handed. The war continued, but on Swedish soil alone.

Spring comes to Peterhof on the Bay of Finland in May. The last ice and the remnants of dirty, slushy snow have melted by then and mild air chases away the memory of the cold. Fountains spew water as a marvel of pipes, canals and nozzles pumps salty seawater up from the bay and into the gardens, where it dances, sparkling, for our pleasure. The young trees, nursed overwinter in the orangery, blossom and bear fruit, and the sea sparkles below the long terraces. Stairs of grey marble lead down into the park, which Peter himself planned so that it is possible to catch a glimpse of our two pavilions: Marly, the marble house with its strict classical beauty, and Mon Plaisir, a simple structure and our first true house in Peterhof. How often had we waited there to watch for the boat from St Petersburg?

Most of the time its passengers were soaked to the skin thanks to a sudden shower above the Bay of Finland. The ladies' make-up would drip from their faces, and musicians were forced to shake water from their instruments. Peter and I would laugh ourselves to tears at the sight, while sitting warm and dry inside Mon Plaisir.

Those happy days were gone forever, though, one morning in May, in the gathering light, when we waited there for Alexey to arrive.

67

I looked out over the troubled waters just to avoid seeing Afrosinja. She sat on a low stool, her face calm, but her loose, long hair flashing around her head like the flames of hell. She had given birth a few days before. Peter had had the child killed immediately. I blinked to chase away my tears, and tasted sea salt on my lips.

Gravel crunched under the soldiers' feet when they marched Alexey towards the house. Afrosinja exhaled sharply. She had not seen him since their separation in Venice a couple of months previously; Peter had sent him to the Trubetzkoi bastion in the Peter and Paul Fortress upon our arrival in St Petersburg. I shuddered. The complete darkness of the cells there shrouded the inmates' minds and dragged them fast into death and despair. No man left those torture chambers in one piece or alive; or if he did, it was only to climb the scaffold.

Peter stood in the middle of the room, his hands folded behind his back. We heard a knock on the door. Afrosinja straightened herself. I held on to the windowsill and glanced outside, to check that there was still life and beauty out there. If I took one step towards Peter, I feared I would fall and crumble to pieces.

'In with the traitor,' he cried, and soldiers placed themselves to right and left of the door as two bullish men dragged in Alexey. Behind them I could see two more soldiers. Alexey's head hung listlessly. He had, if possible, become even leaner. Could he still stand unsupported? The light blinded him. He raised a hand weakly in front of his eyes. Afrosinja eyed her lover coldly and Peter curled his lip.

'Is my son so dangerous that he needs six men to guard him? Look, he is trembling like pig's blubber. Leave us.'

Alexey cowered, burying his face in his bony hands. 'The light . . . I can no longer bear the light. Father, I beg you,' he pleaded.

'Shut up,' Peter told him. 'I'll decide when you can talk.' My fingers busied themselves on the windowsill. Sobs shook Alexey's exhausted body.

'Look up,' Peter coaxed. 'See who is here.'

Alexey finally spotted Afrosinja. He gasped and made as if to embrace her, but Peter roughly pushed him back. Alexey staggered and Peter seized his elbow: he probably did not want his son to fall and die in a stupid accident. No, he was not to escape so lightly.

The girl looked quizzically at Alexey, weeping in Peter's steely grasp. 'Afrosinja! Are you all right?' He looked at her body, which was still heavy, but clearly no longer pregnant. 'What happened to our child?'

She shrugged, a sullen expression on her face. Peter interrupted Alexey's questions. 'You can save your breath. I drowned your child like an autumn kitten and Afrosinja proved to be an upright and loyal subject of the Russian Empire.'

Alexey stared at his mistress. The dawning understanding in his dark eyes was awful to see. He, the fanciful, moody, haughty Tsarevich, had really, truly loved her. Seeing Afrosinja there, sitting calmly amongst us in Mon Plaisir, tortured him worse than any interrogation so far had done. He buckled under the weight of her betrayal. His whole being dissolved in the spring sunshine. I felt like choking and crossed my arms so as not to reach out and comfort him.

'Hand me the letters, Afrosinja,' Peter commanded. She scrabbled in her bodice for a ribbon-tied bundle and she gave it to him with a bland smile. I felt like smacking her.

'Catherine Alexeyevna, dearest stepmother,' Alexey cried. In the mercilessly bright light his skin stretched yellow and waxy over his skull. I could see his ribs showing where his shirt was torn; his face and neck were bruised and swollen. I tried to smile at him encouragingly, but found I could not. Tears rolled down my cheeks.

Peter watched us from the corner of his eye, waving the wad of letters. 'Alexey Petrovich Romanov, did you write these, and did you ask Afrosinja to burn them?'

The prisoner nodded meekly.

'Instead, she has kept the proof of your betrayal safe in her bosom. Close to her warm, soft flesh.' Peter held the bundle under his nose, sniffing at it with exaggerated delight.

Alexey sobbed, 'Why are you so cruel, my father? How have I ever wronged you, apart from being born your son?'

Afrosinja sat frozen on her stool, but Peter strode up to Alexey and kicked him hard, so that he toppled onto the marble floor. 'I will deliver a fair judgment on you. Do not dare to accuse me of anything else.'

Alexey bent double with pain. 'I'm lost,' he gasped.

The sun warmed my fingers: the light, I had to stay close to the light, I thought desperately, and licked my salty lips as Peter circled Alexey like an eagle would a mouse. He read the first letter and shook his head. 'In spite of all the efforts we made with your education, you still have impossible spelling and even worse handwriting.'

Afrosinja gave a little laugh while mute tears ran down Alexey's face. Peter leafed through the letters. 'Ah. Here is a letter to the Emperor in Vienna. Let's see what you had to tell the sot: *"As your Majesty has heard, the bastard son the washer-maid has given my father is sick with fever. My father does what he wants, and God does what he wants."* What do you think of these words, my washer-maid?' Peter mocked, looking at me. He knew how it hurt me to hear that. 'What, in Alexey's opinion, might God want to do with our "bastard son"? Let him perish, perhaps?'

Breathing pained me. The air seared my lungs and hatred spread through my veins, poisoning my heart with its venom. Alexey hated my son; he wished for my boy to die. I avoided his pleading eyes. There were things I could not forgive. Peter knew that. He was like a puppeteer, pulling all the strings.

Peter did not wait for my answer but opened the next letter. 'Ah, this one goes to your cousin Jekaterina Ivanovna in Mecklenburg. Listen to this, it's just too amusing: *"I hope for an uprising of the Russian troops in Mecklenburg, to put an end to my father."*' Here Peter paused.

Alexey was deathly pale. 'Father, please, I don't have the strength for these games.'

But Peter remained unmoved. 'Just one more, for fun. Oh, it is addressed to the Senate of Russia! Brilliant. Listen carefully: *"My father's cruelty has driven me out of the country. Why does he hate me but love the children of his second wife? My half-brother Peter Petrovich is weak and puny. He could die at any time and the Tsar himself might leave us at any moment. I am destined to rule over Russia. Do not consign me to oblivion. It would harm you too."'*

Peter paused and then read aloud, slowly and clearly: *"If I am to be the Tsar, then I shall leave St Petersburg forever and return to Moscow. I shall burn the fleet, dissolve the army and drive away all strangers beyond the borders of our country. I will honour the Church and our God."'*

The silence that followed was deafening. I knew that after writing these words, Alexey did not stand a chance. This was a fight to the death that fate had whimsically decreed between two men: father and son. Alexey lay on the ground as if already dead, and Peter towered over him. Afrosinja had buried her head in her arms. I dared not move.

'Sit up, Alexey Petrovich Romanov,' Peter ordered. Alexey forced himself up. Peter said solemnly, 'As Tsar of All the Russias, I accuse you of high treason. Do you admit your crime?'

I held my breath. Alexey looked at Afrosinja, but I read neither hatred nor anger in his eyes, only pain and loss. She met his gaze, crying by now. Alexey's sallow features twisted in shame. 'I do, my Tsar and father,' he whispered. and his words were almost lost in the sound of the waves washing over the pebbles on the shore below Mon Plaisir.

That moment, I split in half. One part of me stayed at Peter's side, as his faithful wife despite all the hateful events of recent months. This woman would always belong to him and love him for their happy memories. She breathed the same air as he did and shared his bed if he were still to ask it. She shone in the brightness of his light so that no one else dared to approach her; no one heard the hollowness of her heartbeat.

The other woman, though, broke free from the façade that Peter and I so carefully maintained and retreated quietly within. Peter would not get hold of her, no, never again, for she settled silently in the depths of my soul. She drifted there like a boat without a rudder, lost on the stream of my life, until one day another man's love moored her in a last harbour, a place so full of beauty and belief, passion and peace, she could never have imagined it. One day.

At moments I still taste the scented air of Mon Plaisir on my lips, and I hear the wind of Peterhof whispering words of wisdom about the colour of snow, the taste of tears and the vastness of the sea.

68

On the morning that Alexey's fate was to be decided, somebody lightly touched my shoulder, but I slept equally lightly in those days.

'Tsaritsa. You have a visitor,' Alice whispered.

My heartbeat quickened. A visitor meant nothing good at this ungodly hour of the day. 'Who is it?'

'Boris Petrovich Sheremetev. I said it was too early for you to receive him. You are not presentable.'

I climbed out of bed and chuckled. 'If there is one man in the world who has seen me in a less-than-presentable state, it is Sheremetev. I'll be right there.'

I glanced across the quay and the river to the dark, brooding walls of the Peter and Paul Fortress. A beautiful June day was dawning: boats danced on the green waves, and the early, bright sun made the river sparkle when the iron Neva Gate opened. I saw a group of men leave the fortress and step onto the barges that awaited them.

I frowned. 'Should Boris Petrovich not already have taken his seat for Alexey's tribunal?'

Alice nodded mutely.

'Hand me my dressing-gown. Hurry,' I decided, running my fingers through my hair as a makeshift comb.

Sheremetev stood by the window in my antechamber, his narrow shoulders slumped and his neck crooked. He looked small and very alone. My heart went out to him: what would his life have been like if things had taken a different course? He had loved Alice but had been forced to give her away. When I approached, he knelt with a sigh, his gout paining him. I pulled him up to his feet, kissing him three times as a sign of peace. He blushed and adjusted his coat. 'Tsaritsa, thank you for receiving me at such an early hour –'

Alice had stoked the embers in the fireplace while avoiding looking at Boris Petrovich. Sheremetev shuffled closer to the flames, hoping I would not notice.

'I do not know how you feel, but I am so cold these days. Come, sit down with me,' I said, settling on the sofa by the fireplace. He smiled at me gratefully – the warmth of the flames lessened the pain in his swollen limbs – but I knew I had to help him further.

'I have not seen you for so long, Boris Petrovich. Does my old friend come to me only if sorrow weighs him down? But I have to warn you: if your son wants to grow a beard or your daughter wants to wear breeches, I can't help you. Or do you want to own lands that belong to Menshikov? Forget about it, if so.' There, that made him smile.

'If only it were so easy.'

'What is it then?' I asked, taking his hand.

'Tsaritsa,' he said, 'I have devoted my whole life to my Tsar and shall do so until my last breath. I'll fight for Peter, I will ride, I will sail, I will kill –' he gave a pained smile '– as I have done many times before.' He wheezed between sentences. 'But I cannot watch a father judge his own son. You know the verdict on Alexey is already settled.'

If Sheremetev, the man of honour, said so, then it must be true. I bit my lip. 'Tell me how I can help you.'

'I asked to be freed from my duty as a judge at the tribunal, but the Tsar has beaten my messenger with his *dubina*.' My old friend buried his face in my hands; his hair was as white as snow and thin as a spider's web. When he looked up at me, he was weeping. 'It is a yoke I dare not carry. This verdict is against every law of God and nature. A father who wants to try his son, asking for the help of the Church and courts – I cannot die in peace if I am part of this. I don't like Alexey. Among all the bad people of Russia, he might be the worst. But still . . .'

I pondered his words. 'Go back to your palace, *otets*. I will sort it out.'

I leant closer to him, breathing in his bitter scent of age and approaching death. 'Are you sure the verdict is already settled?' I whispered, as in those days the walls had ears.

He looked at me, his eyes veiled. 'Maybe not for the Church or the tribunal. But in the Tsar's heart – yes, I am sure.'

When he left, I took another look at the opposite shore: the boats had rowed over from the fortress to the Admiralty, where Alexey's trial was to take place. Ferrymen leant against street lanterns, chewed tobacco and watched the girls passing by, whistling and catcalling at them. Children gathered around them, eyeing the number of barges and pestering the men with questions. I stepped away. As long as men like Boris Petrovich Sheremetev lived, there was still hope for Russia.

But in the Tsar's heart there was only death.

'But the Tsar's heart is in the hands of God; only He can find the just answer to all questions,' wrote the court of the Russian Church, which refused to pass a judgment on Alexey. For them, the Old Testament, in which a father punishes his misguided and errant son, opposed the New Testament, which preached forgiveness and love.

Peter was furious and called for a secular tribunal; a hundred and twenty-seven Russian dignitaries had gathered in St Petersburg. I myself saw him only once in those days. He took me by surprise, coming into Peter Petrovich's nursery. I was pushing a small wooden boat across the parquet floor and my son made the sound of wind, waves and thunder. 'Boom!' he cried, clapping his hands, and I flipped the boat over as if it had been struck by lightning. He whooped and I embraced him, smelling the June sunshine and the first apples on the trees in his hair. I spent too little time with him alone, had been robbed of so many stages of his life. I held him closer, but he fidgeted and shouted, 'Father! *Batjuschka*!'

I had not seen Peter standing in the doorway with Alexander Menshikov, booted and ready to leave. My skin tingled as Peter lifted up our little boy: how small and vulnerable he looked in his father's hands. Had he also held and kissed Alexey like this?

'I see you've won a naval battle, Tsarevich?' asked Peter. Our son nodded, his cheeks flushed with pride, and placed his hands trustingly on his father's chest. 'I am very proud of you. Let's go to Peterhof soon and you can choose a boat for yourself.'

I rose, forcing myself to sound cheerful. 'Where are you going so early in the morning?'

'To the fortress. The court needs more evidence of Alexey's treason,' Peter said casually.

'More evidence?' I folded my hands on my belly. It was a mere few weeks until I would give birth again. Menshikov laughed and playfully pinched Peter Petrovich's cheek. 'Thirty lashes with the knout loosens every tongue.'

My stomach churned and I stepped up to Peter, ready to plead with him. He caressed my hair. 'This is nothing a woman in your condition should worry about,' he said, but I searched for his fingers, taking advantage of this rare moment of closeness.

'Peter, I beg you,' I whispered. 'Don't do this. Do not sully your glory with blood from your blood. Do not torment the flesh of your flesh. Ban him. Send him to the sawmills, to the mines, or to a monastery. But do not let his death come upon us and our children.'

Peter's expression was unfathomable. 'Menshikov, call the Tsaritsa's ladies. She is not well, she needs rest,' he ordered. Before he left, our son pressed against him once more and Peter kissed him tenderly. He would not look at me anymore and my heart knotted with dread.

After the first round of questioning by the Tsar, Alexey had to rest for three days, Alexandra Tolstoya told me. Only then was he strong enough to meet his father once more. Evil and cruelty lured Peter into their dark embrace, and he was intoxicated by his power and the stench of sweat, fire and blood in the torture chambers; the long hours in the Trubetzkoi bastion seemed to have fogged his brain. Whatever Alexey said, Peter used it against his son. He would stop only when there was nothing more to confess, or if nothing could be confessed anymore.

After another day and countless hours of agony for Alexey, Peter had convinced the tribunal of his son's high treason: Alexey was to be publicly executed. Peter himself did not pass the death sentence; he left that to the court he had called upon to judge his son.

Prince Alexander Danilovich Menshikov was the first to sign the verdict with a cross beside his name. Peter's own hands were clean. But what if there was something else to know? Perhaps Alexey had not bared his soul completely yet, despite all the tortures he had endured? Somewhere in Peter's vast realm a group of conspirators might just be waiting for the right moment to free Alexey. The seagulls shrieked above the Trubetzkoi bastion before the breeze lifted them towards the Bay of Finland when Peter and his men took the barge from the Summer Palace's jetty one last time, on the afternoon that the tribunal's judgment had been delivered.

I knew them all. Peter Shafirov was already sitting in the boat, staring at the water, while Prince Trubetzkoi chatted to him. Tolstoy and Menshikov shared passage with the Tsar, who held his balance on the boat, wide-legged like a seaman. Why did they go and see Alexey again? What for? He had confessed. The verdict had already been passed.

When the darkness of the fortress's star-shaped walls had swallowed Peter and his men, I knelt below a small icon of the Virgin. My fingers trembled as I folded them, searching for words in my memory while I prayed for Alexey's soul. Alice blended me a potion of hot wine, St John's Wort and laudanum. It brought me some hours of restless sleep, plagued by nightmares in which I gave birth to a monster, welcomed by Peter as his child without hesitation.

69

When a fist banged against my bedroom door towards midnight, I sat bolt upright, drenched in sweat. Was I still dreaming? Alice's face was ghostly pale. 'Who can that be, mistress?' she whispered anxiously. 'Are they coming to get us?'

I could not move for dread when there was another knock on the door, hard and demanding. My fear gave way to anger: if the Devil himself was at the door, I should offer him a glass of vodka before he took me. 'We shall see,' I said, padding across the floor to open the door to a familiar figure. I placed my hands on my hips and demanded, 'Alexander Danilovich, what is the meaning of this?'

Menshikov leant heavily against the door frame, as if his legs would no longer carry him. A crippled guard stood awkwardly behind him, holding up a lantern. It cast an unsteady light, lengthening their shadows against the wall. I could not see the guard's face because of his hooded coat, but that was probably for the best. Menshikov seized my wrists. 'Catherine Alexeyevna, come with me, please. Right now. He's going mad,' he stammered. He reeked of sweat and blood, his eyes sunk deep in their sockets and his face and arms speckled with dark spots. I freed myself from his grip and ran a finger over his skin, sniffing at it.

'This is blood. Have you been in a brawl? Has something happened to the Tsar?' I asked. Instead of an answer, the cripple raised his lantern and I stifled a scream. Menshikov's entire cloak was soaked with blood.

'Come, I beg you,' he whispered. 'Come quickly.'

'Not alone,' I said, suspicious. 'Alice, put on your cloak,' I ordered the girl while I slipped into my boots.

We followed Menshikov and his guard down to the river. In the white hours of the night, mist veiled the Neva, thickening into fog on the far bank. Once we were on the flat-bottomed barge, dewy swathes swirled around my ankles and soaked the hem of my nightgown. The magic of these hours no longer touched me.

Alice squatted on the planks as the cripple drove the barge forward with steady pushes, the water giving way silently. Menshikov and I stood close together; he twisted his fingers to stop their trembling. Neither of us spoke. When we reached the Neva Gate, Shafirov stepped out of the shadows and helped me disembark, while Menshikov handed Alice onto the pier. We walked along narrow passageways into the darkness of the Trubetzkoi bastion; water dripped from the roughly hewn walls and pooled on the uneven stone floor. Tar dropped from the torches, hissing, and rats scurried into the shadows. The place reeked of blood and death. Alice's fingers clung to mine like a drowning man's to a plank until we halted before an oak door studded with iron nails. The small window in it was nailed shut. Was this a trap? What if I couldn't even trust Menshikov anymore?

I pulled my cloak tighter around my neck while the cripple turned a key in the lock and retreated into the shadows. The door shrieked on its hinges, but I raised my chin and took a step forward. In a corner of the dingy, windowless cell a man lay on a bunk. He was asleep, a blanket drawn up to his chin. My eyes were still adjusting to the dim light cast by two candle flames when a figure threw itself at me from the darkness, clasping my knees. I staggered, but Menshikov caught me.

'Menshikov, help!' I cried, before I recognised Peter's dark head. He buried his face in my cloak, sobbing, soaking my already damp nightshirt with his tears, his sweat – and blood.

'Catherinushka,' he moaned. 'Thank God! I did not do anything, do you hear me? It wasn't me, whatever they say. Help me. It is not my fault,' he cried, his pleas resounding from the cell's bare walls.

'Help me, help me, help me –' He bent forward, rocking and howling like an animal.

'Give me a hand, Menshikov,' I said, and we dragged Peter to a stool. He embraced my waist and I felt his hot breath through my dress. 'Now you're here, everything will be fine. I did not do anything. It was not my fault,' he stammered again. Alice knelt, taking Peter's hands in hers, and I went over to the bunk. Only then did I spot the man sitting next to it, with his head buried in his hands. I touched his shoulder. It was Tolstoy, his face empty. The blood in my veins thickened with fear and I had a presentiment that made me want to turn on my heels and flee. Instead, I leant over the bunk and looked closely at the sleeping man. It was Alexey, and yet it wasn't him. His skin was blackened and the eyes bulged from their sockets; the mouth was open, jaw hanging slack and broken, the teeth cracked or missing. The swollen tongue had been torn and hung to one side. The nose was thick and twisted, the ears half ripped off his head. He did not sleep: no, he was dead.

'Alexey,' I whispered in shock, struggling against my rising nausea and trying to stroke his eyelids shut. But they would not close and stared out at me, charging us all with his death. When I tried to pull the blanket from his body, Tolstoy held me back. 'For the love of God, don't, my Tsaritsa,' he begged. 'You're pregnant.'

I shrugged him off, but Alexey's state made me recoil in horror, despite Peter Andreyevich's warning. Menshikov held me tight until my head stopped spinning and my nausea dwindled. Alexey's flesh had been torn from his limbs with burning tongs and all his bones broken. Their ragged, sharp ends pierced his skin, which was blackened from burn marks and streaked with whiplashes, at his knees, hips and chest. On no battlefield had I ever seen such a sight; no wild animal treated his prey this way.

'Good God!' I panted.

Peter raised his head from Alice's lap. 'I've done nothing, believe me!' She held him and he sobbed like a child at her breast.

I overcame my disgust and dread and stroked Alexey's thin, straggly hair. 'Now you have peace,' I murmured. Tolstoy sucked his teeth when Alexey's head came loose from his body and rolled to one side, like a ball. He had been beheaded! I pressed my hands against my mouth, aghast, but Menshikov stopped me from running away.

'It was the Tsar who did it,' he whispered. 'Peter was beside himself when Alexey died during the second torture. It was a miracle the boy had lived so long, with God or the Devil's help. Peter was so furious that he grabbed my sword and beheaded Alexey's dead body. Now he's going mad.' I heard Menshikov's words but did not understand them. My teeth were chattering and I felt searing pain in my lower belly. Was I going into labour, here, in the midst of this horror?

'Catherine, what should we do?' urged Menshikov. 'Alexey must be laid out in state, otherwise there will be rumours that the Tsar killed him.'

'Rumours? What other cause could there be?' I said, choked,

Menshikov ruffled his bloodstained hair and considered this. 'A stroke, maybe. Or else his weak chest? Everyone knows that he was in poor health …' His voice trailed off. If he himself was not convinced, how could Russia hope to deceive the whole of Europe?

I bit my lip until I tasted blood, thinking hard. I glanced at Alice. Peter was still crying in her lap, dampening her skirt.

'Menshikov, fetch the garrison's doctor. Tell him to bring his medical supplies and instruments,' I ordered. Minutes later he returned with the man who had obviously been chased out of bed, for he still wore his nightcap and under his cloak I spotted his bare legs and feet. He bowed, peering at the corpse on the bunk. 'Give us everything we need to tend to wounds,' I said, taking his doctor's satchel. 'We also need alcohol. Lots of it. You are free to leave, but forget what you have seen, if your life is dear to you.'

Menshikov pushed him back out and I unscrewed the bottle of vodka and passed a coarse thread through a needle's wide eye. Then I went to Alice and took her hands in mine. I felt her fingers tremble.

'Alice, I must ask you to do something for me. It is monstrous, but both the Tsar and I will never forget it if you help us tonight.'

'What is it, mistress?'

My heart pounded with dread and revulsion as I requested, 'Please wash Alexey's body with the vodka; clean him and settle his bones back into place. He must look like a man again.' She wanted to rise and step over to the corpse, but I held her back. 'Alice, you will also have to sew his head on again.' I spoke very softly, as if I myself hoped not to hear those horrid words. In the cell's dull twilight, Alice nodded mutely. I held out the needle and thread to her. She went to Alexey's bunk, nightdress rustling, shoulders hunched, clutching the vodka, a rag and the needle. Tolstoy silently rose to leave her his place next to the corpse.

'Help me, men,' she whispered as she sat down. Tolstoy and Menshikov turned Alexey, so that his shoulders rested on her knees, his head rolling loose in her lap. Her gaze met his wide stare. She gagged, but made the first stitch through his blackened skin, sewing the throat to the trunk, placing a knot after each stitch and cutting the thread with the sharp small knife from the doctor's satchel. With each stitch her fingers became steadier and she worked in silence while we looked on. Silent tears ran down her cheeks, dripping hotly on to Alexey's dead face. In the candlelight Alice looked so mild and mournful that the men around her cast down their eyes in shame.

The day's first colours filled the white night sky when Peter and I took the barge back to the Summer Palace. The water swallowed the rudder with a hollow splash. Peter clenched my hands in silence, numbing my fingers. Only when we reached the palace's footbridge did he raise his head. 'Tell me I'm not an animal, Catherinushka. Tell me,' he whispered, as the morning light reached his red, exhausted eyes. 'Tell me you will stay with me always,' he pleaded, clutching the hem of my skirt, as the waves splashed against the bow of the boat. While I cast about for words, he peered up into the sallow sky.

'Do you know what the executioners back in the bastion swore? That Alexey's soul had fled his body in the form of a crow.' He sank his face into his hands. When I wanted to console him, he leapt to his feet. The small vessel swayed as he threatened the skies with his fist: 'I will get you! Just you wait! All of you …'

His heavy, pained breathing filled the silence around us. The Neva streamed towards the Bay of Finland. A pale night drifted away, blending into bright day. The first rays of sunshine warmed me after the horror I had witnessed. I helped Peter towards the two footmen waiting for us at the bridge and in his bedroom handed him a heavy sleeping-potion.

The following evening, Peter celebrated the ninth anniversary of the victory of Poltava. He laughed and cheered as never before and forced more people than ever to keep sleep, and his demons, at bay by their sheer presence. I felt hot as I sat covered in heavy robes, jewels and the pasty make-up I had applied on his orders. Peter drank like a horse, downing one eagle cup after another, but I secretly poured every second glass of my Tokay away. The feast of Poltava blended with the celebrations for Peter's name-day, and in the days that followed I endured long Masses, suppers, fireworks, parades and drinking games. Envoys from all over Europe were forbidden to mention Alexey: he had died a traitor and nobody was to mourn him. I saw the French Ambassador, Campredon, eagerly recording everything in his little book.

Alexey's enbalmed corpse was laid in state underneath a white canopy in the Trinity Church. His coffin was guarded by a tall, bulky soldier whose real task was to hinder anyone from coming too close. A magnificent Persian silk scarf had been wrapped around Alexey's neck: no one should ever see Alice's stitches. The people passed by the former Tsarevich in dull, dumb adoration, praying silently and wiping their eyes. The court itself was still stupefied from the recent days' feasts.

Menshikov leant towards me and whispered, 'In my head, drinking songs are mixed up with the hymns, so I had better shut up.'

During the service, Peter was in floods of tears, his hands clasped in prayer. When Feofan Prokopovich read out the story of the son Absalom, a traitor to his father, the Tsar listened intently. Once the service ended, he stepped up to Alexey's coffin: he swayed and held onto its edge until he'd regained his balance enough to kiss Alexey's cold lips, which would never again doubt his father's work in Russia. Then the Tsar straightened up, his cheeks flushed and his eyes bright and focused. He looked ahead, over the crowd's heads, far ahead into the future.

70

Tolstoy was made a Count as his reward for hunting down Alexey, and the only person I would have wished flogged and tortured got away unscathed: Afrosinja married an officer and led a life of peace and prosperity. In Hell, I hoped, she would receive just punishment for her heartlessness. Two months after Alexey's death, I gave birth to a daughter. 'Next time it's a son, Catherinushka,' Peter said lightly, as the little Tsarevna Natalya clenched his finger. 'She is strong as a bear.'

I made Alice Natalya's first lady-in-waiting. Icy strands had appeared prematurely in Alice's ash-blonde hair. She was not yet thirty. Yet the night of Alexey's death had stolen her youth.

The first flakes tumbled from the sky throughout the night as we celebrated St Andrew's Day in Menshikov's palace on Vassilyev Island, which was his sole property. Dishes were just being laid down as the double doors of the gilded hall opened and a messenger slid in. He was caked with mud and could barely fight his fatigue enough to speak.

Menshikov got up to go to him while Peter toyed with the colourful talking birds that the Moorish slave Abraham Petrovich Hannibal was showing him: Peter treated this man like family and had even sent him to Paris for his studies. 'Give me a drink. Give me to drink, scoundrel, miser!' cried one bird. 'Shut up, shit head!' the other replied. Peter roared with laughter and filled the birds' trough with vodka. 'That should make them even more talkative.'

Menshikov reached the messenger, listened, and placed his hand over his mouth in amazement. His eyes searched out Peter, who was tugging at a bird's red and blue tail-feathers. 'What a beautiful present! Thank you. I'll keep them in Mon Plaisir,' he said. Abraham bowed to him and muscles played under his dark, velvety skin; the watching ladies sighed softly.

The messenger drank thirstily from a glass of beer and chewed on a pork bone as Menshikov made his way through the crowd to Peter, who looked up at him. 'Why the sour face, Alekasha?' he asked with a grin. 'Are you jealous of my birds?'

Alexander Danilovich bowed, 'My Tsar. Your enemy, Charles the Twelfth, King of Sweden, is dead.'

Peter went on stroking the colourful feathers of the bird perched on his shoulder. 'Dead? Charles of Sweden? That's not possible.'

'He was laying siege to a fortress in Norway when a bullet hit him. His soldiers carried him with them for days, but the wound festered.'

Peter handed the bird to Abraham, turned to the hall and slowly clapped his hands: once, twice and then three times. The music stopped and the voices hushed.

'My cousin, the King of the Swedes, has passed away,' he cried, before triumphantly thrusting his fists into the air. 'Charles the Twelfth is dead. Russia's enemy is no more.' His words fell like stones into a lake and cast circles of astonished silence. Charles had been part of our lives for so long, a world without him seemed unthinkable. Peter grabbed his eagle cup in both hands. 'The dark clouds have drifted; long live the light,' he cried, ready to drink deeply.

But before the guests could join his toast and his merriment, somebody gave a desperate sob. Peter spun around, his face dark, and I caught my breath. On a table near us sat the most beautiful woman I had ever seen. She wept, but her tears did not dull the lustre of her almond-shaped, amber- and gold-speckled eyes; her heavy honey-blonde tresses had come undone and her full breasts rose and fell with anguish.

'Why are you crying, girl, when the greatest enemy of your fatherland has died? Do you mourn the dog?' Peter thundered, but she bore his look of blazing anger with no sign of fear.

'I do not mourn our enemy. On the contrary,' she said, in a voice as mellow as a bronze bell.

'Why then do you grieve?' Peter towered above her and she rose to her feet, refusing to be dominated. Their eyes locked.

'I weep because now peace is further away than ever. Only confusion and a struggle for power can follow Charles's death, my Tsar.'

Peter considered this. I saw him softening. 'What is your name?' he asked, before wiping a tear from her cheek.

'Maria Kantemir, Princess of Moldavia.'

Peter kissed her fingers. 'Princess, does your beauty surpass your wisdom or is it the other way around?' Her long black eyelashes shadowed the bloom on her cheeks, I noticed. Peter did not let go of her hand but cried, 'Let us drink to the wisdom of the Princess of Moldova. And let us weep for peace, which is ever-more elusive.'

Everyone obediently sobbed into their cups and drank, yet I eyed Maria Kantemir. I remembered her well from our campaign on the River Pruth so many years ago. Back then she had been an unbelievably pretty child, but promise of this sort is easily marred by illness or early death. Tonight the feathers of Abraham's birds paled in comparison with the princess's beauty, her glowing skin the colour of wild honey.

'God protect us and give us peace,' she toasted Peter, never once taking her eyes off him. The colourful birds shrieked, and their cries rose to a screech in my ears, swallowing the music, the cheers and the laughter of the crowd. I had never feared Peter's other mistresses, or his niece, the child Jekaterina Ivanovna. This woman, I knew, would make me suffer.

71

God gave us peace, though only after the jockeying for power that Maria Kantemir had predicted: the new Queen of Sweden, Ulrica Eleonora, first turned to England for help. Admiral Norris dutifully attacked Russian bastions on the shores of southern Sweden, but a stray dog was the only casualty of that skirmish and a bath-house burst into flames. The story made both Menshikov and Peter cry with laughter. In the first spring following Alexey's death, the second Peace Congress of Åland began.

Yet there was no peace in my heart: while the *ottepel* thawed land and minds, my little son caught a fever. One day after the first angry scarlet spots appeared on the skin behind his ears and down his arms, Peter Petrovich lost consciousness. I did not leave his bedside but set up camp in his nursery, talking to him, washing down his hot skin, kissing his face and fingers, and fanning him with cool air. When I sank onto my mattress on the floor, exhausted, I would pray, offering God a quiet, desperate trade. He could take everything I had, or everything I might ever have wanted to have, if he only left me my little boy. I heard myself whisper despicable words, which might have turned the Almighty even more against me. 'Take me. Take Anna, my God. Take Elizabeth. Take them both, take us all, but please let him live.' The sight of his slight, feverish body robbed me of my mind; in those hours my tears never dried.

The Tsar was on his way back from Peterhof: I prayed that he would soon be with me, to help me bear this trial. The next night I never stopped praying, but when day broke, my son could not hear me anymore. His eyes were glassy and he squinted as if the light hurt him. His skin was so flushed that every touch of mine left a white mark on his hot, tender body. Neither my words nor my love reached him; his little fingers lay slack in mine. Blumentrost wanted to bleed him; Menshikov held me back with all his strength so that I did not whip the quack.

In the evening my little son took his last, tormented breath. Peter Petrovich, the Tsarevich, was dead. When his narrow chest no longer rose and fell, I heard someone scream. It sounded like an animal in the slaughterhouse. Only later did I realise that this had been me. I remember nothing else; not scratching my own face bloody nor tearing out tufts of my own hair. My hands and arms were bloodstained from smashing my fists against the walls, breaking mirrors and cutting myself with the shards, all over my body, just to dull the pain in my soul.

It was Peter who brought me back to my senses with his own pain and sorrow: it was impossible for him to find comfort in the belief that this was God's will; the scale of the loss was too overwhelming. I lay over our son's body, cuddling, caressing and kissing him. The door flew open. The Tsar still wore his muddy boots and his face was blackened by rainwater and muck.

My son!' he cried, taking us both in his arms and holding us so tight that I gasped for air, before I gave in to the closeness and the pain. When Peter let go, he lifted his son's corpse carefully, as if our boy were made of glass. Tears streamed down Peter's face while he pleaded, 'Tell me that you're alive, my little angel. Do not leave your father alone. I need you. Tsarevich. Say something!' Strangled by grief, he stood looking down at the deathly pale small face: our son looked as if he was hewn from ivory. The Tsar drew him close, pressing the slight body against his huge chest before he looked to the heavens and let out a scream that made the priest, crouching in the corner, cross himself with dread.

We sat holding each other and holding our child for a long time. I would not stir, but breathed in the faint scent of Peter Petrovich's hair that already was starting to fade. His skin turned waxy, but still I squeezed his fingers, hoping he would answer. It was in vain. The Tsarevich was dead, and with him all our hope.

Hours, if not a day later, it was Menshikov who finally dared to take our little boy from us. I slapped, scratched and bit him, but he would not let go of him. Finally, it was the Tsar who led me to my rooms, where my ladies awaited me, already dressed in black and thickly veiled.

Peter himself did not stay: where he went, I did not know.

Alexander Danilovich Menshikov and Peter Shafirov took care of the Tsarevich's funeral. The Tsar, so I heard later when the madness lifted from my mind, locked himself in his rooms for days, drinking bottles of brandy and vodka. Birds of sorrow nestled in every corner of my soul. More than once I thought of taking my own life. Why could God not leave me this one child, just my son, whose life meant so much to Peter and to me, to a whole country and its countless people?

Russia needed an heir.

Weeks later I woke in the late morning and heard a noise from my study. When I walked over, barefoot and in my nightshirt, Peter was standing by the window. My heart leapt: he was still there; he was still with me. 'My love?' I said quietly.

He turned and I was startled: it was Peter, and yet it wasn't. His face was swollen and his eyes bloodshot with pupils as tiny as needle-heads: he must be drunk or in some other sort of stupor, I thought. He laughed bitterly. 'Do not worry, Catherinushka. We are both as ugly as the night. Peter Petrovich has taken all beauty with him to his grave.' He reached out for my hand. 'Come here.'

He was right, I knew: I only kept the birds of sorrow at bay with vodka, and had to drink vats of it before they sullenly clawed their way back into their nests, leaving me in peace. I stepped up to him at the window, taking his hand. His fingers laced themselves with mine; it felt like old times.

'What are you watching?' I asked.

'Them,' he said. 'Alexey's children.'

Among the rose bushes, Alexey's son Petrushka played with his elder sister. The children had stretched a rope between two statues and were jumping, playing pony and ringmaster. How healthy they looked; laughing, their cheeks flushed by the fresh air. Peter thought the same as I did: meanwhile, the maggots ate our son.

'Why is my grandson so strong and handsome?' he murmured. Since Alexey's death, nobody had dared to speak of him. 'And look at his sister. She is pretty. The daughter of that scrawny German cat has shiny hair and straight white teeth.'

I leant in to him. 'Do not hate them just because they're his,' I whispered. 'Raise them to be good children of your house. They are not to blame for who their father was.'

The children's joy was comforting to me, but Peter shook his head in dismissal. 'Their birthdays shall not be part of the court calendar. Petrushka shall never be Tsarevich, let alone Tsar. It's enough if he learns to read and write. More education than that is unnecessary. Alexey's son is never to rule Russia,' he decreed, his expression implacable. He freed himself from my embrace and stepped away.

'Peter –' I began, but he shook his head.

'God has punished me too much for me to reach an accord with him. I am in Peterhof, should you care to look for me.'

The grief in his voice still hung in my heart long after he had left me. I closed the curtains, shutting out the bright spring light, but the fabric would not stifle the children's joyful cries. I spooned far too much laudanum into warm wine and went back to bed, in the middle of the day. In my dreams the shrieking of the birds of sorrow sounded like children's laughter.

Peter barely alluded to the death of our little son in his weekly letters to Europe, but the news spread like wildfire. Of course he knew, as did I and everybody else, what was thought all over Russia and Europe: an eye for an eye, a tooth for a tooth, a son for a son. The world saw our little Peter's death as a punishment for Alexey's suffering, just as we ourselves did. No one dared to say this aloud bar a monk living in one of Menshikov's monasteries. The man was boiled to death in a great cauldron. The cruel punishment did not hide the bitter truth.

After the Tsarevich's death, Peter fled from St Petersburg. I knew he would not spend his nights alone, but I had never before felt so frightened of losing everything I had ever cared for.

In autumn, the Congress of Åland failed for the second time to end the Great Northern War. Pavel Jagushinsky, James Bruce and

Ostermann blamed Queen Ulrica Eleonora of Sweden. 'She does not wish for peace and is as stubborn as a peasant girl,' Jagushinsky said over dinner. 'A woman on the throne, what an idea! She should have her husband crowned.'

I slapped him playfully with my fan. 'I do not see why a woman should rule worse than a man!'

He shook his head. 'I beg your pardon, Tsaritsa, but women cannot keep their minds together. They scatter their thoughts; women are like chickens, jumping at five grains at a time.'

Peter winked at me over his lamb stew, smacking his lips. 'What do you think, Ostermann?' he asked his Chancellor, amused.

The German kept his gaze lowered. He never met anyone's eyes so as not to betray his true thoughts and feelings. 'I agree. Women cannot tell important matters from trivial ones. As a man, you set your mind to one thing and you succeed. Therefore, the Tsar is the Tsar.'

I did not wish to spoil the merriment but I sensed we all thought the same. The Tsar was the Tsar, but he had three healthy daughters and no son.

Peter's niece, Duchess Jekaterina Ivanovna, fled Mecklenburg upon the arrival of the British together with her little daughter. I'd heard that her husband had regularly beaten and raped her, so an invading army must have made a welcome excuse to leave. When she happily moved back in with her mother, the Tsaritsa Praskovia, I raised the little Mecklenburg princess together with my daughters. It was a small thank you to Praskovia, who had looked after Anna and Elizabeth so well each time I'd had to follow Peter.

Shortly afterwards, in a brief, private ceremony, their father gave the title of Tsesarevna to both girls. Natalya had to wait for this honour until she came of age. My heart soared for them, now Crown Princesses of All the Russias; Anna, all dark curls and blue eyes like her father, winked at me when I wiped away more than a few tears; Elizabeth smiled, her teeth shiny as pearls and her gaze as lively as a bird's, when Peter cut the gossamer-thin veil of a mantle from her shoulders, thus marking her as a grown woman. Of course, we all knew that they were only place-holders until another little brother was born, but their bright faces and their proud demeanour gave me endless joy.

In the following May, England retreated from the Baltic Sea for good and peace talks begun for the third time in the Finnish town of Nystad. At that time I had not bled for three months in a row: had the hurried encounters, for which Peter had just about found time and desire, helped me once again to blessed circumstances? I counted on my fingers: yes, it seemed a child was to be born in the autumn. I had to tell Peter the good news – we would laugh and be merry together, just as we used to! I rang the silver bell on my bedside table, and Agneta hurried in, her cheeks flushed and eyes shiny. I swung my legs over the side of the bed. 'Agneta, you're getting lazy. If your dead mother knew, she would make you sweep the stove as a punishment.' Agneta giggled and hid something in the folds of her skirt.

'What do you have there?'

She blushed. 'Nothing, Tsaritsa. Just a little book.'

I held out my hand. 'You are as red as a cherry, so it cannot be quite so harmless. Give it to me, even if I cannot read.'

She handed me the book, which was bound in beautiful crimson leather. 'Well, there are lots of very colourful pictures in it,' she giggled.

The cover smelt of jasmine and sandalwood and when I opened the first pages, the pictures were indeed more than colourful. I turned the book this way and that, amused by it myself. 'Ohhhhhh, that looks very difficult! Do people really do that? Where did you get this from?'

'It's from China, and in the *gostiny dvor* it is worth its weight in gold. Look here, Tsaritsa.' She opened the book at a page where a man was being pleasured by two girls at the same time.

'I must show this to the Tsar. He will be enchanted. I'll give it back to you right away.'

'Shall I dress you, Tsaritsa?'

'My cloak will do. I have something to tell him anyway.'

Her gaze skimmed my belly and she beamed.

I paced along the private corridor leading to Peter's rooms, looking at the other pictures in the sinful book. Unbelievable: I had to try *that* with him! When I pushed open the concealed door to his antechamber, the footman, who slept curled up like a kitten on the Tsar's threshold, rubbed his eyes, and stood to attention looking embarrassed.

'Tsaritsa! I do not think the Tsar is ready to receive,' he stammered. I slapped him on the shoulder, laughing. 'Boy, I've seen the Tsar very often other than ready to receive, so make yourself scarce and go and eat some hot *kasha* in the kitchen.'

But he blocked Peter's bedroom door, blushing. 'Tsaritsa, I beg you. Come back in an hour.' A stunned silence reigned. I heard sounds from Peter's room: laughter, and low talk. Was that him speaking or someone else? My heart chilled.

'Step aside. I can hear that he's awake,' I ordered curtly.

The young man's shoulders slumped as he obeyed. What else could he do? I pushed the heavy door open, my heart pounding. The room was dusky, the dark green velvet curtains with the golden embroidery soaking up the light. It took a moment for my eyes to grow accustomed to the twilight; I heard Peter mutter, and tiptoed over to the bed. Golden thighs were wrapped around his heaving hips and a pair of hands clasped his neck. His whole body rose and fell; he groaned and panted. The woman spurred him on with endearments that made my ears burn.

'*Batjuschka*!' I said. Just the night before I had put his haste and absent-mindedness with me down to his many burdens when, in truth, he had wanted to save his strength for someone else. 'Peter!' I said, this time louder, and he jerked around, slackening at the sight of me. That served him and his whore right!

'Catherinushka! Who let you in?' he asked, sounding helpless. He seemed embarrassed. Maria Kantemir let her taut thighs linger on the Tsar's back, her slender fingers still toying with his frizzled grey chest hair. She smiled at me, full lips parting, and her peculia gold-speckled eyes as narrow as a cat's. Honey-coloured tresses spread like rays of sunshine over the pillow's starched linen; her breasts were full, high and round.

She made no effort to cover herself, but said cheekily, 'Tsaritsa, my everlasting fidelity and devotion. *Batjuschka*, you giant of a man, you crush me. Let me move.'

'Of course, my princess,' 'Peter stammered. He scrambled out of bed, throwing on his old green dressing gown, and came to me.

'*Matka*, why do you visit me so early?' he asked unhappily when he saw the tears in my eyes.

'I wanted to tell you something, my Tsar,' I said, swallowing my grief. He led me to one of the windows.

'What is it?' He glanced back at his bed where Maria Kantemir watched us with raised eyebrows. I leant closer to him.

'I am once more pregnant with a Tsarevich for the realm.'

He squeezed my arm, 'How wonderful, Catherinushka. Splendid. Shall we celebrate that this evening?' I beamed at him, but then he said, 'Is there anything else you wanted to tell me?'

'No, but –'

'Well, then.'

Maria Kantemir lay on her belly, her hands cupping her face. She idly swung her legs, watching us.

'I will see you in the evening, at table,' he said, steering me towards the concealed door: I was given my dismissal. My cheeks burnt with shame. From the corner of my eye, I saw my husband approach the bed, where he flipped Maria onto her back and pulled her hips upwards.

The door closed behind me and I asked the young footman: 'Who gave you the order not to let me in? The Tsar or the Princess Kantemir?'

'The Princess Kantemir.'

'And you obeyed her?'

He dared neither answer nor look at me.

Only once I was back in the corridor did I notice that I was still clutching the naughty Chinese book. My knees buckled and I sank to the ground, wiping tears from my cheeks. I remembered the night I had fled from Vassily's house. True, my shirt was now of silk instead of coarse wool, and the floor beneath my feet was made of fine wood instead of bare earth. But other than that, little had changed for me in the past twenty years. I was helpless against fate. My son was dead, and a younger woman lay in my husband's bed. The past was gone and there was no future for me. The shadows of the corridor gave life to the colourful pictures in the book: in the flickering candlelight the women's bodies looked as nubile, taut and shiny as golden coils. I slowly tore page after page from the book, ripping them to shreds.

72

The very cold spring brought the first of four years of hail, devastating storms and famine to Russia. Locusts plagued the land, devouring all the grain and then even the stubble. Villages were haunted by hungry wolves and bears, and the village councils had to prepare for an autumn and winter of strict rationing. Everywhere in the country Alexey's ghost was spotted. Wherever he stepped, so we heard, flowers bloomed and grain sprouted. Peter had the people who spread such nonsense, knouted or killed.

My son was to be born into a new era. In September 1721, Andrej Ostermann finally negotiated peace between Russia and Sweden, which ceased all counter-claims to the Baltics for eternity.

When Peter arrived back in Russia in the early-morning hours, he rushed straight into my bedroom, shaking me awake and shouting with joy. 'Catherinushka, wake up! Do you know what has happened?' He was jumping up and down on my mattress like a child, smelling of sweat, the sea and the wind. I rubbed my eyes, still half-asleep.

'What is it, *starik*?' I asked happily. He pulled me onto my knees on the crumpled sheets.

'Listen,' he said, raising one finger and holding me close. I held my breath just as the first bells of the city began to toll into the black stillness of the night. The sound filled the sky over St Petersburg as all the other bells joined in, their joy resounding in my heart.

'These are the bells of peace, *matka*. The Peace of Nystad. The war is over!'

I started sobbing. The war had lasted my whole life. 'Peace!' cried Peter. '*Mir!*' He leapt off my bed, ran to the door and tore it open. The young guard outside wanted to throw himself to the ground when he saw the Tsar, but Peter caught hold of him. 'You – give me your gun, then you can kneel down. You do not need it anymore because there is peace!'

Peter ran to the window, holding the gun, and struggled with the curtains. I laughed as I saw him tangle himself up in the heavy fabric and rushed to help him. Together we pushed the window open and Peter fired shot after shot into the velvety sky of his city. People gathered on the quay and looked up to the Winter Palace: scared, yet full of surprise, as Peter shouted for more ammunition and then cheered, his voice breaking with sobs: 'Peace! *Mir! Mir!*' He reloaded and shot another salute. I held him around his waist, so as to lessen the weapon's recoil, sharing his laughter and his tears.

'Do not be frightened, you asses!' he laughed, waving at the people below. 'Peace, we have peace! The Great Northern War is over,' he proclaimed, the words drowned out by the volleys of shots that answered his own from all over town. The church towers of Russia carried the news far across the country. People ran onto the streets in their nightgowns, dancing, laughing and embracing each other. They grabbed everything they could find, as long as it made a mighty racket: drums rolled next to the rattling of pots and clinking of swords, sickles and scythes. Just a moment later fireworks lit up the sky above Menshikov's palace. Peter watched with damp eyes. 'My Alekasha. Let us go to him. Now, at once!'

Down on the quay musicians were playing, and those who saw Peter knelt and tried to kiss his feet. In the midst of that raging mass of people we set out in a ferry-boat for Vassilyev Island. The waters of the Neva mirrored flames from the bonfires lit all along the banks. No wonder a Russian calls peace and the world the same word: *mir*. People's joy at the Peace of Nystad was louder than any battle-cry but sounded like the sweetest song.

*

It took Peter three full days to sober up enough to think about a suitable celebration for the Peace of Nystad in the cities of St Petersburg and Moscow. His fingertips were still blackened and blistered from the fireworks he personally had sent into the sky, and his arms ached from tirelessly hitting the drums in celebration, marching up and down the prospects of the city. Nevertheless, he reached for paper and ink. 'Let's start. I only want to hear new ideas. After all, this is the end of the Great Northern War,' he ordered.

Maria Kantemir slid into the room and settled next to him. She was dressed according to the custom of her country, and the narrow tunics and embroidered leggings suited her as did her heavy silver jewellery. Her scent of musk and patchouli clouded my spirits: my *damy* whispered that she blended her perfume with some drops of her very own moisture, to make it more bewitching. Peter placed his hand on her knee and gave her his list of ideas: 'Have a look and tell me what you think.'

She read and gave it a moment of thought. 'All this sounds fitting, but it's not quite enough. A ruler like you must add a strong, almost divine note.' Her gold-flecked amber eyes challenged him.

'What do you suggest?' Peter urged, as if pearls of wisdom were about to drip from her full lips. Under my lashes I studied the others present: Peter's friends, pupils and advisers, who were also the companions of my life. There was Menshikov, of course. My saviour Count Sheremetev, and Count Tolstoy, with whom I had faced my fate so many years ago, whose hair had since turned as white as snow. How did these men bear themselves towards Maria Kantemir? We had all fought and feasted together; many times I had saved them from the harsh punishments Peter could decree so easily in his anger. Thanks to me, their estates had escaped confiscation, they had avoided exile to Siberia and dodged death on the scaffold. But gratitude and loyalty are easily eroded by the first hint of impending disgrace, I thought. Was I being overlooked while they eagerly listened to Maria's words? Currently she held the Tsar captive between her thighs. They nodded their agreement to her words, be it from fear, courtesy, diplomacy or true admiration.

'Come as Poseidon, God of the Sea. Sail with the fleet that you have created up to the city you founded. Celebrate all your achievements, my Tsar. We can think about Moscow later,' she advised.

Peter beamed at her. 'My beautiful Maria, how clever you are.' He kissed her and she pushed him away, her smile full of promise. 'Later, my Tsar,' she murmured, lowering her dark lashes. My fingernails dug into my palms as I forced a smile. This woman was more dangerous than hail, fire and plague put together. I placed my hands on my swollen belly, and the unborn child answered with a small kick. Whatever Maria Kantemir planned, it was I who bore the future Tsarevich underneath my heart. Any protest I made now would look like jealousy and drive him further into her arms. Only the sweetest of joys would win him back to my side – I prayed that God would grant me a healthy son.

I cannot fail Maria Kantemir's work in planning the celebrations for the Peace of Nystad. We sailed up the Neva like an image from a dream; on the foaming grey-green waters flashed the brilliant, blinding white of the sails of hundreds of ships. Thousands upon thousands of bright flags, banners and strings of bunting fluttered in the breeze; the shores were black with people. I looked like a real Tsaritsa, wearing a dress of blue-green shining silk, my glossy, thick hair all piled up and secured with emerald combs. There was a heavy matching choker around my neck. Under my bosom, too, I wore a belt of emeralds and sapphires to distract attention from my already heavy stomach.

'You shine like the sun, Catherinushka. No wonder even the magpies are jealous,' Peter teased me after the holy Mass when we rode through the town for the whole evening before returning to the palace to change for a masked ball. I looked like a Dutch peasant woman, with flowers in my hair and a blue-and-white patterned dress, while Peter had dressed as a sailor from Friesland. So we mingled with the fools and the fairies, the shepherds and the Persian princes, until the early hours of the morning. I felt happy and strong, until Peter forced Maria Kantemir onto a divan near my throne, pushing her robe all the way up to her naked hips, spreading her thighs. The little bells she wore on her ankles and wrists clinked softly as he began to lick her. Her fingers laced his dense hair, like poisonous snakes in tall grass, and she let her head fall back, her eyes closed. After she gave a cry, he took a bottle of vodka in one hand and held her over his shoulder with the other. She hung as limp as a young cat when they disappeared into the corridors of the palace.

A week after the celebrations of Nystad I began to bleed in the early-morning hours and my little son was stillborn in the first days of October. Peter's face was as ashen as the morning when he came to see me. After my body tore, my heart broke as well, seeing him like that.

'What happened, Blumentrost?' he asked the doctor, avoiding my gaze.

Blumentrost shrugged helplessly. 'I do not know, my Tsar. He was a healthy and strong boy, but the umbilical cord was wrapped around his neck. He suffocated in his mother's body. That's why birth set in so early.'

Peter briefly cupped his face in his hands, his shoulders slumped. He would not look at me but rose, as if he had heard enough. Blumentrost however held him back. 'My Tsar –'

'Yes, what?' Peter asked impatiently. Where was he going so urgently? Had Maria summoned him and would he leave me here, weak and alone after giving birth? I sensed the birds of sorrow settling upon me again, their claws sharpened. The prospect seared my soul.

Blumentrost sighed. 'It was a difficult birth, my Tsar. The Tsaritsa has lost a lot of blood ...' I decided I would prefer not to hear his words but was too weak to place my hands over my ears. 'I think it is better if the Tsaritsa does not have more children.'

I realised the seriousness of what he had just said; every word was another stone in the high wall that was rapidly growing between the Tsar and me. Twelve times God had given me the chance to give Russia an heir. Twelve times I had failed. That night, I heard, Peter attended a feast in Menshikov's palace together with Maria Kantemir. Menshikov had arranged seats of honour for them in a little tent set back from the crowd where she drank from the Tsar's glass and he fed her little bites from his own plate.

73

A few days later, while I dressed for the service to celebrate peace to be held in the Trinity Church, Peter came to my rooms. I was still weak and my ladies fluttered around me, attending to every detail of my appearance: 'Keep going, my *damy*! I want you to be sure to make the Tsaritsa beautiful as never before today,' said the Tsar. He winked at me and gave a secretive smile.

'Am I not beautiful enough for the reading of the Peace Treaty?' I said, forcing cheer into my voice. He gave me a peck on the cheek.

'You never know what the day will bring,' he said. 'Agneta, adorn the Tsaritsa with the necklace I gave her on our wedding day.' I was amazed by this order but Peter himself helped to place the heavy choker around my throat; the pearls cooled my skin, and the colourful gemstones in the wings of the Russian double eagle sparkled in unspoken challenge.

Peter tilted his head. 'Not bad. Now the red velvet gown.'

I had wanted to wear the Imperial green silk, but he raised his hand. 'Silence. Do not contradict me in front of your ladies or else I'll have you whipped, *matka*,' he joked. 'That's good. Let us go.'

He led me down into the courtyard where the sleighs were waiting. The servants jumped from foot to foot because of the early frost. In the carriage, Peter asked: 'Do you think I need this wig?' He had placed it haphazardly on his head, and his own hair, streaked with grey, hung out here and there above his ears and his forehead. I nodded and he shrugged. 'Oh, well. So be it. But I feel like a monkey.'

Peter was unable to listen to Prokopovich's address during the service of thanksgiving, his feet tap-tapping the floor. I looked questioningly at Alexander Menshikov but he just shrugged. I forced my thoughts back to Feofan's words, which were like pearls on a string, echoing from the Trinity Church's golden-domed ceiling. 'I wish we all fully realised what our Tsar has done for us ... For do we ever want Russia to suffer the same fate as the Greeks and their kings?' I shook my head, without knowing what their fate had been. Alexander Danilovich did the same, and I stifled a giggle. We were both so simple.

But just as the crowd settled for a last prayer, Prokopovich gave Peter Shafirov a sign by touching the *panagia* on his chest. Shafirov rose: the once spindly man had grown into a powerful, self-indulgent prince. His blue silk coat did nothing to disguise his bulk and heavy legs. Even if the bows on the toes of his shoes made him look like a fool, he was a dangerous man: his five daughters had married into the best families in the country, he did lucrative business with Menshikov and was said to have offered a magnificent sapphire necklace to Maria Kantemir. When Shafirov took a scroll from his sleeve, Peter drew me to my feet.

'Thanks to the Tsar's glorious deeds, we have left behind the age of darkness and Russia has found her place on the world's stage,' I heard Shafirov say. Peter's fingers squeezed mine. My eyes met Menshikov's startled gaze. Alexander Danilovich clearly understood not only that something very important was happening, but also that Peter Shafirov had trumped him. I straightened my back, which still hurt from the hours of a labour that once more had been in vain.

Shafirov cleared his throat. 'The Senate begs the Tsar to take the title of Emperor. You have risen from the East, now be a ruler of the West! Tsar Peter, become our Peter the First. Tsar Peter, become Peter the Great, Father of Your Country, Emperor of All the Russias.'

His last words were swallowed by an immediate outbreak of jubilation. Feofan made the Sign of the Cross over Peter's head. Peter gave Shafirov the kiss of peace, looking surprised and embarrassed, and raised his hand. Silence fell in the church. 'I cannot help but accept this honour,' he cried, and I felt his pride and joy: Tsar was an archaic title for a ruler of the East, something akin to a king. He had risen above that in rank and power, shifting Russia to the West.

'*Vivant* the Emperor and Empress of Russia!' voices thundered a thousandfold, through the church and across the square, reaching the Neva and blending with the hundreds of celebratory volleys fired by ships' cannon, before the waters carried the news far, far out into the world.

I was now the Empress of Russia. *Imperatriza*.

In the following weeks, the Neva began to rise. First, the waters reached the steps of the moorings, before lapping over the quay. The following morning, neither horses nor carts could pass through the flooded streets. Come nightfall, the courtyard of the Winter Palace and the castle's ground floor were underwater. Footmen and servants barricaded the building with bags of sand, but the whiff of mould was tangible only a few hours later. Dark clouds gathered on the horizon and it began to rain. The sea raged into the river, tearing down houses and carrying away walls. Soon the bloated corpses of animals and human beings drifted in the flooded streets; disease and plague festered. Peter had dykes built. People drained water from their houses by forming long chains, passing full buckets and vessels of every kind from hand to hand. Yet still they clung to their accustomed way of life, playing cards on the roofs of their houses and wading through thigh-high waters to reach their flooded *kabaki*.

Despite the damage to his city, Peter celebrated St Andrew's Day as usual with the first snowfall. Once again Menshikov had invited us to his palace, as Peter loved a spectacle of splendour without having to foot the bill for it. That evening our sleighs made their way through the city, horses snorting and bells jingling in their harnesses. Snow slanted in front of the glowing lanterns. Peter's hopes and dreams for his New Jerusalem had come true: the shabby wooden structures that once stood here had been replaced by towering palaces and merchants' houses, each three or four storeys high and blazing with lights. Church spires rose into the night sky. Pillars and posts along the quays and bridges were snow-capped; soon it would be time for the ferrymen to exchange their barges for sleighs as winter took hold. The barriers in the wide roads and prospects were all raised and people were out and about everywhere, clad in furs. The air was scented with roasted chestnuts, grilled meats and mulled wine. Proud frigates were rolling on the Neva's steel-coloured waves next to broad-beamed barges. Wares were unloaded and new goods hauled aboard the bigger ships, while instructions, jokes and insults in all the languages of Russia and Europe could be heard, reminding us of the value the city's ice-free harbour held for our country.

Peter sat next to me, warm underneath the bearskins the footman had hooked up to left and right of the sleigh's door. I saw his face glow as he took in the impressive scene. He had willed this beauty of a place from nothing, I thought, and I had been by his side as it was built. I, no one else, least of all Maria Kantemir. Nobody could take that away.

Once at Menshikov's palace, however, the feeling dissolved, like our breath and the moisture from our furs in the sudden warmth of fires and candles – thousands of them. Maria Kantemir leant close to Peter while they ate, telling him amusing stories about the floods. He laughed so much that eventually he pleaded for mercy, so she seized her whip and lashed Peter's fools on their legs. 'Don't you see? The Tsar wants to laugh at the flood. Get on your boat or I'll teach you a lesson.' The fools hastily turned a small table upside down and hopped inside it, looking like two castaways on the Neva. Maria Kantemir circled them, whip in hand, looking as dangerous as the wild cats in her homeland's mountains. Every time she came close to the boat, the two fools paled with fear and acted more and more wildly.

It was not until Peter raised his hand and gasped, 'Enough, enough, I cannot laugh anymore!', that she gave them leave to go. When she sat down with a haughty smile, Menshikov kissed her fingertips.

*

I returned to my rooms. Agneta saw my sullen mood and helped me out of my heavy dress, my petticoats and linen, without asking any questions. She didn't need to. Everybody knew. When she unclasped the jewellery from my earlobes, throat and wrists, I breathed a sigh of relief. The tiled stove warmed the room pleasantly, and I looked at my bare, beautiful self while Agneta cleansed my face with rosewater In the dimly lit room, I saw the bed that Peter had avoided ever since I'd last given birth. Any reason for him to meet me there was gone. There would be no son for him from me, but rumour had it that Maria Kantemir laced Peter's drink with love potions made from either the ground horn of an African animal or the dried, crushed sex of an Indian tiger, so that he would take her three or four times a night. I had also heard that she had not bled in the past months, which made my own blood curdle with fear.

I closed my eyes to let the November moonlight flow into my heart. Agneta, though, had heard something else: 'My Empress,' she said, smiling, 'the people say that the latest flood is the fault of this Moldavian witch.' She lathered my shoulders with jasmine oil and I breathed in the heady perfume. 'Kantemir is said to have summoned the waters. When she took her barge to the Winter Palace last week, the people bombarded her with horseshit.'

For the first time in ages I laughed, and Agneta joined in. The merriment made me feel more ready to face the world. Maria Kantemir, take my place in Peter's bed and heart? I neither could, nor would allow this to happen.

74

All of Europe apart from Austria recognised Peter's new title as Emperor of Russia: Vienna had not forgotten its sympathy for the dead Tsarevich and the manhandling it had suffered at the Tsar's hands.

But Peter's gaze turned to the East as his ambassador to Isfahan, Prince Volynsky, spoke in the Senate. He looked impossibly well groomed compared with most of the senators there. It was common to see their real hair straggling down untidily beneath their wigs; their skin was veined and red; and they picked their noses openly, flinging their findings into all corners of the Senate. Volynsky's dark oiled hair fell to his shoulders, he was clean-shaven and his fingernails were spotless and short. Compared with him, the other senators looked like savages.

'Welcome home, Volynsky. You look like a true Persian. Do you still eat pork? If not, I'll have you flogged.' Peter was only half joking, I knew, but the Senate laughed obediently. 'What is going on in Persia? Tell me all about Isfahan.'

Volynsky hesitated. 'I have some good news. More and more trade leads through Russia, and we have been able largely to suppress the attacks of the Cossack tribes along the riverbanks. This ensures safety for our sturgeon fisheries as well as the transportation of caviar.'

'And the bad news? Or will you bore us with talk of fish eggs any longer?'

Volynsky's expression turned grave. 'Russian trading stations have been attacked and the whole country is in turmoil – I am glad to have made it across the border. I have since heard that the Shah of Persia has been overthrown ...'

'Why didn't you say that sooner?' Peter cried, and lashed out at him with his knout, tearing the silk sleeve of his Persian overcoat and drawing blood from Volynsky's pale skin. 'Who has started the rebellion, and when?'

'Afghan rebels have occupied Isfahan. They burn, plunder, embezzle and kill. Their wild customs spread throughout the land and the law is breaking down there; no one knows any longer what is right or wrong.'

Persia was important to us, I knew; gold, silver, copper, lead, oils, pigments, cashmere wool, silk, fruits and spices, were all loaded onto barges there before the wares travelled West to be traded for gold. What better time could Russia choose to attack the weakened region and return with valuable spoils?

Peter stroked his moustache and grinned. 'You really did not deserve that knouting, Volynsky. Take it as a sign of my love. The next time I wish to chastise you, tell me it has already been done.' Then he frowned. 'All right. Let's get going. Where are the rebels located? Only in Isfahan or all over the country?'

One month later, Russia declared war on Persia. Peter's own country was still exhausted; the princes cursed at having to leave their families and estates once again. I alone was elated. This campaign would allow me to escape St Petersburg, where all and everybody watched me, waiting with bated breath for me to be ousted permanently instead of merely sliding out of favour. Also, the simple life we led in the field had always brought us closer. There, I was sure, Maria Kantemir could not harm me. I pondered Blumentrost's warning while instructing Alice to pack some light, lacy undergarments and nightshirts. Blast him! I would fall pregnant another time and all would be well. My spirits were high when my chests were finally packed. For once I was not leaving behind an infant. My daughters Anna and Elizabeth were young women by now, and our little Natalya was strong and healthy.

On the eve of our departure from Moscow I paid Anna and Elizabeth a visit to say goodbye: sometimes I felt that I did little else with my girls. Their rooms were the picture of peacefulness. Natalya was being comforted at her wet-nurse's full breast. The child's cheeks were rosy and her hair thick and dark. She was soon to be four years old.

Anna worked at her embroidery, sitting close to an open window and comparing her own botched stitches with her maid's fine work. When she spotted me, she came flying over. 'Mother, how wonderful of you to come! Ever since I heard about the campaign to Persia, I thought I would not see you again.' She blushed slightly. 'You know, there's so much for us to speak about.'

I embraced her. Why did children grow up so fast? Had not I just given birth to her a year before the Battle of Poltava? She was fourteen years old and had inherited Peter's bright blue eyes as well as his fair skin and dark hair. I knew what she wanted to speak about: the young Duke of Holstein had been asking Peter for one of our daughters' hands in marriage. Anna as eldest felt that she was entitled to this match, though I knew that the young duke had fallen in love with Elizabeth. At his last visit he'd sailed up and down the Neva, hoping to catch a glimpse of her; but each time I had sent Anna out onto the balcony. Finally, he had stuck to his offer to marry either of the princesses.

'Let me look at you,' I said, and spun Anna round by the waist. The pink silk mousseline layers of her dress flew up like gossamer wings. Her ladies laughed and clapped. Elizabeth looked up from her chess game against Wilhelm Mons. He had that air of gaiety and ease about him that no court manners could ever destroy. It had been a long time, with my travels and all the troubles in the land, since I had seen him. My heart missed a beat.

'Really, Anna, as silly as you are, no peasant in his *izba* would want to marry you, let alone a duke!' Elizabeth chided her sister, and I frowned.

Mons faced Elizabeth over a small table littered with captured chess figures. He said, 'Really, Tsarevna. Is there a greater joy for a young woman than to marry a young man of standing and fortune?' Did he tease her? She blushed and her fingers silently twisted a fallen pawn against the board.

I watched them closely, which was a pleasure to me – I could have looked at Wilhelm's handsome face all day long, hoping for a look or a smile. No wonder that at court more than one person joked about my daughter's closeness to him. So far, I had not paid it any heed; but where there was smoke, there was fire.

'Do you not wish to bid me farewell before I go to Persia, Elizabeth?' I asked, trying to ignore Wilhelm, who rose and bowed to me. Time had taken no toll on him; if anything, it made him more handsome. A few fine laughter lines had appeared around his eyes and at the corners of his mouth. There – he smiled, showing the tooth with the little chip missing – what had caused that, a brawl or gravel in a piece of bread?

'Tsaritsa. May the sun shine on you and your happiness for many years to come,' he said. I saw so much warmth and understanding in his eyes that my soul and my spirit soared towards him. Yet I nodded curtly and turned my back on him.

Elizabeth watched us and then rose to curtsey to me sullenly. 'I'll be glad to greet you, Mother. But I needn't wish you farewell; it is said that you are staying here in St Petersburg.'

Her words hit me as painfully as an arrow. 'Who says that?' I asked, struggling for composure.

Elizabeth shrugged. 'Everybody. Father, the court.' She craned her neck and hurriedly curtseyed even lower than before: I turned. Peter stood on the threshold together with Maria Kantemir. They had spent the last days in Peterhof – our Peterhof! – planning the campaign and she looked like a beautiful savage. She wore an embroidered suede tunic fitted tightly over patterned silk leggings. It was slit to just below her breasts, showing her softly curved belly, and secured with a heavy silver belt; her wrists appeared too slender for the chunky bracelets she wore stacked on top of each other. Instead of painting her face white, her skin was bare and lightly tanned. She carried a small pet monkey on her shoulder, which she fed with nuts and dried fruit. Daria Menshikova had told me that the Princess bathed naked in the Bay of Finland before allowing the sun to dry her off on the pebbly beach outside Mon Bijou. The water – a mirror of the grey, wild sky – was allegedly tamed by her presence. Even the waves lapped her toes obediently.

'My Tsaritsa,' Peter said smoothly to me. 'What luck. Now I can take my leave of all the ladies close to my heart.'

Elizabeth lowered her eyes tactfully. I felt I was but a heartbeat away from Wilhelm Mons. Without looking at him, I sensed his presence with all my being and it kept me steady. Anna looked stricken. She lacked her younger sister's resilience and suffered with me in this defeat.

'Take leave? Why is that? My chests are packed ...' I began, but Peter stopped me short.

'At your age, such a journey is no longer suitable for a woman. You will be my worthy steward here. Who else would serve me so faithfully?' He gave me a peck on the cheek, his lips and moustache barely skimming my skin. Elizabeth pressed herself against him, and Anna curtseyed before he lifted Natalya up. I felt utterly helpless. If he left for Persia with Maria Kantemir by his side, I might as well have my head shorn here and now, ready for the convent he would choose for me upon his return.

'I shall be gone for a while. Keep me in your heart and in your prayers, my Empress,' Peter said formally, and kissed my hands before he turned to leave.

Just then the monkey jumped from Maria Kantemir's shoulder and seized some of Elizabeth's chess pieces; it nibbled at the queen, but shrieked with disappointment on finding the wood inedible and chucked the piece to the floor. Maria Kantemir's voice lashed through the room. 'Come here!' The monkey swung himself back onto her shoulder and Peter kissed her on the mouth.

'Always so imperious, my lady,' he chuckled fondly. She looked at me, her eyes glowing like those of a wild thing looming out of the dark around a campfire. Her threat was clear: upon his return, Peter should no longer be my husband. I curtseyed lower than anyone else when they left the room together. There was no time for me to lose.

75

My Cherkessk maid Jakovlena understood the order: I had sent for her at a very late hour, in secret, and she had come to my rooms from Felten's kitchens. Her grey hair was tousled from her sleep near the warm ashes of the fireplace, yet despite her advanced years her skin was smooth and fair, a feature of her tribe who sold their light-skinned daughters for the highest prices to the court in Istanbul. Her people had tamed the smallpox; fathers scratched their baby daughters' skins and trickled droplets of blood laced with cowpox into their veins. The illness that the babies caught after this was much milder than the smallpox, and so saved them for a lifetime from that disfiguring and often fatal disease. Jakovlena had never wanted more than to work in Felten's kitchen, though I had richly rewarded her for many additional secret services to me over the years: her stone house stood in the third street behind the Moika. I had not only paid for her daughter's education, but had also given the girl good pin-money; Jakovlena's two sons were officers in Peter's regiment.

'Persia,' my maid said, weighing the word, before leaving to pack what little she had this very night. She slipped away, another dark shadow in the bright night of my city, gliding effortlessly between worlds like the secret she was.

On the pier, the day broke bright and blue and seagulls hovered, hoping for rich pickings. The air was alive with all the languages of the giant Empire that Peter ruled. Our three-masters had a long hull but a low keel, as this allowed for an easier journey to the Caspian Sea without the many shallows and sandbanks in the streams holding us back. Flags blazed in the wind; watchmen kept an eye on the cargo, and the crowded quays were buzzing. Sailors swung from mast to mast, their wives wailing onshore and their watchful children pale and sad. Ship's boys were kept busy running last-minute errands; jugglers with colourful birds and monkeys asked for money or pilfered food and purses; pedlars hawked pots, knives, ropes, tools, lucky charms, icons and potions against sea sickness and other ailments, crooked daggers and swords. Through the colourful hustle and bustle I spotted Peter on his horse from afar, studying a map together with his Cossack leader while Menshikov shouted orders.

Peter didn't notice me until I was very close to him, taking in the sight blankly. His face twitched, which could be a sign of anything: anger or mirth. Did the sailors suddenly slow down the loading of the cargo? There seemed to be a lull all around as everyone held their breath, watching us. I steadied my mare and trotted it close to Peter's stallion. The horses nuzzled and chewed each other's bridles. Menshikov hid his smile behind a cough while Peter reached for his *dubina*. I sought his eyes, before saying in a low voice, for his ears only: 'You did not really think that I'd let you go to Persia alone?'

His fingers slid from the knout's pommel. 'No. If I'm honest, I did not believe that, *matka*. I'd rather believe in black snow.'

I smiled and spoke up. 'My Tsar, forgive my tardiness and my delay. Where shall my chests be loaded?'

Peter hailed Ambassador Volynsky, who was busy riding up and down the quay. His fine Arabian steed suffered in the stifling air of our May morning: its nostrils foamed, and mosquitoes attacked the delicate skin around its eyes. 'Volynsky. Let the Tsaritsa's luggage be loaded on my frigate. And see to it that she has everything she might need in her cabin,' Peter ordered.

Volynsky hid his surprise wisely, but just when I felt ready for a last joke with Peter, a sedan chair made of painted wood, the flag of Moldavia waving on its roof, was set down next to us. A narrow hand pushed aside the curtains. Peter chewed uneasily on his moustache, and Maria Kantemir looked at me in surprise while he bent down to kiss her. 'Take good care of yourself, my darling,' he murmured, before saying to me, '*Matka*, we'll see each other on board.' He galloped off and Menshikov winked at me, bowed to both of us and followed Peter, his horse's hooves sending sparks into the morning air.

Maria Kantemir and I were face to face in the midst of the crowd. I stood in my stirrups. 'Since when do you arrive in a litter? Even your Empress comes on horseback,' I said curtly.

Her gaze was mocking when she stroked her loose honey-coloured hair back from her forehead. 'My Empress, have you not been told? How shameful,' she said. Despite the sunshine, frost settled on my heart. I dreaded her next words: 'I am pregnant with the son of the Tsar of All the Russias. He does not wish me to ride.'

I took care to be out and about on deck and had a friendly word for everybody, be it a lowly sailor or an admiral of the fleet. I took my seat at the campaign table together with Peter and Volynsky and followed our progress towards Persia on the map: the Moskva met the Oka, a stream as wide as the sea, with densely populated banks and lush, fertile fields behind. Wherever we anchored, the villagers came down to our ships with musicians and gifts such as freshly slaughtered cattle and poultry, barrels of beer and brandy, oven-warm loaves of sourdough bread, eggs and vegetables. Peter took it all with gratitude in his eyes, assuring the people of his grace. They themselves were suffering a second summer of famine and the hungry gazes of the pale, skinny village children followed our ships upstream.

When we reached Nizhny Novgorod, continuing southwards towards Isfahan, we were stranded on some Volga sandbanks. The still summer air held our ship becalmed. Ashore, Peter spotted Tatar scouts, grim-faced with their deep-set eyes, high cheekbones and smooth tresses as black as ravens' wings. Quivers full of long arrows hung across their shoulders, and I heard that they rode their ponies tender before feasting on them. They were known to be a predatory people, so Volynsky doubled the guards on board.

Maria Kantemir made an unbelievable fuss about her pregnancy. Looking at her frightened me, for now her clearly pregnant belly was more pointed than round, and her skin blotchy and blemished, indicating she carried a boy. The sea journey made her twice as sick; I prayed for a storm so that she would vomit her black soul out of her body. But Peter was so worried about her that I made sure to ask every day after her well-being. 'How is the Princess of Moldavia? Has she had some air today? Let me send her my Cherkessk maid. She knows all sorts of healing herbs and potions.'

But Maria Kantemir would have none of it. 'You do not really think that I am drinking anything the Tsaritsa has sent me?' she snarled, pouring the hot brew on Jakovlena's bare feet. Only when her sickness would not abate did she accept my help and after a while she even sent for the tea.

Behind Kazan, the water gained speed; the rapids carried our boats but with the Cossacks and Kalmucks about, the riverbanks were deserted. We anchored on a peninsula behind the city of Tsaritsyn; I had my glass already filled to the brim when Peter stepped out of Maria Kantemir's cabin. The night air was still as hot as the Devil's breath and I had washed myself down with luke-warm water to freshen up. My skin was scented with rosewater and jasmine, a potion that Jakovlena blended for me.

Peter appeared, buckling up his belt and running his fingers through his sweaty hair; Maria followed him on deck. She clearly hated making love with him in this hot weather and in her condition. By the pale light of the full moon I could see that her eyes lay deep in their sockets. She settled between Peter and me, but refused the fresh fruit I offered with a sullen shake of her head. Peter forced a grape as big as a walnut into her palm. 'Eat that. Here. In front of my eyes,' he threatened. 'I want a healthy son. Children are born strong when their mother is well fed,' he joked, then pinched my cheek. 'When you were pregnant with Elizabeth, you ate like a horse, didn't you, Catherinushka? So, let us have a toast to the strapping recruit that our beautiful Maria is expecting. A strong son for Russia.' He drank deeply from the fresh, foaming beer and burped. Maria paled and pressed her hand to her mouth.

'Princess, was the tea Jakovlena brewed you not helpful?' I asked, sounding worried and kind. Maria nodded, but gagged again.

'You're sending her remedies through one of your ladies?' Peter asked, and I lowered my eyes.

'Yes, my Tsar. No one knows more about ensuring a healthy birth than my maid. And on a troublesome journey like this, one must take no risks.'

'Oh,' Peter said, and burped again. He pulled a fishbone from his teeth before cleaning his fingernails, stained by gunpowder and tobacco, with it. Maria Kantemir poked listlessly at the fish that Felten's men had caught for us in the afternoon. 'You mean the journey does not help the princess's pregnancy?'

My eyes filled with tears. 'After what I have suffered, I know how strenuous a campaign can be for a pregnant woman,' I said haltingly. 'That is why I wanted Jakovlena to look after the Princess Kantemir. It's for Russia, after all.'

Peter kissed my hand. 'Do not cry or worry, my wonderful Catherinushka. This child will be born in good health.'

Maria Kantemir stared at me, her eyes as dangerous as a snake's, but Peter had made his mind up: 'Dearest, as soon as we reach Astrakhan, you will set up camp there and this Jakovlena will be your attendant.'

She wanted to complain, but before she could I cried out, 'No, my Tsar, I need Jakovlena. Without her herbal tea I cannot sleep. Do not take her away from me, please, I beg you.'

Peter hesitated, but Maria Kantemir said, 'All right. I shall settle in Astrakhan together with Jakovlena. Her brew does help me.'

Hot tar dripped from the torches and hit the black surface of the water with a hiss. Peter patted my hand briefly. 'So you can't sleep? What a worry. Well, once we are standing in the field, you'll be so tired that you'll no longer need Jakovlena and her drinks. Now we must ensure the healthy birth of the Tsarevich.' *The Tsarevich.* My heart skipped a beat, and Maria rose and kissed the Tsar with a catty sideways smile for me.

'Allow me to retire. The prince needs rest,' she said, laying a slender hand on her stomach. How far gone was she? Four or five months?

Peter and I sat quietly for a moment. The torchlight speckled my skin with golden hues, and I moved closer to him so that he could inhale my familiar scent. As I filled his cup my hair fell loose and shiny over his naked arm, and his eyes gleamed in the moonlight. 'Who would have thought, Catherinushka, that we would be in the field together once more?' he said, brushing back my curls and sliding his hands over my neck and down my bosom: its flesh shimmered rosily through the delicate linen of my dress. I slid off my chair and knelt down in front of him; he sighed as I tasted him before climbing on top of him. I rode Peter first slowly and then faster, and he came with a muffled scream, throwing his head back, his gaze searching the moon and the stars.

Afterwards, he raised his jug to me. 'It will be a son, won't it, Catherinushka?'

'Of course, my Tsar. To the Tsarevich's health,' I toasted. The clouds across the moon hid the expression in my eyes.

My Jakovlena stayed behind with Maria Kantemir in Astrakhan, the city of a thousand turrets, fragrant fruits and lingering moonlight. I kissed the old woman three times as a sign of peace when she took leave of me. 'Peace be with you, mother,' I repeated the Persian salutation the ambassador had taught me.

'And with you. May God guard you and yours, Tsaritsa. You're a good woman,' she replied, heaving two saddlebags heavy with gold over her shoulders. She would be able to retire a wealthy woman. Jakovlena did not turn to look back at me when she left. I knew that I should never see her again.

76

We slaughtered, baked and brewed outside Astrakhan's walls. The Russian traders, who felt safeguarded by our presence, sent us melons, apples, peaches, apricots and grapes. Nearly twenty-three thousand foot soldiers joined us in the stifling July heat on our march to Derbent on the Caspian Sea. More than a hundred thousand men followed us from further across the country. But fatigue, heat, hunger and thirst robbed them of their senses and our supplies were too puny for all of us, even if we quartered each ration, as a dozen of our flat-bottomed cargo barges had sunk in a storm on the Caspian Sea. Felten and I oversaw the slaughtering of thousands of starving horses. It was horrific, but thanks to their meagre flesh our men had the strength to move on to Baku.

In the evening, after I had treated the last cases of sunstroke and burnt skin, I asked for Peter's Italian barber to come to my tent,

'What can I do for you, my Tsaritsa? Do you need fresh talcum for your body? I still have a little bit of powder. But your perfume from Grasse has unfortunately dried up.' He gladly sipped the cup of cold, sour milk I offered him.

'None of this, maestro. Cut my hair,' I ordered.

'I beg your pardon, my Tsaritsa?' In his eyes a woman without a long, full mane was not a woman, I understood.

'My hair hinders me in this heat and in the sun. My scalp steams. Off with it,' I said. He hesitated, got up and wanted to reach for the jug of water. 'No,' I decided. 'The water is too valuable. Cut it off dry, just like that.' His fingers stroked my scalp. 'Go on,' I encouraged him, smiling at our reflections in the mirror. He raised my tresses and placed his blade at the nape of my neck, where I felt its cool, sharp metal. I enjoyed the snip with which each curl fell to the tent's bare earth, until the barber cleaned his blade and wrapped it back in its leather sheath. Like a woman of the mountains, I wrapped a scarf around my shorn head in a turban, allowing me to spend the whole day outside with the troops.

By night-time, Peter's gaze was empty, not even taking in my changed appearance. 'We cannot go on to Baku, *matka*,' he said, exhausted. 'The men would not survive the thirty-day march. Let's return to Astrakhan,' he decided. 'I shall be with Maria in time for the birth of the Tsarevich.'

'To the Tsarevich and his mother, the Princess Kantemir.' I raised my glass and emptied it in a single draft.

The house in Astrakhan lay eerily quiet. No children were playing on the flat roof; no women sat on cushions in its courtyard, sipping tea and chatting. No servants were running errands, filling the air with the patter of their bare feet and the jingle of the silver bells tied to their ankles. Even the princess's faithful guard of Moldavian soldiers was nowhere to be seen.

Peter and I rode into the shady courtyard, followed by our cook Felten and two dwarves mounted on asses. Birds swarmed through the air; their wings made the mulberry leaves rustle. Water fell into a basin inlaid with colourful, shiny stones. Goldfish swam there, but the surface was covered with green weed. In the heating pans in the corner of the courtyard the ashes were cold.

'Hello?' Peter called, but everything remained silent. I got off my horse. In the basin I washed the dust and the heat from the long ride off my face, despite the water's sour stench. Suddenly I had the feeling of being watched and looked up to the gallery. Had a slight, veiled figure just slipped behind a column there?

'Maria?' Peter called and dismounted as well, walking ahead into the house. I followed him through the darkened rooms and his footsteps echoed in my heart. He pushed open the door to the room where he had taken leave from Maria Kantemir so tenderly just a few weeks ago. The suffocating stench of sweat and camphor took my breath away. Peter gasped, covering his mouth and nose. I took a look around: cushions lay scattered on a divan covered with *kilim* rugs, and on a low table inlaid with ivory stood a silver tray with a cup of mint tea. I dipped my finger in the drink: it was cold and an oily film covered its surface. The marble floor was covered with silk rugs, and in front of a folding screen I spotted a bowl filled with yellow slime. Filthy sheets had been cast off the empty bedstead, as if someone had hurriedly stood up. Peter fought for breath and called again, 'Maria? Where are you, my love?'

My skin prickled with fear and caution when we heard a noise and spun around: a woman stepped out from behind the folding screen. She was densely veiled and said huskily, 'I am here, my Tsar.'

The veil stifled her voice. When Peter stepped up to her, looking delighted, wanting to lift it away, she seized his wrists. 'Let it be. I can do that myself. I'm used to it by now,' she said with threatening calm. I lingered in the shadows; my heart raced when Maria Kantemir threw off her veil and stepped naked into the merciless light of the Persian morning. Peter gasped with horror and shrank back. I, too, only just suppressed a disgusted cry when I saw what Jakovlena had achieved.

Smallpox had had a feast with the stunning beauty of the Princess of Moldavia. Her honey-tinted hair had fallen out, except for a couple of straggly strands, and her bare scalp was covered with scabs and bruises. Her skin was grey and pale, the once even features blemished by deep, crater-like scars. Thin, pale lips barely covered her gums where once there had been an alluring full mouth. The pox had ravaged her body, too: her breasts hung flat and wilted over pointy, sharp ribs; on her arms the illness still lingered – she scratched distractedly at the blisters and pimples on them – and on her legs the ashen skin looked sore over her long bones.

'What happened to you, Maria? Our child –' Peter began, scanning her waist. I clenched my fists: her stomach was flat. Maria

Kantemir had lost the child she'd expected from my husband, the child that would have put an end to my happiness and life as I knew it. Peter stood blank-faced as if struck by lightning. Suddenly she pounced towards me like a wildcat. One of the soldiers just about held her back, but she fought his grip, spitting and biting with rage, while I ordered curtly, 'Get the Tsar out of here. He must not contract smallpox.'

Felten and the soldiers dragged Peter out of the house. At the door, he turned back and I saw the expression of sheer dread in his eyes: only he looked at me, and not at Maria. What did he see? A tall, strong woman with her hair cut as short as thistles; the mother of his children, the companion of his years, the Empress of his realm. He left me to it.

'Hold her,' I ordered the soldier coldly. He grabbed one of the sheets and bundled the princess into it. I stepped up to her. I had won the game she'd felt so safe playing.

'Princess,' I asked gleefully, 'what has happened to your beauty? And the Tsarevich, the child on whom we had placed such hopes? How dreadful! Who could have guessed that the pox was raging here in Astrakhan?'

She spat at me and I shrank back, just avoiding the poisonous saliva. 'Devil of a woman! I know your maid passed the disease to me. She bled me one day and afterwards I caught a fever and the smallpox. You are to blame!' she shrieked, before she was strangled by sobs. 'My son was to rule Russia.'

'Save your breath,' I said. 'This is less than you deserve. If it is Jakovlena's fault we'll have her tortured until she confesses. Where is she?'

Maria Kantemir howled and wanted to strike me once more, but the soldier held her back. 'She ran away, just like everyone else did, when I fell ill. I gave birth to a stillborn child on my own. Nobody wanted to help me,' she shrieked. 'Just look at me!'

'I am looking at you,' I said. 'Is this not what you had in mind for me? Being cast aside and forgotten?'

The soldier pushed her away, wiping his hands in worry and disgust, and we hurried out: Maria Kantemir's crying and cursing rang eerily through the vaulted gallery as we left.

Peter had already returned to the ship; the courtyard was empty. I myself locked the door to Maria's house and let the key slip into my pocket where it should be forgotten. With Volynsky's help I hired an old woman and told her to push plain food and water through a flap in the entrance gate, as if feeding a cat. If the bowls were untouched several days in a row, the house was to be set alight.

But I certainly hoped that Maria Kantemir would live for many years to come.

77

The war against Persia ended the following autumn. A messenger interrupted one of Alexander Danilovich Menshikov's splendid masked balls with news of the victory at Baku. Before midnight struck, more than a thousand bottles of sparkling wine were emptied.

The only peaceful year of Peter's rule began.

I so wanted to recognise the man, but after all these years it was almost impossible. He knelt, and I saw only his prostrate back and callused hands. He was partly bald and his sandals were stuffed with straw for want of proper shoes.

'Look up,' I said, and he did so, trembling with fear. Peter's fingers drummed on his armrest. 'And? Does he tell the truth? If the dog has lied, I'll have his tongue torn out.'

The man moaned and curled up even more tightly.

'Let me look at you.' I stepped down from my throne and stooped over him. Neither the guards nor Peter, Anna, Elizabeth and Wilhelm Mons – without him, my daughter barely took a step – let us out of their sight. The man trembled like pig's blubber but met my gaze. His thin blond hair reminded me of my father's, but he had my stepmother's deep-set eyes and thin lips.

'Are you telling the truth, man?' My voice was raw with feeling.

When he spoke, I saw rotten yellow stumps in his mouth instead of healthy teeth. 'I swear by God Almighty, Marta: I am your brother Fyodor.'

He was a coach–driver's helper on the road between St Petersburg and Riga, where he travelled strapped to the carriage's roof, watching the luggage or looking for scoundrels and obstacles. The sun beat down on him in fine weather; he was soaked by rain or his buttocks froze to the carriage in bad conditions. When one day a traveller threatened him with a good hiding, he had shouted, 'I am our Empress's brother. If you hit me, you'll have to pay for it.' For his temerity, and still in a stupor, he was dragged to St Petersburg to account for his remark.

'How is Christina? Is she alive?' I asked. The question tasted of days long gone by.

'*Ach, Herr Gott*, she brought us nothing but shame. Mother caught her with a man and gave her a hiding. She ran away and today she is a whore in Riga.' He looked as if he wanted to spit, but the splendour of the Winter Palace's marble floor made him change his mind.

'What happened to the rest of the family?'

He pulled a face. 'Maggie married a shoemaker in Riga. The man makes a lot of money but he sets the dogs on me when he sees me.'

'How did Father die?' I asked him.

'Our new master killed him, just after the first famine.'

My poor father. 'And Tanya?' My voice was hoarse. 'Your mother?'

Fyodor grinned. 'She moved in with our new master. He liked her, in spite of her years.'

'I am still not sure I believe you,' I said, searching his face. One more question, to quench all doubts, forever. 'Which animal attacked us, and you crushed its skull with a stone?'

He thought hard, lines furrowing his ruddy forehead. Silence fell in the small throne room. Then his face softened and he said, 'It was a snake, sister.'

Peter showed generosity: Fyodor and Maggie received a pension, but my pleas on Christina's behalf fell on deaf ears. He smiled at me sardonically when the soldiers led Fyodor Skawronski out. 'A whore in Riga? No, really, Catherinushka,' he mocked me. 'I'll send her to a convent where she will be looked after. Now, forgive me, this thief and scoundrel Menshikov has been trying to cheat the Imperial buyers once more. I must attend to it.' He left, merrily lashing his boots with his *dubina* as if in readiness to use it on Menshikov's back. Anna also took her leave; my eyes met Wilhelm Mons's gaze when he bowed and followed Elizabeth. I quickly looked away. Once they had gone, I waved Jagushinsky closer. 'Pavel Ivanovich, is it right that the Tsarevna Elizabeth is with Mons at all times? Does that seem disreputable?'

'It does not *seem* disreputable, it *is* disreputable, my Empress,' Jagushinsky said cautiously.

I pondered his words, rose and smoothed my skirt. 'I am grateful for his services,' I decided. 'But Elizabeth must preside over a household worthy of an adult Tsarevna. Mons is to be my chamberlain from now on. At my age, I should be above suspicion.' I playfully slapped Jagushinsky's shoulder with my fan. 'Now off you go, the Tsar is waiting for you. Do not worry: the *dubina* is already busy enough for today.'

I watched him go, my heart clenching. Was I asking for my own undoing? Nonsense. Wilhelm Mons could easily be my son: my handsome, healthy son.

The yelling and shouting coming from Peter's rooms could be heard from fifty feet away; I heard Menshikov's protests and, in between them, the high-pitched voice of Peter Shafirov. I hastened my steps: had Alekasha gone too far this time? Inside, Menshikov and Shafirov were rolling on the ground, kicking, hitting and biting each other like two drunkards in a *kabak*: fists flew and bones cracked. Peter himself circled the two men and lashed them with his *dubina* wherever he could.

'Stop it, you scoundrels! Fighting in front of your Tsar as if I was one of your whores, how dare you?' he bellowed, when Menshikov grabbed Shafirov by his hair and the latter bit his arm.

I threw myself at Peter, holding him back. '*Starik*! What's the matter?'

Shafirov sobbed while checking his torn, richly embroidered coat and Menshikov sat down, panting. Pearls and silver threads were scattered all over the room and his wig was messed up.

Peter placed his head on my bosom, gasping for air. 'Both of them are liars and cheats, Catherinushka!' he said. 'Thank God, I can always trust *you*. Menshikov should have had his bones broken on the wheel a long time ago for all his lies and frauds.'

Menshikov, who could cross Peter's Empire from Riga to Derbent and spend every night on an estate of his own, pulled himself to his feet. Every Russian knew a different story about his greed, as he wished to be rewarded for every service rendered, be it in roubles or kopeks, a noble horse for his stables or a beautiful girl for the night. He had more titles and honours than hairs on his head, his food was prepared by French cooks, his princely carriage pulled by ten purebreds, and at times Daria wore more magnificent jewels than I did.

Nevertheless, I would not forget a friend who had done me a good deed. In St Petersburg, a man was either the plaintiff or the accused. If Menshikov fell into disgrace, and was duly punished, none of us was safe from Peter's wrath.

'What's the matter?' I asked.

'Menshikov has sold Russian troops stale bread and thin soup. The money for proper supplies is dangling in diamonds around his wife's fat neck instead. Worse than that, he stole fifteen thousand souls from the Cossacks, and now I have to quench an uprising,' Peter spat furiously.

'Well, I have heard worse. Is not Menshikov always Menshikov?' I reminded him, and Alexander Danilovich dared a smile, but Peter was furious, pointing to the door. 'Out! Both of you. Shafirov, I'll check on your business. If you leave town without my permission, I will execute you and your family on the spot. And you ...' he pointed his *dubina* at Alexander Danilovich '... Menshikov! Your bitch of a mother conceived you in sin and shame, and you shall die in sin and shame. Yes, you shall end where you started!'

78

Daria Menshikova came to see me the same evening, just when we – my ladies-in-waiting, Wilhelm Mons and I – were listening to my reader by the fireplace. The book was of questionable content and my younger ladies giggled. Peter's illness hindered him from knowing them as well as he would have done in earlier years, I thought: in the past few weeks his suffering had worsened and his swollen body sometimes made him scream in pain.

My eyes were drawn to Wilhelm Mons; I could not help it. He lay on a chaise-longue and stared into the flames, which lent his skin a golden hue. His long, well-shaped legs were outstretched and crossed. Did the reader's words make his heart race, as they did mine? Was the feel of his lips, which smiled so easily, soft or demanding when they touched a woman's mouth? He moved, folding his arms behind his head and sighing, while looking into the flames. How would it feel to be caressed by these long, slender fingers; those hands that he so casually folded beneath his head? Again, it was easy to imagine him out in the open, sleeping under a starry sky and being content sitting around a campfire. I had forced myself to take my eyes off him when Agneta whispered in my ear, 'Daria Menshikova is waiting for you in the Chinese Cabinet, my Tsaritsa.'

I sighed. Of course. In his struggle for survival, Menshikov used the strongest weapon at his disposal: memories of my youth and friendship with Daria. If we met today, we ate sugared violets and made idle marriage plans for our living children, mourning the dead. As I rose, Wilhelm Mons sat up. 'Follow me,' I said briefly.

I felt him close behind me. If I stopped, would our bodies touch? Instead, I hastened my steps. That was not to happen.

In the Chinese Cabinet, candlelight brought to life the birds painted on the colourful silk wall-coverings. Daria paced the small room. On seeing me, she threw herself to her knees, grabbing my ankles, but I raised and embraced her. 'Wilhelm, give Princess Menshikova your handkerchief. No woman is to be left weeping,' I scolded him playfully. Daria sneezed as loudly as a farmer's wife into the silk cloth; her hair was tousled and the tears left unsightly traces on the pasty white make-up she still ordered from Venice.

'Sit,' I said, as Wilhelm pushed a dainty silk-covered chair closer. He helped Daria to her feet and the chair creaked under her weight. Daria rummaged in her cleavage and handed me a small scroll. 'Alekasha won't tell me what's going on. He smashed our green salon to pieces and the cook got the hiding of a lifetime. As I left he was going for the Delft tiles in his study, breaking them one by one with his cane. He sends you this.' I unrolled the scroll on which there was only one sentence, its ink smeared by tears.

'Read it to me,' I told Wilhelm, who stepped up to the fireplace, letting the flames shed some light on the writing.

' "*What am I to do*?" ' he read aloud, looking up in astonishment. Daria's and my disbelief were palpable. We stared at each other: the powerful Prince Menshikov was foundering. She clasped my hands and said, 'Please, Catherine Alexeyevna, by all that once linked us, by all that we once loved – help us.'

'What should your husband do, Daria?' I asked, chuckling, after a moment of silence. Wilhelm watched me, a slight smile playing at the corners of his full, soft lips. He leant against the silk walls as casually if they were a stable's. His presence made me light-hearted, almost giddy. I said: 'Well, quite simply, Menshikov must follow the command of his master and become what he was earlier. Tomorrow night, at supper with me and some friends. Will you join us?' I asked her, but looked straight at Wilhelm.

Daria took my words with her into the frosty winter night.

Our dinner was simple – stuffed cabbage with a creamy sauce of mushrooms – and Peter ate in sulky silence. He needed more money, but already took his tenth share of even a torn fisherman's net being pulled through Russian waters, however big or small its haul. 'Can you think of something else that I could tax?' he asked me testily.

'Let me think. Homesteads, cattle, wood and bricks, housewares, crockery, cutlery, sleds, carts, beehives, ponds, rivers, mills … even *banjas* are already taxed.'

'Yes. Everything I see when I cross my country,' he admitted grumpily.

I dipped my spoon in my soup, fishing for cabbage and pickled gherkins. 'How about taxing vegetables for floating in a soup?' I asked, but Peter said,

'Already done. The only thing that is not taxed is the air for breathing.'

'Well, then …' I said, holding my breath.

Peter chuckled and raised his glass. 'To you and your ability always to make me laugh.' His eyes were moist; candlelight concealed the frosted streaks in his hair and smoothed the deep lines in his puffy face. Wilhelm, who waited on me, refilled my goblet so that I could answer Peter as I should, when we heard a racket from outside the room: banging and a familiar voice shouting, '*Pierogi*! Hot fresh *pierogi*!' Peter listened, surprised, as the doors flew open and in marched Menshikov, dressed in rags and barefoot despite the cold. An over-large baker boy's cap slipped over his eyes as he touted pastries from a large tray held in front of his belly. '*Pierogi! Pierogi!* Buy with me, the baker boy Menshikov.' He shoved his tray at Peter. 'Eat, puny little prince. Everyone knows that that witch, your half-sister Sophia, doesn't let you have a square meal! But one day we'll show her, together, you and me.'

I held my breath. Peter's eyes wandered from his friend's face to the steaming, fragrant *pierogi*, and back again. He tasted one. 'Hmm – still as good as in old times, Menshikov, you scoundrel!' he laughed, and Alexander Danilovich knelt before him, tears filling his eyes.

'Will you forgive me, my heart?' he whispered. 'I have failed you. But if you flog and behead all scoundrels in your Empire, you'll soon have no subjects left.'

Peter threw the remnants of his pastry to his dogs, who leapt at it while he embraced Menshikov, sobbing and laughing at the same time. 'Do not cross me again, Alekasha, or otherwise I must have your hide, as sorry as I'd be.'

Menshikov sat down and the two men chatted, drank and laughed as if nothing had ever happened. From behind my chair, I felt Wilhelm's closeness, breathing in his scent of musk and sandalwood. I felt as helpless as a doe who senses the hunter approaching. So I heard only faintly as Menshikov said to Peter, 'But you ought to keep an eye on that cheat Shafirov ...'

The following morning an adorable boy was sent to my room; his skin was like chocolate and Menshikov's coat-of-arms was embroidered on his crimson velvet cloak. He bowed and opened the heavy jewel case he carried, showing a tiara, necklace and earrings made of flawless diamonds of such size and fire that they had no par in Peter's treasury. The child chirped in broken Russian, 'With gratitude and adoration from Alexander Danilovich Menshikov.' I gladly accepted Menshikov's beautiful present. After all, he had given me so much, why not these gems to commemorate such a moment in our lives? I sent the boy to Abraham Petrovich, Peter's Moor, where he would be educated and want for nothing.

A few weeks later, in Peterhof, Peter sent for me after we had spent the morning together.

The tubby stable cat had had kittens and our little Natalya was besotted with the blind, clumsy bundles of fur. She sat on Peter's knees and he asked: 'Which one do you want, my girl?' The morning sun set Natalya's auburn curls aflame and my heart tightened with love for her. In the autumn she was to receive her first lessons.

'Can't I have them all?' she asked, astonished, and Peter cupped the five kittens in his large hands. 'Of course, my little angel, you *can* have them all. But perhaps your sisters might want one as well?'

Natalya thought for a moment. 'All right. But only one.'

'Open your skirt, we'll put them inside. But let's take the mother cat as well. The kittens still need her,' Peter said. The cat dug her claws in his hands when he turned to me to say: 'Are you coming?'

'Not yet. Elizabeth is breaking in the stallion that the King of France sent her. I'll watch.'

'Hopefully she will not break her neck before we marry her off in Paris,' he chuckled, and stepped together with Natalya from the darkness of the stables into the bright spring sunshine. Alice already waited for them. She took Natalya's free hand, and the little girl skipped along: they disappeared in a swirl of light.

Elizabeth noted my presence at the school with a polite nod. I watched her force her will upon the stallion and knew she had not forgiven me for taking Wilhelm from her. She would be a good Queen in France, even if Versailles had grown curiously quiet in recent months.

Peter and Feofan Prokopovich awaited me. The priest leant against one of the study's walls, his dark robe blending with the panelling. The room's scent of dust, paper, ink and tobacco was laced by a salty breeze and sunbeams drew patterns on the Persian rugs. I kissed Feofan's *panagia*, and he blessed me with the Sign of the Cross. What duties did Feofan have in Peterhof? His manifold talents never ceased to astonish me; he wrote plays as well as a history of the Great Northern War, together with Peter, every Saturday morning. He read the works of scholars, whose names I could scarcely pronounce, in their own language: Spinoza, Descartes, Bacon and Leibniz, to name just a few I could remember. All his work was done to the honour and glory of the Emperor who had made him a Father of the Fatherland.

Peter looked up from the scroll he was reading, with a tender smile for me. '*Matka*, come, sit down with us two old men. We'll talk some nonsense together.' I felt Feofan's gaze intent upon me but closed my face as only we 'souls' knew how.

'We were talking about freedom,' Feofan said.

'I like to talk about it! *Volya*! To do as you like – isn't that the dream of all of us?' I laughed.

Feofan scolded me. 'My Tsaritsa, you speak like the soul you once were. But freedom does not mean doing whatever one feels like, but being delivered from all ideas that hinder our souls' well-being.'

Peter placed his muddy boots on the table. I frowned: what was Feofan going on about? He chose every word carefully. 'There are laws of the heart and of nature. God decides on them, or else his chosen ruler. The Tsar is a father to his people. With God's help, he takes decisions that we can't fathom immediately.'

'Get to the point, honourable Feofan,' Peter said.

'The Tsar has no son,' the priest continued. 'So he will and must decide upon the succession when the day comes.'

'Let that day be far from us,' I said.

'Indeed,' Peter chuckled, and got up, shaking his legs. 'Thank you, Feofan Prokopovich. I will tell the Tsaritsa what I have to tell her when we are alone. But you showed me the way.'

When Feofan had left, I clenched the carved lion's heads on the armrests of my chair and Peter looked at me in silence. I could barely hold myself back: which of his bastards would he appoint as his heir? He had an army of sons born out of wedlock. My heart beat so hard it hurt. To distract myself I rose and stepped over to the window. There was no sound bar the ticking of the room's clocks, which were set to chime together.

Outside, on the bright gravel of the terrace, Elizabeth stood with Wilhelm, her cheeks flushed by the ride. He laughed politely at whatever she said, but kept his distance, I noticed. My gaze skimmed the park's treetops and the fountains, whose water sparkled in all the colours of the rainbow, and then slid out towards the leaden sea of the Finnish Bay. Peter stepped behind me, embracing me and nuzzling my neck.

'Catherinushka. I've learnt that a woman's body does not do my bidding,' he said, sounding sad, his words cutting my soul like a blade. 'God has denied us a strong, healthy son. I cannot be angry with Him, for wrath shall not spoil my latter days. But you and I, we've always stuck together. You have been faithful to me, always; your words were always to be trusted, as was your kindness and your grace.' His voice cracked. I leant my head on his shoulder and closed my eyes so as to not shed the tears I felt coming. Was he sweetening the bitter pill for me?

'I want to thank you,' he breathed into my ear. 'Are you ready for this?'

I opened my eyes and light poured in painfully. 'Ready? Whatever for?'

'To be crowned. Next year, in Moscow, as soon as it is warm and sunny. If I die before my time, you can carry on my work,' he said, his eyes not leaving my face. 'Are you ready? We are both old. I wish to thank you for everything.'

We are both old. His words took root in my soul, but before they could hurt, I nodded. He laughed, delighted, as he bit me playfully on the neck. 'I am so proud of you!' he told me.

Wilhelm looked up at our window. I felt his gaze on me like a caress and stepped out of view. I am not that old yet, I thought. Wilhelm watched with burning eyes as Peter lifted my chin and kissed me.

79

Peter Shafirov trembled like pig's blubber when he mounted the scaffold, barefoot and dressed in a hair shirt: he had been found guilty of treason and embezzlement of public funds. After the weeks of privation in prison he looked once more like the bright young man he had been before greed got the better of him. Alexander Danilovich sat beside me, spinning the diamond-studded knob of his walking stick. To celebrate the day his former friend was to be beheaded, he wore a new wig and a splendid crimson coat.

For April, the Moscow air was unusually stuffy and a small crowd had gathered on the Red Square. After three years of famine, the people looked gaunt; their eyes lay deep-set and their heads were skull-like. I had heard the whispers: *God punishes the murderer on Russia's throne. We pay for the Tsar's sins.* The Moskva carried hardly any water. In some parts of Russia travellers were told not to spend the night alone in an inn, for otherwise they might end up as a juicy stew. Shafirov sobbed when he saw his five princess daughters soaking their handkerchiefs with tears. I tried in vain to meet Peter's eye. He scanned the crowd and then the sky, where pot-bellied clouds gathered.

The night before, I had searched my drawers for the leather pouch which had hung on my belt during the Pruth campaign. Inside it lay the ring Peter had given me back then, when Shafirov had risked his life for the Tsar and for Russia by going as envoy into the Grand Vizier's camp. 'Let us never forget what happened today,' Peter had said back then.

When I placed the ring on his desk, he frowned.

'What is that?' He turned the ring back and forth, so that the candle flame caught the fire of the flawless ruby.

'The ring you gave me on the Pruth twelve years ago.' I reminded him. 'You said then that I should help you never to forget what Shafirov did for Russia.'

Peter had slipped the ring into the pocket of his old green velvet dressing-gown, telling me, 'Go back to sleep, Catherinushka. It will be a hard enough day tomorrow. For all of us.'

Peter stood up on the scaffold, his expression unreadable. As a cruel joke, the guards yanked Shafirov's legs from under him as he was about to kneel down, so that he wobbled like one of Natalya's toys on what was left of his belly. The people jeered while the executioner adjusted his red hood, to see better through the narrow eye slits. The blade of the axe flashed in the morning sun; Shafirov's lips moved in a silent prayer and his wife, the slender, sour Baroness Shafirov, fainted as the steel swung downward in an arc.

I closed my eyes – and heard the crowd gasp. When I dared a peek, I saw the axe stuck in the wood next to Shafirov's head. He cowered on the executioner's block, ashen with sheer dread but still alive. Menshikov blew his nose in his fingers and grunted with anger. 'Really, can't a man like Shafirov even afford a good executioner? Fool.'

Up on the scaffold, Makarov handed Peter a scroll and the Kremlin's walls echoed the Emperor's declaration back at us: Shafirov had been pardoned. A sigh ran through the crowd; the Baroness Shafirov came to. Shafirov's physician had to bleed him twice before he felt truly back amongst the living again, having seen death ready to snatch him.

In the evening, I found the ring from Pruth lying amongst my bottles of perfume, my make-up, brushes and combs. Peter never said a word about it, ever again.

The summer brought long, bright days and I returned to Peterhof on my own: Peter helped me step on my sailboat, kissing me and calling me by the old nicknames as we took leave of each other for some days. It was as if his love for me was refreshed, twenty years on. As the wind filled my boat's sails, I saw him merge with the grey stone of the Summer Palace's jetty, waving me goodbye. He had been held back in St Petersburg but had urged me to seek the country air. I felt the peace and security I had longed for always, but also a sense of unrest and a yearning for something more. Was that the other woman deep inside me, stirring? I willed her to be quiet.

In Peterhof, I knew, Wilhelm Mons awaited me.

After the stifling heat of the city, the sight of the barren, famished land around pained me: for the fourth year in a row, the barns were bare, and starved bodies lay at the roadside, as no one had enough strength left to bury them. Peterhof by contrast was a quiet paradise: the treetops had grown above the palace's roof, from afar the fountains sparkled, colourful birds darted through the air, butterflies tumbled in the reeds, and I heard the shrieking of the little monkeys I kept in Marly.

As I set foot on the jetty, Wilhelm Mons was there to greet me. I slipped on the wet planks and he caught me, his fingers closing tightly around mine and his four talisman rings cutting into my flesh. I bit my lip so as not to cry out. The sweet pain had accompanied what I most longed for: the touch of his hand. When I looked up, confused, his gaze was deeper than the sea around us. Words of gratitude died on my lips; something long forgotten stirred in my heart, and the sheer force of that feeling robbed me of my breath. My other self, the woman who had hidden in my heart ever since Peter had questioned Alexey, rose from the shadows of my soul, and before I could stop her, she stepped out into the sunlight and replied to Wilhelm's longing with all her heart.

Nothing more happened, merely the brush of our fingertips and my skin scalded by his touch. I walked up to the palace, not turning to look at him; no, not yet.

That same evening the first of many messengers from the city reached me. Peter wrote to me as he had not done for years: ' "Matka, *where are you? The palace is so empty without you, and no one makes me laugh. I play with Natalya every day, because of all our daughters I find your soul, your wit and your beauty in her. What prince will be good enough for her, one day? Otherwise, I wander from room to room and find you nowhere. But rest well in Peterhof: it's wonderful to grow old with a loved one …'"*

I stopped the messenger short. 'Enough, man, you have a long ride behind you. The gamekeeper has brought pigeons up to the house, go and eat.'

He handed me the crumpled note and bowed. 'Does the Tsaritsa have an answer for His Majesty?'

'Perhaps tomorrow,' I said, waiting for his steps to fade away. I knelt down at the library's fireplace, which was lit to fight the night chill. I held Peter's letter to the flames: they licked hungrily over the dry paper. The first words to be swallowed were those of his last sentence: *'to grow old'*. His black writing twitched and fought against the fire, but I crouched, patient as a peasant girl, and watched the paper fall to ashes. Suddenly I had to laugh. I laughed and laughed – a sound to scare a sane man witless. Catherine Alexeyevna is not *old*, Peter. She is young, strong and beautiful: she who loves, lives, my husband. My laughter turned to tears, and I was crying, cowering on the rug, sobbing and clawing at the pile, all the despair and shock of the past catching up with me. I wept until eventually I curled up like one of Natalya's kittens, there, in front of the fireplace. When I awoke, I shivered. A summer storm had pushed open the windows; rainwater pooled on the floor and cold, salty air filled the room. My rug was soaked, too, and the light yellow silk of my dress clung to my body. I tried to pull myself up onto a chair, but it toppled and fell with a clatter. The door flew open and I saw the man whom I had hoped and feared to see.

'My Tsaritsa,' said Wilhelm, his voice unsteady. 'I heard a sound. Have you hurt yourself?' Had he guarded the door all night, watching over me? How else could he have been here so fast? He reached me in a few steps: my hair fell loose and tousled over my bare shoulders, where my dress had slipped during my restless slumber.

Wilhelm knelt next to me; his fingers skimmed my cheeks, touching my mouth like a butterfly's wings. I greedily closed my lips around them and tasted the salt of my tears. He kissed my damp cheeks and muttered: 'The colour of snow, the taste of tears and the vastness of the sea.' I closed my eyes, giving a choked sob.

He embraced me, holding me close. How long had I waited for this moment? Ever since I first met him? 'We mustn't . . .' I started, aware of the danger, the madness, of this.

'I know,' he replied, as the yellow silk of my dress tore like parched paper, and his hands cupped my full breasts before he unlaced me; my nipples hardened under his lips and tongue, my body aching for his caress. I bent backwards, slipping to the floor, splaying my limbs and opening up to him. My skirts rustled as he pushed them up to my waist. He searched my wetness with the tip of his tongue, slowly and softly, taking his time to taste me and giving me all the moments I needed to find pleasure. I cried out, arching my back, lying naked in the bright daylight. He would not allow me to cover myself. 'You are so beautiful, Catherine Alexeyevna. The most beautiful woman under the sun, so full, soft and warm.'

His words made me at ease; his lips found each fold of my flesh and let no part of me escape; his tongue soft and moist, his fingers supple, his hands strong, as he lifted my hips up towards him. I opened my legs wider and wider, greedily pressing towards him and his cock. He was so big and hard that I gasped when he came into my slippery flesh, filling me up, open and wet as I was, and then pulling me on his legs while he knelt. I gave a muffled moan to have him so deeply and still feel him grow, but he placed his hand over my mouth. 'Move,' he whispered.

'I can't,' I gasped, but he made me, slowly, strongly, and a new wave of lust came over me, riding him until I felt sore with pleasure. He cupped my buttocks, pushing me closer, his fingers digging into my flesh as I came a second time. I screamed and in my ecstasy bit his fingers with their four rings bloody, as he tried to stifle the sound. I licked the crimson sweetness off his flesh like a kitten would cream. In his arms, I was a woman once more, not just an Empress. I struck all weapons in a defeat sweeter than any victory could ever be.

*

It was late afternoon when I walked barefoot to the window to close it. It was raining again, and the window swung in the wind. How reckless we were: we had not even shut it before making love. This was madness – if Peter heard of it, it would be our undoing. He had tortured, maimed and killed for so much less than this betrayal. I turned, my heart racing and raindrops wetting my cheeks. My body ached where Wilhelm had touched me, yet already I yearned for more. It felt as if I belonged to him.

He lay sleeping on the rug, breathing softly, sated, his cheeks rosy and his open lips smiling. I lowered myself down by the wall next to the fireplace and sat there looking at him: he was my husband, my son, my youth, my love, my life. I took wood chippings from the basket next to the fireplace and rekindled the flames, just as I had learnt to do as a girl. Sparks fed on the dry straw I had stuffed between the logs, and I sat back on my heels and hummed a little song as I guarded Wilhelm's slumber. How wonderful life was; I neither wanted to sleep, nor to cover myself, nor or eat. My love refreshed, warmed and nourished me. I knew this must never happen again.

The following months forever belonged to Wilhelm. How we lived our love so fully, I do not know. A special God protects lovers: we shared every heartbeat, every thought, every hope and every fear. In the glorious Peterhof dawn we crossed the park down to the sea, chasing each other and playing hide and seek. We bathed in the bay, splashing and laughing. We moved among the trees until they spun around us; the sea breeze crusted the salt on our skin and blue clouds piled up on the horizon while we sipped at the scented summer rain. Amongst the trees, on the soft earth, Wilhelm and I became one creature with two heads, four arms and four legs. What sounds like a monster from Peter's Kunstkamera was the most beautiful state of being I was ever to know. The summer in Peterhof was our world, and this world was good and great.

Elizabeth avoided me. She ate with her sisters in their apartments, kept to the company of her ladies, and when I met them in the park she walked away. The sea breeze blew the fountain's droplets in a rainbow in front of her colourful skirts, which faded amongst the trees as she left me behind.

One morning, I paid her a visit in her schoolroom: the blue silk curtains were drawn back and the books' polished leather bindings gleamed in the sunlight. In one corner of the room stood a man of glass that the girls used to study human anatomy. He was cross-eyed, as one of his ceramic eyes stared at me, the other one down at his feet, ever since Elizabeth had torn it out, and Madame de la Tour, her governess, had twisted it back in askew. Next to the piano of German manufacture I spotted Anna's silver music stand, for she had singing lessons to please the young Duke of Holstein. The wind ruffled the sheets, despite the hooks of ivory holding the paper down.

This sound did not bother Elizabeth: her head was bent studiously as she wrote a note. I crept up to her; some blonde curls had loosened themselves from her plaits and the nape of her neck was touchingly childlike. Before I knew what I was doing, I caressed her head with more tenderness than I had truly ever felt for her.

Elizabeth started. 'You!' she hissed and the look in her eyes, which were as lively as a bird's, pierced me. But I asked in a friendly fashion: 'What are you doing, Elizabeth? How diligent of you still to be here after your lessons with Madame de la Tour.'

'I have not written in my diary for so long and the weather is not fine enough for us to go riding,' she said. I looked outside, where a light wind swept the sunny treetops. What could I say to her? It was clear she wanted me to go. So I cast a glance at the page before her, and while I could not read her writing, I noticed how strong and slanted her letters were. This was not a child's hand, but a woman's.

80

Peter sent me letter after letter to Peterhof, and every line spoke of love and longing: '"*Unfortunately, I cannot be with you, Catherinushka. My old illness plagues me more than ever, and I am glad to spare you the sight. My stomach is as bloated as a horse's, and the pain binds my chest with iron straps; the ulcers on my legs make every step a torment. At least Alekasha has given me a magnificent stallion. So I drink to forget the pain and go riding, even though it takes three footmen to lift me in the saddle.*"'

When the summer turned into damp autumn, I returned to St Petersburg with a heavy heart. At least Wilhelm was with me on the voyage back. I asked the sailors to tie up my barge in a secluded creek well before town. I gave them two hours' leave and was alone with Wilhelm once more. 'This has to be the last time,' I said, as his fingers slid into me before I could even undress. 'If we do this in Petersburg, the Tsar will kill us both.'

'If I have to die, I want to die for you, with you,' was his answer.

He pushed me onto the bed and turned me, raising my hips so he could slide into me. His holding me down and closing my legs while thrusting into me gave me more strength than I had thought possible. I bit the cushions so as not to make a sound, yet wanted to cry for more with every breath.

*

Just when I would have been as happy to tend a fire with Wilhelm in a little *izba*, I had to plan my Coronation. Was I but a soul after all? I felt utter dread: never before had a Tsaritsa been crowned; the Moscow ceremony should make the importance of Peter's step clear to everybody, be they a wealthy prince or a pauper in this vast realm. My spirit, my body and my soul dreaded the weight of the crown, and Peter must have felt my unease when he drew me close to him one day in his study in the Winter Palace. 'Do not worry,' he said. 'I shall be with you, every step of the way.' He smiled, misunderstanding my feelings. I shied away because I longed so much for Wilhelm that I wanted to avoid Peter's touch. But then I gave in and caressed my husband's tousled hair. The table was covered with drawings for robes, uniforms, jewels.

'Look. We drive from Menshikov's house to the Kremlin, cross-ing the Red Square, which will be full of flags. The route to the Uspensky Cathedral is not long, but all the people should see you and it must be an unforgettable spectacle.' He rustled through the papers with his tobacco-stained fingers. 'Here: the list of the people who will carry your train. I have, of course, thought of Sheremetev ...'

If anyone deserved to be with me on that day it was Boris Petrovich, I thought, but asked: 'And who, my Tsar, shall crown me? Feofan Prokopovich?'

Peter dropped the scroll, placed his hands on my bare shoul-ders and kissed my forehead. His voice quivered as he said, 'No, Catherinushka. I myself shall crown you, and no one else.'

That night, I sat on the broad windowsill of my bedroom window: darkness had fallen like a curtain over my splendid city in the snow. Wilhelm pulled the floor-length sable coat off my naked body, pressed me against the pane, parted my thighs and slid into me. My calves lay against his shoulders and I arched against the window that was dripping with our breath, sweat and lust. Wilhelm forced me deeper amongst the velvet curtains to muffle my sighs, moans and then a cry. He felt my heart race against his, his mouth laughing as he kissed his own taste from my lips. We lived our love shamelessly, as if there was no tomorrow: the fear of discovery, and what might happen then, made our feelings even stronger and our passion more burning. But the boost of life and pleasure was as heady as no lasting happiness can ever be.

Peter set the date for my Coronation at the end of May. 'No other month is golden enough to celebrate this day,' he said at a meal during which his two dwarves wrestled, the Moor Abraham Petrovich being their referee. I ate lots of caviar, as Wilhelm had told me that it was good for love. When I looked up, he was giving me a tender smile, which Peter noticed. My heart chilled as my husband asked lightly, 'How is young Mons doing in your retinue?'

'Very well. I have not heard any complaints,' I replied, feeding Peter with a *blinchiki* of smoked sturgeon.

'Mmmm, delicious.' He smacked his lips and sucked my fingertips, then drizzled lemon juice over my neck and licked it off my skin, but stopped short when he noticed my diamond necklace: Menshikov's gift. He frowned. 'Such stones are rare in my kingdom. Who gave it to you?'

'Alekasha. He was grateful to me for my advice,' I said merrily, but Peter shook his head reproachfully.

'*Matka*. You above all others should not accept gifts, and certainly not from Menshikov. No breath of scandal must ever besmirch you, don't you understand? There must be one person in my kingdom who remains incorruptible and I wish this to be you.' He sounded upset.

'Of course. How thoughtless of me. Come now, *starik*, this is not an evening for harsh lessons. Drink with me.' My tenderness soothed him. I refilled his jug to the brim. My body ached for Wilhelm, who stood behind us. But for tonight I had to be Peter's wife.

The robes and uniforms for my Coronation were delivered from Paris; but my crown was made in St Petersburg: the Nevsky Prospect was cloaked in fresh snow when we first visited the jeweller there. Peter did not wish him to travel with his valuable work. The slight man and his apprentices bowed, moving backwards into the small premises while guards manned the door. Peter and I sipped tea with vodka from dainty china as a casket was placed in front of us.

'Put the cup down or you'll spill it,' Peter warned me tenderly.

The jeweller glowed with pride in his creation: 'Are Their Most Gracious Majesties ready?'

Peter nodded, and the man blew out his cheeks as he unlocked the box, ordering: 'Light more candles. I want this to sparkle like the sun, moon and stars.' I almost had to laugh, he sounded so thrilled by his own work.

'More than a million roubles, just for your crown,' Peter murmured, kissing my fingers. Goose-bumps covered my arms: one million roubles was an unimaginable sum, enough to feed generations of Russians in their small, filthy, stinking *izby*. I blinked my tears away: this crown was a miracle and so different from the jewelled domes I knew. A border of diamonds sparkled at the lower rim: each stone was as big as a hazelnut, resting on a band of ermine so as not to press into my forehead. Grey, pink and white pearls alternated with diamonds on the arches forming the upper part of the crown, whilst in between, sapphires, emeralds and again diamonds sparkled. The splendour was topped by a ruby cross; the stone at its heart was as large as a dove's egg, radiating crimson and gold sparks.

'Can I try it on?' I asked hoarsely, but Peter looked at me, horrified.

'A crown is not a cap or a hat, Catherine, that you *try on*, but a sacred sign of the power that God in His grace grants you. You may wear it only once you have been anointed. No water in this world can wash the blessed oil from your forehead: only then are you ready for a crown.'

Back in the sleigh, dusk blotted out the light of the early afternoon. Peter pushed his hands into my sable muff, lacing my fingers with his. 'Thank you for being with me. It hasn't always been easy. I hope this will make it up to you.'

Candles burnt behind the windows on the Nevsky Prospect and in the lanterns along the canals. Snow glowed under the clear, star-studded sky, as shiny as Wilhelm's eyes were after making love. Could I hope that he would look at me like that forever and ever? A thousand eyes watch a Tsar's wife. Stepan Glebov had paid the highest price for loving Evdokia, and she had been but a discarded encumbrance to Peter while I was to be honoured in a way that no Tsar had ever done before. It wasn't even worth thinking about what he'd do to us if he found out. And still I could not let go of Wilhelm. That same evening, I ordered Maître Duval from the *gostiny dvor* to the palace: he had moved his business to St Petersburg. While all my robes were made in France, I wanted to sew Peter's Coronation coat myself, stitch by stitch. I ordered many *arshin* of sky-blue taffeta from Paris and chose silver braid to trim the knee-length jacket. Out of coquetry, I settled upon flaming red silk thread for the stockings. The price that Duval quoted me made my head spin: one silver thread alone could pay a dragoon's salary for two years. Yet I did not hesitate, and when Maître Duval got his order book out, I said to Wilhelm: 'Sign it in my name, will you?'

At the end of March, St Petersburg's noble families left for Moscow. The last icicles still hung in the trees lining the Nevsky Prospect, but milder air and the first rays of sunlight spoke of the approach of spring. An endless train of carriages and wagons crossed the countryside: thirty thousand people were on the road. Ships used the early arrival of the *ottepel* to sail to Moscow, and children ran along the banks as the Imperial vessel cast off, waving and cheering. Clouds rolled overhead and the wind blew away the worries and the shame from my heart, scattering them across the vastness of the realm.

I had to retreat below decks to reflect on what was about to happen. Twenty-five years ago, in another life, a man had bought me for a piece of silver. Now I should be crowned Tsaritsa of All the Russias. Wilhelm dared to slip into my cabin, holding me tightly and whispering sweet nothings until I could breathe again. My fear was mirrored in his eyes, but he kissed me until his strong, steady heartbeat calmed me: how should I do without him? He supported me, felt for me as no man had ever done before. Was there a chance for us to be happy together? I thought, just when I saw the thousand turrets, spires and towers of Moscow. It was not my city, but the place of my most splendid hour. Yet the brightest sun casts the darkest shadow.

On the seventh day of May 1724 I climbed into a golden carriage in the innermost courtyard of Alexander Danilovich Menshikov's house. Peter himself steadied me in my heavy gown. My hand trembled as I placed my fingers in his. 'Stand tall, Catherinushka. Have no fear,' he reassured me, but I felt dazed and the weight of my velvet robes crushed me. Peter had insisted on the warm fabric and the high-necked dress was stiff as a board with gold embroidery. Four of the twelve pageboys appointed to carry my train, lifted it so that I could get into the coach. The boys, all of them sons of Peter's most faithful confidants, looked adorable in green velvet and matching caps adorned with white ostrich feathers. I gasped under the sudden pressure of the diamond clasps at my throat, but by now cannon were starting to thunder and the bells of the city called; the gates opened, and as soon as the Imperial coach rolled onto the Red Square, cheers and clapping rose. The guards stood to attention; trumpets were blown. Drummers rolled a fast, upbeat rhythm. The musicians of Peter's two regiments vied against each other. Two swallows buzzed by my carriage, their beady eyes mocking me. The twelve mares pulling it reared, and the coachman sweated in his silk livery. My hand rose of its own accord. I smiled and waved. There was no turning back.

Outside the Uspensky Cathedral, the newly created Cavalry Guard, to which Alexander Danilovich belonged, awaited me. Sheremetev reached out to steady me. He murmured, 'I am so glad, my lady, I could die.'

Suddenly, the colours were even brighter, the music even gayer. Step by step, I made my way down the nave of the cathedral. The courtiers had had to purchase tickets for the event. A sea of familiar faces turned towards me but I looked straight ahead, to where General James Bruce stood, holding my crown on a velvet cushion, beads of sweat glistening on his upper lip. I struggled to sit at Peter's side in my stiff robes, but tried to copy his calmness and dignity. He briefly winked at me then turned stone-faced, looking straight ahead.

As Archbishop of Novgorod, Feofan Prokopovich read the Mass. With the help of my cavaliers, I knelt before him. His voice echoed in the silence of the cathedral. If I had felt unbearably hot before, chills now chased over my skin. The twelve young pageboys pressed their foreheads to the cathedral's cold stone floor. Silence ruled, inside and outside the holy place. With warm, fragrant oil, Feofan Prokopovich drew a cross on my forehead and muttered his blessing.

The world spun: only Peter remained still, the calm in the eye of the storm. He had done nothing but this for his whole life, I understood, when he lifted the crown, its gemstones catching the light, and I sensed more than saw him. The crowd sighed longingly; blood roared in my ears when the weight of the crown sent a sharp pain through my tense neck down into my rigid shoulders. I placed my fingers in Peter's. I wanted to kiss his feet, but he did not allow it. '*Starik,*' I murmured, and the pain ebbed away as I stood, and music flooded the cathedral. Perhaps only then did I understand what he was willing to share with me. Tears streamed down my cheeks, leaving traces in my thick white make-up. Peter held the sceptre to his breast and raised my hand in his: together, we had lived and loved, and together, we ruled.

The Court rose for the final blessing and the choir's voices carried my gratitude out onto the squares of the city, to the glare of the gold coins Menshikov had thrown into the crowd and the gurgling of the fountains spewing red and white wine. The festivities lasted a week. Then the whole court, with its servants, families, livestock and luggage, left again for St Petersburg where Peter planned to celebrate his name-day on the Neva with sea games and a new round of celebrations.

81

'Now I have gone too far.' Peter flinched. 'As soon as I have battled one pain, I feel a hundred others rearing up.' His face was unhealthily flushed as he had been bedridden for the past four months. Blumentrost had called in other doctors to give advice, which worried me. If a quack admits his own uselessness, things are serious indeed. Doctor Bidloo arrived from Moscow, but finally it was Doctor Horn who drained almost a litre of blood, urine and pus from Peter's bladder.

Wilhelm brought me reminders of freedom, wind and sunshine, telling me funny stories about the estate with five thousand souls I had given him. To him, ten days were long enough to gather the adventures of a lifetime. 'I can't wait until you come and see me in the *dacha*,' he said – that was what he called the little estate close to the Bay of Finland, as if it were a hut. 'Do you still know how to get an egg out from under a chicken? Are you good at milking?' he teased me.

'I've forgotten it all,' I laughed. 'You'll have to start from the beginning then, with me, in the stables,' he said, and I chuckled, going down on my knees and opening his breeches. I sensed his hesitation.

'Come,' I whispered. 'I command it.' His eyes shone like jewels as I, the crowned Empress of Russia, took him slowly, fully, in my mouth, as if I was a maid. His lust was the only realm I ever wished to rule.

*

One autumn evening, Peter asked for supper to be served in my rooms. I ordered his favourite food from Felten – pork sausages with sauerkraut, fresh flatbread and cold beer – and adorned the table with evergreens from the Summer Palace's garden.

Peter arrived accompanied by Jagushinsky, Makarov and Menshikov. Wilhelm waited on me as well as Daria Menshikova and Agneta: the more, the merrier, I thought. My dress was of simple dark-green cotton, yet I wore Menshikov's necklace to flatter him. When Peter entered the room he gave me a dark look.

'Are you in pain?' I asked but he would not answer, so I filled his plate to the brim and broke the bread. He did not thank me. I chatted all the more feverishly. Then, after an hour's mute chewing and gloomy looks, Peter growled, 'Tsaritsa, what time is it?'

The table fell curiously silent as I reached for the delicate watch hanging on a gold chain around my neck: a gift from Peter to me, bought in Berlin. 'Only nine o'clock, *starik*, so there is time left for more food and enjoyment.'

But Peter lunged at me and tore the chain from my neck. I gasped with pain as the links broke and the ladies screamed. Peter thrust the watch's diamond hands forward so roughly that one of them broke. 'You are mistaken, Catherine Alexeyevna,' he shouted. 'It's already midnight, and all but you, me and him –' Here he pointed at Wilhelm ' are to leave.'

My heart pounded and I felt sweat tingling on my neck and in my armpits. Yet I smiled and said: 'Your wish is our command. Goodnight, my friends.' I clapped my hands as if this were a routine matter, yet I saw the dread in our guests' faces and felt faint with fear. Wilhelm stood as still as a statue, his face pale. He steadied himself on the back of a chair, his knuckles turning white. Only the crackling of the logs in the fire was to be heard as Peter's dark gaze went from me to Wilhelm, and from him back to me. I sat down once more, sipping from my glass. My calm goaded Peter and made him unsure, just as I had hoped it would. He pulled a letter from his chest pocket; the paper had been read and folded many times, and some of the wide, slanted letters were smeared by tears. Peter looked at me, his expression full of contempt, before throwing the letter at Wilhelm. 'Unfortunately, I have married an uneducated washerwoman. Read, you vain monkey!' he thundered.

Wilhelm's fingers trembled as he read soundlessly, before looking up. He fell on his knees, gasping for breath, wrung his hands and stammered, 'My Tsar. That's a shameless, ill-intentioned lie.'

Peter did not leave him any time to protest further but struck Wilhelm in the face with his clenched fist, knocking him over. I called out in horror and leapt to my feet, but Peter grabbed and shook me until my teeth chattered, before shoving me away, staring at me with his face full of hatred: 'I have married you and made you an Empress. I have crowned you, and this is how you thank me? Rotten to the core as you are, even daring to flaunt the spoils of your corruption before me.'

He lunged at me and tore Menshikov's necklace from my throat: priceless diamonds rained down upon the rugs in a sparkling shower. Peter pushed me up against the panelling. Wilhelm crawled to him, kissing the rough leather of his boots, sobbing and pleading. 'My Tsar, for all the love and all the honour you have given my family, please do not believe this. I would never besmirch the Tsaritsa's name, never betray you.'

'Son of a bitch!' Peter kicked Wilhelm several times in the face, chest and belly, making ribs and cheekbones crack and then breaking his strong, white teeth. Wilhelm moaned and spat blood. He bent double with pain. I did not move, cowering against the wall. 'Do not dare to name the Tsaritsa together with your damned brethren. All the Mons family will pay for this!' Furious, he seized a porcelain jug and hurled it against a priceless Venetian mirror, smashing it to pieces; I ducked as shards flew. 'This, Catherine Alexeyevna, shall be done with you and yours,' he cried.

I crossed my arms. 'Fabulous. You have just destroyed one of the most exquisite possessions in your palace. Do you feel better now?' I knew he would take any sign of fear or pleading from me as a sign of guilt. I held his gaze as he pulled me close and I saw doubt in his eyes; that might save me, if not Wilhelm.

'Damn you and your guts, woman!' he hissed, before he turned to the door. 'Guards, to me!' Four tall men stormed into the room. They must have been stationed outside, waiting for his signal.

Peter pointed at the crouching, bleeding Wilhelm. 'Arrest that man!' he ordered breathlessly. 'Throw him into the Trubetzkoi bastion. Torture him until he confesses his theft and embezzlement from the Tsaritsa's treasures. I shall have the proof I need.'

'No!' I gasped, and Peter caught me as I fainted.

82

On the day of Wilhelm's execution, I made sure to be seen practising together with my daughters and a dance master from Paris,
hiding my pallor and my dread with painted cheeks and glittering
jewels. 'I heard of a new minuet from Paris, teach it to us!' I clapped
my hands and ate sugared violets to force my lips into a smile.
The master showed us the series of steps, and Elizabeth repeatedly
glanced at me. I thought of the slanted writing that had sealed
Wilhelm's fate: but no, I told myself, that was impossible. She was
my *daughter*. As Wilhelm was dragged from the Trubetzkoi bastion
to the scaffold, I moved to the light, floating melody and danced
across the pieces of my broken heart.

Peter's guards entered the ballroom: I was to attend the execution.

The crowd was eerily quiet as the whole Mons family was led close
to the executioner's block so they did not miss a single detail of his
death. Wilhelm himself could not walk anymore. Rough hands had
thrown him onto a sledge piled with rotten straw, before he was
heaved onto the executioner's broad shoulders. Peter would not let
me out of his sight but I smiled at him, crunching more sugared
violets until my teeth and cheeks hurt.

'Well, Catherine Alexeyevna, what do you feel now?' he asked,
beady-eyed. I tightened my fur collar around my neck and
shrugged.

'I took him for a trusted employee. If he really stole my jewels then he deserves just punishment,' I said, looking at Wilhelm, feeling ready to faint. I had asked God in vain for the strength to face this moment. My love was no longer a man, but a miserable lump of flesh as he was dragged up the steps to the scaffold. He sighed and fresh drops of blood splattered. I knew that he had not betrayed me or our love, despite Peter's torturers plying their cruel trade to the best of their knowledge.

'Oh, yes,' Peter mocked me. 'He tried to pocket crown jewels, as you know very well. I even have proof of him embezzling your funds.'

He shoved a piece of paper into my hand. I gave a sob when I unfolded it. It was my order for the fabrics for Peter's Coronation garments that Wilhelm had signed in my name, at my order. The clothes I had sewn with my own hands, as a sign of my love and gratitude to my husband.

'He signed his own undoing, young Mons,' Peter smiled. 'Look. Look well, Catherinushka.' Wilhelm whimpered and I dug my nails deep into my palms. I loved him; loved him too much, and yet did I love him enough? Why did I not confess and join him on the scaffold there and then? If I once despised Afrosinja for sacrificing Alexey, then the thought of my own silence shall haunt me until my dying day.

Peter tore me to my feet, shoving me closer to the scaffold. 'You can't see well enough from here,' he snarled, and I staggered along, straight to the block, where Wilhelm's body hung. He could no longer lift his head and I was glad of it, for I could not have borne to meet his gaze.

Peter kissed my cheek and shouted, 'The Tsaritsa wants to see up close how the common thief Wilhelm Mons, traitor of her trust, is being judged!'

A murmur rose from the people; they knew all too well why Wilhelm had to suffer. On Peter's sign his men started and I could not hold back anymore. My tears flowed freely, blinding me and blotting out the sheer horror of Wilhelm's death. I know they broke him on the wheel; they slit him open and tore his guts from his body, roasting them on a spit and feeding them to the crows in front of his eyes, before finally beheading him. Peter held me in an iron grip and let me weep until Wilhelm, my wonderful Wilhelm, so full of life, love and lust, was no more.

83

Oh, yes, Peter knew what he was doing. In the following days he forced me to the scaffold again and again; our sleigh would stop where Wilhelm's corpse still hung. His limbs had been torn off by wild dogs. 'Come on, Catherinushka, we'll stretch our legs,' Peter would say merrily, steering me so close to Wilhelm that my skirts brushed his butchered body. I obeyed, but chatted about trivial matters until it got too much for Peter himself. 'You and your damn' courage. If my generals had had but a sliver of it, I would have won more wars,' he growled as he pushed me back into the sleigh.

I cast a last glance at Wilhelm's beheaded torso and took leave of all the love left in my heart. The sleigh jerked forward, its silver bells jingling in the frosty air, and a gust of icy wind hid the scaffold in a cloud of fresh powdery snow.

The same evening, I left the dinner table in Peter's rooms early. My heart longed for the stillness of the night. I needed all my strength for the days to come. Peter had already forbidden his ministers from obeying any of my orders and had sealed my treasurer's office. I had no money left and ran up debts with my ladies.

In my bedroom, Alexandra Tolstoya loosened my hair, unclasped my jewellery and unlaced my dress. A few candles were alight. Had someone already been here? I slipped out of my soft shoes, holding on to my dainty bedside table, when my hand skimmed glass. Had I ordered a sleeping-potion? I raised my night light – and gave a scream; the candle slipped from my fingers and flames licked at the sheets. Alexandra Tolstoya rushed in. 'Milady, what happened?' She suffocated the flames by tearing the sheets from my bed and stamping on them. I sobbed and gasped, pointing to the night table.

'Oh my God, the animal!' she whispered.

Next to my bed stood a tall glass jar, the type used to steep apples in vodka during the winter. Yet no fruit floated in this one, but the head of my beloved Wilhelm. His blue eyes were wide open and his lips pulled back from his gums in agony and fear. He stared at me; his gaze pleading, but not accusing. I gagged with disgust and tears. 'Take that away, Alexandra,' I stammered. She lifted the jar with unsteady fingers, but when she turned around, Peter stood in the doorway, towering over us. We both shrank back, horrified. He took a deep sip from his brandy flask, swaying as he did so.

'Your room is so bare, Catherinushka. What's wrong with keeping a little jar next to your bed?' His voice was slurred yet still threatening. 'Alexandra Tolstoya, whoever moves this jar will pay with their life. In recognition of your faithful service to date, I will allow you to replace it where it belongs and take no action against you. This time.' Alexandra looked at me. What else could I do?

'Put it down, Alexandra,' I muttered and curtseyed to my visitor: 'How kind of the Tsar to think of this adornment to my room.' Was that it? Hadn't he punished me enough? No. Peter pointed at me. 'That's just the beginning. Now, Catherine Alexeyevna, I'll think about what's going to happen to you.' His cold, hard eyes made me shiver. He had already won, and I had lost everything: what else could he want? Alexandra made me a sleeping-potion and in my nightmares Wilhelm's eyes filled the sky like stars.

No one at court was ready to wager a kopek on my future by Peter's side; my destiny was sealed. The only puzzling thing was *what* exactly might happen. To which convent should I commit myself, shorn and lonely? Or was there a cell prepared in the Peter and Paul Fortress, where he would torture and kill me as he had done Alexey? Under the first blow of the knout, I would confess all that I was accused of, and gladly add more. I had suffered when giving birth, but could not bear deliberately inflicted physical pain. I remembered surrendering to Vassily without putting up a fight. Only Menshikov did not forsake me, secretly sending me letters and small gifts to lift my spirits. Agneta told me with tears in her eyes what Peter had said in the Senate: 'I will do to her what England's King Henry has done to Anne Boleyn.'

'What did he do to this Anne?' I asked unhappily. 'And what was her offence?'

'She was an adulteress, Tsaritsa,' she whispered, before drawing her flat hand across her neck.

It was almost midnight when I made my way through the dark, secret corridor that linked Peter's rooms to mine. The night light just about helped me find my way without stumbling over a sleeping footman's body. I pressed my ear against Peter's door: he was in there with Tolstoy and his Chancellor, the German Baron Ostermann. Their voices were muffled.

'My Tsar, do not act rashly. Please consider the betrothal of the Tsarevna Anna to the Duke of Holstein,' Ostermann mumbled.

'I do not see any link there to the Tsaritsa's crime. Just answer me: convent, exile or death?' Peter asked angrily. I chewed my fingers and held my breath. The light at my feet flickered.

'Well,' Ostermann said, 'the Duke could dissolve the engagement if the bride's mother had a bad reputation. With all due respect, the courts of Europe talk enough about the Tsaritsa as it is. If she were to be charged with adultery and beheaded, that would put an end to marriage plans for any of your daughters.' For once, I felt like kissing the wry German who normally was no one's friend.

'Ostermann is right. Not only Anna Petrovna's engagement is at risk here, we would not find a new suitor for Tsarevna Elizabeth once Versailles turns her down,' Tolstoy added.

I heard wood breaking, and Peter cursing. What did he kick and smash in his anger; his desk or his chair? There was a moment of silence. 'How are the marriage plans with France coming along?' he asked.

'Not at all,' Tolstoy said. 'King Louis is silent – insultingly so. The Duc de Chartres, also a possible suitor, married a German princess a few weeks ago without even telling us. Will a king take what a duke despises?'

I pressed my ear so hard against the wood that it hurt.

'So be it. I will wait. But Catherine's hour will come, and it will come soon.' There was cold fury in Peter's voice. I tiptoed back to my room, my heart racing and sweat trickling down my neck despite the chill in the passage. What had I sworn to myself that night in the Summer Palace when he promised me marriage? I would not fear.

Two weeks after Wilhelm's execution, the betrothal of my eldest daughter Anna Petrovna to the young Duke of Holstein was formally announced. The duke gave a concert beneath the windows of the Winter Palace and the musicians' fingertips and lips froze to their instruments. Afterwards, we crossed the Neva in sleds, and heard Mass in the Trinity Church. Feofan Prokopovich blessed the rings and Peter himself placed them on the young couple's fingers. During the feast, the ball and the fireworks that followed, I played the radiant Tsaritsa, for all to see, with the very last of my strength. Yet my mind could neither dismiss memories of Wilhelm's mutilated body, nor of Evdokia's miserable end.

The palace was treacherously peaceful in the first, dark hours of the day: how long had I knelt there in the cold splendour of the corridor outside Peter's door? My fists were scraped raw from banging on it, my stomach growled, my hair was tangled and my cheeks scratched and bloody. I had wept and pleaded myself hoarse until, finally, I'd heard him stir on the other side.

'What do you want, Catherinushka?' he asked warily. I sat up. At least he'd called me that.

'Forgive me, my Tsar, *batjuschka*!' I was strangled by sobs. 'I beg you on my knees. *Starik*, darling, love of my life, please. For all that is dear to us. Our children, Russia – and for all we've been through.' The door opened a crack, and he looked down at me.

'You deceived me,' he said bitterly. I wiped the tears from my cheeks, as helpless as a child, and sat up: it was true.

'Yes. I know. Forgive me. But I do not wish to fight with you, my beloved. I want to make you happy, as I always have. I miss you – everything about you. Take me back into your life, into your heart. Only there do I belong. You are my husband, my brother, my father, my home –'

He opened the door a little further, peering out, and I could see his face. His skin was pasty and his eyes swollen. 'I do not know, Catherinushka,' he faltered. His hesitation frightened me more than any judgment passed in raging anger. Snot and tears ran down my face, and I shivered from cold and tiredness.

'Come in,' Peter sighed, and pulled me to my feet and into his room. The curtains were closed and it reeked of liquor, sweat and smoke. His favourite chair was pushed in front of the fireplace. Had he sat there, his feet close to the warmth, listening to me pleading on the other side for hours on end? He sat down again and I crouched on a cushion at his feet. Peter looked at me, and I was careful not to interrupt his thoughts. His face was unreadable, changed by the shadows.

'What is it with you women?' he said, shaking his head. 'Anna Mons made a fool out of me. Evdokia deceived me even in the convent in which I'd stuck her, while still besieging me with her letters. At least you cannot write, Catherinushka. I will be spared that from you. Maria Kantemir did not keep her pompous promise of an heir for Russia.' I held my breath while he dropped his hand onto my dark, shining curls, wrapping one around his finger. 'But you, Catherine, you have betrayed me at the very moment when I gave you the greatest gift imaginable. Why did you do this?' He sniffed at my hair. 'You're still beautiful. How often were you pregnant? Twelve times, if I'm not mistaken.' He uncorked the brandy bottle which stood beside him on the floor and took a swig. 'Twelve children, and still so stunningly beautiful. But what will the convent's chill do to you? What will you look like, bald and gaunt?' He drank deeply. 'What's worst of all is that in the end, you, too, did not truly understand me. Don't you know how lonely a ruler is; how cold the throne is on the skin of my arse and how far away I still am from even those who are closest to me?'

'I've always been with you. I am always with you. I will always be with you,' I whispered. The flames warmed my bare arms, yet I had goose-bumps all over my body. 'Can you not forgive me?' I had done once what he had done a thousand times. In Russian fairy tales, houses rest on three stilts; was the palace of our love carried by just one pillar: my love and fidelity?

He stared into the fireplace. 'No. I cannot forgive. But I have not decided either what to do with you. Go to bed now, *matka*.'

I took his chilly hands in mine. 'I have borne you twelve children, Peter Alexeyevich Romanov. Can you imagine what it means to give birth twelve times? None of your soldiers has suffered like that or risked his life so often for you. And do you know why I did that? Just for love, my Tsar.'

He gazed mutely into the flames. I let go of his fingers and his limp hands slipped into his lap. At noon the next day, Pavel Jagushinsky picked up Wilhelm's head from my bedside table and brought it to the Kunstkamera where it was to be housed in future.

Evil spirits and memories haunted Peter more than ever; jealousy seared his soul, making him roam his Empire restlessly. Every day I was left unscathed meant hope remained, but in my uncertainty the passing of time was also a punishment. Every day I heard new and wild stories from my *damy*.

'Imagine, the Tsar passed a house where a wedding was being celebrated. So he knocked at the door, sat down at the table and drank more than anyone else.'

'Yesterday, the Tsar visited the Ladoga Canal and drank until dawn with the architects.'

'No, he is at the Ironworks of Olonez, where he chased a blacksmith from his anvil, just to smite six hundred pounds of iron himself. He asked to be paid for his work and bought a pair of long socks at the market.'

He was everywhere at the same time, just not in St Petersburg, not with me.

Peter returned to our city in January. His old fever seized him more violently than ever and he did not even recognise me by his bedside. Few people were admitted and I ordered that little Petrushka, Alexey's son, was not to come to the Winter Palace from his godfather Prince Dolgoruki's house: seeing him would upset Peter unbearably. My orders were listened to once more. I knelt there, hour after hour, or lay down beside him, cuddling up close, whispering memories into his ear. He quietened then and his breath steadied. I embraced him and fell asleep.

Menshikov came to the sick room in the early-morning hours one day and opened the window. When the clear winter air streamed into the room, Peter reeled in his fever, but my weight held him down.

'What made him suddenly relapse?' I asked.

Menshikov stuffed his long pipe and set it alight. 'Well, I wouldn't call that *suddenly*, my Tsaritsa. When we left the ironworks of Olonez, the Tsar already felt cold, despite the new socks he had earnt.' We both smiled before Menshikov turned serious again. 'Yet he pressed on, straight for St Petersburg. It poured with rain; we followed the shoreline, so as not to get lost in the storm, and heard screams coming from the water.' Menshikov blew a few rings into the air, their thin smoke dissolving. 'Some sailors were in distress. Before I could hold back the Tsar, he had already jumped off his horse.'

'And then?'

Menshikov shrugged. 'What else do you expect? He jumped into the icy water, without the least regard for his own safety or health, and swam out to save the men. Once he had brought their boat ashore, they drank like fish, round upon round of hot spirits, before the Tsar got back on his horse. The storm still raged, but we pushed on. He felt feverish before we reached the first of the city's barriers.'

Blumentrost entered the room. 'My Tsaritsa, perhaps it is better for you to leave the room for a while. The mercury cure is not for Your Majesty's eyes.'

I refused. 'I'll stay, Blumentrost. Someone must hold his hand to comfort him.'

Menshikov smiled. 'A true Empress, as always.'

When Blumentrost opened Peter's blanket, I pressed my hand to my lips, fighting the bile that rose in my throat. The skin on his swollen belly had blackened, as if rotting away. Spots and ulcers covered his groin and when the doctor pressed his side, ever so lightly, Peter roared with pain and emerged from his feverish sleep. 'He suffers from kidney stones, Your Majesty,' whispered Blumentrost. 'I'll have to work together with Paulsen and Horn.' Peter's puffed-up body and the stench in the room made me choke, but I took a deep breath and raised his head tenderly. 'I'm ready.'

Blumentrost reached for the mercury ointment and pills.

'How is he now?' Menshikov had slipped back into the room after a few hours' sleep. What should I say? For weeks Peter had hovered between life and death. His gigantic body was weakened by so many struggles: our father Tsar, our protector, just as he'd wanted to be, looked ready to leave us.

Makarov seemed shrunken in his black coat as I waved him close to me, by the window. 'Makarov, I fear that Blumentrost is killing the Tsar,' I whispered. 'Please send a messenger to Berlin. The King of Prussia has a famous physician, Herr von Stahl, of whom Peter has often spoken. Bring him here at any cost.'

Night fell and servants drew the curtains shut, hiding Peter's suffering from his city. Candles were lit, and the warm scent of beeswax as well as the richly spiced Persian incense that smouldered in burning pans softened the stench of the disease. To Peter, the room's shadows were alive with the people who had accompanied us along our way and gone ahead into the underworld. I heard him mumble, 'Mother, do not cry. I am coming. Sophia, leave me alone. And Alexey, you useless boy ...' He groaned and wanted to turn over but Blumentrost would not allow it. Peter settled on his back again. He narrowed his eyes, gazing up into the air. 'Sheremetev! There you are. Actually, it's all your fault –'

I sobbed as Feofan Prokopovich entered the room together with a simple priest. Peter received the last rites for the third time in as many days.

I wept so much that I fainted several times, from fear or sorrow. I could not master either feeling.

When the Tsar was too weak to speak, Feofan Prokopovich, Menshikov and I formed a tight circle around the bed. I knelt once more to be closer to him. Peter's gaze slipped away. The bells started tolling and people gathered on to the quays and the Nevsky Prospect for prayer. What did they wish for? His death or his recovery? Did I myself know what I was hoping for?

He opened his eyes once more, searching my gaze. 'You love me, don't you? Say that you love me, always,' he whispered through lips that were dry and cracked.

I nodded, tears streaming down my face. 'More than my life!'

He sighed. 'You better had.'

I smiled and placed a finger on his lips. 'Do not talk, dear. All will be well.' A glance passed between the doctors: Blumentrost, Paulsen and Horn. Peter whispered something and Feofan Prokopovich bowed his assent, though he frowned as he did so.

'What does the Tsar want?' I asked, my voice unsteady.

'His Majesty asks for paper, ink and guill,' said Feofan. Menshikov rummaged in the desk. Was I mistaken or did he take longer than was necessary? His future, too, was at stake here. Finally, Prokopovich folded Peter's fingers around the quill. Black ink dripped on the starched sheets. I heard the feather scratching over the paper, and Peter's throttled voice. 'Tsesarevna Anna Petrovna. Bring my Anoushka to me, my dear eldest child.' Anna? How would she be able to handle little Petrushka's claim and keep his godfather, the greedy Prince Dolgoruki, at bay? A Tsar's death meant past and present hanging in the balance. The wind strengthened, whistling around the Winter Palace's walls. Who had heard his words after all? Neither I nor Menshikov followed his order. Feofan locked eyes with me and then crossed himself in silence.

Peter's fingers tried to unroll the paper, but the scroll slipped away. All of Russia held its breath.

'Oh, my God,' we spoke his last words together.

INTERREGNUM, 1725

As Menshikov opens the door, the corridor outside the small study is full of men. I spot members of the Synod, the Senate and the Admiralty. For one night we have fooled them and Russia. I rise and ready myself for the nasal voice of Prince Dolgoruki, arresting us in the name of Petrushka, the new Tsar of All the Russias, Emperor Peter II. I fold my hands in silent prayer and close my eyes. The light is so bright, it pierces my closed lids. Am I already dead?

'Tsarina,' Menshikov says huskily, and I look up. The Privy Council kneels in front of me: Ostermann, Tolstoy and Jagushinsky – all of them. Menshikov stares at me with bloodshot eyes, looking like the scoundrel he is.

I straighten up. The icons on my dress jingle and my jewellery sparkles in the candlelight as I speak. 'The great and gracious Tsar, Emperor Peter the First, has passed away. We are torn by grief and numb with pain. For We, Catherine Alexeyevna, Empress and Tsarina of All the Russias, are aware of the responsibility God places on Our shoulders.' My voice fills the room as I lift my right hand. 'We swear to do justice to God's grace, and to love all Russians as Our own children. We will righteously reign, and trust in your experienced advice and guidance.' I look into the Privy Council members' eyes, man after man. The choice is theirs: rule with me or perish with me.

Menshikov is first to decide, swift and cunning as always. If there is any muttering of discontent among the princes, the boyars and above all, the Church, he can call upon the army; planted bayonets will quell any calls for resistance and turn doubters into fervent supporters: 'Hail, Catherine Alexeyevna, Tsarina of All the Russias! Hail, the Tsarina,' he thunders, and the Council joins his cheering.

The call goes forth into the corridor, the courtyard, our city, and finally all over the country. Above the Winter Palace's gate, the flag with the double-headed eagle is lowered to half-mast. From the Peter and Paul Fortress, one hundred and one cannon shots tear the morning air. The bells of the Trinity Cathedral toll dully, and then all the churches of the city follow: The Tsar is dead; long live the Tsarina!

Feofan Prokopovich has returned, just in time, as is his custom. He kisses my fingers and swears his loyalty to me; Makarov unrolls the hurried *ukaz* that proclaims me Russia's ruler. The Princes Dolgoruky come into the room, clutching Petrushka's hands. They must have torn the boy from his sleep, as the young prince blinks, confused by the light of many candles. His hair is tousled and his feet are bare. I feel no remorse: Alexey's son is still so young, and his time will come. The palace guard secures the steps and stairs before which many hundred voices roar, 'Hail Catherine! Hail the mother of the nation, hail our Tsarina!'

The generals kneel; countless times I have sat with them by the campfire, celebrating their victories and lamenting their defeats. I tended to their wounds at Poltava, and spooned thin soup into their bowls underneath the beating Persian sun. I was always there, for as long as they can remember. I protected them, their goods and their families from Peter's wrath. At his side, I had learnt what it took to rule Russia. This is the way it should be: Peter is dead. My beloved husband, the mighty Emperor and Tsar of All the Russias, has died, and not a moment too soon.

Excerpt from the diary of Jean-Jacques Campredon, French Envoy to the Imperial Court of St Petersburg, 16 May 1727

I return from the Palace, where Prince Menshikov told us about the Tsarina's failing health. In all the years I have lived in Russia on behalf of His Most Gracious Majesty, the King of France, I have not seen so much grief in the people's faces. Even Menshikov is stricken and he'd better ponder his own future. For what will happen to him once the Tsarina passes away, only two years after the death of the great Tsar Peter? Menshikov has more enemies than hairs on his head, and in his grandeur and ambition ignores this fact blithely. He betrothed his daughter to the Tsarevich Petrushka, but engagements are made to be broken. Oh, there will be a lot to write about in the coming weeks, I'm sure!

The Tsarina is dying, and one can only marvel at the divine will that has raised her so far, so unbelievably far beyond her birth. Even my queen, who came from humble Poland as Princess Maria, is impressed by her, although she of course would never admit to it. The Tsarina wanted the King of France as a husband for her own daughter, the Tsarevna Elizabeth. But a washerwoman's daughter on the throne of France? Mon Dieu.

At the great Tsar's funeral, Catherine claimed the throne by her display of sheer mourning and despair. How may one woman have so many tears – or maybe we just do not meet any decent women anymore? Tsar Peter had loved her. But had she loved him truly, so much that her tears at his wake could be trusted? He was too terrible. Only a few moons earlier Wilhelm Mons had been beheaded and there was no doubt as to the nature of his true crime. All that was forgotten at the Tsar's funeral: her ladies-in-waiting, their faces thickly veiled, tried to hold her back, but she threw herself to the ground, clawing at the two coffins and howling like a wounded beast.

It took her weeks to let Feofan Prokopovich close the dead Tsar's coffin at all. He lay in state surrounded by the signs of his greatness. Then, just five weeks after his death, the little Tsarevna Natalya died suddenly, at the age of only seven years. The Lord gives, and the Lord takes. The young lady-in-waiting Alice Kramer fell victim to Natalya's death; her mind clouded and she took her leave. The court gossiped for days about the princely pension the Tsarina paid her. What had the true nature of her services to the Tsar and Tsarina been?

On the tenth day of March 1725, both young Princess Natalya and her father, Peter I of Russia, were buried in the Peter and Paul Cathedral in his glorious city of St Petersburg. Tens of thousands of soldiers of all regiments gathered at dawn on the ice of the Neva; thirty-two hundred noble horses were tethered around them, chewing on their silver bridles. Twelve officers carried Peter's coffin and eight general majors held up the canopy of green velvet with its golden tassels, shielding the coffin from the snow. Peter's closest friends and the high dignitaries of the Empire held a piece of the coffin cover each, the snowflakes mingling with their tears.

Once the funeral was over, everyday life resumed. The Tsarina broke the Court mourning period to marry her daughter Anna Petrovna to the Duke of Holstein in a most splendid wedding. Tsarevna Elizabeth is still unmarried, and she does everything possible to spoil her reputation. She is a beauty – parbleu! *I have never seen such cleavage, not even in Versailles – her only faults lie in her behaviour and her nature. Unfortunately, I am too old and not a guard, so she doesn't look at me. I was right to dissuade my king from marrying this princess. Her morals would have surprised even Versailles.*

Menshikov says the Tsarina's lungs are swollen. Yet barely two weeks ago, at the first signs of the ottepel, I rode with her and could hardly keep up as she chased through the woods. At a river, she made us dismount. We fell behind as she walked down to its shores and slipped out of her shoes. We watched her picking up pebbles and talking to herself. She felt the cold of the water, wading into it with bare feet, before she turned to us, frowned and asked: 'Do you hear the horses on the road? What could these men possibly want?' I turned, yet there was nothing to be seen.

She is still a fine woman, with very graceful movements, a bright, clear mind and always in the best of moods. No wonder the people love her: the Tsarina has never forgotten where she came from, but I believe she is bored without the Tsar. In the mornings she is known to dip five warm pretzels into a heady, hot Burgundy, to boost her spirits. On the first day of April she had the fire bells rung and watched the people rush into the streets in their nightshirts, though there was neither fire nor flood. To make up for her prank, the Tsarina served vodka to all and no one was allowed to go to bed before noon, just as if Tsar Peter were still alive. God, how I feared and hated his feasts; sometimes the eagle cup is part of my nightmares. Many times I have prayed that His Majesty King Louis should call me back to Paris. Why did I ever learn Russian?

Lights wander restlessly behind the Winter Palace's windows. Menshikov, who knows so well how to sow and harvest, may call on us at any time.

Horsemen gallop out of the palace's gates. The Tsarina has not waged wars, she has not plundered and has razed neither cities nor countries. These last were two good years in Russia; we lived happily and created new happiness. Blumentrost, the quack, teaches at the Academy of Sciences now, and the St Petersburg Gymnasium is open to gifted children from all over Russia. Last year Vitus Bering carried on with his travels. Only the Tsarina herself never learnt how to read or to write. 'An old mule does not turn into a horse, Campredon,' she said to me.

The carriage of the count Skawronski enters the Winter Palace: are they really and truly the Tsarina's lost family? Everybody wants to belong, and even a Tsarina should not die alone. After twelve pregnancies, only one daughter and a supposed brother hold her hand in her very last hour. Her pain comes in waves, so it is said, and sometimes so violently as to strangle her.

After my supper

The month of May brings the first brighter nights to St Petersburg, their darkness turning milky, a sight that never fails to enchant me. The city is awake, the palace lit up. If I am to report to Paris later tonight that the Tsarina has passed away, we will again have a Tsar Peter, Petrushka, the young son of poor, haunted Alexey. When I looked for sealing wax in the drawer, I found an old leaflet I had forgotten about: 'One could forever and ever praise the merits of the dead Tsar Peter, the greatness, the uniqueness, the wisdom of his rule. But his work brought pain to all the people who came close to him. He disturbed peace, prosperity, the strength of his empire. He violated the dignity, rights, and well-being of his subjects. He meddled insultingly in all matters: from religion to the family to the holy church. Can one love such a despot? No, never. Such a ruler is nothing but hateful.'

There is a knock on the door. It must be the Court's messenger: a Tsarina does not die as a woman, but as a ruler; even if she was always much more a woman than a ruler. I ready myself to leave. Have I ever before spotted the silky sliver of blue haze setting the Neva apart from its shore at dusk? Tonight, the fireflies dance for her alone. Duty calls me, but before I go, I read through the leaflet again.

Can one love such a despot? No. But a man who also happens to be Tsar —?

The Tsarina had made her choice.

Acknowledgements

I first discovered Marta / Catherine I aged thirteen when reading Leo Sievers' fabulous book *Germans and Russians*, which charted the millennial history of these two countries and their peoples. That was it for me: writing about Marta's incredible destiny was an all-encompassing endeavour. I was never able to thank Lindsey Hughes, Professor of Russian History at the School of Slavonic and East European Studies, UCL, for her outstanding oeuvre *Russia in the Age of Peter the Great* – it was my bible while writing *Tsarina*. Nothing would have happened without Jonny Geller and the amazing Alice Lutyens at Curtis Brown, agents *par excellence* and best guiding spirits, who took on the gamble that *Tsarina* was. The day you first answered my query letter, a heron settled in my garden – the most auspicious of signs! Thank you, too, to the elegant and capable Deborah Schneider of Gelfman Schneider / ICM Partners, Literary Scout Daniela Schlingmann – a fine, feisty woman of the first hour – and the whole fabulous Foreign Rights Team at Curtis Brown for spreading the word further. Hats off to my first international publishers and editors such as Faiza Khan at Bloomsbury, Charlie Spicer at St. Martin's Press, Francesca Cristoffanini from Planeta DeAgostini as well as Dr Nora Haller and Tilo Eckhardt at Heyne PRH. You are the magical core 'Team Tsarina', and always happy to welcome others to your ranks. Special thanks to Charlotte Collins, who first translated the Prologue, as well as chapters 1–8, from the original German manuscript. It gave me a brilliant base to work with and the courage to write on, as words are a moveable feast and like clay.

A brief word for the sake of historical accuracy: the beginnings of Marta's life are shrouded in mystery. She emerges from the mist of time when she took a position as a maid with Ernst Glück. While Field Marshall Sheremetev captured her at the siege of Marienburg, his persona in the manuscript is later blended with Peter's crony Fedor Matveev Apraxin. It was Apraxin who took the Baltic girl Alice Kramer in. Likewise, Alice Kramer was called Anna, as were Rasia Menshikova and Alexandra Tolstoya. Other than that, I took very few liberties with happenings and timelines: the Petrine era is incredibly well documented. Also, Marta's tale could only have been invented by life itself.

A Note on the Author

Ellen Alpsten was born and raised in the Kenyan highlands, before attending Instituts d'études politiques de Paris. Whilst studying for her Msc in PPE she won the Grande École short story competition with her novella *Meeting Mr. Gandhi* and was encouraged to continue writing. Upon graduating, she worked as a producer and presenter for Bloomberg TV in London. She contributes to international publications such as *Vogue, Standpoint* and *Condé Nast Traveller*. *Tsarina* is her first novel. She lives in London with her husband and three children.

A Note on the Type

The text of this book is set Adobe Garamond. It is one of several versions of Garamond based on the designs of Claude Garamond. It is thought that Garamond based his font on Bembo, cut in 1495 by Francesco Griffo in collaboration with the Italian printer Aldus Manutius. Garamond types were first used in books printed in Paris around 1532. Many of the present-day versions of this type are based on the *Typi Academiae* of Jean Jannon cut in Sedan in 1615.

Claude Garamond was born in Paris in 1480. He learned how to cut type from his father and by the age of fifteen he was able to fashion steel punches the size of a pica with great precision. At the age of sixty he was commissioned by King Francis I to design a Greek alphabet, and for this he was given the honourable title of royal type founder. He died in 1561.